PENGUIN B

AS MUSIC AND S

Kate O'Brien was born in Limerick in 1897. She became a boarder at the Laurel Hill convent school at the age of five following the death of her mother, and subsequently won a scholarship to University College, Dublin. After graduating from UCD in 1919 she moved to England, where she worked for the *Manchester Guardian* and then taught at a convent school in London. After spending a year as a governess in Bilbao in 1922–3 – an experience that inspired her novel *Mary Lavelle* – she returned to London and married a Dutch journalist; the marriage ended within a year. Her first play, *Distinguished Villa*, was produced in 1926. For *Without My Cloak* (1931), her first novel, she was awarded the Hawthornden and James Tait Black Memorial prizes. Subsequent novels were *The Ante-Room* (1934), *Mary Lavelle* (1936), *Pray for the Wanderer* (1938), *The Land of Spices* (1941), *The Last of Summer* (1943), *That Lady* (1946), *The Flower of May* (1953), and *As Music and Splendour* (1958). Her non-fiction works include *Farewell Spain* (1937) – which caused the Franco regime to bar her from the country until 1957 – *Teresa of Avila* (1951), and *Presentation Parlour* (1963). She lived in England until 1950, when she bought a house in Connemara and moved there. In 1961 she moved back to England, where she lived until her death in 1974.

Anne Enright was born in Dublin in 1962. She is the author of a collection of short stories, *The Portable Virgin*, for which she was awarded the Rooney Prize in 1991, and of three novels: *The Wig My Father Wore*, *What Are You Like?*, which was awarded the Encore Prize in 2000, and *The Pleasure of Eliza Lynch*. Her most recent book is *Making Babies: Stumbling into Motherhood*. She lives in Co. Wicklow.

KATE O'BRIEN

As Music and Splendour

With an Introduction by ANNE ENRIGHT

PENGUIN BOOKS

PENGUIN IRELAND

Published by the Penguin Group
Penguin Ireland, 25 St Stephen's Green, Dublin 2, Ireland
(a division of Penguin Books Ltd)
Penguin Books Ltd, 80 Strand, London WC2R ORL, England
Penguin Group (USA) Inc., 375 Hudson Street, New York, New York 10014, USA
Penguin Group (Canada), 90 Eglington Avenue East, Suite 700,
Toronto, Ontario, Canada M4P 2Y3 (a division of Pearson Penguin Canada Inc.)
Penguin Group (Australia), 250 Camberwell Road,
Camberwell, Victoria 3124, Australia (a division of Pearson Australia Group Pty Ltd)
Penguin Books India Pvt Ltd, 11 Community Centre,
Panchsheel Park, New Delhi – 110 017, India
Penguin Group (NZ), cnr Airborne and Rosedale Roads, Albany,
Auckland 1310, New Zealand (a division of Pearson New Zealand Ltd)
Penguin Books (South Africa) (Pty) Ltd, 24 Sturdee Avenue,
Rosebank, Johannesburg 2196, South Africa

Penguin Books Ltd, Registered Offices: 80 Strand, London WC2R ORL, England

www.penguin.com

First published by William Heinemann 1958
Published in Penguin Books 2005
1

Set in 10.25/12.25 pt Adobe Sabon
Typeset by Rowland Phototypesetting Ltd, Bury St Edmunds, Suffolk
Printed in England by Clays Ltd, St Ives plc

Introduction

The twenty-first century presents a new problem to the writer discussing human intimacy. Anything buried or half hidden or forbidden can be found, explicit and open and wrapped in carry-out latex, on the Internet. This blight of the obvious infects, not just the secrets in a novel, but the way in which those secrets are revealed. It is useful – when our methods are so undermined – to look at writers on the other side of this river of flesh; ones for whom the obvious was not allowed.

Two of Kate O'Brien's earlier novels, *Mary Lavelle* (1936) and *The Land of Spices* (1941), were banned in Ireland – the latter because of a passing reference to homosexuality. This hurt her deeply, but O'Brien was a flower of the Irish convent school system, and not easily thwarted. She was also very proud. Clare, one of the two protagonists in *As Music and Splendour*, may be a lesbian, but this is not the point of her character, quite. The novel – O'Brien's last – was published in 1958. Irish censorship had grown less severe, but to speak of sex between women would still have been inflammatory. O'Brien solved the problem, quite deftly, by speaking about love instead.

Lesbianism is not Clare's problem; her problem is the same as that of her great friend, Rose: she must find her voice. The girls meet at a school in Paris where they have been sent, fresh from provincial Ireland, to train for the great opera houses of Europe. They are young, they can sing – they could break your heart. The novel follows them to a *maestro*'s house in Rome, where they fall in and out of love with their fellow students, and then through their first seasons as fledgling *divas*, aiming for La Scala, and beyond.

O'Brien loves greatness – she loves to talk of it and imagine it, and the final humility it might require. 'Don't you know that nothing can be settled about us while we live?' says a character in *The Land of Spices*, echoing, perhaps, the weary megalomania of writers everywhere. Greatness is the fantasy of the novel and its romance. Opera provides O'Brien with a world of high endeavour, in which a woman can become an *assoluta*: something absolute, something beyond. For this she will need talent, discipline, emotional complexity and purity of intent. This is an ideal that is also available to readers, whether they can sing or not, because the only way to attain it is to become more completely yourself. *As Music and Splendour* produced in me a huge and sighing nostalgia for a time when 'self-expression' meant the expression of something fine. O'Brien is a convent existentialist. She believes in girls. She believes in what they can become. Her belief is made more fierce – more pure, even – by the fact that she wrote at a time when girls rarely became anything much, as the world saw these things.

Still, this relentless interest in the educated heart. O'Brien believes in teachers in a way that is rare among writers; the *Bildungsroman* usually prefers the more accidental lessons that life sends our way. Duarte, Clare's natural maestro, teaches her 'with speed, impatience and merciless accuracy: indeed with a compressed passion in every instruction that compelled her wits to race with him, and that brought – she could hear and feel herself – great elasticity and extension to her voice.' Teaching is a labour of love, to the extent that it is often confused with desire – and when desire is thwarted, then teaching will do. Clare's friend Thomas is gallant enough when disappointed in love, but he flings himself weeping in her lap when she tells him she will study the role of Alceste with someone else.

The self in Kate O'Brien's work is the intractable human substance of Catholicism, it is something that must be moulded and pummelled and broken and reshaped. There is no quarter, and so this most romantic of writers is also the most unsentimental. Perhaps Clare's lesbianism has a function here: it requires a way of writing about girls that is not solved by marriage; it frees up the ending, and allows their lives to be treated with as much uncertainty and rigour as the lives of boys.

Away from Ireland, Clare and Rose leave Catholicism quite simply behind. 'We are sinners,' says Clare, as they take to love, instead. They do this as part of their musical education – who could sing Verdi, if she never had a broken heart? – and they are helped by the simplicity of Catholicism itself: 'Rose and I know perfectly well what we're doing. We are so well instructed that we can decide for ourselves. There's no vagueness in Catholic instruction.' All of this is as pragmatic and uneasy as their feelings about the country they have left behind. Catholicism, like Ireland, is 'over there' – it seems that O'Brien is tired of clawing at both of them from the inside. In this late novel, she retains the questions of Catholicism, while ditching the answers it is so keen to supply.

Clare's problem is, first and foremost, a spiritual one. At the age of sixteen, 'she had to balance herself, unaware of her ordeal, on the sharp and dipping ring – made of light – where the spirit has to decide with the flesh between union and divorce'. This is the challenge set to her voice, which is a cool, androgynous, intellectual instrument, as set against the joyful virtuosity of Rose. The question is not what kind of flesh Clare should indulge in, but whether she should indulge at all. This is not a problem of sexuality, but of art, and it can be resolved only by artistic means. In order to become a true artist, however, Clare must experience sexual love.

Many arias run through *As Music and Splendour*, but one that lingers is '*Che faro . . .*' from Glück's *Orfeo ed Euridice*. If you look behind to see if she is following, Euridice will be lost to you. This is the discovery Clare makes – that all love is impossible, that it fades as you try to grasp it. In the face of this realization, gender is a detail; gender is just a question, sometimes, of logistics.

And still, the music yearns and insists that love is possible so long as we are true. Gender may be a detail, but it is an essential one. Clare has no other option. There is no one else for her to be. When Thomas does finally rage at her, she thinks, 'I can't be stormed at. There is nothing here for him to storm.'

There is something about Clare's heart that cannot be altered, and this romantic essentialism is echoed in the way she harkens to the Irish landscape, to ideas of purity and home. She dreams of being back 'under a rain she knew, among stones and empty lanes, and looking at grey sea and a wet pier, and hearing her grandmother's sweet, good voice calling her in out of the wet to her tea'. These images of authenticity were the stock of Catholic nationalism, whose ideal of the lovely Irish girl did not include her falling in love with other women, in a carnal sort of way. With these images of Ireland, O'Brien, at her most haughty and subversive, claims the higher ground.

O'Brien loves her characters' Irishness. Rose is hailed as La Rosa d'Irlanda by the Italian audience. She possesses, in her easy emotional grace, a large helping of what O'Brien calls the 'over-saluted and over-mocked Irish charm'. For all her wanderings, there is a core that does not change in Rose, either. Perhaps O'Brien is as partisan as any narrow Catholic nationalist when she says that you can take a nice Irish girl anywhere – anywhere at all: 'she did not change in anything, save to grow more like herself, the honest and merry and tender-hearted one, the level-headed and benevolent one, that she could have been foreseen to become in any walk of life, from Lackanashee to Milan and back again.'

Then again, perhaps it is true.

But this sense of an essential, unchanging self has its downside too. Clare, new to love, observes herself and her own emotions. 'Another Clare, the familiar one of always, was about her usual business, and was able to watch this newcomer coolly enough from the wings. And the newcomer knew this, and knew it with a sense of relief that puzzled and sometimes saddened her. One does not change, she thought, one does not escape.'

Clare never does have a great moment of revelation about her sexuality. In a world where the obvious is never stated – can never be stated – things merely are. She comes back from a day spent with her lover, and Thomas sees her on the stairs, and knows more about her than she, perhaps, knows about herself.

Much later, he will call her a 'stinking lily', a phrase that is quite marvellously unpleasant, combining the image of chastity with that of rot. But by now Clare is sure of her heart. Thomas insists on the illusion of love, its essential selfishness and impossibility. 'When it's of love we think, Clare, we're alone with it.' Clare replies that it is 'just possible' we are not alone, that love is reasonable, that it can be given and returned. This hint of possibility gives people the ability to 'bear love, and look at it quietly even in themselves'. It also ' "makes them write poems, I suppose, and operas — "

"Makes them sing?"

"Yes, I think so." '

And so the only explicit conversation in the book about Clare's intractable heart turns out not to be about lesbianism, but about the absolute and the possible, and the space between the two where the artist and the lover both make their home. O'Brien is too proud to discuss something so delicate and important as sexuality on other people's terms.

Perhaps it is my convent education that makes me think there is something thrilling in writing about women's problems in this way. The ardency of her beliefs and the ferocity of her disdain make me think of Kate O'Brien as a figure of almost medieval romanticism: a religious knight. She has, in her time, been accused of arrogance, but she is not so much arrogant as *interested* in arrogance, its pitfalls and delights. She is an extraordinarily resilient writer. She resists the dross – of whatever decade – and so endures.

ANNE ENRIGHT

As music and splendour
Survive not the lamp and the lute
The heart's echoes render
No song when the spirit is mute . . .
When hearts have once mingled,
Love first leaves the well-built nest;
The weak one is singled
To endure what it once possessed.
Oh Love who bewailest
The frailty of all things here,
Why choose you the frailest
For your cradle, your home and your bier?

—SHELLEY

The First Chapter

'Stop crying, anyway. Try to, that is.'

The practice-room was cold. It was a small room, with thin walls of pitch-pine, and with a glass door leading on to a dark passage. All its furniture was an upright piano, a piano-stool, one wooden chair, a metronome, and an oleograph of a young woman with a palm branch in her hand. There was also a bench and a shelf on which some sheets of music were laid. There was a tuning fork on the shelf.

Rain beat against a tall window, which was screened to half its height in black wire.

A childish-seeming girl sat on the bench with her hands knotted round her knees, and gazed up at the running raindrops and the sky. Another child sat on the piano-stool; her head was in her arms and they were on the keyboard. She was crying. Her curly brown hair looked pretty and babyish; the other girl's hair was straight and very fair. The two wore dresses of black serge, full-skirted and very long, with tightly buttoned bodices and stiff, shiny white collars.

Paris lay about them, beyond the ugly window; and the building in which they sat was the Couvent des Pieuses Filles de Sainte Hélène. It was a Sunday afternoon in mid-October.

They were both strangers to these surroundings; the little one who was crying over the keyboard was very desperately a stranger; she had arrived in this place only nine days earlier, quite simply dazed with fright, fatigue and homesickness, and it sometimes seemed to her fellow-exile that the little thing might indeed go mad with fretting if someone could not help her to calm down.

Clare Halvey would hardly have said, if speaking truthfully, that she had herself calmed down yet in relation to the unforeseen life of this convent. But she was already here five weeks, and she was, she had discovered, nearly six months older than Rose Lennane. Moreover, the plan and purpose of her coming here had been discussed for nearly a year, and in her presence, by her father, her aunt and her well-off uncle Matt; and she had come here from Dublin, where her father had lived for the last four years. Moreover, she had attended a convent day school in the city where she had received some elementary instruction in the French language.

But Rose, it seemed, had been snatched by enthusiastic patrons from her mother's cottage in a small village on the borders of Mellick and Tipperary; from a widowed mother and an only sister, from the village school and the village street, and without being allowed to utter 'yes, no or nay' had been landed into the vast, beeswaxed parlour of this house, and given in charge to Mère Supérieure – but especially, of course, into the trust of Mère Marie Brunel.

'Sh! Don't cry,' Clare repeated uneasily.

Rose lifted her head, drew a large handkerchief from the pocket of her skirt and blew her nose.

'It's a mercy *you* talk English anyway,' she said.

'It'd be funny if I didn't. Who sent you here, Rose?'

'The – what is this you call it? – the Comma-*tee*.'

'What's that? What's a Comma-*tee*?'

'It's Father Lucius – he brought me here in the train, and in the ships. Father Lucius and Dr Waldron and Lady O'Dowd, and Colonel Parkinson, and Miss French.'

'Are they your relations?'

'No! I've no relations. I've only Mamma and Aggie—'

'Ah! Don't cry—'

'But Mr McMahon told me – Mr Chris we call him, he has a lovely shop, easily the best shop in Lackanashee – he's going to send me some jelly babies and conversation lozenges – do you know conversation lozenges?'

Clare nodded. 'Does he sell almond toffee?'

'I'm not sure. I'll ask Aggie to ask him. Anyway he said, Mr

Chris said, that I must be very grateful to the Comma-*tee* and do all they said and be a good girl, because this was God's reward to Mamma for all her sufferings and sacrifices.'

'Did your mamma have a lot of sufferings and sacrifices?'

'I don't know, Father Lucius said she did, and so did Mr Chris. So then I told Mamma that I'd do what the Comma-*tee* said. And she said I was a good girl and God would protect and reward me.'

'Is your father dead?'

'Oh yes. He died when I was two. We had two brothers that died too – when they were small, of course. Father died in Glasgow. He died of the drink. Mr Chris told me that.'

'I suppose he was a bad man,' Clare said.

'I think he was. Well – you wouldn't tell anyone, would you, Clare? – Mamma's poor, you know. Well, she's a dress-maker.'

Clare turned and smiled.

'Is she? Auntie is too.'

'Is she? Your auntie in Dublin?'

'Yes, Auntie Joe. She's good at it. She has one of those ladies, false ladies – you know – that you fit the things on. You can turn it around—'

'Oh, I know! Mamma's dying for one of those!'

'Auntie Joe finds it a great help, she says.'

'It *should* be a great help, I'd say,' said Rose. 'Mamma has a sewing machine. Did you ever see one?'

'Yes. Auntie Joe has one.'

'I suppose she's rich – from the dressmaking? Is she?'

'Auntie Joe? Oh – I don't know. Not rich, I'd say. She has a big brass plate and that—'

'I thought being in Dublin—?' There was a pause. 'You see,' said Rose then on a new tone, 'you see, Mamma really can't make much on the sewing in Lackanashee. It's only a small little place. Well – you, you wouldn't say this to any of them here, would you? I mean, to Anne de Hauteville? Would you?'

Clare shook her head.

'Mamma has to go out sometimes to these places – to Miss French, you know, and to Lady O'Dowd – to do their washing

– oh, only their private things, you know, and sewing and ironing and that. You'd never tell, would you?'

'Who would I tell?' said Clare.

'Oh, some of them seem very grand here—'

'Yes. That's true. They seem grand.'

'I wonder when I'll get another letter? Mamma and Aggie said they'd write every week, and I've only had one letter yet. Miss French said she'd write too.'

'You might tomorrow. I notice I get letters on Monday, sometimes.'

'Do you get a lot of letters?'

'Gracious, no! Only from Dadda – but he rather likes writing letters, I think. None of the others would write at all – well, Auntie Joe's busy. And Tom's just gone to Maynooth. He didn't take any interest in me anyway. And the two small ones, you know, Evie and Lulu – they're at home with Grandma. They hardly know me now.'

'Why? Where's at home, Clare?'

'Oh, far away. In County Galway.'

'But I thought you lived in Dublin?'

'No. I was born in Grandma's. We were all born there – like Mother. Grandma is called Mrs Doolin. Dadda is a western man too, from Galway City though. He's in the Excise and Customs, and he was in charge at Ballykerin Harbour. That's how he met Mother. But when she died he got tired of Ballykerin – he's great for cities always – so he went off to Dublin to live with Auntie Joe. She's his sister and she never got married. And then, you see, he took Tom and me – to send us to school. Dadda works in the Custom House in Dublin. He loves it, I think.'

'And don't you like Dublin?'

Clare shook her head.

'I liked school. Not Dublin. I don't live there at all. I live in Ballykerin.'

'So you're like me, really – more like me than I thought. I mean! You're from the country?'

Clare nodded.

'Oh, listen!'

'Señorita Luisa.'

Both girls lifted their heads and listened.

A clear, steady voice, very young, sang the scale of C Major in a nearby practice-room. After a pause it moved on, in careful routine, through an elementary scale-practice.

Rose and Clare listened with total attention.

After a few scales the singing ceased.

'Mère Marie is pleased with Luisa, I think,' said Clare.

'How long was she here before she was let sing a scale?' asked Rose.

'More than a year, she told me. She's eighteen, you know.'

'Goodness!'

'Signor Manci is letting her begin the exercises now – you know, those ones that we read for breathing—'

'Oh, I wish we were let *sing* them!'

'So do I.'

'It's like being a dummy,' said Rose.

Clare laughed.

'You're not a bit like a dummy,' she said. 'There was a dummy at home – he used to sit on the pier, poor Michael Shawn O!'

'But why can't we sing *at all*, Clare? The Comma-*tee* told me that if I was a good girl and came here and learnt to sing, I'd be able to get a lot of money for singing – and pay them back, and look after Mamma, and all! And I must, in that case! But I sang for Mère Marie – what day was it? I'm here nine days, amn't I—?'

'She gave you your test this day week, I think. What happened?'

'I was terrified. But mind you, she was nice to me, and just asked me a bit about Mamma and school and that. Then she asked me if I knew anything at all about clefs and keys and scales, and things – and I told her how Miss French used to teach me, and how I knew a little bit, I thought. Well, then she asked me to take some deep breaths – and then she made me sing the scale of C Major. Then she gave me E Flat, and I sang that. And then she stood up and shut the piano.'

'Was that all?'

'No. She walked over to the window then, and I didn't know whether I was to go or not. But she turned around and said that I was please to sing her a few bars of any song that came into my head.'

'What did you do?'

'I didn't know what to do. So I said a Hail Mary – and then I thought of Mamma; and so I began "The Last Rose of Summer". But I'd only sung the first line when she put up her hand – aren't they awful hands, Clare? – and she told me that would do. I'd have liked to finish the first verse anyway. Mamma sings "The Last Rose of Summer". Well, anyway then she went into English – very funny English, but she said she spoke it so that I'd be sure to understand, and she said that I wasn't to sing another *note* – but *not* another *note*, she said – until I had her permission. Not a note!'

'I know, it's the same for me!'

'But what does it mean? I said, couldn't I sing in the choir? Mightn't I sing in chapel? And she said *non, absolument non*. She went back to French for that. But then she said in English again, that I wouldn't *be* in the choir, and that I was on no account to sing in chapel.'

'What happened then?'

'I – well, I began to cry. You see, it's all very well, but I have to learn singing now – I've promised I would. But I couldn't explain anything to her. And when she saw I was crying she just laughed at me; then she gave me a kind of a slap on my head – quite a hard slap. And she told me to go away.'

'I heard you singing in the *Adoremus* the other evening, you boldie,' said Clare. 'It's lucky Mère Marie wasn't at Benediction that evening.'

'That's why I joined in,' said Rose with a sweet giggle. 'But I was absolutely *pianissimo* – you couldn't have known it was me. You've never heard me singing.'

'That's one reason why I knew it was you. Another reason was that your voice was coming from across the aisle, where the choir wasn't. Didn't you think of that? Anyway, there are only those eight whom she allows to sing for weekday Benediction, and I've been listening to them for five weeks now. I know those eight voices, and I heard you the instant you came in. It's enough to get you packed off home, you know – to disobey her like that!'

'Is it? Oh goodness! But what would the Comma-*tee* say? And Mamma'd be upset, I think. Still – I'd love to sing at Benediction, like at home. It's a lovely choir here.'

'It's famous in Paris. It's a mania of Mère Marie. And Luisa was telling me that on special feast days the music experts come to High Mass or Benediction here, but only on her written invitation.'

'Well – then, I really don't see – after all, if we're sent all this way because we're supposed to be good singers – why can't we be in the choir?'

'We may be in it yet!' said Clare. 'But anyway, at present we wouldn't be let in on any terms! We're not trained. We might be let sing and learn in the sub-choir – but *not* in the chapel, you can be sure!'

'Oh, goodness!'

Clare was leaning against the wire screen of the window.

'I hate this street,' she said.

'I'm sure I do,' said Rose. 'Those houses opposite look awful – but I don't think I've seen the actual street yet.'

'There's no hurry,' said Clare.

She leant against the window pane and closed her eyes.

'I'd like a piece of hot soda-bread,' said Rose. 'Did your grandma make soda-bread?'

Clare smelt her grandma's bread in the other child's words; smelt sea-weed too, and smoke and silence, and her little sisters' sand-filled, oily, curly heads. Evening moved down, coldly here and coldly there.

Clare Halvey was sixteen and younger than those sixteen years. Yet, by chance she had travelled innocently to an outward rim of the human circles. Young, she had to balance herself, un- aware of her ordeal, on the sharp and dipping ring – made of light – where the spirit has to decide with the flesh between union and divorce. In this child, it happened, the two, the enemies, were strong. She knew nothing now, aged sixteen, of their eternal and, in her, expressive life, or of their ferocious enmity. She was a vessel, a battlefield, a minuscule and casual pausing place for argument.

She felt argument rising in her – but only within herself; and only about the nothings that she thought to be nothings. What she did not know, sixteen years old and looking out in wretched alienation at the rain as it fell on a dull street of Paris – what she did not know then, or ever, that her desire to be back under a rain she knew, among stones and empty lanes, and looking at grey sea and a wet pier, and hearing her grandmother's sweet, good voice calling her in out of the wet to her tea – she did not know then that in such agony she was meeting one of mankind's least manageable pains. Neither did she know that she drew her mannerliness about that pain, her calm, her ability to turn and help a lighter kind of suffering, from perhaps those wintry stones, those lanes, that civilized, good voice of grandmother – grandmother saying: 'Come in, child. I have the tea wet. Come in out of the wind, my love.'

The child heard the long-ago words. Out of the wind, my love. She was on her way, involuntarily, into horrid winds, whence no one would call her back, come in, my love. But she knew none of that. She was on a trackless road. And she did not know that she carried armour.

Her story may tell what the armour was. Let us wait. Let the captured lark behave as she learnt at home to behave. Let her go down the dark foreign corridors to goûter – come in to your tea, my child, my love.

The convent in Paris of Les Pieuses Filles de Sainte Hélène, where these two Irish children had been placed in cold October, in 1886, was – save for its music-mistress – a school of no account. Since the expulsion from France of the Jesuits and of the dominant clerical teachers in 1880, religious houses had had to tread cautiously, if education was their source of liveli-hood – and the unremarkable fifty-year-old foundation of the Daughters of Saint Helen would have been of no matter save that here in their ugly Mother-house in Paris happened to work a nun who was a musician.

Mère Marie Brunel – the nuns of her order kept and used

their surnames for political reasons – was a puzzle to the sophisticated in Paris. She was discussed often in their drawing-rooms. It is probable that she knew this, and even enjoyed the knowledge. But why she was a nun, in the Convent of Rue des Lauriers, in the dreary headquarters of the undistinguished order which her great-aunt had founded in her ugly house in 1850, no one knew. The brilliant girl had quarrelled with her family – so far as gossip could remember – around the early 1860s. She had disappeared into Italy, with a singing voice of great promise, and an unusual intelligence about music. She was forgotten – the troubles of 1870 and afterwards had intervened, and her parents had died. But then, unexplained, unannounced, she reappeared – a nun – in Rue des Lauriers.

What had happened to her in Italy, when she had returned, why she was a nun in this dull little order, no one seemed to know. The clouded years had clouded more important hopes and lives than hers – but by the turn into the 1880s, no matter what the mystery, Mère Marie Brunel was important in Paris as a teacher of singing. And the religious order which her depressed great-aunt had founded, in the holy boredom of widowhood in 1850, took its first usefulness, its first whiff of importance, from her success as a teacher of singing.

This success was interesting – yet not accidental. No one in Paris or London knew, to swear to it, with whom Marie Brunel had studied in Milan; yet almost everyone interested in singing was afraid of her.

There was no apparent reason for this; she was a very good nun; she was beautiful, gifted and even important. She was of impeccably respectable, dull lineage, but she happened to possess this gift which Paris appreciated – she was a mistress of human singing. And she made this fact so indubitable in her school for young ladies in the Rue des Lauriers that some of the musically informed, even those who truly disliked Mère Marie Brunel, found themselves wondering if in Europe there existed one more masterly in leading the untrained singing voice into song.

She was a woman of powerful kind – tedious, possibly, because she was single-tracked; cruel sometimes, because she was

single-tracked. She was, perhaps, a born teacher. Also, she had
a passionate and fastidious knowledge of that which it was her
duty to teach. Two such powers endanger others within a gifted
personality. But they worked well in Mère Marie Brunel for the
community and school she served. Driven by them she became
an exaggeration of herself, perhaps. And as a minor expression
of this exaggeration, it is arguable that between the years 1882
and 1887, nowhere in France were the Palestrina and Vittoria
liturgical musics sung more accurately than by a number of
stupid, snobbish little girls in the Rue des Lauriers.

'Rose! Little Rose! We've found you! Come, come—' The
sweet, gay voice of Anne de Hauteville rang in the dusty room.
'Come to goûter, come! My father has sent a very superb
chocolate cake – so I looked for you everywhere! Come,
Rosette!'

All this was in French, but it was evident that Rose Lennane
already understood more than she knew she did. She laughed
and sped to goûter with her little aristocratic friend. The two
left the glass door open, and Clare heard their clatter as they
sped along the corridor. She stayed by the sad, silent window,
looking without seeing it at the respectable street. Then, since
she knew that by rule, by the voice of the bell, she must, she
also went downstairs to goûter.

'Yes, Mother Superior. Luisa Carriaga is under discussion. It is
probable that she will be tried out in Naples and Rome next
year. I cannot say how much I regret that her voice is indisputably mezzo-soprano. It is, however, an excellent voice – but it
is, of course, operatic – and therefore it is unlucky that she is
mezzo—'

The three nuns who governed the Convent of Rue des
Lauriers were in their weekly session. This took place at five
o'clock on every Friday. Mère Matilde de Jouvenel, the Superior
and General of the Order, Mère Marie Brunel, Assistant-
General, and Mère Sabine Dubris, the Mother Bursar. These
three women disliked each other; but Mère Matilde, the eldest,
was a holy woman, and sought to bear with the others. More-

over, although she understood very well how much the Paris house and thereafter the other houses of the congregation owed to the accident of Mère Marie Brunel, she knew nothing of music, let alone of singing; so she accepted in tranquil darkness the importance which this convent held in music. She saw, on paper, that its musical eminence was profitable – even if sometimes at a long throw. She was indeed a holy woman, Mère Matilde – but she was also lazy, and might have chosen to conduct her small congregation in a decent unambitious style. But accident had forced Mère Marie Brunel upon her – and that meant that the world and the devil must intrude upon her easy conduct of the pious daughters of Saint Helen. The world and the devil – mercifully not the flesh. Mère Matilde always noted, with lazy relief, that Mère Marie was ascetic even to exaggeration.

However, there was this matter of the human singing voice, which had become a remunerative business for the Pieuses Filles – and which gave much argument every Friday night.

Mère Sabine, Mother Bursar, approved of the convent's traffic in singing voices, because she saw, to her constant surprise, that it showed profits; on paper, in spite of the long chances taken and the mistakes and disappointments, it was demonstrable that Mère Marie Brunel's fanaticism made money. Nevertheless Mère Sabine disliked Mère Marie, and moreover cared less than nothing for music in any of its forms.

So, they were an ill-assorted three who ran the business of Les Pieuses Filles de Sainte Hélène.

'You have imported two girls from Ireland, at absolutely rock-bottom rates, Mère Marie—'

'I know. I'm coming to them—'

'But they're only on probation, aren't they?' said Mère Matilde, peaceably.

'That is so, Mère Supérieure,' said Mère Marie. 'You know the usual arrangement. If after two months I, Signor Manci and Frau Sturz have decided that they have *not* got voices worth gambling on – their parents or guardians can either remove them, or let them stay on on the terms of the general school. The arrangements are perfectly clear – as Mother Bursar knows.'

Mère Matilde smiled.

'I remember those little Irish creatures, I think,' she said. 'Especially I remember the little one who arrived – was it a fortnight ago? Her name – is she Rose – Rose something?'

'Yes, Mother Superior. That little one is called Rose Lennane. Now you know I will not prophesy. This is a very under-developed and under-educated child. But the people who arranged to send her here made no mistake. It is quite possible that we have a good soprano in this little girl. *But*, she has everything to learn in any case – apart from singing.'

'That is what I wish to question,' said Mère Sabine. 'We take into our house this possible *diva*, at the lowest conceivable rates. We educate her, for almost nothing—'

'We do not offer real education,' said Mère Matilde, wearily.

'We teach her French and manners, and we give her access to education,' said Mère Sabine impatiently. 'Then it may turn out that she can't sing at all, by your standards, Mère Marie!'

'In which case, as you know, her guardians have the option to allow her to remain at the normal fee, or to remove her. I always know within six weeks whether a voice is worth our gamble, or to be dismissed to the choir and general singing.'

'You always know. But meantime we have taken on these young ladies at our lowest rate, Mère Marie.'

'Yes, Mère Sabine,' snapped Mère Marie.

'Patience,' said Mère Matilde. 'Patience, my sisters. There are things I want to know. You are disappointed, Mère Marie, that this beautiful Luisa has a mezzo-soprano voice. Why does that disappoint you?'

'Only because the voice is operatic – the temperament oper-atic, Mère Supérieure. Luisa has a singing voice which is flexible and promising; but her range is strictly middle – and she is, alas, operatic. She can sing the German Lieder, of course, and she can sing religious music. In fact, Luisa will be able to sing anything – but, her temperament is operatic, and she should have been soprano. Instead, she has this exquisite mezzo-soprano voice – and she is too young for most of the greater music that has been written for her kind of voice. In fact, Mère Supérieure, I do not know what to do about Luisa.'

'Wonderful!' said Mère Sabine. 'We have had Luisa here at minimum fees, which are not even paid up to date, Mère Supérieure, and now we are to wonder what to do with her talent!'

Mère Matilde smiled.

'Luisa will find her way. She is a gifted creature. I am no musician, but I take pleasure in the sounds she makes. I think there are many like me, who will like always to hear Luisa sing. But now, as to this evening's business – what is particularly to be discussed, my children?'

Mère Sabine looked up from her note-book.

'The accounts are as I presented, Mère Supérieure,' she said. 'You must examine them, and question them next week. They are in reasonable order. What I wish to discuss is the terms on which we keep on accepting these singing candidates. I'm not sure that our arrangement is the best possible. For instance, these two young girls from Ireland – both have been offered to us because of the reputation of Mère Marie—'

Mère Marie smiled at her Superior.

'Mère Supérieure,' she said. 'In so far as I am useful to this community I serve it through my interest in the singing voice. So I have taken a chance with these two voices – which are being paid for, and will not cost us a penny, may I say?'

Mère Matilde smiled.

'You don't have to dispute, my children,' she said lazily. 'Nevertheless, what of these two new protégées?'

'Mère Supérieure, they are interesting, surmisable, *quâ* voices. They are temperamentally contrasted. But in background – or rather in its lack, in being poor, in being Irish – they are valuable to each other at this stage; they are in sympathy, and they run near together. It is a fortunate accident that they have met in this house – may be here together for the probation period paid for – until we see what we think of them.'

'Well, what are we likely to think of them, Mère Marie? Has Signor Manci tested them?'

This was a formal question. Everybody knew that Signor Manci's judgment, although important in Paris, could not influence Mère Marie. But also it was accepted that, being a nun,

Mère Marie took cover under the solemn mantle of the *maestro*. So now she answered her Mother Superior, as if for Signor Manci.

'Certainly these two voices have been tested. *Quâ* voices, in embryo, there is no doubt as to either. They are potentially excellent. They are as good material as the voice of any sixteen-year-old girl can be guessed to be. But for a while there must be silence – musical education, intensive; also general and linguistic education – and no singing whatsoever for some months. We are in no doubt that, allowing for physical accident or breakdown, or some unusual degree of stupidity – and neither of these ignorant girls is stupid, Mère Supérieure – the two can be shaped into valuable soprano singers. Luckily, also, both are likely to be handsome women. That is a great asset.'

'I agree,' said Mère Matilde. 'In fact I have no serious qualms about these Irish investments, nor, I believe, has Mother Bursar. In any case, we can only trust our expert –' she smiled at Mère Marie – 'and you will agree, Mère Sabine, that the convent owes a good deal to the judgment of its musical directress?'

Mère Sabine nodded grudgingly.

Mère Marie Brunel, encouraged by the drawled benevolences of Mère Matilde, thought of enlarging somewhat her argument about the Irish girls; but she decided on silence. That which she had in mind to say was to her, a musician who listened with cold exactitude to sounds, accurate, and moreover it contained the problem which gave her much to pause upon in the matter of the two in question. But, she reminded herself, to an ordinary person the analogy that teased her in regard to Rose Lennane and Clare Halvey would be a pretty sentimentality – no more. So, impatient and unsentimental, she held her tongue now, and kept, as usual, her own counsel.

'Thank you, Mère Supérieure,' she said demurely.

Mère Matilde eyed her Mother Assistant with caution.

'You smile oddly, Mère Marie! Are you in possession of a secret?'

'Only, perhaps, the secret of how people should sing, Mère Supérieure!'

'And after all you can't share that with us, who are more than half deaf, you'd say!'

'Oh, I beg you, Mère Supérieure—'

A lay-sister came in to announce that Frau Sturz was in the parlour and desired to see Mère Marie Brunel.

The latter looked to her Superior, who flicked a lazy hand.

'Yes, of course. Rather you than I, Mère Marie! How can you suffer that woman?'

'She is a real musician, Mère Supérieure.'

'Yes, she's real. But it's curious that such an appalling amount of reality should be married to music!'

Mère Marie, standing up, laughed.

'Go, Mère Marie; and greet Frau Sturz for me. And now, Mother Bursar, let me look at that black account book, and all the bills and grumbles.' The door closed on Mère Marie and the lay sister. The old Mother Superior passed her fat, wrinkled hand across her eyes.

'Thank God!' she said.

Mère Sabine tried to look unamused.

'Do you recall when Mère Marie entered the religious life, Mère Sabine?'

'No, Mère Supérieure. I was in Rheims, as you know, until 1880.'

'Ah, of course. I think it would have been about 1871 – yes, about sixteen years ago? Difficult to understand`– ah, yes, let us face your old black book, Mère Sabine!'

The winter moved on. The two girls from Ireland were not allowed to sing. But, according to their natures, they spread and grew. They were lonely; they were lively – and they had, however unexplored and undefined, musical gift, musical need and desire.

By March of 1887 both were fluent, if not accurate, in French, and beginning to feel their way in Italian.

'Well, you see what I mean, Rose – even if we don't become singers, we are receiving education, which we can turn to account, and with which we can repay whatever has been put out for us. Oh, Rose – have sense! It's much better to know

French and Italian than to be working a sewing machine in Lackanashee.'

'I suppose so,' said Rose. 'But now I've got the bit between my teeth – and I'd like to be good at singing.'

'I wouldn't,' said Clare.

Rose stared at the other.

'It's what we've got to be, now,' she said.

'I know,' said Clare. 'I wish it weren't.'

They were walking in crocodile past the Madeleine, on their way from a Sunday afternoon concert at the Conservatoire. Ten of the pupils of Rue des Lauriers were being escorted home by Frau Sturz. The evening was cold and hailswept.

Luisa Carriaga came and put her arm through Clare's.

'You're depressed,' she said in French. 'I know by the back of your neck.'

'She doesn't want to be good at singing,' said Rose.

'Well, that's no use,' said Luisa, 'because I'm afraid they think she's going to be good.'

'Still, good or not, I needn't sing if I don't want to.'

Luisa, who loved Clare, laughed delightedly.

'What would you do instead?' she asked.

'I'll go home, after a bit, and teach French and Italian, when I know them properly. I'll teach music too. And I'll be a nun.'

'Oh no, stop it!' said Rose. 'You're not to be a nun.'

'This concert annoyed you,' said Luisa. 'Why, Clare?'

'I was thinking,' said Clare, 'that it was unlikely that any of us three, say, will ever sing better than Madame Varonde, whom we heard today. And that's all it comes to, standing up there, tired and ugly, going through all the tedious antics of the *Winterreise*.'

Rose and Luisa gasped together.

'Schubert!' Rose squealed.

'I know. I'm only saying that I don't care for that kind of thing, and I don't want to be doing it when I'm as old as Madame Varonde.'

Luisa laughed and looked bewildered.

'It's lovely music, Clare – and very difficult to sing.'

'Oh, it's music, fair enough. I wouldn't call it lovely music,

Luisa – but it's music. And of course it's difficult to sing. Only – it isn't worth the trouble. No singing music *is* worth all this fuss about the voice, it seems to me.'

'Clare! You're exaggeratedly depressed today,' Luisa cried.

'Am I? I hate the idea of singing! I want to go home!'

Tears poured down her white face.

The three girls crowded together for warmth as they crossed the Pont de la Concorde.

'You're not to dream of going home,' said Rose. 'How dare you say such a thing, you cruel creature you!'

'Clare,' said Luisa, 'it's only that Schubert's bored you. You won't be a nun, I think.'

Frau Sturz came and rapped Luisa on the shoulder.

'Relax, young ladies! No embracing, if you please! Decorum, decorum.'

'Decorum,' said Luisa, removing her arm from Clare's. 'Decorum requires that you stop crying, Clare.'

'I'm starving,' said Rose. 'I'm frozen.'

'So am I,' said Luisa. 'But I've got some quince preserve – very nourishing, Rose. We'll guzzle it at supper.'

'Thank God!' said Rose. 'I'm dying to guzzle something.'

'You'll get fat,' said Clare.

'And so shall I,' said Luisa. 'A sign that we'll be better singers than you!'

When Frau Sturz escorted the chosen young ladies of Rue des Lauriers to a Conservatoire concert, the route of the long march home never deviated. They crossed the river by the Pont de la Concorde, they followed the Quai d'Orsay to the Champ de Mars, re-crossed the Seine at Pont d'Iena into the Quai de Passy, and shortly, through dull and solemn streets, reached the ugly Rue des Lauriers. When Mademoiselle Perrin was in charge the return home sometimes became fantastically adventurous, and never repeated itself. Rose and her friend, Anne de Haute-ville, and Luisa too, became clever at misleading the fussy old lady, who had little sense of direction and whom Paris terrified. But Frau Sturz had in all things a sense of direction, and nothing terrified her. So on this cold Sunday evening her crocodile crossed the Pont d'Iena exactly at the time they should.

Mère Marie Brunel was expert and industrious in arranging for her pupils to attend such concerts, operas and performances of the Théâtre Français as she deemed necessary for them. She always obtained for them, without charge, excellent seats. But this done, and reliable escort appointed, she gave no further thought to her forthright educational programmes. In winter, in snow, with coughs, colds, headaches, bilious attacks, with thick coats or thin, with or without gloves, in broken shoes or satin slippers, those whom she wished to hear *Don Giovanni* or *Phèdre* or the Goldberg Variations, set out when she said so, and trudged about Paris, and made what they might of the bleak, uncomforted experiences she insisted upon.

There was much to be commended in her arbitrariness. Her charges were young; were they to advance in the careers she could initiate for them they must be assumed to have basically good health. So, did the health of any one of them give way under the rigours of a cold and uncosseted life in Rue des Lauriers, and of a Paris winter unprotected by cabs, umbrellas, warm coats or loving-kindness – so much the better and quicker. If a sixteen–seventeen-year-old girl could not, in meeting the first essentials of what her talent required, ride above a few physical hardships and humiliations, the sooner that was discovered the simpler for everyone, thought Mère Marie Brunel.

Indisputable, so far as it went. There had been a time in her own life – a happy, flowing, young-girl time which the rigid nun had forgotten now in her late thirties – a time when she might have been able to admit, and dreamily, that youth, *naïveté*, courage and burning curiosity will take a racing spirit over terrifying fences, which are not even seen as the young heart rushes and rides them. She might in her pliant days have guessed – what she was to learn for herself – that failure and sorrow more often lie in wait for innocent *élan*, for radiance, than for drill and discipline. But if now she ever considered the sad question – and sometimes, as she listened for instance to the arpeggio-practices of Luisa Carriaga, it did indeed make her pause – the more did it confirm her in the rightness of drill and discipline.

It is possible that Mère Marie, in so far as she was trainer and educator, which was now what she totally was, believed that the artist – and her concern was entirely with the singing artist – must not be allowed to be other than an organ, almost a mechanism, until the technical power, the instrument which is all that the creature is or needs to be, has been brought to its limit of excellence – established and finished strength. Then, she might say, let life come in, if it must, and human desires, and all the commonplace troubles. But first we shall have built a singing voice. And, because of our method, it will be pure of vulgarity.

The crocodile shuddered home, under hailstones and through the ugly streets about the Place du Roi de Rome. The girls reached their dormitories and red-curtained cells. If they had dry stockings and slippers to change into there they were lucky.

Clare sat on her bed and considered what she had heard in the afternoon. She hummed over a Schubert-phrase – and realized as she did so that it was not from the *Winterreise* but from the *Schöne Müllerin*. Worse, she said, worse. Why can we only sing about what isn't true?

But she was only sixteen – and she was cross, uncertain and at bay.

'Come on! Come on down to supper!' cried Rose. 'Here are two letters for you! And I have a big letter from Mamma! Oh, come on!'

The letters from Ireland often arrived on Sunday evening, and such as they were had frequently during the winter been of exaggerated comfort against the chilly, gas-lit melancholy, the sanctimonious twilights of Rue des Lauriers. So the two clutched their letters gladly now and raced down the slippery stairs to the refectory. They would read them in peace, after supper. For the moment, it was enough to have them and hold them.

The Second Chapter

Dearest Mamma,

Thank you very much for Tuesday's letters. Why do you write such short letters, Mamma? I am very glad that you and Aggie are well and that Mrs Parkinson was pleased with the petticoats. Were they silk? Did you have to pleat them? But I do not see how you could do that. All the petticoats are pleated here. We see the *blanchisseuses* doing the pleating sometimes, in the windows they do it. We look at everything when we are walking to our lessons with Signor Manci, or to the Opera. But of course Frau Sturz makes us walk very fast.

Now, Mamma, please will you ask Miss French this for me, because I can only write one letter on Sunday, and this question is urgent. Will you ask Miss French please to see that I can come home for the summer holidays. They will be in the middle of July, so there is not much time. I suppose the Committee are told by Mère Marie how I am getting on. I do not know at all how I am getting on. Mère Marie allows no questions, and Frau Sturz is always very cross. Signor Manci is nice, and would answer me, I think, but I am not allowed to address him except when he addresses me about my lessons. So I do not know where I am. But I must go home, Mamma, for the summer holidays. Please tell Miss French, and tell her to tell this please to the Committee.

Clare is writing to her father to tell him the same. She wants

to go to her grandmother in Ballykerin, just like I want to go to
you to Lackanashee. Only the thing is we must have the money
for our tickets, and a little money for food. We both agree that
we could travel without Father Lucius or anyone now, because
we can speak French and we understand about francs and pounds
and things. We would not stop anywhere, Mamma. There would
be no need to. If we just had our tickets and money for sandwiches
we would keep on going, as we know about the trains and
boats, until we got home. So please ask Miss French to ask the
Committee to write to Mère Supérieure, and if they can be so
kind as to send the money. The cheapest ticket would be the
best. It will be lovely to go home, Mamma. I am ashamed to ask
the Committee to let me go home to see you, but I will repay
them. Even if I am not a very rich singer I will be able to earn
money teaching people French and things. That is what Clare
says, and it makes me steady when she says it, because I think it
is sensible.

We have learnt a great deal of things already, as you know.
They are very pleased with our French and Italian, but we also
learn German, and correct English from Lady Maud Hartingale,
and then we learn etiquette and Shakespeare, and all about operas
and oratorios and breathing, and how to behave in public. But
there is a great deal we do not know yet. Still, I wonder if you
and Aggie will know me, Mamma? How is Shep? Is his paw
better? Tell Mr McMahon that I think I am as tall as him now.
The caramels he sent last week were simply lovely. Please thank
him very much until I see him.

This is a long letter, Mamma, as long as about six of yours.
But it is *urgent*. I will tell you now really why it is urgent. It is
because Clare and I have to sing to some special gentlemen, in
private, on the 6th July. That happened to Luisa Carriaga in
March, and the next thing we knew she was gone, to Rome.
Mère Marie told us nothing, and Luisa was not even allowed to
say goodbye to Clare – her best friend. So we are a bit uneasy.
Of course, neither of us sings nearly as well as Luisa yet, and I
think the gentlemen will say so. One of them is an English lord.
Could you believe that? Would you ever think English lords
would know about singing? And another of these gentlemen is a

cousin of the Pope. And Mère Marie says there will be two gentlemen from Milan. We are both frightened, but we think they will surely say that we are no good yet. So then we can go home until October, like all the others in the school.

My hand is stiff, I never wrote a letter like this – but it is urgent. You see that, please? Dear Mamma, please speak quickly to Miss French. I am nearly sick with wanting to go home and see you. Give my love to Aggie and Shep and Mr McMahon and Miss French and everyone.

Love and kisses and hugs, Mamma,

Your ever-loving daughter,

Rose

P.S. Please show this letter to Miss French. That will be best. I will have no presents to bring home. That is an awful pity, but then I have no money at all, as you know, Love and kisses, X X X X X – Rose

Rose sighed with relief. Her hand burnt from this sustained effort of writing; so did her eyes and her cheeks. She looked across the desk.

'It's nearly Benediction time, Clare. Are you finished?'

Clare looked up from her letter, nodded, wrote another line, and carefully blotted the sheet. She also sighed, and her eyes burnt anxiously, like Rose's.

'You didn't write as much as me?'

'Father doesn't like long letters.'

'But you *did* explain? You did say it was urgent?'

'Yes. Do you think they'll send the money, Rose? Do you think we'll be let go home?'

'Oh, we must go!' Rose wailed. 'Look at how *good* we've been! Look at all we've put up with!'

'I'm afraid of Mère Marie. Rose, we're not just at school like the others – we're kind of prisoners, in a way—'

'Oh goodness! Oh, don't say that—'

The first bell rang for Vespers and Benediction, so the two put their letters into envelopes and addressed them carefully. They did not close the envelopes, as Mère Supérieure must read every letter that left or entered the convent; but there was a general belief that she was lazy in the task, and especially lazy when letters were written in languages, such as English, of which she knew little. Neither did they stamp their letters, these two, as they had no pocket money. Their postings to Grandmother, to Mamma, to Father, to Miss French – were charged on their general bill.

So they took their black veils and missals from their desks, placed their letters in the basket by the door of the study hall, and descended to their places in the chapel.

Later that evening Mère Supérieure *did* read the two letters to Ireland. Through some whim of interest in Clare and Rose she always read their letters. The handwritings of both were clear and childish, and their sentences were simple; thus the old nun's dimly-retained knowledge of English supported her curiosity sufficiently, so that after eight months she now knew far more about Father and Mamma and Miss French and Grandmother than the girls who wrote to them imagined.

She read these two letters slowly, and then re-read them. She did not smile, as almost always she smiled over Rose's letters. And when she refolded the sheets and placed them in their envelopes, she sat and tapped them with her fat fingers for some minutes. Then, decisively, she sealed and stamped them, and gave them with the rest of the school's mail to Soeur Antoine. Mademoiselle Perrin would go to the post before supper.

'Poor children! Poor little girls!' said Mère Supérieure. She polished her spectacles, adjusted herself in her cushioned chair, opened a volume of pious meditations, and quietly dozed off.

By this end of June 1887 Clare and Rose had undergone eight months of intensive and narrowly directed education. During the first three of those months, loneliness, bewilderment, ignorance and linguistic confusion had made them feel sometimes as if drowning. But they had each other to cling to – buoyant pieces of flotsam. Also each had a fretted sense of obligation towards the mysterious scheme which had been undertaken for them; they took it with solemnity, and knew that in later life they would somehow have to justify all this for which they had not asked. They were quick-witted, too, and friendly, and

almost without effort rapidly gathered up enough French to
enjoy the company of their school friends and to become an
easy-fitting part of the strange routine of Rue des Lauriers, and
of that fraction of Paris which they were allowed to see and
study.

They were both in their eighteenth year now. Clare had
become seventeen on the 2nd November and Rose on the
5th April. Each had grown taller, and Rose was losing her
schoolgirl plumpness, in spite of much and excellent food. Frau
Sturz insisted on lavish food for her singing potentials; and it
was embarrassing to Clare and Rose that they were so much
better fed, as Luisa had been, than their non-singing companions of the refectory. This was all the more embarrassing in
that they had no money at all with which even modestly to
return the kindnesses of these companions, let alone to buy
themselves new hair ribbons or stockings or collars. The two
looked indeed now in June very shabby and down-at-heel, but
Mère Marie never paid any heed to their anxious pleas for small
repairs or renewals in the cheap and limited school outfit which
had been provided for them in October. Other girls received
what they required in order to look neat and ladylike from their
parents, and on Sundays and feast days were allowed to wear
silk frocks from home and pretty hats. But the two from Ireland
grew ragged as spring passed over them and summer came, and
not all their anxious darning and brushing could make them
seem otherwise.

'I sometimes think when we're in the crocodile that we're
like a pair of kitchen-maids that the others have brought along,'
Rose said.

'It won't be long,' said Clare. 'If we work hard we won't be
long here.'

'Anyway, when we get home in July we can fix ourselves a
bit. I know Mamma will make me a nice dress or two.'

'I suppose they'll give us our own clothes to travel home in?'
said Clare. 'The things we came in, I mean. I wonder where
they locked them up?'

But the two were worked so hard, their days were so cram-
full of tasks that were strange and exacting, and they were

always so tired when they got to bed, that there was not much time left to them to brood on their enforced appearance of dilapidation.

They were being crammed, as milk-fed calves, for one purpose.

What might be called their general education, that part of it which they shared with the rest of the school, was kept narrowly but forcefully along linguistic and literary channels – they had to work intensively at French, Italian, German and English; there were the usual religious studies; history was sketchily taught, and for them mainly it was history of art; in particular, musical and dramatic art in Europe since the sixteenth century.

But in their especial field they were slave-driven, and sub-jected to rigid labours that at first had mystified and dis-heartened them; but when in April they were allowed to sing notes, then scales, then exercises, for one half-hour each day, they began to feel a little where they were being led; they grew alert to the purposes of the daily breathing exercises, the vowel practices and the consonant; they began to listen for each other's progress, and to criticize, not only themselves, but the singers they were taken to hear. And they told each other often, for courage, that there might well indeed be point and light somewhere not too far ahead of this period in Rue des Lauriers.

They were good children; and if they were innocent, and still comically unaware of the traps and dangers which would lie all around them when they moved further along the path on which others had planted for them their uncertain feet, they were nevertheless intelligent; and in singing, especially in studying to sing the first songs allowed them, they found exhilaration, and often great fun.

'I don't know what they'll make of me in Lackanashee – I'm so highly educated all of a sudden!' said Rose sometimes.

And Clare laughed too, and saw far-off her grandmother's witty, loving eyes searching her for the changes wrought in a few lonely months.

They each had one thirty-minutes' lesson twice a week with Signor Manci; they went together to his house, chaperoned as a rule by Mademoiselle Perrin, but for every fourth lesson the escort, and commentator, was Frau Sturz. On the other five days of the week they took their thirty-minutes' singing alone, save that on Saturday mornings Mère Marie sat in the practice-room, and took notes. And on every day of the week they had half-hours of breathing exercises, of laryngeal and labial exercises, of vowel and consonant exercises, with Mère Marie. With Frau Sturz they had stern half-hours of pianoforte prac-tice, of musical theory, of score-reading, and of the history of opera.

They were busy. And now at the end of June they were anxiously studying to be ready for the 6th July, when in Mère Marie's sacred music-room they would each have to sing two prepared operatic pieces for the conclave of renowned gentlemen. They had to be ready also, if asked to do so, to sing any third song which they might have studied earlier in the year.

Signor Manci had assigned to Clare 'Caro Nome' from *Rigo-letto*, and 'Regnava nel silenzio' from *Lucia di Lammermoor*. She liked the latter choice, but felt uneasy about 'Caro Nome'. Rose was to study 'Ah fors e lui' from *La Traviata* and Cheru-bino's song, 'Voi che sapete', from *The Marriage of Figaro*.

'Why did he have to give me that? It's a boy's song!'

'I think you're lucky. I wish he'd given me Mozart,' said Clare. 'But you're his pet.'

'Don't you like your ones?'

'Lucia – yes. But Gilda – ah, I don't know!'

'What did Luisa sing for them?'

'Che faro—'

'Oh, lovely!'

'And some lieder, I think. It's ages since I heard from Luisa. I hope I'll have a letter before – before we go home.'

'You're sure to. "Fors e lui" is very difficult, Clare. Do you know that?'

'Yes, I think it is. I'm surprised at his giving it to you for this test. Somehow, "Caro Nome" would suit you better, Rosie.'

'La Traviata – she was, well, she was what you'd call a – a fallen woman, wasn't she?'

'Yes. I think you're a little bit young for – well, for interpretation, pet!'

'I should hope so, you boldie! But, after all, we're only supposed to sing the notes as accurately as we can. That's what Mère Marie is always saying.'

'And she's perfectly right, I think. Anyway, so far as I can make out every second one of these damsels in opera gets to be a fallen woman at some point! It's monotonous! And when you come to think of it, Rosie, isn't it a funny career they're forcing you and me into – to spend our lives singing and acting away as fallen women!'

Rose laughed delightedly.

'What on earth would your grandmother say to that, Clare?'

'Oh grandmother! If she knew the half of it she'd say we were all mad!'

'And yet, Mère Marie is very holy. Do you think she ever sang any of these – bad characters – when she was a singer?'

'I don't see how she could avoid it. They seem all to go either mad or bad – there's no other way out! Except in Mozart and Glück. And they are the best, I'd say.'

They were waiting in a practice-room for Julie Constant – the scores of their prescribed arias, with only pianoforte accompaniment, open on their knees. Mère Marie, very severe about convent rules, of silence during work and against young ladies pairing off together, was shrewdly slack with these two, allowing them often to share a practice-room, and to talk together more than was normally permissible in the house. For she saw that, whereas they were industrious and already far more than they realized mentally engaged with what they had come to Paris to do, yet they were frequently very lonely and puzzled and that to be somewhat free of each other's companionship kept up their morale more efficiently than too much discipline would have done. She said nothing of this, however, so that the two innocents often marvelled at the freedoms which they believed they stole from their hard-driving task-mistress, and wondered if she was in fact as all-seeing as she believed herself to be. But the whole wall between the practice-rooms and the dark corridor beyond was of glass, so that too much giggling, too much leaning on the window-screen, was always concluded, without comment, by the abrupt entrance either of Mère Marie or one of her aides-de-camp.

Julie Constant came in.

'Sorry I'm late, girls! Monsieur Grenaville was as slow as usual – and in a very show-off mood! Who's first? Come on, Rose!'

Julie Constant was nearly twenty, and had finished school, but her parents, who lived in Grenoble, insisted on her boarding at the convent at least during her first year as a student at the Conservatoire of Music. She studied the pianoforte and was held to have a promising talent. She was a big, lively, dark girl, self-confident and good-natured, and she was bored at having to lodge at Rue des Lauriers. She said that in the autumn she would insist on sharing rooms with some other students, somewhere much nearer Rue Poissonière. She was a warm admirer and friend of Luisa Carriaga, and therefore during the winter had resented Clare and Luisa's affection for her. But now, Luisa gone, she was friendly and helpful, and she enjoyed the pretty Rose very much.

'Come on, let's have Cherubino! Naughty boy, are you ready?'

Julie was to be their accompanist on the 6th July. Frau Sturz had commanded her to that responsibility, as herself she would require to sit in the audience and take notes.

So they practised away, singing, repeating, explaining. Although they did not notice this, they enjoyed themselves. While Clare was singing Lucia's story of the lake, Mère Marie came noiselessly into the room, and stood by the door, her hands hidden in her sleeves, the very expression of non-committal attention. When the song ceased she took out her silver watch.

'You have each sung for half an hour,' she said. 'That is all the singing allowed today, young ladies. Ah, there is the Angelus! *Nuntiavit Mariae Angelus Domini . . .*'

The Angelus said, the young ladies bowed to Mère Marie, Clare held the door open for her, and then the three went eagerly downstairs to dinner.

*

On the 1st July Rose heard from Miss French, who said that she had read her letter to her mother to the Committee and that in view of her excellent reports they were all willing – subject to the permission of her teachers in Paris – that she should come home at the end of July, for a month at least; it was probable, Miss French thought, that at present Rose's training should not be broken off for three months, but Lady O'Dowd was writing to Mère Supérieure on behalf of all of them, and when the permission had been received money for Rose's fare would be sent at once. It would also be necessary, of course, to find a suitable person with whom she and her young friend Clare could travel, but that would be more easily arranged from Rue des Lauriers.

I have told your mother of this decision, dear child, and I need hardly say how much she rejoices, and Aggie too, and all your friends in Lackanashee. We shall have to promise solemnly, of course, that you do not sing a note from the time you leave Paris until you return. That will be hard on us all, but I am certain it will be the first condition of your being allowed home so soon. We are longing to see you – you have been very much missed. Your mother keeps well and busy, and sends her love, as does Aggie. I enclose a small present just from myself (one pound). I am sorry it is not more, but you know my circumstances. However, it occurs to me that you may need some fresh laces and ribbons to beautify you for that important 6th, so I trust you will be allowed to buy them with this note. God bless you, Rose. We pray for you here always, but shall say some special prayers on the 6th July . . .

'Oh dear Miss French! Oh, but she shouldn't send a pound! She sent one at Christmas too, you remember, Clare? And really, you know, though she's a great lady, she's very, very poor, and has only a tiny little house! Oh, aren't the Committee good? Isn't this good news?'

(Lady Maud Hartingale had long ago taught Rose how to pronounce the word 'Committee'.)

It was indeed a cheering letter, and it was reinforced for the two by a brief one which Clare received the next day from her father.

4 St Bernard's Crescent,
Drumcondra.
29 June 1887.

My dear daughter,

I see no objection to your coming home for a time, if your teachers allow it. Certainly your grandmother and the young ones will be delighted to see you at Ballykerin, and the western air should do you good after Paris. About your fare, I shall have to get it from your Uncle Matt. But as he is very pleased with your reports and seems to make a great heroine of you in his talk these times, I'm sure he will agree to this extra expense. He and I are not very warm friends at present, so I shall send your Aunt Josie to do the talking. She, by the way, sends this pound, to cheer you up for the 6th. Good luck on that day.

Your fond Father

P.S. When I hear what your Uncle Matt has to say I shall write at once to Mère Supérieure. Good luck again for the 6th. Auntie Josie says she will offer Holy Communion for you on that morning, and she is sending word to Ballykerin to have them all pray for you there.

Father

So, it seemed pretty certain that they would be going home! And here they had two pounds between them – how many francs, Clare? They had never jointly possessed so much, as tips from home had been extremely infrequent and very small. Two pounds! Well, if they sponged and brushed their Sunday black calicoes, then perhaps they could get new white lace collars, new black hair-ribbons, some white cotton gloves, and perhaps even a belt, a glossy black belt each? Could they?

Julie Constant said that indeed they could, and have some change over. But *she* must take them shopping, she said – *not* Mademoiselle Perrin, who was an old fool, and would let them waste their money.

'Leave it to me,' said Julie. 'I'll persuade Mère Marie to give me charge of you! She knows that I've got sense, and that I know Paris. And I've no classes tomorrow afternoon.'

So it was done. Julie, who dressed well on a small allowance, was a vigorous shopper who stood no nonsense, and would not let them pay a sou more than she thought correct for anything. So each one got exactly what she felt to be essential to good order, a pretty lace collar *and* cuffs (the cuffs enchanted them), each a beautiful piece of black silk ribbon with which to secure her hair at the nape of her neck, each a pair of white cotton gloves and a shiny black belt.

'We'll look simply dazzling!' said Rose.

'And see all the change we have! Let's buy *you* something, Julie!' said Clare.

'Oh yes! A shiny belt, Julie?'

'Or a collar and cuffs?' said Clare.

'Nothing of the sort, not a button,' said Julie. 'Don't be such sillies!'

'Ah, but—'

'No buts. Not another word, please. You're simply not going to buy me a thing! But what we're going to do now is go and eat cakes somewhere.'

'Oh, I know! We'll give you a marvellous feast, Julie darling!' said Rose.

'I'm paying for the feast,' said Julie.

Clare turned and faced Julie, laughing.

'If you do that, I won't go to the feast, Julie. Do you hear? Either Rose and I pay for this party, or I'm going home by myself to Rue des Lauriers!'

'And so am I,' said Rose.

'Very well, you proud Irish ladies. But where shall we go?'

'Would we ever have enough for a – a fairly grand place? How much have you got, Clare?'

The two were counting coins in their worn little purses. They were walking along the Boulevard de la Madeleine, and the sun blazed radiantly on them.

'I promised Mère Marie that we'd go to a quiet, respectable chocolate shop,' said Julie.

'Oh no! I'd like to sit, for once, in a grand place. I'd like to see some well-dressed ladies and gentlemen,' said Rose.

'Where I'm going to take you you'll see some,' said Julie, and they crossed the Madeleine steps and entered a small pâtisserie in the corner of the Place. Shady, dark and smelling of rum and coffee. Very elegant. The girls looked around with cautious delight, and seated themselves at a marble table in a window. If the conventual dowdiness and markedly shabby attire of the two younger girls made some of the customers smile, Julie's chic and her air of worldliness reassured the waitress, who took her orders very politely. Clare wanted a *citron pressé*, but Julie said she was already far too thin, and must drink the famous creamed chocolate of this house.

They sat there longer than they should, observing the in-and-out of elegant ladies and gentlemen, and watching the summer afternoon life of Place de la Madeleine, trees, flowers, moving shadows, strong moving light on the grey stones – and life roaring and laughing.

'It's like when we're at the Opera,' said Rose. 'The cut of us – and poor Mademoiselle Perrin, she's worse! – seated in the thick of all those grandees!'

'It won't be long. Rue des Lauriers won't be very long, I think,' said Clare.

'Please God!'

'No, I don't think it'll be long,' said Julie. 'It's sad the way you singing ones just come there for a while and then vanish – for ever.'

'Not for ever, surely, Julie? I mean, you'll vanish too – you won't be always at the Conservatoire, and then goodness knows where we might all meet!'

'When we're famous, and beautifully dressed,' said Rose.

'Goodness knows!' said Julie. 'I wonder where Luisa is? Do you know, Clare?'

'I haven't heard for more than a month. But she was in Rome then.'

'There was some rumour about Naples – I wonder—'

They walked home, meandering by the river, and singing softly, in defiance of orders.

'I'm going to wash my hair tomorrow,' said Rose.

'So am I,' said Clare.

'Mère Marie won't let you.'

'She won't know until it's done.'

'Anne de Hauteville has given us some lovely stuff in a bottle – shampoo she calls it. She brought it back from home on Sunday, so that our hair would look nice for the sixth.'

Julie smiled.

'It's a good idea. But Mère Marie will have a fit! What about sore throats?'

'Oh, nonsense! How could you get a sore throat in this weather?'

Hair-washing was not encouraged at all at Rue des Lauriers; but for her singers Mère Marie regarded it as a major peril and almost an act of insanity. It was well she did not know what was afoot, or about Anne de Hauteville's shampoo; but she knew nothing of what went on in the dormitories.

At a quarter to five on the afternoon of the sixth, Clare and Rose sat with Julie in their usual practice-room, waiting to be fetched by Mère Marie and led to their ordeal. Julie held the portfolio of music on her lap. She had tactfully put on an almost nun-like grey dress, severe and faded-looking.

The two singers sat motionless together opposite her. They looked touchingly immaculate. Helped by their friends they had indeed brushed and sponged their Sunday black dresses of calico, and had persuaded Sœur Antoine to iron them. Their small lace collars and cuffs were perfectly adjusted, the shiny belts clipped in their pathetic waists, their white cotton gloves were on their hands, and their beautifully washed hair – Clare's straight and pale gold, Rose's curly and gold-brown – was smoothly held in place at their napes in the new black silk ribbons. Everything as planned, thought Julie. But the two faces she looked at were almost strange to her, immobile, and startlingly white. Clare was always pale, but now her colour was chalky, and her thin face seemed to have lengthened in a day! But to see Rose so colourless, so un-roselike, was odd indeed. And the usually clear blue eyes of each burnt black now, and shone fiercely.

Neither moved, neither spoke.

I wonder if they're praying, thought Julie.

'You look lovely, my dears,' she said. 'The collars and cuffs are sweet – aren't they?'

Rose tried to smile at her. Clare also made an attempt.

Mère Marie came in and the three stood up.

'Ready, children? How very nice you look! Come now – our visitors are waiting for you.'

They followed her downstairs and into the reception wing of the convent, where her music-room was. They knew this room, having often attended concerts there, and having for the past three days taken their practices there with Julie, so as to get used to the piano and the acoustics. Mère Marie led them past the wide dais and the piano to the centre of the room where Mère Supérieure was playing hostess to five strange gentlemen.

The old nun turned and smiled.

'Ah, here they are, our two Irish songbirds.'

They were presented, Clare curtsying first, then Rose, to a small, bald, hideous man who was an Italian prince – they could not catch his name, but clearly he must be the Pope's cousin. Then they had to curtsy to the English milord, who startled them because he was young, very elegant and fair, and because he giggled when trying to greet them. Lastly they were presented to three middle-sized gentlemen in black, who, they understood, must be two from La Scala and one from the Roman Opera.

They had been told that they were not to speak at all unless directly addressed, and then to answer politely and as briefly as possible. But, thought Julie looking on, there was certainly no need for such injunction. Neither Clare nor Rose could have framed a three-word sentence at that moment, she surmised; and she remembered that, surprisingly, Luisa, whom she had accompanied at her test, had been exactly as nervous and frozen as these two.

The absurd introductions effected, Mère Supérieure excused herself to the strangers, and said she hoped to see them later in the parlour when they would have partaken, she hoped, of a little refection. All the gentlemen bowed low.

As the old nun moved away she patted Clare's cheek and then Rose's.

'Good children, pretty children,' she said. 'Sing prettily now, and God bless you.'

Julie held open the door for her and she was gone.

Signor Manci came forward and led his pupils towards the dais, holding them paternally each by an elbow.

'You are about to sing very pleasingly now,' he said. 'Remember you can only do your best, and you are very young. We will begin with Miss Rose, Mademoiselle Constant. She will sing her two – "Ah fors e lui" first, I think. Then Miss Clare will sing her two. You sit there, to the side – down from the dais, while Miss Rose sings. I do not want her to see you – and the same for her when you sing. God bless you now—'

He went back to his chair beside Frau Sturz, notebook and pencil in hand. Clare, as she took her appointed seat where she would only see Rose in profile, observed that all the five gentlemen, spreading themselves out and pushing their chairs over the parquet, held pencils and writing pads. Mère Marie alone had no such equipment. She stood by herself at the end of the room, her hands in her sleeves, and she appeared to be looking out of the window absentmindedly. But Julie, settling herself at the piano, knew that nothing that happened in this room in the next forty minutes would escape the nun's attention.

Clare turned her eyes away from the gentlemen, whose various faces would have shocked her even had she not felt so sick with fright. She fastened her whole attention on Rose, whose profile was somewhat averted from her. And suddenly filled with fresh amazement at what they were both about to attempt, she prayed calmly for her friend, as out of perfect stillness Julie struck the opening bars.

Mère Marie had disapproved of Signor Manci's choice of 'Ah fors e lui' for a test for either of these almost infant voices. But she had made no protest, because she would have accounted herself officious to do so; also because, despising Manci the man, she had learnt to respect the teacher. Now as Rose sang the hackneyed but exacting and touching aria, the nun saw Signor Manci's point. Although the girl was seventeen, it was a child who sang; yet the form and the difficulties of this piece of music displayed at once the existent purity of her voice and its promise of intelligence and flexibility. Mère Marie observed as she listened that not one of the gentlemen wrote on his pad.

Clare, watching, listening, knew that Rose was singing with all her wits assembled, that courage had come with the first note, that she was putting everything she had been taught into it, and was thinking almost calmly now ahead of every note. She came to the end, having made, Clare thought, no mistake in breathing or timing.

When the aria was over, Rose bowed, and stepped down off the dais to a chair beside Clare's. Julie followed her, and looked at the audience. The gentlemen moved, one or two of them scribbled something on their pads; Leo XIII's very ugly cousin got up, scratching his ear, and spoke a word to Signor Manci; the English milord bent over languidly to whisper something to the Milan gentlemen, then ran his beautiful silk handkerchief over his golden hair.

Signor Manci signalled to Julie and she and Rose returned to the dais. Clare smiled almost normally at the two as they left her.

Cherubino's song rippled out, deliciously – perhaps a little *too* fast, Mère Marie thought, but that again was Signor Manci's decision. In a few minutes Rose's ordeal was over.

The pause was longer now. The gentlemen moved about, muttered together in Italian, helped themselves to drinks of water, made some notes, and had a joke or two with Signor Manci. On these occasions the loquacious Frau Sturz, for reasons of policy, never addressed the visiting experts unless when, all being over, she was called into conference; and Mère Marie did not address them because she could not bear to in such an hour. She stayed upright by the far window, and observed everyone.

Presently seats were resumed, silence fell, and Clare followed Julie to the dais. She began with 'Caro Nome', and Rose, listening and praying for her, thought much as *she* had thought during 'Ah fors e lui', that Clare had courage in hand, and was singing with concentrated accuracy, and with all her brain. Yet, I don't suppose those old fellows know, thought Rose, because it sounds so lovely and easy. Rose had yet to learn how very much old comic men from La Scala know about singing, even the singing of frightened beginners.

Mère Marie, more experienced than Rose, wondered never-theless as she listened and watched if, in these two immature voices, both at present so heavenly pure, elderly men, jaded with hearing singers great and less than great, could at first attending perceive how differently the two girls were going to sing. Blackbird and lark, she had always thought, without sentimentality. The analogy was a mere simplification for her in assessing, as precisely as she could, the two contrasted qualities promised here. Again she observed that nobody took notes.

After a pause, as quiet and commentless as that which fol-lowed Rose's first aria, Clare sang Lucia's 'Regnava nel silenzio'.

Mère Marie admired this aria and thought it very well chosen for Clare's voice. Now she listened in what was for her an almost relaxed contentment.

When silence fell on the dais it lay also for a few seconds over the audience. Then Il Principe, Leo XIII's cousin, stood up, scratching his ear, bowed vaguely towards the three young ladies in the corner, and went into conversation with his col-leagues, who were writing on their tablets. They beckoned Signor Manci, and the anxious girls watched the pointless-seeming laughter and affability from afar off. However, after a few minutes their professor came to them and said that the gentlemen would like to hear each of them sing some song, not operatic, that they had been allowed to study earlier in the year. 'I say nothing, I guess,' said Signor Manci. 'I have a surprise, perhaps.'

Julie had rehearsed each of them in a favourite piece, with Mère Marie's approval and Frau Sturz's supervision, in prep-aration for this possible request.

So Rose went on to the dais again with Julie, and, almost happy now, and thinking of Mamma and the sewing-machine and of going home soon and of all the money she must earn later on, sang, freely, childishly, 'The Last Rose of Summer'.

She was flushed now, and looking her loveliest, and when the song was ended the gentlemen beamed, and murmured: 'Bravo, Signorina.'

Then Clare took the stand. Almost protestingly, Julie

thought, almost in prophetic fear, clearly, poignantly, she sang, 'I know that my Redeemer liveth'.

The attack in her voice was intellectual now, and Mère Marie thought that she felt a subtle wave of surprise go through the gentlemen. Indeed, the nun herself heard something new, something adult and questioning today, often though she had heard Clare work at this too-well-known piece which, herself, she did not admire. It was sung now modestly indeed, but with a quality of holy certainty that spoke questioningly to her, at least, about operatic plans and the obvious mortal destiny of this young girl.

Rose was a little afraid for Clare of this trying, long piece, and had wanted her to sing a Schumann song, since she liked to sing Schumann. But now she felt reassured. It was going beautifully. As it came near the end she looked cautiously at the five gentlemen. They were all completely attentive, and as she studied them she saw Leo XIII's cousin take out a big silk handkerchief and carefully dry his eyes. The sight all but made her so forget the occasion as to gasp.

'Bravo, Signorina, bravo!'

The whole business was through, without noticeable mishap. Oh thank God! Thanks be to heaven!

There was scratching of chairs and a babble of Italian.

Mère Marie came to the three girls. She patted Clare's head, then Rose's.

'Good children,' she said. 'Come and say good evening to the gentlemen.'

Gladly and rapidly they did so, almost giggling back now at milord when he giggled. The Pope's cousin squeezed Clare's hand so that his great ring nearly cut off a finger, she said afterwards. One of the gentlemen from Milan seemed as if he wanted to kiss Rose there and then. But Mère Marie shepherded her three to the door.

'Run off to your goûter now – and enjoy it,' she said.

Delightedly they ran.

They had been allowed, of course, no goûter at the usual four o'clock, but by tradition after this kind of ordeal, the singers had a special festive goûter in the *little* refectory, to which they were allowed to ask two or three of their friends. So Anne de Hauteville, Josephine van de Velde and Teresa Brauch were waiting for the three, with Sister Cléophas to brew the chocolate and pile the plates.

Wildly they laughed while their friends surrounded them; Rose was slightly hysterical; Clare, though she laughed too, felt sick and dizzy.

'What are they like, anyway?'

'A hideous lot!'

'Except the English milord,' said Rose.

'He's rather like an overgrown daffodil,' said Julie.

'But he giggles too much! Oh, girls – the Pope's cousin – do you know what? He cried, he actually cried, when Clare was singing "My Redeemer Liveth"!'

'Nonsense! He *couldn't* cry! It was the heat!'

'Oh no! He wiped his eyes very, very carefully. I saw him, I tell you!'

'Good Lord, Clare,' said Julie. 'If you made one of that pack cry, Heaven knows where you'll end up!'

Clare felt a deadly sense of anti-climax. But she drank her chocolate hungrily, and thought of Ballykerin Strand and of her grandmother.

The party was gay, and handsomely spread. Julie gave as clear an account of the afternoon as she could to the questioning others – Clare and Rose having little more than absurdities to record.

'Oh, and now in a while we'll be going home, and all the fuss is over for the present—'

'The fuss is never over in voice-training,' said Julie warningly.

'Oh, it can be, it must be – sometimes', said Clare. 'Otherwise, what's the good of it?'

'It's going to be over for us for a while anyway,' said Rose, 'and, what's more, I'm going to sing at Benediction tonight!'

'They won't *let* you, Rose!' said Teresa.

'Who's going to stop me? Mère Marie will be busy with all her ugly gentlemen. Will you sing too, Clare?'

'I will – indeed I will!'

'I haven't sung "Tantum Ergo" since I left Lackanashee! Isn't that ridiculous?'

'Well, Miss Rose,' said Sister Cléophas, 'if you're not to put everyone out of tune tonight, you'd better stop eating those cream cakes!'

'Put everyone out of tune? How dare you, Sister Cléophas?'

'Didn't you know, Sister Cléophas,' said Julie, 'that she *can't* sing out of tune? She and Miss Clare suffer from a thing called absolute pitch – it's prevalent in Ireland!'

'Peculiar I call that,' said Sister Cléophas.

The party went on eating and laughing until the Benediction bell rang. Then they went to the chapel and sang all through the service.

'It's almost like being at home already,' Rose whispered to Clare.

Clare smiled; home, to her, still seemed far off.

The Third Chapter

The heat of July in Rome could not do less than impose languor upon grief and rage; or so Clare thought. Yet in the first days it was no ally, but only another of their thousand enemies. In the first days Rose was dangerously distracted by woe and anger, and Clare, though less clamorous, felt defeated and savage too.

She supposed that neither she nor Rose would ever forget their last day, the 8th July, in Rue des Lauriers, when out of a blue sky and without having uttered any kind of preliminary warning, Mère Marie commanded them to pack their trunks, as they were leaving for Rome that night, under the escort of Frau Sturz.

Uncertain whether she had heard aright, each girl had torn into a vociferous scene of protest and refusal. But Mère Marie smiled and repeated her command. Together they swept it aside, and insisted that they would not go to Rome at six hours' notice, that they must be allowed to consult their people at home, that they were sick and tired of slavery. Clare said she did not care if she never sang again; Rose said that she was not an orphan, and would stand no more of being ordered around in darkness.

Mère Marie let them rave. Then she said, gently, that their homesickness was understandable, but that it was a part of what they had to pay to their future, and that no one with a vestigial understanding of their potential talents could tolerate the idea of their taking a vacation at this very precarious and elementary stage in their development. And – a vacation in Ireland! she added with a dry laugh.

'What's wrong with Ireland?' asked Rose in a fury.

'Nothing, child, save its total ignorance about music.'

'If Ireland is totally ignorant about music,' asked Clare, 'why are Rose and I so idiotically important?'

'Because, by accident and by God's goodness, you each hold promise of possessing soon an exceptionally good operatic soprano voice. That is a very delicate possession, and its growth must be the charge of experts, and only of experts. You are two wilful and ignorant young girls, who clearly do not begin to apprehend the difficult thing you have been sent to Europe to do. But you will apprehend it. You will be taught to. Proceed now with your packing. I shall send Sister Cléophas to the dormitory to help you.'

They had demanded to see Mère Supérieure, and were allowed to see her.

The old nun patted their heads and told them to dry their tears, that Rome, the Holy and Eternal City, was the most beautiful and interesting place on earth in which to study and be young; that she was writing that very day to their parents and guardians, to report how satisfactorily both had sung at their test on the sixth, and that the experts from Italy insisted on their immediate transfer to Rome, to begin the serious part of their training. All of this had been foreseen at the initiation of their plan, she said, and would therefore cause no surprise to their people in Ireland. It was routine when a voice promised well. And they would love Rome; she would send their Roman address to their families and the Committee; and in conclusion she enjoined them to be good and dutiful, and always to be faithful to Holy Church. She gave them each a useless little ivory-bound prayer-book in which she inscribed a pious wish and her name and the date, 8th July, 1887. Then she kissed them – a nun's kiss, a brief touch of the cold old mouth on either cheek – and waved them away.

So, after a day of blind storm and fuss, the stresses of which were increased by the sympathetic wrath of their especial friends, at evening they had to climb into a cab and set out for the Gare de Lyon.

Mère Marie stood in the hall to oversee their departure.

'Such unbridled weeping is very bad for your throat, Rose,' she said.

'I'm sick of my throat,' said Rose.

'In a little time you won't say that. Yes, Frau Sturz, everything has gone out to the cab, I think. Goodbye, my children – and try some day to forgive me for knowing what is best for you.'

'Goodbye, Mère Marie.'

She stroked Rose's bent head, and kissed erect, exhausted-looking Clare.

'*Vaya con Dios*,' she said to her softly.

Clare's attention was held by the words, and by some desolate quality in the voice.

'That isn't Italian, is it, Mère Marie?'

'No, child, Spaniards say it, Go with God.'

'*Vaya con Dios*,' Clare repeated. 'Go with God.'

Frau Sturz chased them into the cab, and that was the end of Rue des Lauriers.

Their journey through the hot night and hotter day was for the most part a miserable memory, although Frau Sturz, for the brisk bully she was, proved almost sympathetic, and did at least allow them to grieve and grumble together in peace in their corner of the crammed second-class carriage. For her part she made herself acquainted with their fellow-passengers, and counselled them to pay little attention to the tears and red eyes of her two young Irish charges.

'Ah, Irish!' said one sparkling old gentleman. 'A sorrowful people! They weep much, much!'

This observation actually made the Irish laugh, and thus created all-round relief. And thereafter, when Frau Sturz and others opened their creaking baskets, splendid collations were spread, of cold, sweet coffee, and cold meats and bread and butter and peaches and lemonade. And for a great part of the night the mourners slept uneasily in each other's arms, and Frau Sturz snored firmly, and so did others of the company.

By morning and when Turin was passed, Clare could not but be amazed by the brilliant land and coast through which they raced; but Rose, too much exhausted now to cry any more, would not be bothered to look out upon wonders. Even at Pisa she had to be dragged to the window to consider the Baptistery and the Leaning Tower.

'What of it?' she said cantankerously. And then, with a return to her usual mischievousness: 'The towers at home don't do that.'

This observation pleased the sparkling old gentleman, and from thence to Rome was developed a measure of polite conviviality which reassured Frau Sturz as to the nervous stamina of her erratic pupils.

Upon arrival in Rome she accompanied the two at once to the apartment in Via di Ripetta of Signor and Signora Buonatoli. The former, she explained to them, would be their teacher of singing in his own home, and would control their studies at the Academy of Saint Cecilia, where he was a director and professor. The signora was a kindly lady, half French, half Italian, who had once been a promising opera singer but who, it was said, had not had sufficient health to continue in the career. She would be responsible for their physical well-being, for their conduct, for the hours they kept, etc. Naturally, as students in Rome, they would be less well guarded than they were at Rue des Lauriers, but she trusted them to take no advantage of that – and to work hard and carefully, as was their duty.

After they had had a dazed and long night's sleep in their new quarters, Frau Sturz had called for the two and taken them for their first morning walk in Rome.

Crossing the Corso Umberto, she had shown them the unimpressive façade of their Academy, in Via Vittoria; then through the Piazza del Popolo, having delivered herself of a concise history of its monuments, she took them up to the Pincio, and sat them down on the parapet while she identified the Seven Hills, and pointed out Saint Peter's and the Capitol. Thereafter they descended the Spanish Steps and by way of the fashionable Via Condotti reached home again. Handing them in at her great dark doorway to Signora Buonatoli, Frau Sturz pecked at their cheeks, admonished them once more to be good, turned and disappeared down the stairs. She was to return to Paris that evening.

*

'Tomorrow, my dear friend,' said Signora Buonatoli to her husband, 'tomorrow we all celebrate the great day of Our Lady—'

'What great day, my dear?'

'Why, stupid man, the day of Maria Assunta – our favourite feast in this household! And we are going to celebrate it with an expedition, my children – an expedition into the Castelli! A long day among the Alban Hills – a picnic, as the English say, husband, a *fête champêtre*!'

'Ah no, Vittoria, my dearest! It is too hot! We are too busy!'

'No one is busy on the feast of Maria Assunta, Giacomino *mio*! Besides, it is all arranged! I arranged it in my mind completely, before dawn today! All these dear charges of ours will disport on the Roman hillsides with us – the Irish girls for the first time! And since it is her feast day, Assunta will be with us too – no?' She tapped the hand of her strong young serving-maid, who smiled and nodded as she helped her mistress for the second time to a steaming platter of *pasta*.

Professor Buonatoli shrugged.

'We shall be murdered in the crowds! Still – if you have arranged it, I know, my dear! We'll go! We'll go! Naturally – and God protect us!'

He laughed softly and went on eating.

The dear charges, five of them, smiled at each other, and interestedly, pleased with her notion, at the Signora.

She was a benevolent but moody lady. For luncheon just now she had swept from her room to greet them all after a period of forty-eight hours during which they had not seen her. She was a large presence; above her big powdered face was heaped a great luxury of hair, dyed a rich blackberry shade. She was wrapped in a trailing peignoir of creamy wool, in need of laundering, and she wore many rings and bracelets.

'All ready to sing Norma,' Thomas, the Welsh boy, had whispered to Clare.

The five young lodger-students liked her, but already Clare and Rose had agreed that Frau Sturz and Mère Marie knew less about Roman chaperonage than they imagined – for Signora Vittoria, as she desired her household to call her, was – it seemed to them – as haphazard and lazy as she was good-natured. When she was in the company of her 'charges' she was all theirs, gay, authoritative, and even of educational value to them, because she knew the world they were entering, and her reminiscences had a kind of rakish, dusty brilliance which was novel and informative. But she was a lie-abed, and also she spent long, careless hours with old cronies, laughing and singing and disputing, behind the folded doors of her private *salotto*.

Signor Giacomo it was who saw to the routine of his lodgers' days, who doled them out their weekly pocket-money allowances, who, assisted by Assunta and by his maiden sister who lived in a small apartment a floor below, saw to it that all five were in their rooms before eleven o'clock, and that in no circumstances, save when escorted by him or his sister to opera or concert, did any one of the young ladies leave the apartment after seven o'clock.

For the rest, Assunta and a strong old laundress-scrubber looked after the rambling place – it was in fact two dark and awkward apartments thrown into one – with energy. There was plenty of simple food, everything was Romanly clean, punctuality at meals was insisted on, and curfew for the girls at seven. But, so long as they attended to their lessons and got through all required practice-work – 'Well,' said Rose, 'less guarded than at Rue des Lauriers! Oh, poor Frau Sturz!'

'Mère Marie would faint if she saw the way we're living here!' said Clare.

And the two laughed aloud often in their bed as they considered, in half-alarm, their astonishing, sudden freedom.

But Signora Vittoria *was* the queen of the household nevertheless, as everyone perfectly understood. Assunta adored her, which was odd, as she exacted unflagging attention. Clare was not quite sure that Signor Giacomo adored her as warmly as Assunta did. But she imagined that once he had done so, and he was a too-industrious man who seemed to find more than enough to be adored and to exact attention in his work.

So, on the morning of the 15th August, with all of Rome, the party from Apartment 9, Via di Ripetta 170, set out for the

Alban Hills. Everyone – except perhaps Signora Vittoria – having attended Mass at nearby San Carlo, a very early start was made. Clare, Rose and the Sicilian girl Mariana Fogli were allowed to go to the station by omnibus from San Silvestro, under the escort of Thomas and Tonio. The Professor, Signora Vittoria and Assunta made the transit by open carriage, bringing the baskets.

To a stranger it might have seemed impossible to board the little train for Castel Gandolfo which Signora Vittoria had decided upon. But, inexplicably and almost without a struggle, her whole party of eight got placed, with baskets, shawls and parasols.

The morning was already burnished and blazing, loud with Roman noise, and swollen with feast-day stress and press. But it was Signora Vittoria's intention to reach her chosen place of picnic before the real heat of the day assaulted her; and so she did.

At the little clamorous country station Assunta seized upon two open pony carriages, and well before noon, leaving the high walls of Castel Gandolfo behind, the party found itself paradisially encamped, under great, deep chestnut trees, and resting on moss and fern, low down beside the strange waters of Albano – in a silent grove where few would come, even today.

'Ah, the poor Pope! Our dear Holiness! How he will be disturbed now up there, in his summer fortress!'

'Not at all, Vittoria my dear. He's extremely well walled in – from everything.'

'I hope so, Giacomino. A saintly man, my children. Not a statesman, of course, like Pio Nono. But a gentleman – a very great gentleman!'

Assunta had found a smooth and welcoming tree-trunk for her mistress's back, and now with shawls and cushions throned her about for a rest. Then the devoted girl set to work upon the luncheon baskets. The Professor stretched out a little way off upon cool moss and in sweet shade. The five young ones moved down to the water's edge.

'Here you are, Signora.'

'Thank you, Assunta. Thank you. Again please. That's it.'

The Professor tried not to hear the surreptitious clink of glass or his wife's greedy whisper. He closed his eyes and thought of Verdi's new and great *Otello*, of Tamagno's treatment of the unusually written duet in Act I. '*Gia nella notte densa . . .*' he began to hum, wonderingly.

Antonio de Luca was a Tuscan, but he had been studying in Rome for two years and knew the country of the Castelli.

'We must take you up there some day,' he said. 'You see, Rocca di Papa? It is lovely – and you can ride on donkeys from there to the top of Monte Cavo.'

As Mariana Fogli and Antonio each knew as little French and English as Clare and Rose at present knew of Italian, conversation was not always rapid, but Thomas Evans had Welsh nimbleness with tongues, and having lived nine months in Rome was a helpful guide and interpreter. And now all five, rejoicing in the radiant day, stimulated by the surprises and comedies of their little journey and startled, some of them, by the emphatic, sharp magnificence of the immediate scene, talked or not as they chose, in holiday fashion, and hardly aware if they were listened to, or even whether they spoke or only thought.

'Does anything ever happen in this lake?' asked Rose, in French.

'Much!' said Tonio in Italian. 'Much sailing, swimming – many are drowned.'

'It's very cold and very deep, they say,' said Thomas.

'It looks treacherous,' said Clare.

'Yes,' said the Sicilian Mariana, 'some of the waters further south, some of our Mediterranean bays, look like this. Worse really—'

They all laughed.

'Worse?'

'Oh, I think it is beautiful,' said Rose. 'But it's certainly very still. That might frighten one a bit. Now, our lake at home, where I live—'

'Oh, an Irish lake, Miss Rose! I know what you mean! Ours must be like yours, in Wales?'

'You call yours of Killarney – no?' asked Tonio.

'Not *mine*, Signor Tonio!'

'Nor any of mine,' said Clare.

Assunta was calling, so they turned back into the grove. Luncheon was spread on white cloths, looking very beautiful and copious. The Signora was already at work with glass and fork, and enjoined the others, through a full mouth, to help themselves. They ate with leisurely greed, and drank from the great flasks of Frascati which had been bought in Castel Gandolfo as they drove through.

'We should have made a little fire, and caught and cooked some trout!' cried the Signora. 'Oh, why didn't we think of that, Giacomo?'

'Because such an undertaking would have taken at least an hour and a half, my dear, and you were hungry!'

'But now I'm hungry for those trout I am imagining! How silly we are, Assunta!'

'Are the trout from this lake a funny colour, Signora?' asked Rose.

'A delicious silver-pink, child – fairy fish!'

'Mostly brown,' said the Professor.

'Silver and pink, husband. Beautiful fat fishes.'

'This wine!' Clare held her glass up to the light.

'You like it, Miss Clare?'

'It looks – it looks like music, Signor.'

'It's rather tricky music to drink,' said Rose.

Signora Vittoria chuckled.

'And you for your age, Rosita,' she said. 'I hear you practise, and for your age I say you promise to be graceful with tricky music!'

'Then let us give her another tricky passage,' said Tonio, pouring wine into her glass.

'This will be a very tricky bit!' said Rose. 'Goodness Clare, how we grow up!'

Clare laughed.

'It seems we have to, Rosie. That's being forced on us!'

'Naturally, child,' said Signora Vittoria. 'Drink your Frascati, and grow up and sing! No one will ever sing Italian opera who does not drink Italian wine! And why is my glass empty, may I ask?'

Assunta filled it to the brim.

Thomas leant on his elbow beside Clare, and bit into a dripping peach.

'You like this day, this scene, Miss Clare? You laugh more today than seems to be your habit.'

'Is it the wine?'

'But you drink wine in Via di Ripetta, looking grave as a rule.'

'It's true – I do like today. Or rather, I'm seeing it very clearly – all this—' she waved her hand comprehensively.

'All this – well, what?'

'I'm bad at talking.' He smiled at her. 'Well, it's as marked out as if – as if I were remembering it. Or as if I were, perhaps – seeing it on the stage – oh, silly—'

'I wonder why that is? After all, you're now five weeks in Rome, aren't you?'

'Yes. And I'm still in total confusion. This, though, today – is a separate thing – separate from the other impressions. And then, it's a *first* thing. The first thing of its kind in my life ever. *Fête champêtre*! You see, we – we didn't have them where I was a child. We were poor, and everyone worked hard at my grandmother's, and we stayed where we were always.'

'Ah! So did we at home.'

'I think somehow that we'll all remember today.'

He looked at her kindly.

'You say that as if it were a sad idea.'

'I don't think it's sad. Could you give me some grapes?'

At last the party ceased to eat and drink and the young ones helped Assunta to tidy up and pack the baskets. The Professor commanded them that siesta be observed and that no one was to leave this mossy grove until he gave permission. Those who did not desire to sleep must sit or lie still; they might talk together, but softly. And he presumed he need not repeat – he glared at Rose, who had in fact been heard to hum while packing up, forgetting herself in Frascati, perhaps – must he repeat that no one, no one was to sing as much as a bar in the open air? That said, he lay down and covered his face with a silk handkerchief.

Signora Vittoria was already veiled in muslin, cushioned and a-snore. Assunta sat beside her and drew a piece of embroidery from her workbag. The five moved off somewhat from this settled group, towards where, still under the trees, they could see the green lake and the austere hills beyond it.

'This is just the time I'd like to sing,' giggled Mariana to Antonio, as she seated herself against a tree-trunk, and patted the moss beside her in invitation to him.

'Me too,' said Rose. 'Why, we could have a lovely little practice now, the five of us – very softly—'

'What would you suggest, Miss Rose?'

'Rossini – something from *The Barber*?'

'Great fun! Isn't it a pity? Where are you going to sit, Miss Rose?'

'Here, against this lovely little rock. I can see the lake splendidly now!'

Antonio seated himself tailor-wise between Mariana and Rose. He was a young man of good Florentine family, handsome and with a very promising baritone voice, the cultivation of which displeased his parents. But he was ambitious and cared only for singing, and as they were indulgent and had other sons he had his way.

Clare sat on a fallen tree-trunk at the very edge of the grove, almost in the sunlight; Thomas leant against a tree beside her.

'Why do you stay in Rome, Mariana,' Clare asked her, 'you and Signor Tonio, at this time? I mean, with the Academy shut and everything. After all, you've both been studying for two years, haven't you? And you aren't far away from home, like us others?'

'Oh, you have to stay with your maestro almost unbrokenly for the first years – they're terrified to let a singer out of their reach – almost until they consider you fully trained!'

'Dear heavens!' said Rose.

'Singers have an awful life, Miss Rose,' said Tonio gaily. 'Until you are fit for public performance you are treated like a defective child – indeed, even then you are so treated, I believe!'

'But Rome can't be good, for voices or anything, in this heat?'

'It isn't,' said Thomas. 'And if poor old Giacomo could afford it, like some of his colleagues, he'd have a summer villa somewhere to shift us all to. But he can't do that. He works like a demon – he has a lot of pupils in Rome, you know – and he writes on music for many papers and publications.'

'Why isn't he as well off as his colleagues?'

'I don't know – he's great at his work.'

'I think he's the best teacher in Rome,' said Tonio. 'Certainly he's the most painstaking. They say he has a lot of relatives hanging on to his earnings. But I wouldn't study with anyone else, now I know him so well.'

'He's a fanatical Garcia disciple,' said Thomas.

'We've gathered that,' said Rose.

'But he's not slavish; he's developed some ideas of his own,' said Mariana.

'Yes, and written well on them,' said Thomas.

'His *Italian Voice* is on our reading schedule,' said Clare, 'but my Italian isn't equal to it yet.'

'It won't be for some time,' said Thomas. 'The old man has a crotchety style.'

Thomas dropped to the ground, leant his head against Clare's tree-trunk and closed his eyes.

'A sail!' said Rose softly.

Tawny, sharp-cut, it moved about the ice-green water. Someone, a shrill-noted boy, sang as he steered it, filling the hot silence. The five listened and grew lazy.

Out of shut-seeming eyes Mariana observed Antonio.

She had known him nine months, having come to Via di Ripetta from other lodgings and another maestro in December. She was in love with him now, but with cunning older than herself made little show of that. Indeed she guessed and was even shrewd enough to hope that what she felt was a transitory and juvenile passion. For a Sicilian she talked little and guarded herself almost stolidly; but she was sharp in assessing her world and could calculate realistically what she might hope to extract from it. Success in her profession she would work for with all her strength, and with it, when it came, she would look for domestic security, with a respectable husband and children whom she would love very much.

She was a good girl of peasant stock; neither beautiful nor ugly, she had the bright colour and glow of southern Italy; she was squarely built, had good health, sufficient brains, and a fine contralto voice. She was twenty now, and after two years' hard work in Rome believed that soon she might be allowed to try out her talents in some provincial opera houses. She had been sent to Rome with a scholarship provided by the City of Palermo, and this success had so much pleased her peasant father that he supplemented the scholarship regularly and as liberally as he could. She was very grateful for all of this, and intended to justify it as fully as possible.

Therefore she did not welcome in herself her strong attraction towards Antonio; but indeed had she been older and with thoughts of marriage in her head, she would have welcomed it still less; because she understood well that this young de Luca, while electing to be a singer, a vagabond among vagabonds, was still, and rightly, she conceded, conscious of his social origins and of his duty to them; and he would certainly never, at any point of his life, consider marriage with a peasant.

So she viewed her emotion calmly, and even with amusement. Yet it persisted; it grew. And she observed him now, stretched in strong beauty on the moss, and happily, smilingly observing Rose.

'Young ladies,' said Thomas in his careful, slow Italian which Clare and Rose could follow easily, 'young ladies, since we five are going to be together for many months, would you consider allowing Tonio and me to call you by your Christian names *without* the polite formality – for simplicity's sake?'

The girls all laughed and said that of course they agreed. Tonio sat up.

'Well done, Thomas! Well done indeed! And you ladies in your turn will call us just Tonio and Thomas?'

This also was conceded.

'It's high time, really,' said Rose. 'It's a big, awkward word, Signorina.'

'Prettier than *Miss* though, don't you think?' said Tonio.

'As for you two,' said Rose to Clare and Thomas, 'do you know what? I was looking at the pair of you just now when you were asleep—'

'I haven't been asleep,' said Clare.

'Well, you had your eyes shut – and do you know, it suddenly struck me, you could nearly be brother and sister – really, you're almost twins, aren't they, Mariana?'

'It's a little true – I have noticed it,' said Mariana.

'But it can't be!' said Thomas. 'I've an old scarecrow of a face – and look at Miss Clare!'

'Oh, I didn't say you're as handsome as Clare!'

'How could you be, you silly Thomas?' said Tonio.

'It's just that you're like her. Do you see what I mean, Clare?'

'Well, I see that he's more like me than my own brother Tom.'

'Ah, you have a brother Tom?' said Thomas. 'What a pity! What is he like?'

'He's two years older than me; he's dark-haired, and a bit – chubby. He's going to be a priest.'

'You make many priests in Ireland,' said Tonio. 'We have some of your young ones in Rome. You see them, Rose? They wear the purple sash?'

'Yes. I'd like to know some of them, to talk to them. Only that wouldn't be allowed.'

'Indeed it wouldn't, quite rightly!' said Tonio. 'But why wish to talk to seminarists?'

'Because I'm lonely.'

'As lonely as that? Oh, we must indeed cheer you up!'

Clare rose and walked out towards the lake. Thomas moved after her.

'You'll get into trouble if you're caught,' he said.

'Oh, only for a minute! You can't see anything under the trees. And it's not so very hot.'

They moved across the path and stood above the green water.

'What's it like when the Academy is open, Mariana?' asked Rose.

'Busy, very busy. You'll have a lot to do.'

'I have a lot to do already! What with Italian with Signorina Caterina – the Professor's maiden sister – and German with Herr Stüfel, and all the work Signor Giacomo expects done, all the reading if it was nothing else—'

The other two laughed.

'A mere nothing, Rose!' said Tonio. 'When term begins they'll wear you out!'

'Still, Rome must be exciting when everything is going full blast. When the opera is on, and everything. Is the standard good at Costanzi's?'

'It varies. The important singers move about very much in Italy, you know – and after La Scala they like best engagements at Costanzi's or at San Carlo in Naples. But we sometimes hear very good opera at the Argentina or the Valle. Don't we, Tonio?'

'Yes – but it's a pity, Rose, that you weren't here for the Roman première of *Otello*!'

'Heavens, yes!' said Mariana.

'After the Scala première in February, they sang it at Costanzi's – in March. Tamagno, Maurel! Marvellous! I wonder if I'll ever sing Iago?'

'Very likely you will,' said Mariana.

'With you as Emilia? And Rose as Desdemona! What a wonderful cast!'

Mariana laughed.

'The *maestro* Verdi writes too many mezzo-soprano parts for my taste,' she said.

'Oh, you could sing Emilia. You're not a real contralto, Mari—'

Movement was stealing back into the afternoon stillness. Shouts of swimming boys rang out; a mandolinist strummed as he passed by under the trees, his country love upon his arm. A white sail sped past the idle tawny one.

'La Signora wishes that you come and amuse her, if you please,' said Assunta.

Signora Vittoria, unveiled and refreshed, was in happy humour. Signor Giacomo still lay motionless and with covered face.

'Look at that lazy figure,' his wife said good-temperedly. 'You'd be justified in imagining that he does not sleep at night! But where is Thomas, and our grey-eyed Chiara?'

'They're here on the rocks, Signora,' said Tonio, and, running back, he called them. They returned into the grove.

'You ventured from under the trees at the crest of the day?' said Signora Vittoria; and Signor Giacomo peeped out as if exasperated from under his handkerchief. 'Oh, you creatures of the north! Will you never understand?'

'Never, Signora,' said Thomas, dropping on his knees beside her. 'Understand Italy? How could we?'

'Understand Italy? But no – of course not! All we ask is that you try to understand how to *live* in Italy!'

'We'll try. Won't we, Clare?'

'You must.' She eyed the two shrewdly. 'And now let us all eat some grapes and cakes. Assunta!'

'No cakes for you, Signora,' said Tonio. 'You're going to sing for us, aren't you?'

'Am I?'

'Oh yes! Please yes!' they all cried.

'Some of those songs from your village,' said Thomas.

Signora Vittoria's childhood had been spent high up in Etruria, near Volterra. And when she felt so inclined she made dramatic play with the Etruscan idea, in relation to herself, her forbears and her scattered talents and beauties.

So now, with style and accuracy, she sang songs she had heard in her mountains long ago. Clearly she loved to sing them, and she knew how to sing. Clare and Rose guessed, from amused lights in the others' eyes, from Assunta's open laughs, from Signor Giacomo's sitting up and listening with an anxious expression, that some of the lines she sang, in sad songs or gay, were not such as Thomas would readily translate for them; but as they were in a dialect which probably he did not understand, they were little troubled, and enjoyed what they could appreciate, the delicious, skilful singing, the deeply-schooled art concealing an art which had been abandoned but was not dead.

After a slow, sad song, the singer laughed and said: 'Now I *will* have some cakes, at once, Assunta!'

Said Clare: 'Forgive me, Signora, but that which you have just sung—'

'It is a burial song, Clare. It is known in my village as "Her Music for His Tomb"—'

'It seems a good name, Signora. But – it reminded me of something I heard a girl singing once, in a boat in the bay at home. I couldn't write music down, and it's a long time ago – but this—'

'All sorrowful peoples echo each other somewhat when they sing, Clare – especially when they sing. And your race is old and sorrowful. But we, Etruscans, we are like no one, and none have captured anything we had. We are a mystery, the oldest of Europe's mysteries, and we are quite alone. We are as we are, and like no one else – there are no echoes anywhere—'

'That is perfectly true, my dear,' said the Professor. 'There are no echoes, and you are precisely as Etruscan as is Thomas here, from Wales, or our dear Mariana!'

'You say these impatient things, my dear Giacomino! But I do not blame you, as you know. He is a good man, children, and a good musician. That is a lot to be.'

'If you can't be Etruscan,' said Tonio gaily. He was allowed much by the Signora, who liked good looks.

'Signora,' said Rose, 'I've been told that you were a very great Traviata.'

'Who told you, child?'

'Signorina Caterina.'

'Ah, my dear sister-in-law, bless her! Is she right, Giacomo?' Her husband smiled gently.

'Vittoria, you know as well as I do that you were the most beautiful Violetta that has yet sung the part anywhere. That you will ever be matched in it I beg to doubt.'

'You see! What he says is true – and look at me now! Look at me now! Now, children, I am exactly like all the Traviatas that are to be seen in every opera house in Europe! But the difference is that I do know the music.'

'Would you – would you ever sing us a little bit of it, Signora?' said Rose.

Signor Giacomo sprang to his feet.

'Sing an aria, sing two bars of an operatic air, out here, sitting down, unaccompanied, and with your throat full of cake – my God!'

'What's cake, man! Sit down! Give me a glass of wine, Assunta!' She gulped a drink. 'Listen now – you have heard, you study this opera?'

She leant her great, hair-laden head against the tree-trunk, and shut her overlidded eyes.

'Say to thy daughter . . .' she sang. It was as if she whispered. *Dite alla giovine* . . . She seemed to make no effort, hardly it seemed that she used her lungs, yet each note came in its place, gently taking its part in what the song said.

Her audience, knowing the opera, followed her closely, but lost sight of the ageing woman who sang; they only heard the voice, or what they accepted momentarily as the voice, of Violetta. What they heard in truth was interpretation, under-standing, memory, and art – art neglected, flung aside, but when as now for a lazy whim picked up, still gold, pure gold.

'I shall die . . .' she sang, and to the end of that passage. And then she stopped, opened her eyes, and flung up her hands.

'Oh God! Oh God! How lovely that was once! What are you thinking, Giacomo?'

'I'm thinking that your ear and memory and control are so good that you could teach singing, Vittoria, if only you'd exert yourself!'

'*Teach* singing! I? Heaven defend us, I haven't sunk that far! Or have I, husband?'

'As low as I? Ah no, my dear.'

'See how he trips me up! Do not marry, young ones! Sing and wander the world, and do not marry! Above all, do not marry a serious person!'

'But, to marry – it must be a serious person,' said Mariana.

'I disagree. And you'll hardly find a serious person on the opera stage, my little Mariana!'

'Then I shan't marry!'

'Nonsense, Mariana,' said Tonio. 'You'll make a serious person of whatever vagabond you're generous enough to love!'

'So she will! A sad story,' said Signora Vittoria. 'And what of our strangers do you think, gentlemen? Our two young virgins from the land of saints?'

Tonio and Thomas smiled with apologetic benevolence at Clare and Rose.

'Leave surmise about them, wife,' said the Professor. 'They sing like birds; it may be that I'll get them to sing like angels. That is a rare hope with young ladies, but when it appears it comes out of Ireland. So, let me make two angels sing if I can. Afterwards, they can fall, if they want to!'

'Angels do fall, don't they?' said Tonio.

'Only an occasional one, I think,' said Clare.

'What a pity!' said Thomas.

'Why did you give up singing, Signora?' asked Rose.

'I can't explain that, child,' the Signora said gravely.

'All to do with being an ancient Etruscan,' said Tonio.

The Professor laughed.

'Isn't it cool enough now? Can't we walk somewhere?' said Clare.

'Yes; we can start climbing up to Albano any time now,' said the Professor. 'Do you want me to wait with you for your pony carriage, Vittoria?'

'By no means. You must chaperone the walkers, as you know. How could I let all those young people loose in these woods today, Giacomo?'

'Oh, we can trust them to these chivalrous boys for an hour or so, surely?'

'Indeed you can, sir,' said Thomas.

'No, no, Giacomo; it wouldn't look correct. You go with them, and Assunta will wait with me here for the carriage.'

'Very good, my dear. It's a pity you can't walk with us, because I believe there are some supposedly Etruscan tombs in this wood, somewhere between here and Albano. You might find an ancestor or two!'

Vittoria laughed delightedly.

'By no means, Giacomo. *My* Etruscan people never condescended to the Campagna. No, away with you all – I shall read to Assunta awhile, and she will sew; and we shall all meet at that great café – you know – in the Piazza Umberto—'

'Carone's?'

'That's it. We'll eat salami there and drink wine – at about six o'clock, my friends. So – away! It is a lovely walk, up to Albano. I knew it when I was as young as you are now.'

It was a lovely walk. Under chestnut trees at first, sweet-smelling, and over leaf-fed moss. Small wild flowers and jaded greater ones broke through the cool green, and now and then as they climbed they saw a flash of the sultry lake below. Broken, ancient stones lay south and north of them under the old trees, and young sweethearts of the feast day lay against them, locked in peace. Higher up they walked under scattered, deep-bent olive trees, heavy for harvest; here they were in the light, and could look down on the expanse of Lake Albano, and upward to the glittering little town.

'They say that some of these olive trees are as old as Christianity,' Signor Giacomo told Clare. 'But I don't think any tree can live two thousand years, do you?'

'I don't know,' said Clare. 'But olive trees look prematurely old, I'd say.'

The Professor chuckled.

'Anyway, this little town of Albano – doesn't it look pleasant there? – it's said to have been a favourite resort of the awful creature, Domitian. However, Pompey had a villa there too, I believe – and he was relatively respectable.'

Rose and Tonio raced ahead, stealing olives, playing with goats; Thomas walked politely with Mariana; Clare was content with the Professor's kind company; he left her inner mind free to range over the Campagna and the long day.

The Fourth Chapter

'No word from home?' said Clare.

'Oh, no – but I gave no address. I said I'd stay in Europe awhile, and teach, and that I'd write soon again. I couldn't face what they'd say.'

'How is the teaching job?'

'All right. I've two jobs now – both boys are invalids; one isn't right in his head. But they want to learn Latin and English – and I'm paid enough to live on.'

'You don't look as if you were living.'

'Oh, that's only nerves. I should leave Rome – but I don't want to yet. And I have these jobs.'

The two shabby figures, gaunt, untidy young man in black and Clare in a darned and faded print dress of her Rue des Lauriers wardrobe, sat on a stone bench on the Pincio parapet.

'It's nice that I met you this evening; I often look for you.'

'And you often find me,' said Clare.

He laughed.

'I'm beginning to know your haunts and habits,' he said. 'I often watch for you in Via di Ripetta, or round the Academy.'

'Have you so much time on your hands?'

'Well, one of my pupils lives up there off the Flaminia – convenient! I like talking with you – if you can put up with me? The other one too, pretty Rosa – but you especially.'

'Why? Are you very homesick?'

'No. I love Rome.'

'I don't.'

'I know you don't – yet. But I've been here over three years, you know.'

'Oh, it's an amazing place – I'm – I'm glad to be here,' said Clare.

'And God knows I'm glad you're here!'

She raised her brows, shy of his vehemence.

'You see – when you've done what I've done – to them at home, I mean; to my mother and all – no matter how right you believe yourself to be, you're haunted – God, you're haunted! They're poor, you see – and they're very holy, and they made great sacrifices for me. Well, that's awful to think of now! And it's a relief to be able to say something about it sometimes – to someone like you. After all, you know what I mean, you come from the same country and the same kind of people – these Romans, what do they know or care about people like us?'

'Nothing. They sometimes seem to me more Roman than can possibly be true!'

'Oh, they're true enough – and they know it!'

Both looked out in silence over the great stretch of roofs and campaniles, domes and columns, to Saint Peter's and beyond. It was an evening of May, high-lighted and exquisite, and up here noisy only with the cries of playing children and the ring of harness bells.

'I think that's the silver of the sea, at Ostia,' said Clare.

'I like when you see it right across Rome from the Alban Hills. I think it might be worth a man's while to stay all his life in Rome, and learn it. But other people would go away, of course. How's the work?'

'Unceasing. I get awfully tired of it. It's funny – they're so careful of our voices – but they're merciless with all the other parts of the training, We never stop working!'

'But look at you now? Is this work?'

'Oh, one is encouraged to take some air and exercise on fine evenings. But I get to feel so crammed and overweighted with opera lore – opera, opera all day and night – that I get the idea sometimes that there can be no more to know, and that I'm a fully-fledged *prima donna* already! But I'd like to see what would happen if I said that to Signor Giacomo! Or even to Thomas!'

'Thomas. That's the Welsh genius, isn't it, that I met you with along by the Tiber the other day?'

'Yes. Thomas has strength of purpose – he's very ambitious. He gives me courage.'

'H'm. And you give me courage, I think.'

He bent forward staring west, and twisted his big hands together.

'I'll have to find out how to be ambitious now,' he said. 'That's a thing I've never been. But – after a while – I'll have to see.'

'Good evening, Clare,' said Thomas, standing in front of her. 'Good evening, Mr Flynn.'

'Good evening.' Patrick Flynn stood and picked up his black hat from the bench. 'Good evening, Miss Clare,' he said.

'Don't go, Paddy!'

'I must, I've work to do. I'll meet you again soon, I hope.'

He bowed to her, nodded to Thomas and walked away in the direction of the Spanish Steps.

'Consoling the afflicted?'

'Paddy isn't afflicted.'

'He looks it. May I sit down? But I thought you told me that to be what you call a "spoilt priest" in Ireland is a very sad thing?'

'Yes – but I also told you that Paddy isn't that! He left in time. He was only a seminarist.'

'But he looks tragic, all the same.'

'I think he's only temporarily troubled and upset. It's a hard thing to do – there's his family, you know – at home it's a very great honour to have a son a priest.'

Some weeks earlier, on a Sunday morning of Lent, Clare and Rose, having heard Mass in Saint Peter's, had sat awhile in the shadow of the colonnades, watching the life of the Piazza and talking of letters they had had, exchanging news of Lackanashee and of Ballykerin.

'Irish voices, Irish places. May I speak to you, I wonder, young ladies?'

A tall, white-faced young man in threadbare black clothes was bowing to them, hat in hand.

Gladly they invited him to talk. He sat on a broken column near them, and told them that his name was Patrick Flynn. He came from County Clare, near Miltown Malbay, and for three years had studied for the priesthood here in Rome, at the Irish College. But he had known for some time that he could not and would not seek ordination and at last, during this Lent, had left the College and had written home of his decision. He was looking for work now; he could at least teach. He could not go home yet, to face the grief and anger of his parents; moreover, there was nothing he could do for a living at home, and he did not think his people would wish him to return to the village for some time.

The two girls were happy to talk to an Irishman; they understood his remorse and anxiety about the people at home, and they spoke kindly to him. And he for his part was interested in their unexpected story, and heard much about Mamma and Grandmother, and Rue des Lauriers, and Via di Ripetta, and Signor Giacomo and the Signora. So the audacious encounter – for these young ladies were strongly bound not to converse with strange gentlemen – became happy and even merry.

But soon it was time they sought their tram. Mr Flynn escorted them to it, and stood waving his hat as the tram-horses rolled the young ladies away. He was the first acquaintance they had made outside the world of their work in their more than eighteen months of exile, and they found him interesting and sad, and they were pleased that he was one like themselves, and from Country Clare.

He was, however, only one encounter among many. Their days as poor and unknown students, foreign students, in Rome were immeasurably more free than could ever be the lives of respectable Italian young ladies. No one save the household at Via di Ripetta and their colleagues and teachers at Santa Cecilia knew or cared who they were, and still very shabbily dressed in the remains of their Rue des Lauriers equipment, still modest and maidenly of aspect, they looked indeed on Rome's streets, these two from Ireland, like well-conducted young maidservants sent on errands from some old-fashioned palazzo. But the frock does not prove the monk, and ten months of hard and busy life in Rome had rapidly extended Clare and Rose. Living at ease with an extraordinary city and able to understand its language, working at pressure and competitively in a particular small group dedicated to ideas and situations which were adult, worldly, exacting, ambitious, emotional and alarming – the two had grown up, were growing up much faster than they knew. From having been as lost and foolish as babies when they reached Paris from Ireland, now though only eighteen, each of them was, according to her nature, far more alert to the battling and advancing world than she had any means of guessing. Each was visited by great homesickness still, and very often; each, in her own heart, was sometimes frightened of the fantastic future which had been thrust upon her; each hated her poverty and shabbiness and dependence on a pittance of pocket-money; but each saw now the scope of her work, and except in inescapable moods of depression felt conscientious about it, and equal to it; or if not all of the latter, knew herself to be challenged and engaged by it. And each, in ways and deviations all her own and not the other's, thought very much about singing, her own singing, and its assumption, its chance and arbitrary possession of her and of her desires for life.

They were learning every day and every night; about music, about Italy, about themselves, and their fellow-creatures. They had grown tall – Clare was growing *too* tall, Signor Giacomo warned her – and they had deportment now, and poise. They had friendships, troubles, angers, headaches and exasperations. They were admired, they were snubbed; they were disliked; they were often disturbed by the whirlings of temperament, jealousy, vanity, ambition and impatience in the midst of which they lived, and of which they found themselves partakers. And often they were sick for home.

Still, they worked well, ate well, and slept well. And every night and morning each said, word for word, the prayers which morning and night she had said throughout childhood.

Thomas stretched his long legs.

'You're in love with these little acacia trees, it seems?' He pointed to them, white-flowering, just below where they sat.

'I was thinking a minute ago that *they*, now, would be something to sing about! Instead of all those personal feelings of mad or frivolous ladies that one has to learn to simulate!'

'Oh Clare! Their feelings are excuses for music!'

'Does music need such poor excuse? Anyway, those acacias practically are a song – even if it's never sung.'

'Song without music?'

'If you like,' said Clare, who was shy of fancifulness, even her own. 'All I meant was that they are lovely, indisputably lovely – which is more than can be said of a lot of the things we wrestle with all day.'

'True. And you're welcome to consider the lilies of the field. But art is man's business. Nature is God's, clearly enough – and we don't know where He got or perfected His idea of an acacia tree. But we work at ideas that appear to be our own – and some of them come off. And we have brought off some things which will outlive all possible white acacia flowers—'

'That's true – under God, Thomas.'

'Oh, agreed – one has to say "under God", because we don't know the first cause. Still, as handicapped men we have imposed art on nature – oh, I'm a bore.' He smiled at her. 'All the same, I'm having at this minute that exhausting visitation, an idea. I think I'll write a song about these white acacia flowers – I hear it a little now, I think. Where shall I get the words?'

'Write them yourself.'

'Maybe.' He took a note-book from his pocket and a pencil. He stared towards Ostia awhile, and then made some scribbled notes.

'What's today's date?' he asked.

'Fifteenth of May, 1888 – in six months I'll be nineteen, Thomas.'

He put his note-book in his pocket.

'The name of the song will be "Clare", I think,' he said. 'It'll be what you have in mind.'

A bell tolled from Trinita dei Monti.

Thomas looked sideways at Clare.

'Now, I've silenced you,' he said.

'Yes, Thomas. Often you do.'

'Why?'

'Oh! I'm awkward – and you're always flinging generous implications at me!'

'They're not generous implications. I've told you before now how much I admire and resent you. What more natural? What more annoying? If only you weren't an Irish lady, my God!'

'I don't think I'm a lady, Thomas!'

'Oh, I'm no judge – I come from a public house in Cardiff. But you're my idea of a lady, I'm sorry to say.'

They both laughed.

'Will you come to Benediction with me at Trinita dei Monti?' said Clare.

'But, child – the singing there! The way those poor nuns sing!'

'I know. I get homesick for *bad* singing, Thomas!'

He laughed delightedly.

'That's such a good argument that I'd almost go with you – but, do you know, I think there's a great deal in the wind in Ripetta, about us all – and I think old Giacomo may be going to address us about his plans before supper. Tonio has heard some plots—'

'Plots? What is it?'

'Summer plans – scatterings, trial runs. Come down to the Piazza di Spagna and I'll give you an ice on the way home, and prepare you for what you may hear!'

Thomas, about four years older than Clare, was ambitious and very industrious. He studied singing only as a part of his education, although his tenor voice was pure and strong, and he had – as Clare had observed in Academy performances – a good operatic style. But his real studies were pianoforte, composition, and orchestral and operatic structure and direction. Before he came to Rome he had worked for two years at the Leipzig Conservatorium, and intended soon to work in Vienna. His father was a prosperous publican in Cardiff, and proud of his gifted son, to whom he grudged nothing. But Thomas was thrifty, and considerate of his parent, and made money when and where he could, taking summer jobs with touring opera, coaching first-year composition students, and writing pieces about Italian life for newspapers at home. His days were therefore full, and it surprised Clare, who admired his capacity for work, that he found time to loaf with her, finding her out on her walks very often with curious accuracy. But he had established himself as her mentor, and was indeed a friend who interested and pleased her. He was self-confident and widely-read, and he called himself a rationalist.

They went down the steps together, winding their way round the idle groups who sat at ease in their path.

'How would you like to be a model, and sit here cooing with the Margutta boys at the end of the day?'

Clare laughed.

'I wouldn't like it at all!'

Thomas nodded to a bearded young man who leapt to his feet and seemed anxious to greet him.

'*Buona sera,*' said Thomas, and took Clare's elbow. 'This way, Clare – they're thick on the ground this evening. So you'd rather sing Rossini's light-headed ladies?'

'Oh, any of those gentlemen's ladies! Because at least, however idiotic, I'd be doing the thing myself! Not just sitting having it done!'

Thomas threw her an amused look.

'That reminds me,' he said. 'The other day I was drinking beer with a painter fellow – a German I used to know in Leipzig – in Della Croce. And you went by, all alone and innocent! And poor Kalmann nearly went mad! Must see you again! Must paint you! Must follow you! Couldn't we follow you and try to see where you lived? What was the matter with me? Had I any eye for a woman? Did I know anything about you? Did I, for God's sake?'

'And what did you say?'

'I said I didn't know you at all, that I wasn't even clear who he was talking about – and I bought him another beer. By that time you had vanished round the corner into the Corso.'

'You were taking a lot on yourself, weren't you?'

'Certainly I was.'

'Is he a good painter?'

'Oh middling – but we don't require him to paint you, do we?'

They sat in the window of an English tea-room, and asked for *cassate*.

'Oh, Thomas, did I tell you I had a letter from Luisa Carriaga yesterday?'

'No. What's her news?'

Thomas had known Luisa only a little during her period of study in Rome. Her teacher, in whose house she lodged, lived on the Aventino, and she had Spanish friends in the city; but he had admired what he heard of her work in the Academy, and when Clare wanted to know where she was, had found out during the winter her address in Milan, whither she had been sent to study with a very exacting and expensive professor. So thereafter she and Clare corresponded.

'It's exciting, because I may see her soon. You know she has been understudying for *three* operas at La Scala—'

'Which?'

'*Orfeo*, and *Faust*, and *The Barber* – and now she *thinks*, she's not sure, she thinks, she's going to be asked to sing one or two parts in the summer season here, at the Argentina!'

'Well! That's funny!' said Thomas.

When the season at La Scala closed in May, so did the Neapolitan opera season at San Carlo, and likewise Costanzi's season in Rome. But opera was not silenced in Italy then. Good and less good short seasons were given throughout the summer, in towns of the north and centre, and – in Rome – in the Argentina and Valle Theatres. Great singers sometimes liked to condescend to these performances, and certainly many very good singers and conductors were glad to engage in them; and they were used also to try out cadets leaving the schools.

'Only what are you saying about scatterings? It'll be just my luck if I'm sent off to do my breathing exercises in Bologna or some place the very week Luisa comes to Rome!'

'I don't think – from what I hear – that you'll be sent north immediately. Rose will – some of them seemed to think in the schools – but no one knows what's going on, really!'

'Rose! Ah – perhaps that would be just as well, for a bit—' Thomas smiled at her.

'Wherever she's sent Antonio's determined to be sent!'

'I suppose so. I believe Mariana's coming back next week.'

Since Easter Mariana had been attached to a minor opera company performing at the Teatro Verdi in Florence, and was said to have made a successful beginning.

'Who said that?'

'Assunta, I think.'

'Well, shall we go home and eavesdrop around?'

They strolled through the beautiful cool evening and its clamorous life.

'Does Signor Giacomo ever rest or take a holiday, Thomas?'

'Not that I've heard. But he wouldn't know what to do with one – now. Usually at some moment of the summer he takes the Signora up to some health resort – I've forgotten the name, but it's in Etruria, need I say? He leaves her there with Assunta for as long as she'll stay. And that period in Ripetta *is* his vacation, I think.'

'She's bad these days, isn't she?'

'Yes; and all of a sudden she'll be fine. They say she really *was* a great artist, no nonsense. But then, so was he. Well, I sometimes wonder if I'll end up like him – gifted and dusty and forgotten!'

'You won't, I'd say.'

'Why?'

'Well – you're, you're not soft, like him.'

'No. Perhaps that's where he has the laugh on me?'

'It might be.'

As they crossed the Corso towards Via Canova, Thomas raised his hat to a tall, lean man with very dark eyes, who raised his also and bowed.

'There's another disappointed man,' said Thomas. 'Younger than Giacomo, of course, and more enigmatic.'

'What does he do?'

'He lectures on orchestra and sacred music. Mostly he takes private pupils.'

'Oh, he's the Spaniard, Duarte?'

'Iago Maria Duarte, that's he. Very Castilian and standoffish. Good at his work. I don't know why he hangs around in Rome . . .'

The *portiera* sat in the doorway, with seven or eight of her cats in her spread lap. Clare stroked the nearest black and white head as she passed, but the old woman did not smile or answer her greeting.

'She's a sullen old thing, isn't she?'

'Just Roman,' said Thomas. 'Hold your breath now for the climb.'

He took her fingers lightly in his.

'It's like a very long C in Alt,' said Clare.

'Oh no, Clare! Quite wrong. It's a darker, duller note – just requires chest and training! Lower mezzo – nothing at all like your C in Alt!'

'All the same, some day I'll try going up all the way on C in Alt.'

'Just you dare!'

Surprisingly the apartment was quiet. There was no one in the *salotto*. The only signs of life were the smells of supper and, far away, from the Signora's room, a thread of singing.

'That sounds nice,' said Thomas.

Clare went along the corridor to the room she shared with Rose. The latter was standing at the window brushing her hair. Assunta stood at an open cupboard, and folded into it some newly ironed linen.

'You're an angel, Assunta,' said Rose.

'Nothing, signorina,' said Assunta. 'And it is you who are the angel.' She smiled at Rose as she closed the cupboard, and Clare noticed as she left the room that she had been crying.

'What's up with Assunta?'

'Oh, just tiredness, poor girl. The Signora appears to have been perfectly awful this last time—'

'Oh Lord! Poor Assunta! Why does she stand it?'

'Well – she, in a way she adores Signora Vittoria, I think—'

'But – she can't really?'

'Ah, you know—'

'Yes – Thomas said something once—'

Rose turned and laughed at Clare.

'Does Thomas talk of things like that to you?'

'Things like what? He said something, in a joke I imagine, about blackmail.'

Clare flung her hat on the bed, took her hairbrush and, pulling hairpins from her chignon, joined Rose at the window.

Both liked the now familiar, proscribed view of life which this grey courtyard afforded them, and through the perpetual and tantalizing criss-cross screens of sheets and shirts slung out to dry they followed the lively days and nights of their neighbours as closely as they could.

'Those puppies have no sense,' said Clare. 'It isn't nearly their supper-time yet, the sillies. But, why was poor Assunta crying? Anything extra?'

'Yes. She was to have gone home yesterday for the day, to Nettuno. It was her mother's feast day, and her sister's last Sunday at home. Her sister is sailing to America from Naples on Friday – and Assunta has presents to take her, things she's been sewing. They're very, very poor, you know, her people. Well, she couldn't go, of course, with the Signora the way she was – and she had to send a telegram to her mother. I got Tonio to send it for her, as she couldn't get out even to go to Mass. But now today the Signora seems – well, all right again – and so Assunta asked her this afternoon if she might take the evening train to Nettuno tomorrow, just to say goodbye to her sister – she said she'd only be away about five hours—'

'So—?'

'The Signora said nothing – but just simply slapped her face.'

'Oh! But Rosie! Why on earth does Assunta stand it?'

'She has to.'

'No one has to.'

Rose leant back against the window-frame. As she brushed her shining hair and twisted a hand through the geranium plant that tossed itself almost into the room – with the evening west of Rome falling about her and catching her eyes, she looked, Clare thought, the idealization of any one of say ten unfortunate young virgins of opera that she might soon be singing to the world. In the hard and lively months of Rome she had shed all baby vagueness of line, had grown taller and was almost as slender as Clare. She had assumed the whole grace of girlhood and her lovely face and head were like a swaying rose in early summer.

She surveyed Clare in affectionate amusement now.

'Listen, Clarabelle,' she said. 'You and I have been forced abroad to do nothing else, you might say, except study and interpret the "amatory predicaments" – your words, Clare! – of a lot of unbalanced maidens of high and low degree! Isn't that so?'

'It is indeed!'

'And aren't you always grumbling about those poor maidens? You don't believe in them. You'll have to some time. But, listen now. There was a tenor student here a year ago – he's still at Santa Cecilia, and as a matter of fact you've sung with him sometimes, but I won't tell you in what. Well, one night when the Signora recovered unexpectedly from one of her attacks – she found Assunta in that student's room. In his bed. And – and, well – with no clothes on. Assunta told me this herself.'

'Well – then?'

'Assunta adores her mother, who has had a hard life, and is very pious and strict. Also there is an uncle who is a missionary, and a great glory in the family. Assunta is terrified of him. Naturally she thought she'd be sent away in the morning, without a character, and that a terrible letter would be written to her mother. But – it was the student who disappeared in the morning, Not a word was said to Assunta – but she's been made into a slave.'

'She's so exceptionally useful – I suppose the old woman saw her chance to chain her here for life?'

'That's it.'

'But it's – it's grotesque, it's almost silly!'

'Yes, you see it's an opera really – nearly as silly as all the ones you laugh at, Clare!'

'I can't think of one quite as realistic, Rosie – can you?'

'No. Poor Assunta!'

'Did she – did she love that student?'

'I – I don't know. I don't imagine she did, in the way one reads about!'

The two paused, hardly knowing what to say next.

'How you grow up, Rose! Being the confidante of strange stories—'

'Hardly strange, I suppose?'

'Perhaps not – speaking generally, but to me it *is* strange – it's almost impossibly strange – what Assunta did.'

'Oh, you!' Rose laughed delightedly. 'If it were *you*, then it would be strange, I grant you!'

'No letters, I suppose?'

Rose shook her head, and began to arrange her chignon before the mirror.

'Do you think we'll be involved in these summer engagements they're all talking about, Rosie?'

Rose looked troubled.

'I don't know – I'm a bit afraid – oh, if they let us go home! Even for half the summer!'

'Even for a week! But somehow, we might be lucky. Little Giacomino is still terrified of letting us sing outside his studio—'

'Yes, but he hasn't the last word!'

'Where would we get our tickets, anyway? Oh, heaven – it's too long!'

'Don't – oh don't !' said Rose. 'I don't want to cry. Ah, here's the collar I thought was lost!'

'They're quarrelling again,' said Clare. Rose came back to the window. 'He's just pushed his soup nearly off the table, and flung his napkin at her!'

They peered down into a window of the floor below.

'He's a very bad-tempered young man,' said Rose.

'I expect being married is on his nerves.'

A hand-bell rang in the corridor.

'Come on, I'm hungry,' said Rose.

'I'm not – I had a *cassata* just now.'

'With Thomas?'

'Yes. Oh, and I met Paddy Flynn on the Pincio – I'll tell you later—'

They ran to the *salotto*. But on its threshold Clare stopped and put her arm across Rose to stop her. Behind the tattered silk screen at the far end of the room someone was singing.

'*Che puro ciel . . .*'

'Luisa!' said Clare.

She swept across the room singing.

'*E quest' asilo ameno . . .*'

Luisa, followed by Signor Giacomo, came in great laughter from behind the screen, and she and Clare fell into each other's arms.

'*Che faro . . .*' Luisa began.

'No, no – no more of this random singing,' cried Signor Giacomo.

'No more,' said Luisa. 'Oh Clare! So you've been studying. Eurydice? Oh Clare, how lovely this is!'

'But where did you come from?'

Both had gone straight into French, which was the language in which they had known each other.

'From Milan, silly! Where else?'

'Oh, I know! But tonight – and here?'

'I'm staying in the Aventino – I got to Rome this afternoon. But I had to see *you* at once! Oh, and Rose! Little Rose, grown tall and lovely!'

Clare stood quiet. The beauty of Luisa's singing shocked her.

Thomas came across the room.

'Aren't you glad, Clare?'

Signora Vittoria swept into the room.

'Who was singing Orfeo?' she cried. 'Oh, child, whoever you are, you must be forgiven! You are not Viardot. Do you imagine that anyone who heard her could bear to hear you?'

Luisa laughed with grace.

'Signora,' said Thomas, '*you* could only have heard Viardot when her voice was gone, surely?'

La Vittoria was pleased by this tactful intervention, which was true. She swayed vaguely towards Thomas.

'Indeed, she was pitiful the only time I heard her – in Germany somewhere. Was it, was it twenty years ago?'

'More than that, wife,' said Giacomo.

'Ah well – maybe! But they always said—'

'Rightly, I'm sure,' said Antonio.

'So am I,' said Thomas, 'La Viardot was no myth. And Luisa will be pitiful also, thirty years on, in Berlin or Buenos Ayres – and so will Rose and so will Chiara—'

The girls laughed.

'We may not wait for that,' said Rose.

'You will,' said Signor Giacomo. 'Please God you will! Please God you are singers, and will accept that fate, wherever it leads you.'

'I'm hungry,' said Antonio, who sometimes noticed distress in others and took simple ways to help it.

'So am I,' said everyone. But La Vittoria would not be deflected.

'You think this Spanish girl sings well, Thomas? Because she sings mezzo-soprano? What nonsense!'

'My dear—' said Signor Giacomo.

'My dear, be quiet,' said Signora Vittoria. 'Spaniards tend to sing mezzo-soprano. Curious. It's a pity, my child!' She made a vague gesture towards Luisa. 'Oh – oh, supper – where is Assunta?'

Everyone, sorry for Signor Giacomo, pressed towards the dining-room. Assunta took her mistress by the arm.

Thomas walked slowly to supper beside Clare and Luisa. He paid no heed to their rapid and happy interchanges. His thoughts, sped by their gay singing of the Glück phrases, had leapt forward, far from this hour and its confusions of pathos.

The general mood during supper was tense and illumined – the more delicately because everyone felt obliged to present a normal face, so as to conceal from Signor Giacomo any hint of their pity for him.

Signora Vittoria had indeed this afternoon drunk deeply; and that, though its results were an embarrassment which her young household grew skilful to conceal, was tonight more difficult to bear than customarily, because all knew that change, ideas and discussions in regard to their immediate future were whirling in Signor Giacomo's anxious head; also the sudden return of Luisa was sweet and exciting, and pointed the direction, perhaps, for some of the others in the coming months. But when the Signora was as far removed from rationality as on this evening, did she then choose to sit at the head of her supper-table, dominating it, all surface wit must be given up to the pretence that there was no oddness anywhere, and to helping her sad husband through one more wasteful and comic hour.

Assuredly, against the barrage of her intoxicated arrogance, her sometimes quite brilliant drunkenness, the weary *maestro* would enter upon no discussion with his pupils of their actual work. For she, in her cups, was a great confuser and a trailer of red herrings; and whereas the young people, used to her now, found her often as amusing as they must concede that she was sadly monitory, yet they understood somehow – far though they all still were from marriage as from other repetitious monotonies of mature life – that this woman's husband, still loving her it must be supposed, was sick to danger point of exhibitions in her of her failure, and of his; and they knew that they must pretend not to see this failure at all.

Signora Vittoria made this disciplinary exercise difficult, loving and demanding as she did attention and adulation, so that when she was as highly lighted as on this evening, she could place the young and polite in the position of seeming to draw her out, seeming to make fun of her. And this was a predicament which, in the presence of Signor Giacomo and at his table, could become painful.

Tonight all were stressed and uncertain. Clare watched Signor Giacomo, and decided to be quiet and get through supper quickly. Antonio took a similar watching brief, and settled to his wine and *pasta* bowl with gratitude. Luisa, the stranger here, looked on. Rose thought that conversation should be tried.

'Signor Mazzaglia's lecture on the *leit-motif* was puzzling this morning,' she said. 'Were you at it, Clare?'

'Wagner?'

La Vittoria's heavy head rose slowly, as a snake's in venom. 'They speak to singers in Italy, even at the Accademia, of that charlatan and his *leit-motif*. Ah yes, I know, I know!'

Clare shook her head at Rose. This was not the evening to drag in Wagner. But Thomas followed up.

'You never knew him, Signora? You never met him?'

Clare frowned at Thomas. They had heard so many times what was to come.

'Meet him? Know him? In – oh what year—'

'In 1869, my dear,' said Giacomo.

'So long ago? Well then – he heard me sing – in Brussels, I believe? I sang Norma and Alceste—'

'You sang Alceste, Signora?' said Luisa, startled, forgetting herself.

'Yes, Alceste,' said La Vittoria sleepily, and she lifted her glass. Her husband put his face into his hands. 'Alceste . . . I remember. And that extraordinary German came to me and begged me, begged me, children, to study for him Eva, of *Die Meistersinger*, and Isolde – *I* – to sing in such an uproar!' She drank again.

Luisa spoke softly to Signor Giacomo.

'Richard Wagner asked her to study Eva and Isolde, Signor?' Giacomo smiled.

'He did indeed, Signorina. I was conducting *Norma* and *Alceste* that season in Brussels. We were not married then.'

Luisa turned to La Vittoria.

'Why did you *not* study those parts, Signora?'

La Vittoria lifted her purple eyelids.

'Because the human voice is music, child, and if we use it we must have it heard. It must be clear. Those who listen to it – please, Assunta!' Assunta filled her glass. 'Those who listen – excuse me! – must know what it is saying, and why—'

'There's the point of the *leit-motif*,' said Thomas.

'You silly boy!' La Vittoria pitched a little over her glass. 'The *leit-motif* is the sentimental gossip of the orchestra . . .'

Clare laughed, and so did Giacomo. They had not heard that before. La Vittoria smiled drunkenly.

'So when you come on, the voice, the supreme instrument, not only has all been said, but you have to scream it all out again against an orchestration of – oh, of elephants and giraffes and – and – crocodiles, perhaps?'

'And a few canaries,' said Antonio.

'Oh yes, canaries! Canaries. To be lost – but what did Richard Wagner care?'

La Vittoria laid her huge head down on her fruit plate.

Signor Giacomo, the peach he was peeling in his hand, stood up.

'Come to my workroom at once, all of you,' he said, and thrust the silver knife sharply into the dripping peach.

'Yes, yes, to the workroom,' said La Vittoria, raising her head.

'Assunta, in God's name,' said Giacomo. Then he strode out of the room, and the five students followed him.

In his workroom he was the master they worked for and who made them work. Domestic embarrassments vanished behind its huge doors, and they forgot pity, and attended only to their own business.

It was a big, ugly room, bare, untidy and, besides two grand pianos and a bench, an armchair and some shabby stools, given over to the spread and mess of a student of one subject. For all those entering it now, except Luisa, it was the everyday place where they were anxious and on their mettle.

'Yes, yes – you come in too, Signorina Luisa. I shall not keep them long – and you are related to what I wish to say.'

Thomas dropped on to a piano-bench, and fooled his hands along the keyboard.

'Shall we make up some *leit-motifs*?' he said. 'Clare, now—?'

Antonio went to the other piano.

'Come on; I'll get one for Rose—'

Signor Giacomo lifted his hand.

'Quiet, gentlemen. Sit down, all of you.'

He conveyed what he had to say with his customary anxious authoritativeness. All five of his pupils, he said, were to be offered places in one or other of the touring opera companies which would be at work in about a month from this evening. For Thomas and Antonio this was a routine expectation, and he foresaw that a professional season would be important and directive for them; but, 'as to our Irish young ladies, whereas I am pleased, my dears, that your work is rousing interest and whereas I know that this is what we have been preparing for – I am also a little uncertain, even alarmed. However, my colleagues and the directors of certain opera groups are overruling me – and I know that my tendency is perhaps overmuch to *protect* voices. In any case, the season will only be for ten weeks, the experience is absolutely essential – your patrons in

Ireland desire you to make the trial – and, admittedly, you are no longer so very young—'

Everyone laughed, but they knew what the master meant; that even he acknowledged that a voice may be allowed somewhat to take its chance once its possessor is approaching the twentieth year of life.

'We acknowledge our age, Signor,' said Rose. 'Indeed, compared with Patti and Madame Lind, Clare and I are a pair of very old non-starters!'

Within ten days, therefore, they would be at rehearsal with a professional opera company; each of them would make study of two or three leading rôles, chosen from among operas within their scope and upon which they had in some measure worked during the year, and these they would be allowed or expected to sing about once, each, within every two weeks of the tour. Also, they would understudy the chief singers, attend all rehearsals, and sing small parts as required. They would not sing in the chorus. They would be suitably chaperoned and watched over, and they would receive salaries – these to be arranged. A just proportion of these salaries would be paid directly to him, for restoration to the patrons in Ireland. The rest they must learn to manage wisely. He would give them all details and any advice they required within the coming days, which would indeed be busy for them. He was not yet sure as to the works to which Thomas and Antonio might be appointed, but he believed that Rose would be required to be proficient in the parts of Zerlina in *Don Giovanni*, Gilda in *Rigoletto*, and possibly Violetta in *La Traviata* – or Cherubino in *Figaro*. Clare was to study Eurydice in *Orfeo*, Lucia in *Lucia di Lammermoor*, and probably Isabella in *Don Carlos*.

'You are to work here in Rome, at the Valle Theatre, Signorina Chiara, where your friend, Signorina Luisa, will also be singing. You, Rosa, will be attached to Signor Prezzoli's very good company, which will tour cities north of Bologna, beginning there—'

'Ah! Prezzoli,' murmured Antonio.

'I'm to go away – without Clare?' cried Rose.

'That is all for now,' said Signor Giacomo wearily. 'We

shall have details to arrange – but that is the plan. May it be fortunate!'

He waved them off with a half-smile. He felt sad.

'Thank you, sir,' said the young men.

'Thank you, Signor, good night.'

'We are all going out now, sir, to celebrate the news,' said Antonio.

'Moderately, I trust.'

'Naturally, sir. We won't be late.'

'But we'll get the keys from the *portiera* all the same,' said Thomas.

Giacomo was leaning out of the window. Clare thought that he looked extremely small and grey.

For herself, she had been made desperate by the news which he had announced with such finality, and she was afraid to go away from this room, where she would have to think about it, discuss it. And ah! at home they had known of all this plan, *and* had consented to it, without a word to them, and while Rose and she were in the dark!

In Italy in the nineteenth century, through the persistence of a long tradition, theatre meant almost entirely *il teatro lirico* – opera. Almost every Italian town which was not a village had an opera house, a *teatro lirico* which was held in veneration by its citizens. These theatres were used throughout the year for local concerts, lectures and amateur, or hired, performances of opera or drama. But opera was what they had been built for, and opera the people liked to have presented in them, professionally and as well as could be afforded, at least once if not twice in the year, for a *festa* or *stagione musicale*, musical season, of one or two weeks. The tours stretched, in importance and in place, between, say, Naples and Treviso, Turin and Bari. They presented therefore, up and down the peninsula, a considerable field for the speculation of impresarios. These business men liked well to reap the summer profits of this field; because in June, July, August and September, when all the great opera houses were dark, it was possible to get singers and conductors of standing, and even of fame, to perform in the lesser theatres – they always needing money, and also desiring to extend their experience and their repertoires. Further, for the summer months it was possible to handpick singers, orchestral players and conductors out of the thousands of cadets and hopefuls thronging the musical academies and conservatoires of Italy. Also, in a season when the rich and the ennobled were scattered to their country estates, mostly dominating the lesser towns, the good-humoured summer patronage of such could be counted upon, and perhaps eventually turned to serious use.

The business arrangements of these impresarios were more or less as follows: while bargaining, slowly and secretively, throughout the winter for the summer *festa* dates of the best towns he could get or afford, each was listening, scouting, gossiping, watching, and seeking the opinions of the musically informed, for the operatic group he must assemble before June. Such a group would consist basically of a conductor, as renowned as might be afforded, and two assistant conductors; a chorus master and assistant; a stage manager and crew; a wardrobe mistress and half a dozen experienced dressers, male and female. Thereafter, and only matchable in importance by the conductor, a tenor, a baritone, a bass, a soprano, a mezzo-soprano and a contralto – all of these, the leaders of the company, to be as good as could be tempted and paid for; and each to be supplemented by two young ones of his or her kind, selected from the schools and the beginners in the city operas.

Orchestra and chorus were not engaged. Most Italian towns had orchestral and choral clubs, which in the more fortunate towns were of the local conservatoire, and amused themselves with musical entertainments during the eight darker months of the year. And these groups were in every city the real enthusiasts for the summer seasonal arrangements. Because it was then that they were tested, and could really show their town what they could do. And it was the exacting duty of each impresario's hired assistant conductors and chorus-masters to go ahead of his company by two or three days into each scheduled town, and assemble and rehearse the proffered orchestra and chorus. Naturally such an arrangement, whilst attractive to each town's musicians, and unattractive to the anxious professionals, limited the choice of a seasonal programme to within the knowledge of the available orchestra and chorus. But many of these were ambitious and well-trained, and worked through the winter at scores they hoped to shine in in the *stagione*.

That was the general plan of Italian summer opera. But no one singer or conductor, engaged, say, by Signor Prezzoli, as Rose was to be, need be sure of work in his company throughout his arranged season. Any member of any troupe had to agree to possible dismissal at a week's notice; or to the Italian mania for exchange – for instance, Antonio might be singing Nabucco in Ancona on any Saturday night and after curtain fall be told that he was promised to another management, say in Perugia, for Monday, to sing – no one could remember exactly what.

These were the terms – with, for beginners, the poorest pay that the impresarios could hammer down to. But young students were used to simple and cheap living; life in Italy in little towns in summer was enough, without money; and the schooling of the small opera houses was what they sought, and needed.

As they walked down the Corso, Clare reached for Luisa's hand.

'Why not mine?' said Thomas. 'It's very strong. You're as white as a sheet!'

'We must drink wine,' said Antonio. 'Aragno's?'

'Excellent,' said Thomas.

'Too dear,' said the girls.

'Let's go where there's air,' said Clare. 'You know that place, Thomas, just up from the Piazza Venezia—'

'Oh yes – on the corner of Santi Apostoli—'

They went there; Trajan's Forum was across the street; beyond the old Venetian Palace rose solemn Ara Coeli and the Capitol. And in the deepening blue darkness they could see some broken pillars of the Great Forum. The air was made aromatic by breezes from across the flowery Palatine.

They drank Velletri wine from the Alban Hills, and the young men insisted on the extravagance of little sugared *biscotti*.

Clare looked at Rose and saw that she was all but stricken

by the *maestro's* news. The piteous quiet of the lovely face was hardly to be suffered, and she stretched her hands across the table to the other's baby wrists.

'Rosie, it's come! Oh God!'

'I can't do it, Clare! I won't, I won't! Oh, they're mean at home! Oh, what's the matter with Mamma? Are we in penal servitude, you and I?'

'We are, I think.'

Rose's head went down upon the table. The bright curls fell across the pretty biscuits. Clare stroked them back, and let her own tears fall.

'Oh God,' she whispered. 'Oh God, let us give this up! Let us go home, dear God!'

'Make them drink their wine,' said Luisa to Thomas. 'Rosa, Clara – come, don't you remember how desperate you often were in Paris?'

'They're frightened!' said Thomas, in puzzled consternation.

'But, of course! Terrified,' said Antonio. He put his arm about Rose and lifted her head. 'Come, lovely Rose,' he said. 'Come, drink, and then we'll talk about all these new affairs – come, sweetest Rose—'

He held the glass; she leant on his shoulder and drank some wine; her eyelids were down and tears splashed into the glass and on to Antonio's hand.

Clare understood, with relief, as she looked at the two together that for Rose there could be no escape from the vocation which the faraway Committee had imposed upon her. As the girl drank the pale wine and spilt her tears, as she leant on the shoulder of the beautiful young man and accepted the kindness of his hands, she was – Clare saw, as so indeed did Thomas and Luisa – a pure presentment of the art she was to work in. The Committee had made no mistake.

Rose would many times be frightened, always she would be homesick, and often she would cry; but, thought Thomas, who could hear himself composing the muted orchestration of this moment that he looked upon, she is *given* to Italian opera. She will bear it, because she is it, and it is she. She flows in it, and it flows through her.

Not so this other, he thought. These tears that Clare is licking in with that bright, pointed tongue are, he reflected, the first of her tears that I have seen. And they are *not* Italian opera. How would one orchestrate for them?

He lifted Clare's glass, and touched her hand.

'Drink, Iphigenia,' he said. 'Drink, Alceste.'

Luisa laughed. 'Drink, Eurydice,' said she.

Clare drank, and smiled at them.

'We make theatre, Rosie and I,' she said. 'Forgive us, please. We can't help it.'

'Shall we forgive them, Luisa?'

'Oh, no! We'll punish them!'

'Good idea. Now, Clare, here is your penance. Sing us this instant an ascending chromatic scale, with trill and double shake – that's easy, isn't it?'

'And supposing Signor Giacomo passed by?'

'He'd be enthralled. Go on!'

'I'll go on drinking wine, that's what I'll do,' said Clare, and held her glass towards him.

'You'll not succeed in life,' said Thomas. 'You are too self-indulgent.' He filled her glass.

'Go on, Clare,' said Rose. 'You're very good at ascending chromatics.'

Rose was laughing now, and her tears shone as they dried on her face.

'You're in penance too, young lady,' said Thomas. 'You're to oblige this instant with a diatonic shake. Can you remember one – or will you compose one for us?'

Rose swept her curls back from her forehead, smiled amusedly at Thomas and sang a long phrase from *Anna Bolena*: '. . . *col perdonno sul labbro si scenda* . . .'

Her friends smiled at this familiar exercise from Manuel Garcia's hand-book, but they acknowledged that the challenge was brilliantly taken. And indeed it silenced the café, immobilized the hurrying waiter, and brought passers-by on the hilly street to pause. None of this through excitement or surprise. People sing in Italy, and are pleased and accustomed to hear their fellows sing. The brief hush that fell about Rose's notes, and marked their range of audience when they ceased, was simply of pleasure, alert and critical pleasure. That was well done, that was good, one heard the attentive moment of silence say. And then Rome moved on, waiter and all – some of the citizens humming the outline of the Donizetti phrase.

'Bravo, La Rosa,' said Thomas and Luisa. And Clare marvelled all over again at the ease of Rose within the yoke that had been laid upon her.

But, for the moment, if there was not peace, if fear was not quietened or any of the loneliest questions answered in either of these naïve and fretting Irish breasts, their immediate mood had been turned by wine, by Rose's singing and by the friendliness within which they sat – so that good manners, if no more, commanded them to forbear from selfish wails and lamentations. So cautiously ignoring a while the evening's dramatic news, the five gossiped in normal fashion, and drank more wine, and engaged Luisa in accounts of Milan, of how her work was there, and whom she worked with. She had been happy enough, she said. The work was very hard and serious, and life consisted of it, and of nothing else.

'One thinks of nothing but music in La Scala,' she said. 'But it's great fun, and you're very happy at it – most of the time! Or I was anyway, I think.'

'You went on sometimes in your parts, didn't you?' said Thomas.

'Twice I sang Siebel.'

'That wasn't very alarming, I'd say?'

'Well, comparatively no. But I assure you I was glad it was nothing more exacting I had to sing – because Siebel was my first ordeal. Oh, my God! Facing that auditorium! Ah, in a hundred seasons one could never be other than frightened to death!'

'Oh Luisa!' said Rose.

'But you had rehearsed in it, hadn't you?' said Antonio.

'Certainly – with the full chorus and orchestra – and with the curtain up on all those empty, shrouded tiers and tiers of boxes. Always then I found it ghostly and alarming – and, do you know, Clare – sad? *But* – on the night, it's not ghostly, it's not sad! Lord, there it is, full, full, full of people – absolutely quiet people, motionless – listening to you, listening, having come there to do nothing else but listen!'

'Heavens, yes!' said Clare.

'Exciting, exciting!' said Antonio.

'Might easily be too exciting,' said Thomas.

Luisa laughed.

'Very easily! But truly I find it too frightening for that. It's an absolutely terrifying thing to have to do, to have to sing – to sing alone – in La Scala! And do you know, sometimes when I tell myself that I've already done that on five separate nights, without fainting dead or without even disgracing myself – I can't exactly believe it! I try sometimes in the night to remember how it was, how I got through – but I can't—'

Clare nodded her head.

'That must be a great mercy,' she said.

'It probably saved your reason,' said Rose.

'What were the other four appearances?' asked Thomas.

'Siebel again. And Orfeo twice. I sang Orfeo for the second time only last week. Last week was terrible. All the scouts for the summer season were swarming round, and we *cadetti* never knew what we might be asked to do! But I sang Rosina in *The Barber* only once. I don't think they cared for me at all in that in Milan!'

'Why, do you think?'

'Well, my *maestro*, Ferrano, said that the fashion is almost fixed now – anyhow in Milan – to have Rosina sung by a true soprano—'

'At the Academy too,' said Thomas.

'So – those were my five nights!'

'Let's drink to them!' said Antonio.

'And to five hundred more,' said Thomas.

'Five thousand, I'd say,' said Rose.

'What sort of old wheezer would I be, I wonder, after five thousand nights of opera?'

'Well,' said Thomas, 'a hundred performances a year would be too many – but supposing you gave them, you'd only be seventy, my dear – an exquisite Orfeo!'

'And may we all be there to hear it,' said Antonio.

'With Clare, aged only sixty-nine, singing Eurydice!'

'*E quest' asilo ameno* . . .' Clare sang softly, amusedly.

'Go on,' said Thomas.

She shook her head.

'What's making you look so pleased?'

'I'm thinking how lovely it will be to be sixty-nine – because then it's pretty certain one won't be being forced to be an opera singer! Let's go up on the Campidoglio!'

They crossed the Piazza Venezia arm-in-arm in a row.

'There's my Aventino bus,' said Luisa. 'I ought to take it.'

'There'll be others – it's early.'

Antonio began to sing.

'*La ci darem la mano* . . .'

Rose and Luisa both took up Zerlina's part, in rivalry.

'I'll wait for Donna Elvira's entrance,' said Clare to Thomas. 'After all, she speaks the truth.'

But the singing died away in laziness as they climbed the steps under the huge threat of Castor and Pollux. They crossed the piazza past Marcus Aurelius and his horse and went round the Senator's Palace to look out over Rome from the parapet below the Tabularium.

Whenever Clare stood here, at any hour of day or night, in any mood of Roman weather or of her own, she had the grace to feel recompensed for having to be an exile and a student of opera. Not so with Rose, in whom the broken Forum and Colosseum induced an unfruitful worried sadness. She preferred Rome from the Pincio, or from the high gardens of the Janiculum – for she took joy from trees and grass and trotting horses and the shouts of children. The old broken marbles she could take for granted – but they wearied her. Tonight, however, her eyes flicked over them without attention, as indeed did those of her companions. All were familiar with this place of vantage, and had come here now simply to be together a while longer, and to get nearer to the breezes coming over the Palatine from Ostia.

They leant or sat on the parapet.

'May we smoke, dear ones?' asked Antonio.

'Delicious,' said Rose, as the smell of two cheap cigars curled into the sweet air.

Thomas leant back, looking beyond Caesar's Forum.

'I wonder what the Victor Emmanuel Monument is going to be like?'

'It's obviously going to be very big,' said Luisa. 'Look at the extent of the foundations.'

'He was a great man, you know,' said Antonio. 'Truly great and honourable. We owe him a fine monument.'

'Well, you're putting it in a fine place,' said Clare.

'King Umberto's a brave little man,' said Rose. 'They're always shooting and stabbing at him, aren't they? But he's very plain. Do you remember, Clare – we saw him the other day, in his carriage?'

'Naturally he's brave, dear Rose,' said Antonio. 'He's of Piedmont, and he's well bred.'

Thomas smiled, and so indeed did the three girls. None of them was what Antonio would call well bred, but they were all acquainted in their blood with the idea of bravery. Affectionately, however, they let the *cliché* pass, and when Don Giovanni renewed very softly his '*La ci darem . . .*', softly and absent-mindedly three Zerlinas joined him, and Thomas assumed duty for the first violins.

But if the attention of Rose and Clare was not on the great stretch of history and beauty spread below them, neither was it with what they sang to '*il traditore*'. Clare was not, under the shock of the evening's news, undergoing yet more than that degree of homesickness which by now she had learnt to live with, to wake to and to carry in her breast into sleep. Always she carried childhood with her – but she often told herself wearily that she had already been hoist with it in Dublin, in Aunt Josie's house, and then in Paris. She was well used by now to remembering Grandmother, and the rainy street of Ballykerin and the flapping, clear sea against the wall and the screaming birds and her little curly-headed sisters, fighting and barefoot and always damp and hungry. She carried it all with a cautious quiet now, and sometimes allowed herself to wonder what in fact it held in its sad simplicity that made it into a precious, secret reliquary, a treasure which she had to conceal and assess only in the dark privacy of waking and of going to sleep. What made it gleam so constantly, seeing that it was set against the alarming magnificence of Rome, and the curious, imponderable prospects spread out for her to venture upon? She did not know. But she had learnt to live with its reality. And tonight, no doubt, it waited for her as usual in her night prayers and in her last awareness as sleep came down. But now, singing amusedly with the others and determined to come in ahead of anyone as Donna Elvira, she was not homesick. She was looking, without sentiment or backward glance, into her future – that future which in her ignorance and timidity she had accepted from a few authoritative gentlemen in Dublin, and to which now she was indeed committed by the *maestro's* fiat of tonight. It was clear now, crystal-clear as she stared into the relentless Roman night, that she was surrendered to the accident of one imperfectly understood talent. Money had been spent which she must earn and repay; gifts of instruction and guidance had been poured on her; she was being educated and carried out into worlds and opportunities she could never have imagined when she sat by Grandmother's clean fire, listening to the sea outside the wall; moreover, all this endowment of her had stirred up greeds and hopes at home where no one else but she had been selected for such audacious speculation. She was committed; she must go forward and be that which bene-factors had said she would be. Angrily she told herself now not to be dramatic, that since the Rue des Lauriers days she had fully realized her obligation. That was true; yet in secret she had soothed herself in Paris, and even here in Rome, with plans of escape – quite honourable plans of taking all the given education, and equipping herself to teach very expensive pupils – singing and English and French – and rapidly pay back what had been gambled on her. That done, she would be free, and would find her own way, without patrons, without orders, and with no need at all to sing in opera. But tonight she saw that the gates had closed on her. She must accept this decision taken over her head. Angrily she laughed.

Thomas took her hand.

'Only my own joke, Thomas,' she said, 'I mean that I see I have to face the music.'

Luisa jumped off the parapet, and greeted a man coming towards them. She spoke in Spanish, and in Spanish he answered, removing his shadowing black hat.

'Ah, Señor Duarte!' said Thomas.

The Spaniard, still smiling surprisedly on Luisa, bowed to Thomas. Luisa, holding the newcomer's hand, brought him forward and presented him to her friends.

'Don Iago Maria Duarte – but you have known him at the Accademia, no?'

Don Iago bowed to everyone, and then spoke to Clare.

'La Señorita Clara 'Alve?'

Clare bowed, confused by the Spanish address and variation of her name.

'I hear from Signor Giacomo,' Don Iago went on in Italian, 'I hear that you desire to take private lessons in sacred vocal music from me in the autumn?'

Clare acknowledged this.

'That is interesting, Signorina. I shall be glad. So few of the young care to study sacred music. Now this Signorina Luisa, my fellow-countrywoman –' he turned and smiled at her, 'has, I think, a perfect voice for oratorio and for our great Spanish church music. But she will not work at it!'

'Then you should compel her, sir,' said Antonio.

'No, no,' said Rose. 'Luisa is exquisite in opera. And I'd hate to have Clare swept off into oratorio – I'd call it a shame, Signor!'

Don Iago laughed delightedly.

'Some voices are for everything, Signorina! They are the great voices, the Proteans. And you be careful, Signorina Rosa. I have often heard you sing – and your voice will learn that it requires more music than was written by Rossini and Verdi!'

'Amen to that,' said Thomas.

'We were singing Mozart just now,' said Rose, with a flick of irritation.

'Why then, continue, my young friends,' said the Spaniard, and bowing again and with a smile to Luisa he went on his way and down the steps.

'I like Don Iago very much,' said Luisa.

Clare looked at her with sympathy. He speaks her language, he is from home, she thought; this reminded her of Paddy Flynn.

Rose, unlike Clare, was not afraid tonight of her committal to the profession placed upon her; she had embraced that, she looked towards it with terror but also with joy and a kind of begging love. She had no doubt but that she must be what she had been elected to be. She adored her work and she gave herself to it without cloud or question. Cloud? There was always one, which tonight had swelled so black and frightening that she had to fight it off with every kind of wine and flippancy and song and immediate nonsense. This cloud, which varied with every day in shape and size and colour, was simple, childish homesickness. It was indeed her only grief in these pupil years. She was very intelligent, but cared not a whit for the complicated dusts and civilizations over which she tripped either in Paris or in Rome. She absorbed and enjoyed and learnt very nimbly from the general Latin graces; she observed the life of Rome with amusement and appreciation, and she spoke Italian already with admirable grace. She was in fact – by happy accident – in that country which of all on earth could make her what she was to be. Her nerves, her intuitions told her that. But they did not, naturally, warn her of the conflict which this sympathy must set up between her Italian-made self and the little girl who had set out in tears from Lackanashee.

Tonight, however, terrified and shocked by the decision taken over her head, very much shocked that Mamma and Miss French should have cheated her in this way, she was positively afraid to look, until she was alone – or, at least alone with Clare – at her desire for Lackanashee. Oh Mamma! Oh Miss French! Oh Mamma!

She flung back her head against Antonio's arm.

'Antonio, I hate all these old ruins! Couldn't we go and hear a bad mandolinist somewhere?'

'Nothing easier!'

They all went drifting back towards the Corso.

Clare and Luisa went arm-in-arm.

'You haven't said you'll be glad to be singing Eurydice with me,' said Luisa.

'How could I say it? I'll be terrified!'

'But so shall I, you egotist!'

Clare turned and looked, in comfort and pleasure, at Luisa's lovely Spanish face.

'I suppose you will, come to think of it?'

They laughed and kissed each other.

'Oh, there's my bus!'

The old horses were shaking flies off themselves under the trees outside San Marco. Luisa leapt on board.

'Good night! Tomorrow, tomorrow!'

Thomas said: 'That'll do. She's out of hearing. Look, the others are waiting.'

They joined the others.

'A little wine, I think,' said Antonio.

'I want some lemonade,' said Rose.

'I'd like to hear a flat old tenor,' said Clare.

'We can manage both,' said Thomas, '*and* an out-of-tune mandolin.'

They drank wine, the girls too. Clare desired any folly which postponed night-prayers, and their perplexing train of fear. Rose, her eyes burning black, looked into her wineglass and thought: I am *not* going to cry. All right, I must sing this summer. It was mean of Mamma – oh, it was mean of Miss French! Still – I'll do what they say. After all, I must.

'Sweet Rose,' said Antonio, 'what are you thinking of?'

'I'm thinking of Mamma,' she said, 'I'm thinking that she's very unkind to me. Poor Mamma! Ah well – *next* summer, please God . . .'

Next summer, thought Clare, next summer.

The Fifth Chapter

The next summer came – June 1889. It found Rose not famous yet indeed, but known and discussed throughout Italy. After twelve months of singing here, there and everywhere about the peninsula, Rosa d'Irlanda, as the programmes named her, was now not only being looked for and acclaimed by opera-goers, but, of all young sopranos then singing and studying in Italy, it is probable that she was subject to the closest attention of the opera managements. The hard-headed men who owned Italian opera, and who therefore, at that time, controlled opera throughout the world, listened to Rose during the long spring of 1889 with an attentiveness which their non-committal caution could not disguise. And as she was sent from this company to that and from opera house to opera house, under the system of borrowing, lending and experimenting which governs Italian theatre, it became clear to any who watched, in love, jealousy or indifference, that a new star was in ascendant, and that its trajectory was not being guessed, or plotted, with especial greed and passion.

Rose's touring summer of 1888 had been happy, and within it she had shown such educative pace and sympathy with her work that at its end her *maestri* were agreed that it would be wrong to set her back in the student-life of Via di Ripetta. It was clear that she learnt accurately within the hard routine of the profession, in the company of experienced singers, under different conductors, and with varied teaching. So it was decreed that she go on singing in the smaller opera houses of Italy through the winter and spring seasons of 1888–89.

This pleased her, although the constant hard work as adaptable member of a troupe, and the too-frequent changes of directors, made it difficult for her to increase her repertory – and this she knew to be an essential duty. However, gallantly, joyously she sought opportunities to understudy, and spared neither herself nor her masters in her zeal to learn as many scores as they allowed her. It pleased her, simply because she loved the life in which she found herself; but also because, at every change of company throughout the winter, her status and so her salary moved upward by a little; and, having a good head for money, she understood from the proportions of her weekly payments that the debt to the Committee was already lightening, that she was now earning her living, was incurring no more obligations since she had sung at Bologna in June 1888, and was in fact, since she was thrifty, in a position after January 1889 to send small monthly savings to Mamma. She had been unable to do this until she had, very necessarily, replaced the worn-out Rue des Lauriers wardrobe by a few respectable dresses and bonnets and pairs of shoes. But at last, within her second year in Italy, she could live modestly without worrying about the Committee, and could already help Mamma a little.

This gave her satisfaction, and eased her homesickness. But the opera-singing life in itself did these two things for her also. She saw now that she positively loved what she was about, and that she had been very lucky. Often in elated hours she blew kisses westward.

'Where, Rosa?'

'Over the sea! To Lady O'Dowd and Father Lucius, and the Colonel and Miss French – and Mamma!'

Several kisses she would blow then, and speed them with a phrase from the opera she was that week especially studying.

If she loved her life, it was perhaps no more than she should do, in plain gratitude, as spring advanced. For success crept up to her eager feet in ripples small but consecutive, each one, as the tide moved in, lapping somewhat higher than its precursor.

At Carnival she had sung in Venice, in the Goldoni Theatre, under the baton of Arditi. She had sung Cherubino in *Figaro*, a part she disliked, but in which she was already creating the hint of a reputation. Arditi had been delighted with her performance, for the best professional reasons; but Venetian Carnival society had been enchanted simply because, with or without reason, this Irish Cherubino enchanted them. In Turin she had sung four operas under the direction of Luisa's Milanese *maestro*, Luigi Ferrano, and in April, still under Ferrano's direction, when she sang *La Traviata* in Parma, she found that she was singing it to Verdi himself. And the composer was so generous and gracious to her afterwards, orally and in letters, that almost she questioned his renowned sincerity. However, conducted by the great Ponchielli in Florence in May, she again sang *La Traviata*, as well as Zerlina in *Don Giovanni*, and Gilda in *Rigoletto*; and on an evening at the end of that short season the *maestro*, in an unbuttoned mood and much delighted with her, let fall the gossip that on the composer's own commendation she, Rosa d'Irlanda, was being observed and considered for Desdemona at La Scala in the autumn season.

So, as years go for the young and the more or less defenceless, the twelve months that ran between June in 1888 and June in 1889 were vivid and promising for Rose.

Throughout these months she was never in Rome, and did not see Clare, who was still working with Signor Giacomo, and who sang at the Valle Theatre sometimes during the winter, and after Easter 1889 was engaged for a short season at Naples and Palermo. But the two exchanged long letters, full of plots and hopes for meeting again, and even for singing in the same company. Clare was studying sacred and church music with Iago Maria Duarte, and was still living at Via di Ripetta. Thomas was also there; very busy, singing, conducting, directing and composing opera – not yet prepared to go on to Vienna.

The two who during this touring period crossed and recrossed Rose's northern paths were Antonio de Luca, and Mariana Fogli, the young Sicilian contralto.

But when at last in June, at the end of her Florentine engagement, she did after twelve months return to Rome and rented, to Clare's delight, a room in Signor Giacomo's apartment, it became clear that once again the longed-for summer return to Mamma and Lackanashee must be postponed. For something very like fame was now to be offered to Rosa d'Irlanda, and she must stay and work for it.

The hundred-and-fifty-year-old Teatro Nobile del Torre Argentina, which had been closed for nearly twenty years, was re-opened by the City of Rome in spring 1888, as an opera house. Large, brilliantly decorated and electrically lighted, it became fashionable at once, and the excellence of the productions of its first season threatened the leadership of Costanzi's. It had a great history of first performances and of famous voices, so had been welcomed back into Italian musical life with acclaim and excitement. And in its happy second year its management arranged to give Rome and her visitors a more than usually well-planned summer season. And among the young, and less young, elected to carry this through, Rosa d'Irlanda was marked down for many rôles.

This would be a test to decide everything for her, and one which she knew she would not refuse. So in Via di Ripetta she rested in early June, while awaiting her summer contract and assignments.

Clare and she could hardly cease from talking at first. No longer sharing a room, they spent hours of each night one seated on the other's bed, while they exchanged the experiences, developments, adventures and misadventures of the long year. And sometimes if they laughed too much or raised their voices in excitement, Signor Giacomo would knock on the door and beg them in Heaven's name to respect their larynxes, and rest them in silence and sleep.

At times in these long conversations of reunion they turned simultaneously into Italian speech. This amused them very much. But by degrees Clare observed that it was a sign of reserve in both, of unforeseen shyness, of screens coming down.

Inevitable, she thought, and looked at Rose with added attention then, in grave surmise. That each had changed in her first professional year and saw change wrought in the other went without saying; but neither spoke of this at first, save in reference to superficial things.

'Oh, what a lovely dress, Rosie! It is a relief to see you properly dressed at last!'

'And you! Sometimes last year I used to think that we'd never get out of those Rue des Lauriers rags!'

'And now you look as if you'd never heard of them, you elegant creature!'

'I love clothes,' said Rose. 'I'm afraid I could easily go mad on them!'

'Ah, don't! You don't need to!'

'You look simply beautiful now, Clare. But you're still very – very austere, somehow – aren't you?'

'I don't think so. Actually, I've been having quite a worldly kind of life.'

'I should hope so, indeed! But still, you'll never look worldly, no matter what you get up to!'

'Well, you will – and you do, my lady! Goodness, what a success you are! Poor old Giacomo is so excited about you that he's almost afraid to breathe when people speak your name!'

'Anyway, it's a blessing not to be making a mess of things – so far,' said Rose, and she touched the wooden bedpost, and made the sign of the cross. 'On account of the Committee, you know, and all that.'

Assunta came in with a jug of lemonade and some *biscotti*.

'Oh Assunta, you pet! I was dying for some lemonade!' Rose took Assunta's hand and drew her down and kissed her. 'But you should be in bed and asleep hours ago! You're tired!'

'Not very tired, Signorina.'

She stroked Rose's shining hair, smiled and withdrew.

'Her life is always the same,' said Clare.

'I'd love to give her a good holiday – take her to Ireland or somewhere,' said Rose.

'You won't be able to do that just yet, anyway!'

'No. And you? Can you go home?'

Clare shook her head.

'I'll have to take a summer season. I haven't got half as far on with my debt as you have, Rosie. And except for Grandmother I don't think anyone especially wants to see me at home now. But your mother will be disappointed about you, won't she?'

'Truly I don't know,' said Rose in Italian. 'I sometimes get an idea now that Mamma is fonder of the money I send than she is of me.'

'I'm sure that isn't true,' Clare answered vaguely, in Italian too.

One evening in the Piazza Argentina Clare encountered Thomas as he emerged, music-laden, from the new Opera House. He grabbed her arm.

'Wrong direction, girl,' he said. 'Home now to Ripetta – supper-time.'

'I'm having supper in Trastevere.'

'But you're singing tomorrow night!'

'Oh, I won't be late. I'm taking his ticket for tomorrow night to Paddy, and I promised I'd have supper with him.'

'In his rooms – as usual? These Irish seminarists!'

'He's not a seminarist.'

'He always will be. And all this strolling round Trastevere—'

'Well, I'm an actress – I'm a rogue and vagabond—'

'I wish you were! But perhaps you are! Perhaps this pious Paddy Flynn is the hypocrite I take him for?'

'Perhaps – but I don't think so.'

'Well, may I walk a piece of the way with you, over the bridge?'

'Of course. But all those portfolios you're carrying—?'

'*I'm* not an invalid.'

Clare smiled, and inhaled the cool evening air with gratitude.

'Don't be harsh, Thomas. You have a hundred friends. Let me have one.'

'I haven't a hundred lovers.'

'Neither have I.'

'I believe not. But it's time you had one, anyhow. For a start.'

'I sometimes wonder what they'd think at home if they heard some of my conversations with you.'

'But you aren't at home. You're in the world, and you are becoming an interpreter of the world – in one medium – of some of its eternal troubles and excitements—'

Clare laughed, but a little wearily.

'I know. It's a curious obligation – and believe me, Thomas, I consider it. After all, I have to, under your tuition.'

'Sit a minute,' he said, and dragged her down to a café table. 'These portfolios are confoundedly heavy.'

They drank vermouth and soda, and looked back across the lively Piazza at the Tiber and at Rome.

'Tomorrow will be the seventh time that I'll have heard you sing Eurydice – and the fourth time with Luisa.'

'Thank God it is Luisa tomorrow!'

'You prefer singing it with her to L'Amietti?'

'Heavens, yes! And anyway, she *looks* a bit like Orpheus!'

'Poor old Amietti! I wish they'd let me conduct you and Luisa in that opera!'

'It'd be lovely if they did. But I suppose they think that the three of us together would be a bit of a risky group – too young!'

'Nonsense! I'm a great disciplinarian, as you know.'

'Anyway, I'm glad it's Duarte tomorrow night – because I'm used to him, and Rose will be there and that will make me extra nervous.'

'You'll be all right. Duarte will see to that. And I'll be listening like a lynx.'

'So will Rosie. Oh Thomas! Don't talk about it, please!'

The hand that lifted her glass shook, and her profile was strained and sharp. The signs pleased Thomas, who believed in this resistant artist.

'Drink up,' he said. 'We should have had brandy.'

'I must go on – Paddy will be wondering—'

'Let him wonder.'

'I – I always love his company on days like this – days before a performance – because' – answering Thomas's questioning eyes – 'well, you see, with all the best will there is, he simply doesn't know a thing about what it's like – the fear, the terror. Now, with you or Luisa, or Duarte – it's awful! Because you know! Paddy makes me forget it, and we talk about Ireland and Parnell, and we drink tea.'

'I see the point. But don't drink too much tea – not as good for the voice as wine.'

They parted on the corner of Via di Fratte, where Paddy lived.

'A suitable address,' said Thomas. 'And take care of yourself now, among the wild men of Trastevere.'

Paddy lived in two small whitewashed cells at the top of a narrow house. On the landing he shared a cold water tap and a small oil-burning cooking stove with an old German teacher who occupied the room at the rear.

The Irishman was now earning a bare but for him sufficient living through part-time teaching in schools and through private coaching. Also he was working in the University for a doctorate in history.

Lest she forget it, Clare gave him at once his ticket for the morrow's performance at La Valle. He placed it carefully in his wallet.

'Thank you, Clare. It's very good of you. And this will be the last time this season, alas!'

In July she would be going north on summer engagements, following more or less the route which Rose had taken a year before.

'God knows when I'll sing in Rome again!'

'But in October – you said! Clare, you *are* coming back in October?'

'I suppose so. I must do my duty.' She leant against the balcony grid and looked backward along the street. 'I don't like going on tour. Since I can't go home I'd – I'd rather stay in Rome. I used to hate the place, you know, in spite of all its marvels—'

'I remember—'

'But now – oh, it's been an extraordinary year; and I'm afraid I'm in love with Rome – in a reluctant kind of way. But I still hate the Romans,' she said, with some relief in her voice.

'It was the Romans who made Rome.'

'Yes. Strange!'

'I worship Rome,' said Paddy.

He came on to the balcony with two glasses of wine in his hands.

'Extravagance!' said Clare.

'Oh, we have to drink to Eurydice – and her return!'

'No, no – let's forget her, Paddy! I'm frightened of her and Orpheus today! We'll drink to the Land War and Michael Davitt!'

'We'll do that later, if you like, in honest, decent tea. Come and eat, Clare.'

The whitewashed study-cell was modest, in accordance at once with its occupant's means and his taste. He had little money for books, and worked for the most part in the libraries of the Vatican and the Collegio Romano; but the few he had were neatly shelved, and above them stood a brass crucifix and a velvet-framed photograph of his mother. On the opposite wall he had pinned a large photogravure of 'The School of Athens'. This evening he had cleared his working-table and set it with his two straight-backed chairs near the window, laid with plates and bread and salt.

He brought cold food from his cupboard on the landing; they dressed the salad and they ate.

Their friendship had become at once precious and exasperating to the two within its year. Paddy looked more of a boy in his grey alpaca jacket than he used to seem in his clerical black, and his covered-in eyes were now more often fixed, Clare thought, on faraway abstractions of philosophy than on immediate 'shalls' and 'shall-nots' of moral passion. Yet the puzzled half-would-be priest was not dead in him and, uninstructed still as to the world, he feared its sins as he apprehended them in himself and all about him – and stared in dismay at the human prospect. This dismay turned often to fanaticism and impatience; he was indeed unstable and naïve.

Clare was by now perhaps somewhat too little of either; a source of conflict in her might be between her native, too marked stability and her quick acceptance of knowledge of the world in which she found herself and with which it would be necessary and pleasant to make terms. What the terms could be, she being her very self, she did not see, but she was at present no more than cautious in consideration of those advancing problems which from far-off she was beginning to understand. And she could never be fanatical – or so she thought.

Because of their common inheritance she more or less understood and much admired Paddy; and because his face pleased her and his simple manners, as well as his trick of saying illuminative things when they might be least foreseen, he had grown personally dear to her – an escape and refreshment, a presentment of the standards of childhood. Sometimes she surprised herself by the near-tenderness which could creep into her thoughts of him.

Yet they quarrelled often and passionately. But tonight they would not do so.

Paddy knew nothing of the miseries and senseless terrors which a public performer must undergo each time his hour draws up – but he accepted the recurrent sickness in Clare, and it touched him that she found help and oblivion against it, whenever she could, with him. So they would eat well, and exchange their news from home, and he would lend her last week's *Clare Champion* and *Cork Examiner*, and he would talk about his pupils and she would sing the praises of that enigmatic man, Parnell. And they would drink strong, sweet tea, and he would tell her of this or that out of Rome's past that had arrested his attention during the week. And he would then walk home with her over the river and along the Lungatevere, under the trees, to Ripetta. And she would sing as they walked, 'At the mid hour of night,' and 'When he who adores thee . . .'

The first part of the evening went according to this plan; and, supper eaten, washing-up done, they sat by the window on the two hard chairs and drank tea and toasted Michael Davitt.

But they were uneasy.

Clare was always at once restless, guarded and irritable on the days before she had to sing in public; and apart from that tension, there were questions and troubles in her head at present which might not even be hinted at to Paddy. Also she was oppressed by the thought of leaving Rome, and him, soon and for months. This added heaviness of heart, which seemed to be greater than she had reckoned on, made her cautious, and inexpressive save through flippancy.

'I smoked a cigarette last night, with Rose,' she said.

'You what?'

'Smoked. Have you any cigarettes, Paddy?'

'Most certainly not.'

'Well, don't report me to little Giacomo, will you? He'd have a seizure! Our sacred throats!'

'Oh, your throats! But – ladies don't smoke, Clare.'

'Rose says they do – in private. And anyway, I'm not a lady. Grandmother sometimes smokes a pipe, on the quiet.'

'That's different.'

'What way?'

Paddy was uneasy. He never could endure to be out of the Teatro del Valle on nights when Clare sang, yet the approach of each occasion and still more its taking place made him even more irritable than it made Clare. But not at all for similar or sympathetic reasons. He knew little of music, and cared not at all for its operatic forms, and it seemed to him, in his dark ignorance of her profession, that Clare always accomplished what was required of her perfectly – she alone in the cast. The others invariably wearied him. She being therefore in his judgment incapable of error or less than supremacy in the exercise of her surprising art, he was secretly impatient of her recurrent anxieties about it, which he found unreasonable in her, and even a shade feminine and affected. But to see her and hear her on the stage did always distress him for many days after each experience, sickening him into perplexity, idleness and self-dislike. Clare had appeared to him on the first morning that he saw her, in the early spring of sixteen months ago among Saint Peter's colonnades, as beautiful enough for any idealization, any remote and heavenly symbol. An angel or a virgin from some Sienese canvas, he had thought then – and always still, when he saw her coming towards him through sunlight, erect and fair and unearthly slender, he was reminded of annunciations and heavenly messengers.

This admiration of her physical aspect he could manage, and he allowed himself its uneasy pleasure. But when, one of a hot, sibilating, applauding or non-applauding mass of his fellow-creatures, he had to sit and stare at all this far-off beauty across footlights, across music; when he saw it enhanced, exoticized, high-lighted; adapting itself to interpretation of this or that improbable legend of human love and sin and melodrama, and this for all the groundlings, for any comer who was free to clap or spit or seek her out and kiss her hand; this also in the constant company of common troupers whose business it was in public and for the public's delight to treat her as absurdly as an evening's entertainment exacted – to kiss her, to stab her, to snatch her up or throw her down, to roar duets with her, to swoon at her feet or have her swoon at theirs – this tormented Paddy, made him hot, made him black and sulky, gave him headaches, gave him insomnia, made him dully misanthropic, and yet, held him fascinated.

He was glad it was to be *Orfeo* tomorrow night, all the more since it was the last time for months that he would go through the bright anguish of listening, looking while Clare sang, to him and hundreds. The myth itself appealed to him, and by now he knew the opera, and admired very much its economy, purity and grace. Of all the operas he had listened to within the year, either in Clare's company or when she was performing, it was his favourite. And he thought that complicated and contradictory as seemed the character of Glück's Eurydice, yet Clare, simple girl from Ireland, understood her with positive authority, and certainly looked her every inch, in each note and movement of the story.

He often talked about *Orfeo* with her; but when he tried to tell of his especial appreciation of her in it, she only smiled and shrugged him off. He knew she was shy of praise; but also he felt that, whereas she accepted the kindness of his words, she found no more in them than the nervous stammerings of one who was at once ignorant of his subject and sentimentally partial to her.

This sense of barrier made him nervous; also secretly it angered him. He never acknowledged this anger to himself, or more truly, he never sought honestly for its source. But its pain stirred much and easily in his breast these days, as the hour of Clare's departure from Rome rose clear on the horizon. And when he could not bear it, he sometimes sought outward expressions and justifications of it which were superficial and unfair, but were movements of feeling, and so relieved him.

'Silly of Rose,' he said, 'to be showing off to you like that, about cigarettes.'

'Rose never shows off. It was only a bit of fun.'

'Maybe. Of course, she's young for all this wild success she's having.'

'No, she isn't. From now on she's simply got to be ready for anything. You know, with ordinary luck, in about five years from now Rose will be a kind of legend in opera – or so they say.'

'She's very eager for success, I hear.'

'She is indeed – and for two good reasons.'

'Are there good reasons for desiring success, Clare?'

'Well, Rose wants it because, first, she wants to justify all that was done for her by the people at home – and, secondly, she *loves* her work, and she can't help knowing that she's every chance of being superb in it!'

'She'll never be as good as you.'

'Nonsense, Paddy! You don't know what you're talking about!'

'Sorry.'

'Ah, don't be cross!'

'I'm not in the least cross. But sometimes I can't help worrying about you two girls and this extraordinary, dangerous world you're plunged into!'

'Yes – the world's dangerous. It doesn't take long to find that out. But we're all in it, and we've got to live in it somehow, until we die.'

'I was talking about your special world – the theatre world.'

'Ah! But Paddy, why should that worry you more than other possible worlds? I mean – what do you know about it?'

'Only what everyone knows,' he said stiffly.

Clare smiled.

'If that's all—' she said.

'Why are you being so rude to me, Clare?'

'Am I rude? I'm sorry – but don't get pompous, like a good boy.'

'Of course, if it's pompous to worry about your friend Rose—'

'Most certainly it is,' said Clare coldly. 'And anyway, what on earth is there to worry about?'

'I read about her in the papers; I hear you chattering about her from her letters – and when I've met your friends and colleagues, Clare, her name is often in the talk—'

'Of course it is! We love her—'

'Yes, there's too much love! You all use the word too much. Do you know its meaning?'

'Oh, Paddy, there are so many! But don't lecture me tonight!'

'Good heavens, when *have* I lectured you? Perhaps it'd be better if I did! Oh Clare, be careful!'

'Careful of what?'

'Of yourself. Of what you must always be. Of all the old values – of your childhood and your church—'

Clare stood up.

'You're talking like a madman!'

'Better talk like that than like some of your other associates—'

'You don't know my associates!'

'I've met them, in your company! That Evans, for instance – joking, conceited atheist, whose only intention is to break your heart!'

'Don't be such a *fool*, Paddy!'

'And the Spaniard you're so much in awe of – what's his name?'

'Do you mean my teacher, Iago Duarte?'

'Your teacher? Be careful what you let him teach you, Clare! I know more of him than you do. He's a profligate – that's all *he* is!'

'A profligate? Oh Paddy, do *you* know the meaning of *that* word?'

'I do – and so should you! And if you were really Señorita Carriaga's friend, perhaps you'd explain it to her! Or is it too late, in her case?'

Clare stepped away from him.

'You gossip!' Her voice shook, sobs breaking it. 'You mean, uncharitable man! Where on earth do you invent your wretched guesses and surmises?'

'I invent nothing. I study your associates because I care so much for you!'

'Care for me? How dare you say it?'

She picked up her purse and scarf, left the room, and sped down the stairs. Paddy rushed after her and caught her by the arm.

'Go back to your room. I'm going home.'

'I'm taking you home.'

'You are not. Let me go.'

'You're not crossing Rome alone at this hour of the night.'

She jerked her arm out of his hold and sped down to the street as if on wings. But he caught up with her again.

'I insist on escorting you to Via di Ripetta.'

'Do you really think that I never walk about Rome unless you're at hand to protect me? Go away, Paddy, please.'

They strode along the pavement at a pace which amazed the Roman loafers. In the Piazza before the river Clare saw buses turning at a trot on to the Garibaldi Bridge. She tore across the middle of the traffic, caught up with one and leapt on board.

Before Paddy could see what bus she had in mind she was lost, out of sight. But he also raced through carts and carriages and blocking crowds, on to the bridge.

'Clare! Clare! Come back! Forgive me! Oh Clare, forgive me! I'm mad, Clare! Forgive me, come back! Come back!'

Assunta met Clare in the corridor at Via di Ripetta.

'You're early, Signorina. That is good. You'll need a long sleep tonight. I shall bring you some lemonade.'

'Thank you, Assunta.'

She learnt that La Signorina Rosa was dining with the Marchese di Montebirone and some gentleman from Milan, that Signor Tomaso was not in yet, and that Signorina Luisa had called at eight o'clock and left a note on her dressing-table. This said that Luisa was sorry to have missed her, that Duarte required them both to be at the Valle at ten o'clock in the morning, to run through the third act – and that she sent her love.

Clare undressed slowly and knelt to say her prayers. But long after she had finished them she stayed on her knees, and rested her head against the counterpane. She felt sad and was afraid to go to bed. Perhaps Rose would look in to say good night.

But Assunta, bringing lemonade, said that Signorina Rosa would be late and that she would wait up for her. Signorina Chiara looked very tired, and she advised her to go to sleep quickly.

'You look tired, too, Assunta. How is the Signora?'

Assunta sighed and shrugged, and as she closed the door and withdrew Clare felt sadder still, afraid of tomorrow, all the tomorrows, everyone's.

But when the last curtain fell in the Valle on the following night, the mood was other than fearful.

This last performance of the season of *Orfeo* was in no sense a spectacular or significant occasion. Luisa and Clare – against a beautifully disciplined chorus of shepherds and fairies and happy and unhappy shades – under Duarte's calm beat had sung their best-loved opera as well as they at present could, to a full and friendly routine house, an audience of regular patrons who knew them by now, and knew the music that they sang. It was improbable that there were any formidable European opera spies present – save perhaps Rose's important-looking escorts in her box; and they, Clare surmised, were there only for the pleasure of being with Rose. There might be a director from Costanzi's concealed somewhere, or from the Argentina or from Paris. But the atmosphere from the front of the house was more that of friendly send-off and *arrivederci* than of critical attention or professional appraisal. Still, the girls knew that some excellent judges were listening to them – Signor Giacomo, for instance, and other Accademia professors; Signor Ferrano, Luisa's *maestro* from Milan; many of their own contemporaries and rivals – and a few formidable, anxious critics who loved them: Rose, Thomas, Mariana, Antonio. And Clare also knew that Paddy was in front; she would have known he was there even had she not found his desperate letter and a bunch of roses in her dressing-room.

The curtain down then, the gay and friendly calls taken and re-taken from an audience that had been mainly kind throughout the year to their beginnings, there was for the two the customary inrush of relief and peace, as always wild and sweet; and as the lights went out and they turned and ran to their dressing-rooms, hand in hand, they went on singing.

The music they both loved had carried them far tonight, together and above themselves. Their descent was slow and reluctant, and their hands did not fall apart when they paused in Clare's doorway.

Still Orpheus and Eurydice, their brilliantly made-up eyes swept for each the other's face, as if to insist that this disguise of myth in which they stood was their mutual reality, their one true dress wherein they recognized each other, and were free of that full recognition and could sing it as if their very singing was a kind of Greek, immortal light, not singing at all.

'Thank you, thank you,' they both said, and then they laughed at this reciprocal gratitude that always swept them after they had sung together. And in their laughter they became themselves at once, Clare and Luisa; so, lightly they kissed, and turned away to wash and cold-cream themselves back into the ordinary Roman night.

'I'm starved,' Luisa called from her dressing-table.

'Oh, so am I! I'm ravenous!'

'Well, you've earned a real supper,' said Thomas's voice. 'Which of you may I visit first!'

'Not me!' 'Not me!'

'Hurry up then and make yourselves fit to be seen! The whole front of the house is coming round to kiss you! And I want the first kiss from your lips, my darlings, before they're squashed and shapeless!'

'So you're pleased with us, *maestro*?' asked Luisa.

'Ask me that tomorrow! I hate intemperate speech. Tomorrow I'll hear how flat you went, both of you, in *con me viene* . . .'

'Flat! How dare you!'

'Tonight somehow I couldn't hear it! But hurry, ladies – your infatuates are swarming through the stage door!'

Supper, at the Ristorante Colonna, was by invitation of Rose's resplendent escorts – the Marchese di Montebirone, elderly, plump and gay, and a very handsome young Signor Sandroni, heir to industrial fortunes in Milan, whose family were long-time patrons of La Scala. These gentlemen flung their invitation handsomely, so Clare and Rose took hold of protesting Paddy and swept him into one of the waiting victorias.

'Stop fussing, Paddy,' said Rose. 'I want to talk to you! And besides, it's more than time you had a taste of worldliness.' And the large private dining-room at the Colonna, flowered and lighted, and spread to entertain a randomly gathered number of people, all engaged – for life, one might say – in pursuit, promotion, expression or conquest of a human art, an earthly, transient, pleasure, and all as it happened tonight finding themselves happy in this purpose, a little in love with it, for the hour, as with the wine they drank and the eyes they smiled at – and, for final, brief grace, able most of them to carry in their half-listening memories passages of the music which had brought them together here – all of this, gathered into one room, could indeed be called a taste of worldliness.

'I'm not properly dressed,' said Paddy.

'Neither is Thomas,' said Clare, 'nor Gennaro. For that matter, neither am I.'

Clare, compunctious, kept him at her side and made him feel sure that she and he were always friends, and had once again forgiven each other totally. She drank their secret toast with him – 'To the Land War!' – and made him laugh. She told him who this one was and that, and she made Signor Giacomo sit on his left hand, as she felt that the two would like and reassure each other.

'You pleased me tonight, Signorina Chiara,' said the little *maestro*.

'Thank you, Signor. I hope that is really true?'

'Of course it is. We will talk tomorrow – of some details. But Glück – in Glück you please—'

Paddy looked in hurt amazement at the temperately-spoken little man.

'But surely, sir, the Signorina pleases, as you say, in everything?'

Giacomo smiled.

'She pleases you, young man, in everything, we can suppose! But that is irrelevant to being a soprano singer.'

'I thought we were speaking of her singing, sir?'

'I was. Now, listen to me—' and Giacomo tackled at once the cold trout on his plate and Paddy's and the world's fatuity when moved by a singing voice.

The Marchese, a sociable man and facile in curiosity, moved among his twelve or more guests round the large oval table, sitting here and there as a vacant place offered. Luisa had pleased his fancy much tonight, and he lingered beside her to toast and flatter, and find out what he could about her. Meantime Antonio took his vacated chair at Rose's right hand, and set himself gaily to the business of annoying and dispossessing the handsome industrialist from Milan.

Iago Duarte poured wine into Clare's glass.

'It was good tonight,' he said. 'There are nights – rare they are indeed – when a conductor, his singers and his orchestra are *one*. I don't mean that they are perfect then, or even very good – but they are that first essential, they are together, they are *one*. That is the beginning, and we achieved it tonight.'

'Yes, it felt like that. It felt *safe*, at least! And that's no little thing, Signor.'

The Spaniard smiled.

'How experienced you sound, Signorina! And believe me, believe me you are not!'

'Indeed I know I'm not!' said Clare. 'But please don't croak! I've done with being afraid now, for a few days.'

'It's those few days that are always saving us – in everything. Isn't it? They are dark, after all; and we may not cross them as far as the next wild jump.'

'That's true. And yet,' she looked at him uncertainly, 'I suppose one would rather get to it than not?'

'Even if it should be Iphigenia or Isolde or Elvira?'

'God forbid!'

'They'll confront you, Signorina. They are there ahead, be sure!'

But Clare looked about the present scene and shook them from her, those faraway, possible ladies. Tonight, this hour of it, was happy and felt safe – almost as the third act of *Orfeo* had felt safe the hour before. She would admit neither fear nor loneliness to cross the lighted room, and she turned from the closed Spanish face beside her. Rose's face she sought instead, and caught it smiling towards her.

'Oh Clare, we're praising you here!' Rose called to her, and she and Antonio and Signor Sandroni all lifted glasses towards her. 'Dear Eurydice! Most lovely!'

A happy hour – high-lighted for everyone by friendly eyes, and by some eyes that loved or thought they loved each other. Clare held it gladly within a small ring of pleasure; so did Rose; so did Luisa. And if Paddy could not thus relax to it, he did allow its passing grace, and he liked his first experience of champagne. But he noted with disapproval that the Spaniard on Clare's right, the 'profligate' who hardly seemed to speak to her, drank none of this pale gold, but filled and refilled his glass from a dark bottle marked 'Armagnac'.

Iago Duarte liked good food, which he never troubled to give himself; so he ate the excellent dishes of this supper party slowly, with appreciation. He was not a social man, and tonight he felt tired. Indeed, at the end of the year's busiest term at the Accademia and the close of the Valle season, he could claim to be tired. So he wondered why he had not walked home alone through the cool night as he desired to instead of accepting to sit down with all this youthful noisiness and vanity and hope. Smiling a little, he lifted his brandy glass, and his eyes met Luisa's, resting on him from across the table. His smile deepened, and faintly flickered to her his amusement at her elderly and aristocratic new admirer, still by her side.

She sang tonight exactly as she can sing, he thought contentedly. These dukes and millionaires and deaf professors – he shut his eyes – one day, and it is not far off, when she is finally acclaimed, in Milan or Vienna, they will boast that they heard her tonight in the Valle. And the joke of that will be that they didn't hear her. Giacomo, tired old theorist and scholar of the voice, who would have his pupils sing as by compass and protractor – and much was to be said for his mania of caution – poor old Giacomo might still have a vestige left of listening power? Young Evans probably knew what he heard when Luisa sang? And the Irish Eurydice? He looked at her sideways. Yes, she knew; singing with Luisa she, it was crystal clear, knew and heard with her brain what she was matched against; or rather, mated to, he corrected himself. They are good for each other in music, he thought. Both are potential perfectionists and, by God's mercy, they are mutually sympathetic.

However, they are young; they are – look at them! – babies at the threshold. They will be spoilt, they'll grow vain and jealous, they'll quarrel, they'll grow fat – Luisa will, anyway. They'll have lovers, they'll have bullying patrons, they'll refuse to sing together – and worst of all for both, success will sweep them for ever out of my control.

He shrugged, and drank again.

A Spaniard, he did not love Italy; or, overmuch, Italian opera. But his exile's life had long ago been ordained for him in permanent association with both. So the Castilian reserve and habit of silence which his Roman acquaintances sometimes sneered at as theatrical but which was in fact as inescapable a part of him as his eyebrows or his hands – this hard reserve made it impossible for him to expose those enthusiasms, disappointments, passions and rages to which he was as likely and timid a slave as any man. Indeed, he sometimes thought, as the years climbed on him and he observed his own tightening habits of shrug and monosyllable, that his shell of inexpressiveness was at last succeeding in hiding him even from himself. Sometimes he thought, detachedly: I have made myself a fair musician, but in doing that I have unmade myself of being everything else that a man might be. I don't see that happening to all these others? However – and, as was his habit, he would shrug himself off.

But if he accounted himself no longer a person, he knew that he was still that conception, a Spaniard. Spain had inhabited him all his life, and was as closely the prisoner of his spirit as he of its wide, remembered plains. Willy-nilly he carried Castile through all his conscious hours, without thought and without escape; and when he slept, when he dreamt, he slept and dreamt at home. He would never return, yet when his hour came, it might be claimed for him that he would as surely die in Avila as the least travelled of her citizens.

So, since Luisa was a Spaniard and, apparently, worthy to be one, when she appeared at the Accademia Duarte had, secretly, taken as it were possession of her voice, its protection, its training and its future. He was not her private, appointed *maestro*, but she attended many of his classes; and he found ways in which to watch over her talent, and protect it from what he held to be certain vulgarities of Italian method. And by now he was beginning to hope that the honour, the virtue of singing was safe with her. When alone the two spoke always in Castilian, and that made them love to be together. The almost twenty years that separated his weariness from her eager, gifted youth were too many, but the racial accident and their singular accord in music made bonds between them.

The party hummed along; it sparkled and grew warm – too warm, though the windows stood wide open to the night. The refreshments continued to be lavishly commanded, lavishly served, and as many of the guests were young and hungry, this was very pleasant to them, and induced amiability and silliness. But more amiable and silly than any of his guests the Marchese di Montebirone grew, or appeared to grow. He liked to speak, and standing up to proffer toasts or sitting down to court Luisa he made continual speeches which, in so far as they heard them, amused and even in their better turns of bombast delighted some of his hearers. They might not have so much pleased certain older singers who had learnt the hard way how to read the nobleman's affability; but he flattered innocents tonight, not only with his comic eloquence but with too much of his champagne.

Duarte might shut his eyes and his weary ears, and ponder calmly on the injuries that self-inflating patronage can wreak on the silly and helpless gifted; Giacomo, and indeed the two or three of his Accademia colleagues scattered round the table, did not hear a word the Marchese said, nor did they try to. They enjoyed their supper, and fussed in their minds over what they had heard tonight, and over their own pupils, or debts, or wives, or stomach-aches. But the young guests, those who had sung or led the violins or the ballet tonight, or who were hoping that this rich Maecenas might attend while they did so tomorrow – they all listened tolerantly, and with a kind of self-mocking hope, to the patronizing and orotund flourishes which, clearly, the old gentleman enjoyed even more than they did.

Rome knew, he told them – certainly some of Rome's responsible men knew how great was the great city's privilege in nourishing their talents, which were to feed one of Italy's greatest arts – the art of music, music in song, *bel canto*. They must not fear – he and his family, like others, had always been the protectors of opera, and of opera's aspirants – tonight he had been more deeply stirred than he could say, and he felt Rome's privilege all the more in noting that talents of high order came for tuition here from all the world – why, in this room tonight we have the Rose of Ireland, ladies and gentlemen, and – dare I say – with a deep bow to Clare – the Lily of Ireland also? Loud applause. And what is this flower of Spain? Carnation? Camellia? What flower is she, gentlemen?

The Marchese sat down to work this out, his arm across Luisa's chair-back.

'At any rate,' said Thomas, bending over Clare, 'he'll find she's neither a daisy nor a buttercup.'

'Isn't he eloquent?' said Clare.

'It ill becomes me, having attended his fine party, but I don't like that pulpy man,' said Paddy.

Duarte laughed.

'What is that word of English, Signorina?' he asked Clare in Italian. 'An adjective, I think, before the man?'

'Pulpy?'

'Ah – I could never pronounce it – but it is an exact word, I feel.'

'It's hot in here! Oh Thomas, would it be rude to walk over to the window?'

'Would it be rude to walk home?' asked Duarte.

'That's what I debate,' said little Giacomo, whose face was grey, and who had eaten and drunk too much for his weariness and the hour of the night. 'My wife, my dear wife will be anxious—'

Clare smiled to herself; so did Thomas. Neither had ever

known Signora Vittoria to express anxiety about their little *maestro*, and each could guess at this moment, were she waking or sleeping, she did not recall the everyday fact of his existence. Well, champagne, enough of it, brings illusion, Thomas thought; and illusion, oddly enough, is a consolation. Nevertheless, the room was now too hot, and enough of the Marchese's oratory was already enough. Rose, leaning forward, suggested for the hearing of her two hosts, and smiling beautifully towards her fickle old nobleman, that the singers were tired, perhaps . . .

With alacrity the singers, the whole party, were on their feet.

On the refreshed and washed Piazza, under paling stars, farewells and expressions of thanks and pleasure became confused, repetitive and foolish; for the sweet air of the early summer morning struck sharply on heated and unwary heads. So the gathering broke up dreamily, and melted, singing, calling, through the light and shadows; and some who had desired to take each other home got lost, lost the one they sought, and called and sang and vanished.

Clare saw Luisa thrust into an open carriage by Duarte. She waved, feeling sad. 'Tomorrow! tomorrow!' she called, and so did Luisa, her face gleaming ghostily.

'We'll go by the river,' said Thomas. 'Come, sir; a breath of air.'

Paddy already had Giacomo by the arm, and the little man leant against him lovingly.

'You are a kind, good Irishman,' he said.

Thomas took Clare's hand, and with some laughing stragglers from the orchestra they all went loafing past Montecitorio and through narrow streets that for the hour were quiet, across Scrofa to the Lungatevere.

They paused to lean on the parapet under the still trees, and they listened to the silence of the river and the city.

Antonio leant by Clare's side. She was surprised to see him. 'Is Rosie here?'

'No. Her host of this evening swept her away in his carriage.'

'Very correct,' said Thomas. 'The nobleman?'

'No, the industrialist.'

'He's very handsome,' said Mariana.

'It must be near dawn,' said Clare. 'Shall we walk up to the Paolina Fountain?'

'Too far,' said Thomas.

'And very bad for your throats,' said little Giacomo. 'Oh, I must get home. Take me home, Signor Paddy.'

'Me too, Signor Paddy,' said Clare.

'No, I'll take a carriage! Won't you come to the Janiculum, Clare? Will you, Mariana?'

'I'd love to, Tonio,' said Mariana. 'But it would cost a foolish sum of money.'

'Oh, what matter!'

'Anyhow, I have a *Semiramide* rehearsal tomorrow.'

'And so have you, my boy,' said Thomas to Antonio.

They followed the river to the Passegiata di Ripetta – calling good night sometimes as one of their group or another flitted off for home.

When they reached the heavy doors of the apartment house in Via di Ripetta Signor Giacomo would not be parted from Signor Paddy, who must ascend with him, he said, to meet his beloved wife. Paddy protested, half-heartedly, that the Signora would assuredly be in bed. In truth, he desired very much to ascend. In this champagne-clouded morning hour he was loth to part from Clare if he might stay where she was a little longer. Signor Giacomo was assured that his beloved wife held vigil; also he wished to drink a glass of brandy with this Irish friend, and to see if he could sing at all. The Irish tended to sing correctly, he said. Very odd, as they were not musicians – he must test Signor Paddy with a scale. His wife would wish him to. There was brandy in the studio.

Thomas and Antonio looked uncertain, but Clare walked on upstairs.

'Let them be,' she said. 'I've never before seen the *maestro* enjoying himself.'

'But try to turn up the gas jets,' said Mariana, 'or they may have a bad fall.'

As they climbed Giacomo explained the simple *Portamento* exercise to Paddy, and began to sing it. So they all sang it softly, for Paddy.

Assunta opened the apartment door. She showed no amusement when her master was surprised that his beloved wife did not await him in the studio. As naturally as if it were five of the afternoon rather than of the morning she opened the curtains; then brought glasses, bottles and fresh water.

Giacomo sat at a piano and began Paddy's singing lesson. The others gathered round a minute, to encourage – then melted away to their beds. Clare stood, dead weary, by the window. The two men, the gaunt young one and the little grey one, looked sadder than she could explain in the morning light. The *maestro* played an exercise gently – and then fell back against Paddy.

'My beloved wife is – ill. Very ill. I wish I were a holy man like you, Signor Paddy. Are you a priest, Signor Paddy?'

Clare went away to her bed.

Rose's door stood open. Where had she gone through the sweet morning in her gentleman's carriage? Oh Rosie, Rosa d'Irlanda, why do we not go home?

The Sixth Chapter

Clare learnt much of Italy in the summer months of 1889. The Teatro Lirico Pollinari, the opera company by which she was employed, opened its season in Bologna, went thence south-east to Ancona, and onward, zig-zagging in weeks and fortnights to Genoa, Piacenza, Turin, and back again through Brescia, Cremona, Mantua, Parma . . . It was during a hard, hot week in Ferrara that Luisa, who had been singing in Venice, came to be with her for a few days; a refreshment and delight.

Clare did not like the flat and shadeless town, so had it not been for the temptation of Luisa's company might have welcomed her hard work, for besides the routine understudy rehearsals of the repertory she was assigned three leading rôles in the week – Gilda, Lucia di Lammermoor, and The Queen of Night in *The Magic Flute*. And the company was kept on the alert by Signor Pollinari, who warned them that Ferrara's was a theatre in which the great Giuseppe Verdi was apt to appear unannounced, listening for new voices. As besides Clare there were five unknown hopefuls in the troupe, there was tension on the stage every time the curtain rose, and no one knew whether, towards the end of a long, hot summer of uneven work, the famous presence in front was or was not to be desired. No one, that is, save Clare, who wanted not at all at present to sing for the *maestro*.

But Luisa, hearing her in *Rigoletto* on the first night of the week, said it was a pity that the old man had not turned up.

'He'd have been delighted – with you, *and* with Thomas.' Thomas had conducted. 'But truly, truly, Clare – how much you are learning!'

'You have to learn. They work us desperately hard. You've no choice but to learn.'

'Oh, that I know – but you were always a good student. It's something else, something much more than hard work—'

'I don't think so. One does – oh, I suppose, *accept* the curious situation, after a bit? One's in it, after all.'

Luisa looked at Clare attentively.

'What is it?' the latter asked.

'Ah – nothing! It's lovely to be with you!'

'Oh, I've missed you, Luisa – and missed singing with you!'

'Still, I suppose it was as well they separated us, for a while.'

They were strolling about the Piazza Savonarola, tasting such freshened air as the midnight brought, and leaning sometimes on the moat-wall of the Este Palace.

'This is a disappointing place,' said Clare. 'I thought it was on the Po – but it's miles away from it. And I don't care for this – do you?' They looked up at the huge red building.

'Ah, you should see Venice!'

'I know. Please Heaven I will! That at least! Before they send me packing – to teach singing in Dublin.'

'That won't happen.'

'Oh, not yet, I hope. I'm not well enough educated yet to justify all that's been done for me.'

'You and your old conscience!'

'I haven't much conscience, really. I wish we were in Rome – don't you?'

'I thought you hated Rome?'

'In a way. In a way I always will. But I miss it too. I found a novel in Genoa – I don't suppose you've read it – I imagine it hasn't been translated. It's by an American – Hawthorne. It's called *The Marble Faun*. Have you heard of it?'

Luisa shook her head.

'It's a preposterous book, really – the plot is wild, but the characters – well, the leading character, an American girl called Miriam, is indescribably unbalanced – and conceited too – Heaven knows why! She's not altogether unlike me. But I'm not as bad, Luisa, really I'm not! And I hope I'm not so tedious – yet?'

Luisa threw an arm along Clare's shoulder.

'I must read this book. Can't you find it in French, or Italian?'

'No, you don't need to read it. But it's awfully good on Rome – it seems to explain one's quite small memories. It's odd, because naturally as a Catholic I don't feel disgusted with some things which sicken this New Englander – but you know, in the hot trains when I read him he gives me back Rome, the bit of Rome I know – from the Pincio to the Tiber – all that!'

'So you're missing it?'

'I'll miss it for the rest of my days. But that isn't to say that I love it—'

'You sound sophisticated. This is a perverse sort of love-affair you're having—'

'Is she indeed?' said Thomas. 'And is it with old Benevaro, do you think, Luisa?'

'Oh, her Rigoletto?'

'Hers, indeed! Did you notice how I had to hold them down last night? Truly, in the second act—'

'Oh Thomas, be quiet! You're disgusting!'

'Not I, dear Clare, but your ageing eunuch!'

'Benevaro's no eunuch,' said Luisa. 'And he's still a very good voice.'

'Oh, don't mind Thomas! Poor Pietro's a bit clutchy and awkward to sing with sometimes – but all he really wants is to have the curtain down so that he can get to his bowl of *pasta* and his wine and his good wife.'

'Certainly that's all – when the curtain *is* down! But when it's up he's still inclined to go mad – especially if he's got a really young soprano opposite him!'

'I expect he's a sensual old fatty – but he can still sing!' said Luisa.

'Let's go round and look at the Cathedral façade,' said Clare. 'It's innocent and holy – it'll refresh us!'

They laughed, and strolled along.

'But Benevaro *was* a great man for the ladies at the beginning of his career – wasn't he?' said Luisa.

'A devil. Old Giacomo actually chuckled in my hearing over Clare's having to sing with him!'

'How dare he?' said Clare.

' "He always liked the most beautiful women," said Giacomo, "and the most young – and he always got them!" '

'So now he has his memories,' said Clare.

'And I don't think he's going to get this most beautiful and most young one,' said Luisa.

'Well, with whom then is she having this perverse love-affair?'

'Guess, Thomas.'

'I have three guesses.'

'Save them. You wouldn't win.'

Thomas said good night at the door of Clare's lodging in Via Ariosto. They heard him singing some kind of folk-song as he hurried along the empty street.

'He sounds happy,' said Luisa.

'We've a new contralto that he's mad about. He's always in great form when he's mad about someone.'

Luisa leant against the banisters and laughed.

'Clare, my dearest – soon you'll *have* to stop playing the enigmatic juvenile!'

There was no answer. Clare locked the door and turned to mount the stairs. The gaslight accented her fair pallor; she looked weary and even admonitorily old for her nineteen years.

'I must write to Rosie tonight,' she said. 'I wish I weren't so sleepy!'

On the landing of their rooms Luisa saw how darkly burnt Clare's eyes.

'What is it? Have I – said anything to hurt you?'

'No—'

'But you *are* hurt!'

'Ah, Luisa – I've long passed being juvenile. Anyway, who could stay juvenile in the company I keep? But – enigmatic? Oh heavens, to be surrounded by enigmas isn't the same thing as to be an enigma oneself!'

'We're not enigmas – we're strolling singers!' Luisa opened her door; a gas-jet burnt low within. 'Come, Clare – I'll make Spanish chocolate—'

'Have you the equipment, you old trouper?'

'I have indeed. I'll give you a glass of wine if you prefer it.'

'I must get these comforting things to travel with,' said Clare in wonder.

'Do.' Luisa turned up the gas. 'You'll never be a real actress until you know how to mess about in lodgings!' She opened a cupboard. 'Would you clear those books and things off the table, pet?'

'But – I've my prayers to say –' Luisa smiled at her. 'And I want to write to Rosie.'

'I want to talk about Rosie.'

'Ah!'

At the same hour in her lodging in Rome Rose was not talking of Clare, but she may have thought of her. For her rooms were high in a house on Lungatevere di Sangallo, under the shadow of the church of San Giovanni dei Fiorentini, and the view from her windows was uninterruptedly of the Janiculum, across the river. That green hill always reminded her of her first bewildered weeks in Rome, and of how Clare and she had loved to walk about it, seeking cool air, and looking west to Ostia and the sea. And when the lights began to come up in the city, refreshed and amused, it had been fun for the two to walk down again past San Onofrio and over the bridge, back into the nocturnal roaring and shouting of Rome.

So with their view and their chance of fresh air at night, these two small, poor rooms pleased her. They had been found for her by a dresser at the Argentina, whose aunt was the *portiera* of the house; and their poorness did not trouble Rose at all. Rather did she marvel exultantly that she had already reached a position in life which enabled her to be the sole and paying occupant of two rooms in the City of Rome. Such a surprising state of affairs took her, she admitted, a very, very long distance from Lackanashee. But – they had sent her a long way, and she was doing what they had bade her do. And if the doing of it had become for the most part wonderful, and her passionate concern; if moreover it had forced her to grow up, had changed and was daily changing her; if it had by now much blunted her loneliness for home and for childish things – was she to blame? Or if blame there was, might not some of it fall on Lackanashee, where loneliness for her had been blunted somewhat, she suspected, by the money she was able to send?

Naturally she received dear, full letters – proud of her and kind and expressing the Committee's satisfaction in their protégée – from her good Miss French. And Mamma wrote a little line every month, to acknowledge safe receipt of a money order, to tell her that she was a good daughter, and so God would bless her and keep her from all temptation; that it would be lovely to see her again some day, please God; that times were a bit easier now, she was happy to say – and what with Aggie earning too, in Mr Chris's shop; and that this one had died, and that one had gone to Philadelphia; and might God keep her, and she was her loving Mamma.

Mr Chris had naturally long since given up sending jelly babies to La Rosa d'Irlanda, but he always sent his love, and his hope that he'd be cheering her very soon in the Theatre Royal in Dublin. And Father Lucius wrote sometimes, kindly, encouragingly, well pleased with her industry and success, and always ending his letter with a small, stout wedge of moral and spiritual advice.

She hailed these steady signals from home with constant pleasure; they helped her, and they warmed her affectionate heart; and she answered them always, gladly and fluently. But her life lay now committed where those same signallers had directed her blind and silly steps three years before, and there could never be return to Lackanashee in the old and simple sense – for Lackanashee had made her a present of the world.

When she had entered into possession of her two rooms, Rose wrote several letters of rapture to Clare.

. . . I simply can't get over the importance of it! I have to pay the *portiera* every Saturday, and she gives me a receipt. Oh, they're poor little rooms, and the rent is *well within my means!* But my favourite view in Rome – the Tiber and the bridges and the dome of Saint Peter's and the Janiculum! And down under the window those shivering trees that you are so mad about. I make my own coffee in the mornings on a very dangerous kind of old rusty spirit stove. It terrifies me! And I go shopping mostly in the Fiori market. You remember it? It's great fun there and as cheap as possible. You know, Clare, you can buy *one* egg, or *one* peach, or *one* tomato – or one little slice of veal!! What on earth would they say to that in Lackanashee? To go into a shop for one egg? I'd love to try it on Mr Chris!! . . .

She also had much to say in her letters to Clare of what she called their 'debit accounts'. These she inspected with Signor Giacomo at the end of each month. The little grey *maestro* was still in charge of their finances – and this was fortunate, for he was, as both girls knew, almost a maniac of precision and honesty.

The method, established by tradition, by which these endowed students repaid their benefactors was simple, and benevolent. Signor Giacomo made all their contracts, and each management which employed them under contract paid to each girl on every Saturday evening half of her wage. The other half was paid to Signor Giacomo. Every fourth week he made up their 'debit accounts', and – in Clare's absence now – explained them to Rose. His own charges were for board and lodging by the month for the number of months either had spent with him – to which was added his teaching fee, and a five per cent charge for acting as their business agent. So, against his own bill he took each month half of the half he received, sent the other half to Mother Bursar at Rue des Lauriers, and posted detailed accounts of this routine disposition to Rose's Committee and to Clare's Uncle Matt.

Signor Giacomo would make no further charges, once his bill had been paid – no matter how rich or famous either of his pupils might become. But Rue des Lauriers had a clause in its contract – and therein lay Mère Marie's gamble-value to the convent – which exacted that from the date when any of its sponsored singing pupils sang at La Scala, or the Paris Opera or Covent Garden – whichever was the first engagement – the convent received twenty per cent of that pupil's earnings in that first engagement and in her subsequent three contracts.

This was a severe clause, but it was at present remote, and

when it came into action it was probable that all the first liabilities on the young singer would have been discharged. So that in a first two seasons of success Rose or Clare would be themselves receiving eighty per cent of their salaries. Luisa was now arrived at that point, having sung at La Scala; and she was doubtless proving a salve in Mother Bursar's breast, and was a fair help to Mère Marie in committee.

Rose was shrewd and very anxious that she and Clare should be out of debt as soon as possible. She did not grudge that future twenty per cent to Rue des Lauriers, as she more and more realized that Mère Marie's fierce training had truly earned it – and to be successful enough to be liable for it would be a happy state, and would mean the freedom of safety in a danger- ous profession.

So she always studied the 'debit accounts' with zest, and amused Signor Giacomo by her crystal-clear grasp of them. It surprised and rejoiced her to see that, even on her small salaries, her debt to the Committee decreased with speed. But it troubled her that Clare, so good, so brilliant, was far behind her in this race for independence. She had been in constant employment – as she said to Signor Giacomo when they studied business affairs together at the end of July – for fourteen months, and, because she was lucky, with rising salary from engagement to engagement. But Clare had still been in student-status until February, which meant that she had only been earning money – and not good salaries either – for five–six months.

'Couldn't our two payments – what you receive on our behalf, I mean – be treated as one sum by you, and disposed of equally against the debts?'

Giacomo laughed.

'You're as generous as you are shrewd, Rosa. But I couldn't do that. And our dear Chiara would not permit it, be assured.'

'She wouldn't know.'

'I send her details, as to you.'

'She doesn't read them, Signor. She leaves it all to you—'

'And you don't?'

'Oh indeed I do. But I like to understand where I'm going.'

'And so does La Chiara, believe me. And she will be all right too about these debts. Do not trouble, Rosa. Her career moves less than yours at present – but there is no fear.'

'I didn't mean there was . . .'

She wrote of these figures and prospects to Clare, whom she suspected of depression and anxiety – *and I'd be able to have grander rooms, perhaps, only I want to send as much as I can to Mamma. And anyway I don't want grander rooms. These are perfection. If only I could fit you in when you come back to Rome! But you'd never fit – I mean, your clothes and things. It's a fearful squash for my few rags, even. But Assunta's an angel. She does all my washing and ironing, and positively keeps me looking like a lady – or an actress acting a lady! And the poor little thing dashes to and from Ripetta to look after me, in a state of terror, and then bursts into tears when I force a few lire on her! The creature, how good she is . . . !*

In another letter to Clare she lectured:

You bore me with that nonsense about wanting to sing in Haydn's *Creation*. Who's going to ask you to, my girl? And would you blame them? I suppose it's fair sense to be studying *Fidelio* – anyhow, it's hard work – but nobody wants Beethoven in Italy. Can't you be content that they'll always want your adored Glück, and Mozart? But, you know, you *must* surrender to Verdi. It's no use singing Italian opera as if you smelt a bad smell. Oh, forgive me, pet – I'm a bit excited tonight, and your very detached and nunlike letter worried me. I hear only glowing accounts of your performances everywhere – but you write about them your-self as if you were recalling how you dealt with the drains, or something. Please, Clare – don't mind me! I've been drinking champagne – which I don't like. But it's Tonio's birthday tomorrow, and he's been celebrating it tonight, and as I wasn't singing I celebrated with him. We're having a real supper-party in his honour here tomorrow night. We're going to do something *flambé* – kidneys, I think – on my terrible, dangerous stove! We may all go up *flambés* – our own kidneys as well as the ones Tonio is buying! But then I came in, and your letter depressed me. Pet – I thought that with that melancholy Duarte away off conducting Luisa you'd get more Italian-minded, with dear Thomas to shout down all your nonsense – Oh, forgive me, I'm silly . . .

. . . I was silly and bossy in that last letter, pet. Oh, we had great fun at the birthday party last night – and there were some terrible rows too. Tonio doesn't like the French tenor – you know, René Chaloux – who sings with me in *The Barber* – and there were other confusions. Emma was cross because Pecaver didn't arrive – and La Lanci had toothache – oh, there was a lot of distracted emotion! But we had great fun practising my shakes. That's the latest – did I tell you? I have to see what I can do – says Signor Toscaro – in the line of shakes! You know the idiotic things – oscillating away like mad on a minor second! – And the higher the better, naturally. Has any *maestro* set you at them? If he has, you can blame Catherine Hayes. I think they have an idea that it's an Irish talent – so look out! However, I wish you'd heard us all last night, sending our rival shakes out over the Tiber! Luckily the old lady below is stone-deaf, and the man next door does nothing but yell 'bravo' and 'bis' from his balcony . . .

Those were letters of late July and early August. Now August was burning out. But the night, past midnight near one o'clock, was emptied of the day's slow heat. Rose stood at her window and looked towards the darkened Janiculum. Above it stars rode in a clear black sky and sweet-smelling air moved in from Ostia. Below in the Lunga the dried trees rattled their leaves, and she remembered Clare and their first Roman walks together in their first August here.

René Chaloux, the young French tenor, stood beside her. Together tonight they had sung, each for the first time, *I Puritani*.

Both had been very nervous. Rose knew that she knew her singing text, and that so did René know his; but she was dissatis-fied with her direction, she did not know her conductor, had not sung to his baton before, and had never before had to portray insanity. She disliked the opera's scheme, but greatly admired some of its lyric passages. Altogether she had approached the performance in despair – and that René did likewise had not encouraged her. As she had no madness in her and only – pitilessly young – shrank in disgust from it, she needed very intelligent direction for interpretation of Elvira – and her director had not apprehended her fear of the part – and probably thought that all could be left to her sure singing, and to her beauty.

But Rose was afraid of madness that had to be sung *legato*, and wished she was Clare.

The audience at Argentina that summer was alert, because of the open challenge to Costanzi's, and because the management's policy was courageous, in presenting many young voices, but only such young voices as they believed to promise future operatic magnificence, on Italy's terms. The season had proved Rome's interest in the summer experiment. Hot though the nights were, scattered as might be 'society', the Argentina performances were closely watched and reported, by newspaper critics, by talent hunters, and by the ordinary Roman and holidaying public.

Rose, working hard and aware how closely she was listened to, came through without mishap, and with some nights of triumph. René Chaloux had done less certainly – his voice was very promising and he was a serious actor, but a Frenchman could not hope easily to seduce a Roman audience, whereas an Irish girl had only to show them that she could do what was required of her. She had to show them that – but, that done, they were hers. And so it had been with Rose. They were on her side, the ordinary part of every audience, and they waited benevolently for her to show them if or not she could sing.

Always her voice surprised them, and sometimes it had the effect of tricking them into silence – so quietly it could move out over them, making them wonder sometimes, instead of assent, which was their habit.

She was afraid of *I Puritani*. But she had courage, and was forever learning to direct it. So, tonight her voice, which her wits prompted her to relax and under-use, became, as she listened ahead to what she had to sing, an instrument entirely lyrical; non-operatic, meditative, almost somnambulant.

Her audience, less familiar even than she with the character she was presenting, listened with curious, quiet attention while she groped through expression of a madness she did not understand. And she realized, when the long anxiety was over, that she had seemed to prove something, to herself and to her listeners. So that when she and René came together at last in the truly beautiful love-duet – '*Vieni, vieni* . . .' – relieved to have got safely within reach of the final curtain, they had sung with all they knew of joy and lyrical impulse. Tension spent now, confidence, freedom and understanding poured out along the clear young voices. They felt their music; they took control of it and were by it controlled. In grace and beauty, and singing together through a moment of inexplicable light and penetration, they held the house enchanted, and illumined a passage of musical sweetness – accidentally maybe – but poignantly, startlingly, to a radiance wherein Bellini himself might have imagined it.

They walked home together. Triumph and excitement beat in each breast, but for once even Rose had no words – and they were only superficially aware of the streets they passed through. They walked in blazing silence.

Outside a *trattoria* where they and their friends often ate at night, René did say: 'Are you hungry, Rose?' But she shook her head at the little crowded place. 'We'll eat at my window,' she said. So now they stood at her window, still hearing their own singing. '*Vieni* . . . !'

Rose looked out as if in search of something lost in the lively darkness – herself, perhaps. The babbling child that she was when she walked the Janiculum with Clare two Augusts ago. She was not different from that child – she was that child grown up. It was possible that Rose, quickly poised in a world to which she was miraculously suited, would never need to be more sophisticated than she was now. She would have, as do all who live, instructive and individual experiences; she would learn, in error and success, many curious and many ordinary truths; she would take chances, and cause others to take them; and she would mature, and grow middle-aged. But in her two first years of Italian life her intuitions and talents had taught her – conscience looking anxiously on – all that it was essential to know about life ahead.

That life would depend, as had her life in childhood, upon love – the love that she had to give, as she had to breathe; and the love that she had to take. She was distant now, in spirit as in space, from those loves on which she had been nourished at home. But Italy and music had educated her temperament as well as her talent. And she knew now, had known for a long time, in silent anxiety, that she must live with love.

Love, in many kinds, had offered her its education. And at first she had been surprised at how little alarmed she was by any of its suggestions – even the silliest, even the most worldly or the most obscene. But often, in tight, funny corners with elderly gentlemen or in more stormy scenes with younger men, she was reminded of commotions witnessed, or rumoured, at home in Lackanashee – and as then, so now, she always felt perilously on the side of the fool or the drunken one or the too excited. She was, in short, given to life and acceptance of its stresses. And, by now, she was prepared for her second thoughts.

Nevertheless, moving outwards freely and with wide-open eyes towards all that Italy suggested – and the more she sang and studied singing the more understanding what she sang about – still she waited.

She seemed to be almost irresistible to men; her beauty apart, she was gay and young and warm, and inclined always to like rather than dislike a fellow-creature. When to this dangerous grace of spirit was added, in Italy, her operatic promise – she was an open target in the field through which she moved. But she came quickly and without conceit to understand that, and it did not frighten her. Rather the knowledge gave her coolness, and increased her charm. Yet no man's wooing – was he prince or impresario or millionaire or cardinal or ageing tenor or ambitious baritone – none could get from her more than good manners and good night. Not because she missed their point, or any of their various points, and not, after a while, because she was any longer afraid of her Italianated self – she would reckon with it, she and her home-trained conscience – but because she would plunge when she had the gift of her own will, her own desire, in her hands. In singing love and of love she had learnt about adult love – and did not see that its truth differed far from the love she had lived with at home. In that she may have been innocent, but not innocent of the necessities of her own heart, which was tender, and must find a need of its tenderness at least, before it spoke.

Nearest she had been brought to trial of her own expression was by Antonio de Luca. He had made himself dear to her in her beginnings in Rome, and he was a boy, and beautiful and amusing. In his tempestuous first demands on her he had been too harsh with her conscience, with her good Lackanashee standards and her necessity to take her time in the whole Italian assault upon her gaucheness. But she had liked him very much, still liked him dearly. He, however, would have it that she was playing for success, and was therefore more complacent than she admitted with the various princes and impresarios and millionaires who gave her suppers and roses and perfumes, and who sent their carriages to fetch her hither and thither.

The silly battle went on, about untruths. But Antonio had gained affection from her in the days when there was none of this flourish of near-success – and he did not understand how great his advantage was in that. He made mistakes now; he hurt her.

René Chaloux was an unknown stray who spoke bad Italian. He was poor and young, and in Italy on a desperate throw for his luck. He had a lovely tenor voice, little training and no time to lose. He must either prove his worth within a year or go back to Rouen to his father's excellent *charcuterie*. He was a tall, too-tragic, fair-haired boy, starved-looking, who had a romantic and unusual attraction on the stage. Rose had sung with him in end-of-term performances at the Accademia. His shyness and obvious poverty had struck her then – he had seemed to be very much as she was, in worldly terms. Thereafter they had not met until in this Argentina season; she had been glad to find him understudying there, and assigned to sing certain tenor rôles. They had grown friendly. They sang in *La*

Traviata together, and in *Il Barbiere*. They were the same age. He told her about his family in Rouen, his impatient father, his determined ambitious mother, his fears and hopes. She told him about Mamma and Lackanashee and the Committee. He throve in talk with her. She fought day in, day out with Antonio for her right to friendship with René. René fought with Antonio until one night they managed somehow in a row in the Piazza Navona to knock each other back into the central fountain. That did not cool their mutual dislike.

However, on the night when Rose and René sang *I Puritani* at the Argentina, Antonio was singing *Macbeth* in Bologna. Rose, sufficiently nervous, was glad to be sure of that.

Now, they had sung *I Puritani*. It was over, the theatre was dark, and the music of the night was forgotten by all who had heard it and were now asleep. By all save the two who had sung, who still thought they sang the last duet.

Rose leant out of the window and stretched her hand to René.

'Let's sing softly,' she said, and began his tenor opening of their duet: '*Vieni* . . .'

He seized her hand.

'No, no,' he said. 'We couldn't sing it again.'

She gathered up his hand in both of hers and held it to her mouth.

'I could,' she said.

'You are not to kiss my hand,' he said, turning to French from his bad Italian. 'Speak French, Rose. What are you thinking about?'

Rose looked up.

'Don't laugh at me,' she said. 'I was saying a prayer.'

He did not laugh. Their two faces shone in reciprocal, sharp delight.

'Nothing you're saying is a surprise, Luisa.'

'I didn't think it could be. Only – your reserve about, well about everything, makes you a little difficult, pet! And – for Rosie anyhow, perhaps you'd make things easier, make her happier anyway, if you could break it a bit?'

'H'm. But how could I? One can't ask people questions about what is strictly their own business.'

'Ah, Rose isn't like that. She'd never be strict about her own business, as you call it! And you are you, after all, Clare – her only real friend in Italy!'

'I've been trying to make her feel how I love her – simply by not interfering, or seeming to fuss or be protective at all.'

'No one can protect, naturally. And she's taking her fences with great verve. But she'll always want your affection – and she said to me when I was at Costanzi's three weeks ago that she thought that somehow you and she were getting to mis-understand each other. That was only a feeler, of course – a hint.'

'There's *no* misunderstanding. If there were it would come from her. She told me in a letter lately –' Clare smiled with a hint of bitterness – 'that I sing Italian opera as if I smelt a bad smell!'

'Oh, but nonsense! She never could have!'

'Yes – and she went on to say that I wrote to her about my efforts as if I was reporting how I had dealt with the drains!'

Luisa, laughing richly, made as if to take Clare's hands. Instead, she refilled her wineglass.

'She's mad! When last has she heard you sing Rossini or Verdi or any of her darlings? Indeed, I wish she'd heard your Gilda last night! There was much that she, or anyone, could learn from it! But you know the way she loves to amuse and exaggerate in talk! It's part of that sort of flying charm she has! And it's growing on her with success. It delights people – and it's always delighted you, hasn't it, her power to rattle amusingly?'

'Delighted, and amazed.'

'Still, it was bad of her to write such nonsense to you!'

'Oh, she was sorry afterwards – in her next letter she explained that some prim one from me had worried her. Also, she seems to have been flustered in general. People throwing each other into fountains!'

'Yes – I've heard of rows. Tonio is being very jealous and angry—'

'But isn't he her favourite still?'

'He's wild about her, and he's very determined. Oh, he'll get her yet – some day—'

'I don't suppose she has – what's the phrase . . . ?'

'Taken a lover?'

Clare smiled. 'It sounds businesslike. Well, has she, yet?'

'I don't know.'

Clare made as if to speak again, then turned her face to the brilliant sky above Ferrara's roofs. If she felt sad it was no more than in her recurrent vein of self-dissatisfaction, and of perplexity before her small life's fixed or fixing purposes. It puzzled her obstinately that she seemed committed, willy-nilly, to the single idea of exploiting herself, through her unimportant, transient talent and her still less important emotions and brief, uncertain ambitions, self-bound and self-directed. It was within this narrow, small house of herself that for her career's sake she was expected to live, she saw. And she saw that precisely so, within and for themselves, must all these others of her near acquaintance live.

She had expected life to be a free and wide advance, in proportion to its lack of importance. Now she began to fear that the only freedoms waiting along her regulated path were the small personal ones, of mood, of sensation, of free and easy love and of habits of self-indulgence. All the meaner freedoms, which in truth only meant a narrowing-back into an egotism that was frivolous, a self-bound state, a condition of living which might or might not be sinful in the Church's sense, but which seemed to her, as she faced it, limiting, sad and a disappointment.

'It's like being in a sort of a hen-run, isn't it?' she said.

'Isn't what, Clare?'

'Our life – opera-singing.'

Luisa gave a surprised laugh.

'Our life? Well, I suppose any life can be compared to a hen-run. But – after all, the hens do have fun!'

'Yes, that's it. That's what keeps them in the hen-run.'

'Don't you want anyone to have fun, then?'

'I want to have fun myself, you silly! But – Oh Luisa, travelling up and down Italy I stare about me and I feel absurd. Oh, all this confusion of splendour and misery, all this great and terrible story, the outpouring of God's wealth and the cruel poverty of his children, and then the life and the beauty – the children, the singing, the flowers – and *all* the arts, all of them, teeming about everywhere – and the result only social tragedy, power and greed and utter cruelty in a few making a mock of a whole populace, and of all God's gifts – and there we sit in railway carriages and dressing-rooms – and we have no contact with the people we're making money out of, we know nothing about anything except a few old operas – and we've nothing to do with life, outside of the state of our precious larynxes, and the state of our nerves and stomachs and senses.'

'We have to do with life – that's why we sing. Singing is about life. And we can't help having stomachs and senses. All the Italians have them too – and take mighty good care of them! Oh Clare! What's the matter with you?'

Clare laughed ashamedly.

'Forgive me! I'm an ass – but I dislike this Romagna country! And I've been lonely and fussed – and then the sheer relief of seeing you again! Oh, Luisa, I'm afraid I'll talk you to a stand-still! Only . . .'

'Only what?'

'Well – you don't seem quite the same. You've got rather wise – I don't mean really wise – oh I don't know – but anyway, you aren't as *young* as you used to be!'

Luisa did not laugh.

'I'm not wise,' she said. 'But the way you fret me, you make me say these pseudo-wise things, and I can see them getting on your nerves.'

Clare smiled gratefully.

'Ferrara's quiet, for Italy – isn't it? These side-streets, so very well built and yet so dull, don't you think, Luisa? Like something one might imagine somewhere in the Netherlands. We really ought to have put on *Lucrezia Borgia* – just to remind them of old times!'

'Yes. There's a great part I'd like to sing in that – Orsini!'

'Oh, why didn't we think of it in time? I like singing

villainesses and poisoners, you know – and sopranos are hardly ever allowed to be that kind.'

'Certainly Lucrezia is a terror in that opera!'

'Yes – absurd! But I wouldn't mind singing her. We must talk to Thomas about it sometime, Luisa. Ah, and speak of angels! Here he comes! Do you hear him?'

Tenor notes came inward along the street.

'He's not singing in Welsh,' said Clare with amusement. 'That means he's bored. Perhaps the young lady wasn't in his mood.'

'Tom Moore, isn't it? Seems as if he's in an Irish mood – *not* in the young lady's.'

Clare leant out and sang a bar or two with him: '. . . Oh say wilt thou weep when they darken the fame . . .'

Thomas smiled up from under the gas lamp.

'Sh, Clare,' he said. 'We'll annoy the citizens. Why aren't you at your own window?'

'I'm drinking wine with Luisa.'

'Ah! I see. Luisa's bad for you. May I come up and drink too?'

'I'm afraid not, Thomas. This is a respectable town.'

'That's true, I wish I were in Cardiff! Would you like to be in Cardiff, Clare?'

'Ballykerin would do me.'

'And me. I'd love to be in Ballykerin. I'm sick of bloody Italy, bloody opera, bloody, filthy Italy – my God!'

A shutter opened in a house opposite.

Thomas waved to Clare, turned and bowed to the shutter-opener, and went on his way. 'When he who adores thee . . .' he began again, singing loudly now as he trailed down the empty street.

The girls listened, and when the voice vanished into the night seemed disinclined to speak. A clock in a nearby bedroom chimed a half-hour. Clare moved as if to go to her room; Luisa put out a hand to stop her. Clare looked down into the lovely, subtle Spanish face that had a weary shade on it tonight.

'We must sleep, Luisa.'

'Yes. I'm bad for you, as Thomas said.'

'Ah, Thomas! But don't be wise about him at me now, will you?'

Luisa's hand fell away from the other's wrist.

'I wasn't going to say a word. Thomas has plenty of his own words – and so have you, when you like.'

'That's true.'

Clare moved back to the window and leant against the frame.

'Luisa,' she began uncertainly – 'forgive me. But this – this private life you've been explaining to me for Rosie, this life of – love, and love experiment – are you leading it yourself?'

'I was hoping you'd ask me.'

Clare did not speak her next question, but Luisa answered it.

'Duarte,' she said.

'I knew it was he,' said Clare.

'But how could you? It's only since we left Rome—'

'I could see you both thinking of it in Rome!'

'Why didn't you say that to me then?'

'Say that to you? Dearest Luisa, how on earth could I?'

Luisa looked anxiously into all the open questions in Clare's eyes. How far or deep was it to be, this sudden plunge for simple truth? How much must she narrate of herself, of her quite ordinary sensual mistakes and stupidities, to this cold innocent? Better go slowly, Luisa warned herself. I have told her the important thing, the only serious secret that I have. And I am glad to have told it to her, not only for my own sake, but because I am certain that Duarte wants her to know of it.

'He's old, Luisa – isn't he?'

'Yes. He's – he's forty-four.'

'Oh! More than twice your age! But then – you're both Spaniards. That must make you – well, make you very fond of each other, here in Italy.'

'It does. You know, he's of Avila, where my mother was born, and where I often stayed with my grandfather when I was little. Of course, we live in Segovia, my father's town; but I've two uncles in Leon and his grandfather is buried there. And he still owns some houses in Avila – so we share a kind of triangle of Castile.'

'Ah! That could make – love – understandable.'

'I'm not sure. Perhaps it only makes confusion.'

'No. Love itself is what's confusing, I'd say. Things like that, about sharing Castile, should lessen confusion, surely?'

They don't, Luisa thought. Nor do you either, Clare, she thought.

'You had to – be lovers, I mean? Both of you thought—'

'Yes. We've been entangled in each other's feelings for a long time. It was getting tiring!' Luisa laughed very simply. 'He's good, Clare. He's very unaffected and proud. I've liked him since the first day I met him, and that's well over two years ago now. And he seems to me to be the best musician, the most learned and the most fastidious, that I've met, so far.'

'He's not ambitious – is he?'

'No. He likes his chief work, sacred music. He doesn't care for Italian opera – unless you go back to Vivaldi and Monteverdi. But he conducts and directs to keep in training – and because he likes to force the repertory operas back into their written shapes, he says.'

'Hear! Hear!' said Clare softly.

'Oh, you're his present example of what he means! He's often said to me: "Listen, but listen to how *exactly* Clara sings!" We call you Clara in Spanish, you know. "That girl knows every mark and indication on her composer's score, always – and rigidly, rigidly she sings what he wrote."'

'Rigidly seems to be the right word,' said Clare.

'Not at all. He adores your voice, and he'll be wild if you don't go on with your sacred music studies—'

'But I can't, Luisa, at Santa Cecilia. I'm earning my living regularly now.'

'That rule might be waived. Anyway, you'll have to take private lessons with him.'

'Couldn't afford them.'

'We'll see. But anyhow, you're his ideal singer at present, among all us young ones.' She paused. 'It's funny how he can't stand tricks of any kind – though I say to him that music's an art and art is full of tricks. Then he rages! "Find some tricks in Michelangelo," he says; "find me a few in the Ninth Symphony, or in any part of Glück, or in Racine!" We had uproar one night in Milan – you know we gave five performances at the Dal Verme, before we did the Mantua season. And my La Scala *maestro*, Ferrano, came to hear me – and I took some refresher lessons with him. Well, when I told Iago—'

'Iago? Ah yes – Duarte, I'd forgotten—'

'When I told him that Ferrano wants me to study *cadenze*, he went quite mad with anger. And when Ferrano gave me scores with some of Pauline Viardot's famous *cadenze* inserted – I didn't know where the row was going to end. But Ferrano is my *maestro*, whom I admire very much. Iago had never been my teacher – and I intend to try to work as Ferrano wishes.'

'Funny. It reminds me of poor Rose, who's being pestered about "shakes" at present – because Catherine Hayes was famous for shakes. Your fellow countrywoman was great at *cadenze* – so *you* are chosen to emulate *her*! Isn't it silly?'

Both had welcomed this passage of surface-conversation which had carried them temporarily a little away from Luisa's admission about Duarte and the immediate anxious shyness it had created between the two.

But now silence fell.

Clare reflected that the newly acknowledged fact that Luisa was living as the lover of a man – living in sin, as all Clare's elders and betters would say, and have the right of it so far as she knew – this fact seemed as she accepted it to draw her into very close association with the Spanish girl, to make clear a formidable quality in their mutual sympathy – and at the same time to darken it.

Luisa wondered: What would she think if I told her other things, sillier – how very boring I could be! But Clare wouldn't be bored – more likely she'd be distressed, I think. Rue des Lauriers seems more than two and a half years ago. How young we were then – even Julie Constant was young, I see now. But Italy is a forcing house. Clare's growth has been as much forced here as anyone's – differently from Rose's, differently from mine. But certainly forced, and with much grafted on that she doesn't notice yet, perhaps!

Clare sat on the floor and leant against the ironwork across the open window. The moonlight silvered her hair and all her edges.

'I don't think Rose has been going to confession for ages,' she said. 'Of course you don't go.'

'How do you know?'

'Well, I don't know. But, after all you're living in sin and have no firm purpose of amendment . . .'

They both smiled.

'I'm doing something which I don't regard as a sin, and so I *can* have no purpose of amendment. But of course I know it's a sin in the view of the Church, and therefore I can't ask for the Church's absolution – I don't go to confession, naturally.'

'I do.'

'What do you find to confess?'

'Really, Luisa – what cheek! I argue, mostly. I'm not a fervent believer, I never was, even as a small child. But confession and all the rest – it's a discipline. I suppose that I have in spite of myself what Grandmother calls "The Faith". If I have, I'm glad. I imagine I'd be lonely without it.'

'It – "The Faith", I mean – might *make* you lonely?'

'It might. But so might anything – love, or anything. We have to chance it, Luisa. I don't think I'll ever be the slave of the Penny Catechism, but at the same time I'd find it hard – if I ran into a serious moral conflict – I'd find it hard to decide that I was right and the Eternal Church wrong!'

'Still, the question could be left open, couldn't it, until the Judgment Day?'

Clare laughed.

'Is that your way round it?'

'More or less.'

'I can imagine Rosie dodging along that way, too! God knows, it's natural! But it *is* rather easy, don't you admit?'

Luisa said nothing. The open question between, say, God and oneself might be easy – and assuredly there was no need to be pompous and make heavy weather of it. But within the decision, within the conduct which more or less begged that question, the immediate, small situation – let Judgment Day wait! – was not necessarily easy. But that kind of sub-whimper could only be, and very strictly, one's own affair. If – too young, strongly in need of love, strongly attached to one who brought it, and eager for a self-protective gesture which will have deep and inescapable seriousness – one finds oneself, still loving and grateful, in grips with an emotional life too grown-up, too subtle, too anxious and too elderly for it to seem possible either to help it or trust in it – then what to say, and why? In love's name, something has been attempted; and in love's name the attempt must be worked out, proved. What would Clare make of all such talk?

'It's a pity there's no more wine,' Luisa said.

'I must go to bed.'

'You're not singing tomorrow night, I trust?'

'No, no. Lucia on Thursday night. But I've a session with Thomas at eleven. He and I are studying *Fidelio* together. Will you come and criticize?'

'I'd love to.'

Clare had stood up.

'How cool this night is – after the burning day!'

Luisa came to the window and stood beside her.

'Ariosto died in this street,' said Clare. 'You'd never imagine it, would you?'

Three o'clock struck.

'Good night, Luisa.' Clare put her arms about the other. 'It was good of you to tell me about Duarte – and it was necessary for me to know.'

Their eyes met in a shining, puzzled look. But Clare suddenly kissed Luisa's eyelids.

'No more, Orfeo. We must sleep.'

The Seventh Chapter

Although the autumn term had started at Santa Cecilia when Clare got back to Rome, the Buonatolis were able to let her have a room in the apartment in Via di Ripetta. She was very glad of this, and grateful to Signor Giacomo for the modesty of the charge he made. As he had his complement of resident students, Clare had to take a very small room, but it pleased her well, as it looked on the roofs of the Belle Arte Schools, and over them and the tall trees of the Passegiata fresh airs blew in at night from beyond the river.

It made her happy always to return to Signor Giacomo and – also – to Signora Vittoria. She often realized as she came and went at her ease in the large, dark apartment that here was the nearest she had ever attained to the idea of home since as a child she had been taken from Ballykerin to Dublin, and to school.

It amused her now, back from the long tour of provincial seasons, to find herself held to be very grown-up, an experienced professional, someone hardly to be spoken to, by Signor Giacomo's new batch of beginners. Almost *passé*, I expect, she thought, as she watched and listened – and how sad for me that I never even got a chance at La Scala! But in order not to impinge upon the gaiety and cross-talk of the young ones – and perhaps also because she wished to keep bright her own first-term memories; all the nervousness, all the mistakes and fun and freshness – Thomas, Antonio, Mariana, Rose, and the Signora's wonderful outbursts, and the little *maestro's* peppery and loving lectures, and Assunta's anxious face that used to puzzle them – she almost never ate in the dining-room with the newcomers.

In these days of early October, while winter plans were being manœuvred for her by her little *maestro*, and by Thomas, she had some precious freedom; and thought to spend the exquisite days in long-postponed and real exploration of Rome, to which she had come back with a gladness that astonished her. And all the more did she nurse and cherish, and try to keep to herself, the immediate interlude; because within the small circle of her loves and friends – and within herself – she saw troubles crouching, tensions and passions crowding slowly forward over what should be daylight and clear views. Meantime, however, Rome itself was in sweetest mood; *scirocco* gone and *tramontana* far away; high benignant skies shedding incomparable light on all the thousand-coloured stones, flowers everywhere, fountains everywhere, children shouting, old men tuning mandolins.

'That is you, Chiara mia? Come and talk to me!'

The door of Signora Vittoria's *salottino* was open.

'Of course, Signora – if I may.'

'I always know your singing,' said the Signora, who was stretched out immensely on a fragile-seeming sofa.

'Was I singing?' Clare asked in surprise.

'Softly. But my hearing is superb, of course – and I think it was a phrase from the second act of *I Puritani*?'

'Ah! I was thinking of that opera, Signora – because I'm going to hear Rose sing it tonight!'

'And very beautifully she'll sing it! Do you know that I actually went to hear her in it – with my dear husband – about six weeks ago? I expect that is why I recognized your phrase – the mad song – how is it?' She hummed uncertainly, but Clare knew better than to sing with her. 'How long is it, I wonder, since I last sang Elvira? In Naples, I believe, in 'sixty-nine – or was it at the Carlo Felice in Genoa! Ah, the audiences there! Wait, wait, Chiara! These Romans, phoo! It is something quite other to sing to the Genoese!'

'I have sung to them, Signora. But only in the Politeama,' Clare said modestly.

La Vittoria reached for a glass conveniently placed, and drank from it contentedly. And between mouthfuls she struggled to remember aloud the details of her last appearance in *I Puritani*.

Clare was a pet of hers; so, oddly enough, was Thomas. And when they were students either had occasionally been called in here, on one of her good afternoons, if she was short of audience. It was a crowded and airless little room, and only Assunta's energy and tact kept it from being disgusting. But Clare liked to sit there sometimes; and if she did not exactly 'like' La Vittoria that was because the verb did not catch the irrelevant interest and curiosity which this large, blurred personality roused in her. It seemed to Clare – and Thomas agreed with her – that La Vittoria must always have been artist *pur sang*, artist incarnate, without calculation, idea or glimpse of any kind beyond herself and the frame within which she could express herself. And that alarming and almost stupid integrity, which she still quite comically possessed, must have been – beyond whatever beauty she had, beyond her queer power to amuse, and even almost beyond her voice – what made Giacomo her lover once, her anxious slave for years, and for life her weary, faithful, unforgetting husband. Why, however, had this powerful example of egotism, this concentration of self-confidence so far slipped from its podium as to require the glass perpetually in the hand, the bottle forever at the elbow? What had happened, and when? And why had it in fact only half-happened? Because whereas it often seemed to the looker-on that Signora Vittoria lived only to destroy herself, in fact she appeared all but indestructible; and when she was 'well', as the household said, she could be, though odd and battered and absurd – and cruel – almost life-giving; at least, startlingly alive to no purpose, and startlingly her wilful yet comically dignified self.

Clare had heard her rambling when she seemed far out of control, and so had Thomas. And each had more than once suspected point and topicality in the long, authoritative generalizations. La Vittoria was, by her habit, irrational; and her passing likes and dislikes were irrational, and tended to get twisted into the untidy fabric of her habitual phobias and enthusiasms.

'There's something Shakespearean in her drunken talk – only I can't catch it. It isn't quite good enough to get home,' Thomas said.

'It sounds like cunning – but it can't be,' said Clare. 'She isn't cunning. Yet – how does she know, or guess, people's immediate antics?'

'I sometimes wonder if Assunta—?'

'Ah, no! Assunta is a rock of judgment. Besides, she's paying herself for La Vittoria's drunken intuitions – poor Assunta!'

'Well, then – does little Giacomino chat to her, in the deep of the night?'

Clare laughed out loud.

'In the deep of the night "La Traviata" snores, Thomas! Rosie and I had a room near her when we first came – and the noise used to frighten us! Anyhow, what does little Giacomino know, to chat about?'

'Only everything, pet. That's all. Just everything, about his darling pupils.'

Clare listened now, or half-listened; and today more out of amiability than amusement. She had been on her way to her room, to rest and write letters; she had walked about Rome all the morning, alone and in some degree at peace. She had bought bread and figs and eaten them at noon under the dark trees in the Palatine, where she had lain a long time on a flat and ancient stone, singing sometimes, sometimes half-asleep. As she came down into the Forum, Grandmother had taken hold of her thoughts, for which she was glad. So, to please the dear visitant from Ballykerin she had turned into San Ignacio and said some prayers and gone, reluctantly, to confession.

She was glad afterwards that she had made the effort, and the reward seemed to be that it pushed approaching clouds and questions out of the way of that day's light.

Rose, she thought now – for a conversation with Luisa of the night before had been around her breast all day – Rose, you should be happy, for a little, anyway – after all, it *is* first love. Oh, I wish I hadn't said I'd take Paddy to *I Puritani*! Mad of me. He's in such a bad-tempered state – and if he goes on about Rose – ah well!

'I remember a French tenor,' La Vittoria was saying. Is she some kind of thought-reader, Clare wondered? 'I don't like the French. And none of them can sing, you agree? But this unimportant man – why does he come into my head? He sang with me in Vienna one season – and the other soprano, a very pretty German girl – what *was* her name? Ah well, she made a very sad fool of herself. Very undignified indeed, poor girl! I wonder where she is now. She was a type that recurs – in our world especially. Too pretty really, too outgoing . . .'

La Vittoria found her glass empty, and looked cross.

'Assunta still shopping! It is absurd all this *ménage* that she has to do! Giacomo must get me another girl for all that outside work! I need Assunta here *perpetually*!' She struck her fat hand heavily against the table. 'I sometimes wonder . . .'

Clare guessed that, probably rightly, La Vittoria was guessing that not far away in Lunga di Sangallo Assunta was sewing or ironing for Rose. If she was, Clare felt sorry for Assunta's evening, during which no offence would be mentioned, but wherein she would be worked and driven to the last edges of her strength.

'. . . But you all go your ways! I can lie and rot. My husband says – oh, what did he say? But you, Chiara, you want to sing in South America – you, a purist, to have that vulgar fancy—'

Clare looked amazed.

The large arm swung out past the glass to get the bottle, but only hit it. Clare caught it as it staggered. La Vittoria looked up at her, appeased.

'Yes – pour it, please. I'm tired.'

Clare hesitated. The bottle was of Strega, which she knew to be powerful, and which she assumed should be diluted. But she doubted whether it was not mad cruelty to pour any of it at all for La Vittoria now. She wished indeed that Assunta was at home.

'There is the glass, child.'

Clare lifted the glass and began to pour a little Strega into it, cautiously, frowningly.

La Vittoria waited, almost good-tempered again.

'South America – never there, Chiara! Never – South America!'

Thomas came in.

'The *maestro* said I might visit you, Signora.'

She waved him welcome. Thomas, from bowing to her, turned sharply on Clare, who was setting down the bottle.

'She wants some of this,' she said, 'but I didn't know . . . ?' She spoke softly, in English.

He looked at the glass in her hand, and smiled.

'Is that all you were going to give her?'

'Well – but – is it safe?'

'Decidedly unsafe to give her only that much! Do you want one of poor Assunta's black eyes?' He took the bottle and poured a large drink.

'Oh Thomas, no!'

Thomas handed the glass politely to the eager Signora.

'It'll put her to sleep,' he said to Clare in English, 'and if you had a cure in mind, my dear, you're a bit late.'

'It's not polite to talk English,' said La Vittoria.

'That is true,' said Thomas. 'But we get tired in Italian, Signora. We're bad at it.'

'No, you're not. Not bad at all . . . But if Chiara goes to sing across the Atlantic . . .'

'God!' said Thomas in English.

Assunta came hurrying in.

'Signora – I am late—'

With a magnificent swing La Vittoria threw her emptied glass at Assunta's face, but the girl ducked as one in good training for such events – and smiled apologetically at the others.

'Better if you go now, Signorina,' she said. 'La Signora needs to sleep awhile.'

Clare and Thomas withdrew, but not before the Signora's huge purple eyelids had hidden them from her indifferent gaze.

Thomas was agitated, as Clare had known when he came into the *salottino*.

'Where can we talk?'

'Well, nowhere very easily here. Can't we talk another time?'

'No – now.'

'Well, then you'd better come to my room. But not for long, because I have to change. I'm going to the opera.'

'What opera?'

'The Argentina, where else? To hear Rose in *Puritani*.'

'Ah, of course – I'll take you there. Macchio's conducting; I'd like to watch him.'

'No. I'm meeting Paddy in the Galleria Colonna at seven, and I promised to take him.'

'God Almighty! Paddy!'

'Oh, stop cursing,' she said, as she opened the door of her room.

'Any reason why I should?'

'I don't know. What *is* the matter?'

He walked to the window and looked out, then turned and looked about the little cell.

'This was my room when I lived here,' he said.

'Ah yes – so it must have been.'

'It was different then!'

'How?'

'Oh – same furniture. I know every squeak and bang of these pieces of equipment, Clare! And, isn't it a good joke, I know every creak and groan of that little old bed! You can't make a move in it, my lady, but what I know the sound produced – I could write a small descriptive piece, for flute and oboe and bass-viol.'

Clare, who was sitting on the bed, stroked it and laughed.

'It doesn't make a sound,' she said.

'I suppose not – when Psyche rests—'

'Ah, what's the matter, Thomas?'

Gripping the iron window-grille behind him he looked about their small enclosure, as if to find a simple answer. Clare, looking up at him, remembered irrelevantly what Rose had said a long time ago: 'You two might easily be brother and sister.'

He ran his hand through his hair, and then looked down at her out of eyes that were tired, their usually sharp blue washed to grey.

'Too much matter for this little poke of a room,' he said. 'It's your future – and mine, Clare – and what to do for the best.'

'I know.' She was troubled by this look of trouble which he so rarely allowed to cross his face. 'It's your future that's the matter, Thomas. I'm still – a sort of property. But you are only marking time now; and that's wrong.'

'I'm not so sure,' he said, growing combative. 'After all, as you know I have settled now on opera – oh, well, the whole field of orchestrated and vocal music. That means I've a world of work to do in opera.'

'Yes. It means that you should have gone to Bayreuth this summer as you meant to, instead of fooling round at what comes easy—'

'Nothing comes easy, my God! If you think it's easy to conduct or rehearse an opera – *any* opera! Oh, I'm surprised at you!'

'Still, you should be engaging yourself to very hard work at La Scala before the end of this month – or, much better, you should be doing what you always said you'd do this autumn – you should be fixing up for Vienna, where there's everything for you to study, and where you're even a bit known already, and you'd get all you wanted of exacting work! Or else – there's the Berlin Opera. You used to be determined on all these places—'

'And so I am still! When did I say I wasn't going to Austria?'

'Well, you always used to talk so much about your plans. But then this summer you shrugged off the whole idea of Bayreuth – and no one was allowed to mention the place. And it *was* an obsession!'

'It'll be that again, I expect.' He smiled at Clare. 'I suppose a man can only manage one obsession at a time.'

'You seemed to have five or six on hand when I first knew you, Thomas.'

'Had I? Well, Wagner wasn't one of them, really. But the study of him, to get to know him root and branch, through every crevice and twist of his meaning to the very top – to be able really and truly to reproduce his music as he meant it – that is of course a necessity!'

'And you're neglecting it!'

'I'm not, I tell you! I've read and played his scores through and through, night after night last winter. I'll show them to you, with all my queries and notes. It was often a way of getting peaceably through nights when I wanted to be making a fool of myself in obvious ways.'

'Still, that isn't the same thing as going to work in Germany!'

'But who said I'm *not* going to work in Germany? Who said you mightn't be working there with me?'

'I! Oh Thomas – don't be crazy! I'm not nearly ready to sing in those countries yet – and Giacomino wouldn't hear of anything so rash!'

'I'm not saying you're *ready*. Neither are you ready yet to sing in La Scala – but if you were given a booking there this winter you'd have to take a shot at it. And if you're allowed to do that, you're certainly good enough to do the same in a German opera house—'

'Oh, I'm not belittling Italy! Only, the Northern repertories are different, and I know no German—'

'You won't know German until you have to work and sing in it every day. And I'm not saying you'll be asked to sing in the State Opera House anywhere, my pet—'

'No need to sneer—'

'I'm thinking of all the smaller theatres and concert groups, and oratorio and church music opportunities – and the variety of teachers and experience – and the usual repertory taste of Vienna especially, so really suited to your voice and *your taste . . .*'

'I know – and if I'm good enough some day, Thomas! But I've oceans of work to do before I'd dare, oceans to learn – as Giacomo knows, if you don't—'

Thomas came and sat beside her on the bed.

'Giacomo knows your business better than you do, Clare. So if you think that at this stage in your training you're going to be allowed to batter around Latin-America yelling your head off in *Faust* and *Marthe* and *Il Trovatore*, to say nothing of such novelties as *The Gypsy Baron*, and to say less of your screeching away as Michaela while Luisa sweeps the Continent as Carmen – which is to be sung in Spanish, I'm told—'

Clare smiled guiltily.

'I've been getting very small salaries, Thomas; I'm still an awful debit on Uncle Matt and his friends – and this Latin-American tour is being well paid.'

'Well, if you want to throw all of Uncle Matt's money into the Rio Grande you've only got to go off and do so! But you won't be let, my girl!'

'Some good people are going – I believe Pirazzei is a very shrewd impresario—'

'He is, indeed. He has signed on Marisi, who shouldn't leave Europe now. A lovely tenor – do you remember, we heard him at Costanzi's in April in *La Sforza del Destino*? But then, the poor chap's married, and it means six months' certain money—'

'Duarte wouldn't go on a really bad tour—'

'I'm not saying it's really bad – it's just dull and silly. And useless for a young one like you – worse than useless. Indeed, I think it's a mistake for Luisa – but those two are Spaniards, you know, and so Latin-America attracts them; and Duarte's tired of Rome – as well he might be. And I think that he wants Luisa all to himself for a while . . .'

Clare said nothing.

'But what possessed you, Clare, to think that you could manœuvre yourself into this expedition on the quiet?'

She laughed.

'I wasn't manœuvring – how could I? I was just vaguely talking of it, with Luisa – and with Rose.'

'Well, what did Rose say?'

'Oh – she thought I was crazy! In fact, she got very cross with me. "One minute, nothing will do you but *Fidelio* and *Iphigenia in Tauris* – and then you want to be off singing Gounod and Bizet to a continent full of Indians! Oh, you're really not all there, Clare Halvey," she said.'

'You see! Rose is true. She's a serious worker. Oh – she mayn't have all your weight of grey matter, my pet, and she isn't as choosy about this and that – but she's an absolutely honest artist – she's passionate about it, you see—'

Clare buried her face in her hands.

'And I am not?' she said angrily. Then she flung up her head, and he saw that her eyes glittered with hard tears. 'Rose is lucky, Thomas. Blindfold and innocent she was led into – into what she is! She can't escape, she can't fail! Whatever doubts or questions there may be – there is this certainty for her! And it justifies everything. Indeed, it must sweeten everything, I'd say.'

'You're – not jealous of her, Clare?'

'Jealous? Am I? Well, who wouldn't be?'

'Not you. There's no need.'

'Oh yes, there is! Leaving all her lovely singing out of it – look at her courage – look at how open and sunny-hearted she is! Oh Thomas – do you really think that everything should be easy?' The hard tears spilt along her face, and she brushed them away and pushed her fair hair back from her forehead. 'Do you think there's only one kind of passionate artist?'

'We're misunderstanding each other – don't cry, Clare . . .'

He took her hands and kissed them, turned them over lovingly and kissed their upward palms.

'Please – where's my handkerchief?' said Clare, and drew her hands away.

There was a knock on the door.

'Come in,' said Clare, thinking it might be Assunta with coffee, or possibly Luisa on a chance call. But when the door opened it was Paddy Flynn who stood on the threshold.

'Oh, hello, Paddy!'

'I beg your pardon, Clare. But Assunta said I might knock.'

'Of course. Won't you come in?'

Clare had stood up and moved towards him.

'Most certainly not! Simply, I got away from my pupil in Via Valadier rather early, and I had thought, as I was passing, that you might like to take some exercise in the Borghese Gardens—'

'That was kind of you, Paddy. But I walked all over Rome during the morning – and now I have to write some letters, and change my clothes before I meet you for the opera –'

Paddy hardly seemed to listen. He was staring at Thomas who had risen when Clare did and now was leaning out of the window.

155

'– I'll be at Piero's in the Galleria at seven, as I said. Thank you for calling in.'

'Oh, nothing.' Paddy bowed and shut the door. Clare sat down on the bed again. Thomas turned to look at her, and they began to laugh. Clare felt as if she might have to laugh for a long time.

'Oh! Oh Heavens! The evening I'm in for now!'

'Does that seminarist often march into your bedroom?'

'Good God, no! He'd rather die than cross its threshold. But often during last year he's called with a note, or to see if I'd go for a walk – he has pupils in this neighbourhood. And Assunta and everyone knows him, and they just tell him to see if I'm in. You know how unconventional this household is? Indeed I think their casualness horrifies Paddy – he'd much rather wait in the *salotto* and have me fetched. However, needs must and he comes as far as my door – but *never* further. I see that he finds it extraordinary that I should say "come in", as I always do. But then – that's not surprising. Any conventional young man anywhere would think it odd.'

'True – I suppose. One's forgotten it all.'

'Still – oh Lord, the lecture I'm going to get! *You* sitting here on my bed!'

Thomas came and sat there again.

'And you were crying, pet – and I was kissing your hands—'

'No, you weren't when he knocked. Still – you were here and taking your ease! Oh, Heavens, between your bad character and my own, and Rosie's – I won't be allowed to take in a phrase of *I Puritani*—'

'Serves you right. Why do you put up with him?'

'I like him.'

'Like him?'

'I like his face. Don't you?'

'Certainly I don't – a sort of under-done Savonarola!'

'Maybe – but it's wild and unusual. And he has brains. Oh, he reminds me of home, and forgotten things, Thomas – he's very Irish.'

'If he is, I begin to understand the history of your nation.'

'No, you don't.'

'But if he's very Irish, where were you got? What does Rose represent? Where did you two get your singing voices?'

'In Ireland. We're all Irish, the three of us. Oh – I wish I could go alone to *I Puritani* tonight!'

'You're looking tired – and we haven't even begun our quarrel, Clare.'

'No; I know we haven't.'

'Well, we're young still – there's plenty of time. Rest now – I'm off.' He put his arm about her shoulders. 'Lie down on this bed of sin when I'm gone, and prepare to face your father confessor in Piero's at seven o'clock. Have you any chance of absolution?'

'None at all.'

He stood up, and pushed her gently back on to her pillow, and then he bent down and kissed her.

'*Ego te absolvo,*' he said, and smiled and went.

Rose, sitting ready in her dressing-room after the overture call, and hearing the overture begin far-off, made the sign of the cross and slowly said three Hail Marys, as she always did when she heard the first notes of the orchestra. Then she asked her dresser to request Signor René to come to her for a moment.

He came at once, made up and shining, but still in a dressing-gown.

'Not dressed yet, love?'

'Oh, I'll be ready in a minute, Rose. But since you sent for me – naturally I came!'

'Ah yes, I'm sorry. But it's only to say –' she stretched for his hand – 'that I'm extra nervous tonight, so I thought I'd better warn you.'

He looked surprised.

'Of course, sweet Rose. But why? Why extra nervous, I mean?'

'Well, we haven't sung it together since – since that first time—'

'Ah, no! That's true.'

'And my great friend, Clare – you know, you've heard of Clare – will be in front. And she hasn't heard me sing for ages. So, I thought I'd better warn you, René love—'

He laughed, and carefully stroked her hair.

'Of course, dear! Mustn't upset the beautiful maquillage. But –' his bright eyes met her anxious ones in the mirror – 'we'll be all right. And for your Clare I understand that you can do no wrong!'

'Oh, I don't know! She's a terribly good listener.'

'Let her listen! Ah, I must get dressed, love—'

'Indeed you must – fly!'

At the door he turned back, and smiled very gently at her.

'Rose – something I noticed at rehearsal yesterday – forgive me, but your *tempo* in *Credeasi* – will you be sure to take it from me . . . ?'

'From you? But – we take it from Macchio!' She began to laugh. 'We have to, my silly boy – or what would happen?'

'You don't understand? That long *Credeasi* is tremendously difficult for me—'

'We all know that, my love—'

'I know you do. Only don't race it, will you?'

Gioia Lanci, who was singing Henrietta, came into Rose's dressing-room as René hurried out.

'What's he talking about?' La Lanci was an experienced singer.

Rose was looking surprised, but she laughed softly.

'He's still uneducated musically,' she said. 'He seems to think that the *Credeasi* is a sort of steeplechase!'

La Lanci snorted.

'Oh, it's nerves, Gioia! He's in a fuss – and who wouldn't be, with a top F to tackle?'

'He's in no fuss,' said Gioia. 'Any wine?' Rose's dresser ran to fetch a glass and bottle. 'I like to gargle with wine before I go on. Thank you.' She took the filled glass and stepped to the washstand. 'And he isn't so ignorant either – no, Rosa. The matter with your French darling is that he's shocked at your brilliance and determined to tone it down!'

La Lanci gargled.

Rose looked gravely into the mirror; then, obeying the call-boy, she moved towards the wings with Henrietta of France.

*

Clare stood near the white-globed lamp and turned the marked pages of a score of *I Puritani*.

'Oh God! This fiendish thing!' said Rose.

'Mind, Rosie!' said Clare, without turning round. Rose was on her knees before her rusty oil-burner, tilting an omelette in a pan.

'Here! It's ready now! Come on before I burn it!'

Skilfully she divided it and slid it on to two plates.

'Quickly, Clare.' It was lovely, full of vegetables, and running wet and buttery.

'How skilful you are!'

The two ate eagerly, but Clare still kept the opera score beside her on the table.

She had been enchanted, startled even, by Rose's singing of Elvira. She had, in fact, been alone to hear it – greatly to her pleasure. For when she reached Piero's to keep her appointment with Paddy, she found a message left for her there with the young waiter Domenico who had been in the chorus at La Valle and was a friend of hers.

'Signor Paddy regrets, Signorina, but he will be unable to join you here or to accompany you to the opera.' If there was an ironic question in Domenico's eye – for he knew Paddy – Clare's did not acknowledge it. She ate some salad, drank coffee, and walked in peace to the Argentina, to listen to Rose and the young French tenor.

When she had heard that *I Puritani* had been put into Rose's repertory for the Argentina season, Clare had studied the score with Thomas. Actors are each other's best audiences, generally; and singers listen understandingly to singing. But Clare and Rose, young so far and very much frightened of their work, were acutely aware, each for herself and for the other, of the dangers their inexperience must confront; so they always felt that they could not be good listeners to each other. 'The day will come, pet,' Rose used to say, 'when we'll be so sure of our fame and our genius, the pair of us, that we'll be able to criticize each other with the most disgusting coolness – you'll see!' But that day seemed a long way off.

Tonight, however, alone in her stall in the centre of the

second row, Clare had listened with close attention to Bellini's opera, which she knew to be musically graceful and unexacting, but dramatically near the danger-line of the absurd.

'I don't mind silly stories, Thomas,' she had said, when they were playing through the score of *I Puritani* one night in Ancona. 'In themselves, I mean. After all, the best stories are unreal; I mean, unprovable. So the difficulty isn't for the composer – it's only for the unfortunate actor. And in a caper like this you'd need more support than Bellini can give you, I'd say – I mean, it'd take Glück or Mozart to make one accept the nonsense—'

'Or Verdi?'

'Yes – in a different way. I wonder how Rosie will manage the going mad?'

'It's beautifully written – that scene—'

'Yes, lovely, *legato* – but tricky to express madness in, don't you think?'

'You go mad very well as Lucia. You ought to see how here –' Thomas played it over – '*Qui la voce soave . . .*' and Clare sang it with him, and then broke off and laughed.

'I can go mad fairly well in music, Thomas, and Rose can go to the bad, or fall in love – whichever you call it, according to the plots.'

'What's required is to be able to do either or both, at the drop of a hat!'

'Yes. We both know that. We've often talked about it. After all, it looks as if we'll have to live and die with Italian opera.'

'You could do worse, young woman. No need to look so snobbish!'

'Snobbish? I'm frightened – that's what I am!'

Now, exhausted and humbled, the omelette devoured, she watched Rose toss a salad, standing in the window, with the Roman stars and the Janiculum lights behind her head. Clare remembered suddenly the little girl who used to sob, her head bent down, in the dreary practice-rooms of Rue des Lauriers. Somehow, she thought, Rose is perfect.

She cries, Rose cries when she is lonely. She remembers her

mother, and the boats, and sails on Lough Shee. She says the long night prayers that she has always said. She works with gaiety to repay the Committee, and to help Mamma. With every month she travels further, calmly, into adult life. She grows more beautiful with every change of season; she is the more at ease with life and the more its energetic partner as it more commands her. She sang 'Vien, diletto' tonight as if, Clare thought, the mad girl found each note herself, pristine, unforeseen. But Rose, in her dressing-room, was no mad girl – simply a happy, tired singer in love with her beautiful tenor. Making no mystery of that, and dismissing him with tenderness because she wanted to talk to Clare. So then, kneeling down before her little brutal stove to make an omelette, and flushed with triumph at its goodness. Now, tossing the salad – her lovely head bent.

'I think I've overdone the garlic,' she said, and put the bowl on the table.

'Rosie,' said Clare, 'you sang tonight – oh, pet – what can I say?'

Rose lifted radiant eyes.

'You – liked it? It's not your kind of opera—'

'Oh –! But it's music to sing! And you sang it, Rosie! Both of you!'

Rose looked carefully at Clare.

'You liked René's voice?'

'Very much, Rose. I think he sings most delicately.'

'How he'd like to hear that! He's young, you know. He's very nervous.'

She filled Clare's glass.

'You remember this Velletri? It was the first wine we knew in Rome.'

'It's lovely.'

'You're not shocked, Clare – about me and René?'

Clare did not answer. The simple question touched her, but she did not know the answer. By the catechism, by the rules of home and tradition, was she shocked that Rose should be the lover of her first love?

She walked to the window.

'Oh, my pet, don't pester me! Sing "Vien, diletto . . ."'

But Rose shook her head.

'No, I'm still hungry. Come and have some salad.'

There was silence for a minute.

Clare knew that for now at least, for tonight, Rose no more desired than did she to talk of René Chaloux. Each was sure of that; but still, the bare enough had not yet been said.

'Rosie,' Clare said very gently. 'By what right would I be shocked – about you and René?'

Rose looked at her gratefully, but still with a question in her eyes.

'It's – it's a remarkable thing to have done, I think . . .' They both smiled uncertainly. 'I mean, you and I both know that for either of us it *is* a remarkable thing to have done – no matter what all these others may think!' She waved a hand and the two laughed a little towards their absent friends. 'But I imagine you're secretly feeling a bit shocked at yourself – are you?' Rose met her questioning eyes gravely and half-inclined her head. 'Well, after all, you're the only one who need be – aren't you, pet?'

'Oh, Clare, you *are* good. I – I just wanted you to know from me, that's all – not just by gossip.'

'I know.' Clare looked about the shabby, foreign little room, and out to the lights of Trastevere. We are travelling fast, she thought. Already I hardly remember what we were like when we came to Rome two years ago.

She laughed quite clearly, and stretched a hand to lay it on Rose's wrist.

'You're unexpected all the same, Rosie Lennane! A Frenchman, of all unlikely people! And such a baby of a Frenchman too! Hardly a day older than you, is he?'

'A month, I think.'

'The audacity of the creature! Ah well, God bless you, little Rose!'

They drank their wine, and each saw gratefully that bright tears stood in the other's eyes. That is enough for now, Clare thought. That is all we could either of us bear tonight. She is all right now; she only wanted me to know from herself about her lover – and to be sure that I am not horrified. And admittedly it's queer that I'm not.

'I had a letter from Grandmother on Monday—'

'How is she, Clare?'

'Ah, the dear one – her handwriting looks feeble. She sent a lot of scapulars and Agnus Dei's that the nuns made and want me to get blessed by the Pope. "You're to be sure to see the Holy Father personally about it, child, or Sister Liguori won't feel sure about them—"'

'You must tell that to Monsignor Donellan—'

'Yes; I'll give them to him. Grandmother thinks that Leo XIII is more than ever like Grandfather. She saw a new picture of him the other day in *The Irish Rosary*, and she says that if Grandfather had lived to his age, they might as well be twins!'

Rose laughed.

'Your grandfather must have been handsome.'

'According to Grandmother! I must go home to her, without fail, next year! It'll be four years then. Perhaps we could go together in the summer, Rosie?'

'I wonder—'

'After all, if we get a lot of work this winter and spring, we mightn't need to do the summer *stagioni* at all! And we'll really have to be given a holiday by that time. You might come to Ballykerin for a bit – and then perhaps you'd ask me to visit you at Lackanashee?'

'I'd love to show you Lackanashee. I'd love to take you for a sail on the lake—'

'You sound sleepy, pet. I wanted to talk about *I Puritani* to you – but I will, another time.'

'You liked it?'

'I hadn't thought it was nearly so melodious, or so touching! You cast a kind of spell on it, the pair of you, I think. You made it positively romantic and – like lovely music!'

Rose smiled.

'We're both attached to it – now. It was on the first night we sang it that we – told each other we were in love.'

'Ah!' Clare stood up. 'Shall I boil some water and wash up these things?'

'No, pet – we'll just stack them on the table on the landing, and the portiera's cousin will see to them in the morning.'

'Oh, I'm glad. It's lovely here, Rosie – no wonder you're proud of your Roman apartment! Will you go to bed now?'

'Yes. But what about you? Shall we go and look for a cab for you?'

'A cab? Gracious, I've only got to walk down the embankment to Ripetta!'

'I know. But will you be safe? Will you be scared?'

'Rosie, pet! If you're to be scared you couldn't live in Italy at all! And as travelling singers, my goodness!'

'I know. But people fuss—'

'Yes – they fuss. They fuss about a lot of things, Rosie – as perhaps you're finding out?'

They smiled, and kissed each other good night.

'Well, hurry home, let you—'

'I love walking about Rome.'

'Be careful, Clare – the stairs are very dark.'

Clare paused under the trees to wave to Rose, who hung out of the lighted window.

'Good night, Rosie!'

'Who's that?' Rose called sharply. 'Are you all right, Clare? Who *is* that?'

A man in black was standing on the pavement beside Clare. She turned, and recognized him.

'It's Paddy!' she called up to Rose in an impatient voice.

'Oh, I'm glad! That's kind of you, Paddy,' Rose called out. But she could see even from here how much Clare was exasperated by the sight of him. She saw her gesture of dismissal, and the speed with which she strode away along the riverside. She watched them race each other out of sight – they're like angry children, she thought, as she turned back to the lamp-lit room, and to the shadowy and puzzling small chamber of her newly-discovered heart.

The Eighth Chapter

October passed, and when it was gone took more that was beautiful with it than its own Roman beauty.

There had been great manoeuvring and planning, as usual in this month, between impresarios, theatres and *maestros*, and the young had gone about anxiously, feeling cautious, anticipatory and afraid; not daring to speak clearly to their elders about their immediate hopes lest that imperil them; and unable, some of them, to exchange the truth of fears and desires between themselves. Unable, shy, in-driven – and knowing that they were at the mercy of expediency and *il teatro lirico*.

Rose, for whose voice a screened but dogged battle was being fought – on a four-sided front, Thomas said – between the business men of opera, none of whom wanted either to commit himself too far yet *or*, for a trifle, to let her slip to another wolf – Rose who should have enjoyed all this and merrily appreciated its tricks and rumours, was disconcertingly unamused and irritable, and sometimes spoke quite savagely about little Giacomino.

'He's going on as if he was a magician – a silly little fortune-teller!' she said. 'Do you think he has the Evil Eye?'

Mariana Fogli, the Sicilian, gave a cry of fear.

'Oh no, Rosa! Never, never say that!'

'Silly Rosa!' said Gioia Lanci.

Five or six of the Argentina company were seated on the terrace of a café in the Largo Arenula. They were to sing *La Traviata* tonight, with Antonio de Luca, attached to the company for these last weeks of the season, singing Germont père to René Chaloux's Alfred. Antonio sat in handsome boredom now, with his arm along the back of Mariana's chair. The expression in his clear eyes as he considered the young French tenor across the table made Gioia Lanci at least look forward with amusement to the evening's performances of father and son.

'It isn't our little Giacomino who's playing magician with you, Rosa d'Irlanda,' Antonio said. 'Still – look out for the Evil Eye.'

'God forgive you, de Luca,' said La Lanci.

René sat beside Rose. He was still slow in Italian conversation, so he paid no attention to this talk, but went on writing a letter. Rose thought that his fair beauty never looked more astonishing, even on the stage, than when set down as now in a hot Roman street scene, in a crowd of solid Romans. He'll sing Walter and Siegfried one day, she thought. I wonder if I'll ever be able to sing Wagner?

'Laugh, Rosa! Make us laugh, as you can,' said La Lanci. 'After all, you have to start dying on our hands in an hour or two!'

'Well, that's easier than going mad! Though Clare doesn't agree – Oh, hello, Thomas!'

Thomas stood before the group, his arms, as usual, full of opera scores. He smiled at Rose.

'May I sit down?' Antonio pulled him to a chair at his side. 'What doesn't Clare agree to, Rose?'

'That it's easier for a soprano to die than to go mad! Clare says, you know,' she said to La Lanci, 'that the few other fates allowed to sopranos are so false and so conducive to madness, that it would be as well to formalize the thing and have them just always go mad—'

'A fine idea,' said La Lanci, 'and it should make for a lot of splendid singing—'

'*Cadenze galore!*' said Rose.

'But none of you girls would be able to take the strain,' said Thomas. 'Think of what Malibran would have made of Clare's formality!'

'She'd have exploded it,' said an amused old bass-singer called Tosa. 'The world would have had enough of madness – after Malibran.'

Thomas looked interested.

'You're old, I know, Signor Tosa. But – you *couldn't* have sung with *her*?'

Tosa laughed.

'No. I sang with her wonderful sister, though – La Viardot – where are we? Eighteen-eighty-nine? – Yes – thirty, thirty-four years ago, I think – in *Rienzi*.'

'*Rienzi?*'

'Yes – somewhere in Germany. I've forgotten where. I sang Colonna, and she sang the son, Adriano. I was only a youngster. She *was* a bit old for that part then. But she was a master in her art – that's the only word for Viardot – a master!'

La Lanci gave the good-humoured smile of the trouper who has heard a reminiscence once or twice before.

'Is anyone but me going to eat before the performance? All right. A ham omelette, please, and a green salad, Carlo. Watch for the garlic, Rosa, when I'm yelling away above your dying head!'

Thomas signalled to Carlo for more wine.

'Where is Clare, Rose?' he asked.

'Oh – she and Luisa went off at cock-crow to the seashore! At least, that's what she told me they were doing. Didn't you know?'

'No.'

'Yes, they went early,' said Mariana. 'I met her coming out of Mass in Lorenzo in Lucina, and she was simply flying to get the bus for the Ostiense Station!'

Thomas's unashamed preoccupation with Clare was touching, and regrettable, La Lanci thought; and she watched his mobile face with sympathy now. She was only a singer, a well-trained soprano, and in no place to judge Thomas's talents in music; but he had been *répétiteur*, chorus-master, and often within the last year conductor where she had sung, and she knew how ruthless, energetic and ambitious he was. Also, she heard his rivals and colleagues talk of him; and often she listened to him on the subject of himself. Over three years indeed she had known him. She was in these years a lonely woman, from having been one for many lovers; so sometimes she had taken

Thomas home with her, and listened to him, fed him, and taken him to bed. She was not in love with him, but she liked him more than she liked most men. And by now she knew more than perhaps he measured about Clare. For often this Welshman got drunk and when he got drunk he talked until the good-natured Gioia had almost to slap him into silence and sleep.

But this pure passion for the complicated, frosty Clare did not any longer amuse Gioia overmuch, since it seemed to be slowing up the egoist in Thomas, making him indecisive, making him tired.

'They were going to walk along the beaches from Ostia to Palo or somewhere,' said Rose.

'You're singing tonight?' Thomas asked Antonio.

'Yes, curse it!'

'Tonio, that's a bad thing to say!' said Rose.

'I meant it badly, Rosa. I'm insulting you – see? Curse it, I said.'

René Chaloux flushed and sprang from his chair.

'You understood that?' said Antonio to him. 'Your Italian is coming on!'

'Yes – I understand – plenty!'

Rose took his wrist.

'No, René, you don't understand plenty. Sit down, please.'

Antonio put some money on the table and rose lazily.

'Come, Mariana – will you?'

They strolled away.

'You shouldn't bother baiting him like that,' said Mariana.

'Blast him! I hate him! What possessed her, Mariana? A Frenchman. An *evirato*, a *castrato*!'

'He's no *castrato*! And don't shout, dear one! It's easy to see what possessed her. René is made to be a girl's first love, first craze, if you like.'

'Oh, for a fifteen-year-old in a convent! But, Rosa, grown-up, a beautiful, accomplished singer – a woman—'

'Emotionally she's only about fifteen – or was, until this. He's teaching her fast though – poor Rosa! But the Irish are very odd, Antonio. Don't you see that? They're almost unnatural. Look at Chiara!'

'Oh, she's cracked, I know. But Rosa!' He began to laugh. 'I'll let him have it about returning to his "home in fair Provence" tonight – *Di Provenza il mar . . .*' he sang gaily.

'René comes from Normandy,' said Mariana.

Antonio stopped in the street and laughed outright. 'Good! Good! *Di Normandia il mar . . .* It goes beautifully!'

But Mariana was not worried.

'You wouldn't do that! You're too well disciplined about your work,' she said.

Thomas moved round the table to sit beside La Lanci.

'I'd like to talk to you sometime, wiseacre,' he said.

'You've done that often before, my lamb.'

'I know. Are you free for supper tonight?'

'I am.'

'Corradetti's – in Croce? At midnight?'

'Rather expensive.'

'I want decent food. I'm not going to offer you much, though – you're getting fat – and you shouldn't be eating all this now.'

'Oh, Annina is easily sung.'

'I agree. And that's what's wrong with you. You'll only do what's easy.'

'No one is asking me to do anything else.'

'How old are you, Gioia?'

'Thirty-two.'

'Too young to be settling down as *seconda donna*.'

She smiled.

'It's a part I get cast for, Thomas. And I seem to have the necessary brains.'

'Have you? I'm tired of brains – my own and other people's. And they're superfluous in interpretation of music. At Corradetti's, then?' He stood up. 'Good singing tonight, Irish Rose. I'd like to hear *Ditte alla giovine*, but I've work on hand.' He gathered up his scores. 'I'm seeing Giacomino later – any love-words?'

'None at all to the little bully,' said Rose. 'Just a cold kiss on his forehead.'

Thomas bowed and strolled away.

René looked after him, half-smiling.

'How conceited he is, that Thomas,' he said in French.

The whole table protested.

'Thomas? Conceited! Oh heavens, have sense!'

Mariana was right. René was for Rose's *naïveté* the necessary object of first love. In her two quite adventurous first years in Italy no one of the sophisticated, appreciative and sometimes powerful men of the world who had flattered and coaxed, and sometimes sought frankly and with intention to seduce her, had succeeded more than to amuse and somewhat educate her, and occasionally, to her secret surprise, to disturb a hitherto untroubled sensuality. Antonio alone among Rose's admirers had reached the suburbs of her heart, but she was unready nevertheless for his forthright masculinity and its exactions; and she knew – often feeling foolish and embarrassed in her knowledge, though allowing him no such hint – that by his terms of love she was the most inept and timorous of school-girls. Moreover, perhaps she suspected that to love Antonio, to plunge into free love with him direct and naked from the cold rock of the law of God – that that might be too much, too serious for her, and so unfair to him.

Still, the life she led – in Italy, in the sunshine, singing and gypsying around with gay and sceptical companions, hearing their jokes and stories, looking about her, studying drama, drinking wine, travelling from lovely place to lovely place, learning music and how to sing it, hearing it sung, arguing with it and about it night and day – this life which she accepted wholeheartedly and with constant, burning gratitude to God and the Committee, left her always, night after night, because of her very love of it, lonely. Lonely, yet for long unsure – or rather at least sure of this, that when sometimes in her bed she cried uncontrollably, the tears were no longer for Lackanashee and Mamma but for some near and new acceptant of all that she was learning to say and feel when she sang.

At last in summer, at the Argentina, René, who had crossed her path occasionally within their two Italian years, was her vis-à-vis in some operas – and made instant and imperative claim on her waiting love. His beauty, his youth and grace, his poverty and homesickness, his diffidence among the confident Italians, his touchiness, his mistakes and stupidities, his sweetness to her and his absolute trust in her – all took her quick and at last decisive heart; so that, asking God to forgive her, 'saying a prayer', as she told him, she made him take her, she became his lover.

They walked together now along Via Botteghe Oscure. In a street behind the Gesú, René had to fetch some shoes which were being repaired and which he required for the night's performance.

'Was I unpleasant, darling?' he asked. 'Should I not have got angry with Antonio?'

'You weren't at all unpleasant,' she replied almost fatuously, as if to say, How could you be? 'But you shouldn't have got angry.'

'I see. But I don't understand.'

Rose smiled. René often said he saw but did not understand; she supposed that in French there might be a divergence of meaning between the verbs which escaped her superficial knowledge. She believed that many of his apparent mistakes, even his musical mistakes, which enraged conductors, and made other singers describe him as conceited or simply as an ass, arose from the precisions of his French idiom, and his slowness with Italian. And she knew, everybody knew after all, that the French acknowledge only one language, French. For herself, she saw how vulnerable he was, and she remembered her own imbecilities when she was first in Paris. In short, he touched her heart. She loved to look at him, to sing with him, and to lie in his breast and sleep and be his love. And she did not think at all that he was an ass.

And in the last she is perfectly right, La Lanci might have said, or Thomas, or old Tosca. This Lohengrin, this Tristan out of Normandy is no ass, but on the contrary a clever speculator and a bit of a wizard. It is no ass, they might have said, who selects and secures for himself the most promising of all the young sopranos in Italy and quickly turns her into an ass. Clare, however, would have said no such thing. She liked to look on the beauty of Rose and René together, she liked to hear them sing together, and she often prayed, boldly and anxiously against Heaven's rule, for Heaven's protection of their tricky and delicate first love.

When they had got the shoes they strolled back hand-in-hand towards the Argentina.

'Camellias, love—'

The old man with the barrow gave René a rich armful of them, white and heavy, for La Traviata, whom he knew and saluted now with grace. Rose pulled one flower through the pin of René's cravat.

'Look how that becomes him!' she said to the old man. 'Isn't he beautiful?'

'Perhaps he is. But look at you!' said the old man.

Signor Giacomo worked himself into a distressing temper while Thomas was with him. This was not directed against Thomas, although the latter had to accept some censure. He had come by appointment to take his old teacher's counsel about work in Leipzig and Berlin, where the little *maestro* had influence and prestige. Thomas himself knew Leipzig in the Konservatorium, but now sought direction into Opera House circles. Giacomo had been lavish of instruction and with notes of introduction.

'. . . If you go, you backslider! If indeed you try, just for a change, to be the student I knew!'

'Yes – if I do. But not, of course, the student you knew—'

'Don't trip me up! Is that all you're good for now? Oh, I'm irritable – forgive me. But I grow old, and this year, my new young ones – oh, they are to be a poor vintage! I know it already – in ten days! Not one, I think, in the six! Not *one*, Tomaso! I have been misguided, misinstructed! Yet – I must teach, I must bear it—'

'But why, sir, if they're no good? Can't you send them home?'

'An honest man would send them home – and I *am* an honest man, Tomaso. But – this apartment, my dear wife, my old sister downstairs – if I send away my new pupils, I get no others this year, I anger my patrons, I throw all away!'

'But – the Accademia—'

'Yes – from Santa Cecilia and a few visiting pupils – enough, plenty and happy, for me – but – Ah Tomaso, you know! Do not bother me! I have all you see about me, so I must teach the unteachable. I do not mind – often there are unteachables. What I rage about is that I *had* just lately a vintage year – your year – you and Tonio and Mariana and the two Irish flowers – a remarkable year! And every one of you is wasting time, or playing the fool, or going to the devil!'

'But nonsense! What are you talking about, sir? We've all worked hard all this year—'

'You have not! On the contrary, you've all been getting interested in yourselves as romantic individuals – phoo! – when all you're here for is to learn to be musicians, of some kind – artists of music, young man, not commonplace fallers-in-love with yourselves, or each other! You know not which! You, Tomaso – you sicken me!'

'Blast your impertinence!' said Thomas.

'Curse away! I will curse you!' said Giacomo. 'But you know! And I believe you'll do your work and be all right – there is a good hardness in you. Still, did I have the wisdom of Solomon, would I perhaps indeed have *allowed* that mad Chiara to go now to South America? If I cannot save you both, why not save one? Save you, the more important, the real musician – and let her go to her folly – for she is a mere singer!'

Thomas jumped up – but cut whatever he began to say on a kind of gasp.

'Fill our glasses, Tomaso. This is a good Soave – I know the place it was made.'

Thomas paced about the room.

'Where are you sending her this season?'

'Mind your business. Go to Germany.'

'She should go to Germany!'

'Time enough. She has much to learn – and she is not a likely Wagnerian.'

'But Glück and Mozart – and *Fidelio* – and she's very promising in all those Italians that France and Germany like – Bellini, I mean, and Donizetti and Rossini—'

'She will learn them best here – she needs another hard year of Italy. But she is *my* concern, Tomaso – not yours! Attend to your own neglected future, young man!'

'I shall do so.' Thomas's voice was cold. She was not home yet; Assunta had told him that when she let him in. He listened now all through Giacomo's shouting for any sound of key or footfall.

'South America! Duarte's inexplicable,' said Giacomo. 'Let him sign himself up, by all means – even with Pirazzei. He gets sick of Italy – and since he won't go home, I suppose South America attracts him. But, to advise and lure that very promising Luisa into such a mischief! And yet the man has taste! He *is* a musician! And you can't tell me he can't do without his far-too-young young mistress for a few months – he's not all that enamoured, be assured.'

'Oh, let him go, the bore!' said Thomas. 'Luisa must be cracked!'

'You are all cracked! But Luisa is not my concern. I will save Chiara's pure voice from that South American massacre. I have saved it – because while she is in debt to her protectors she must do as I say – but, oh, she is angry!'

'What a fool she is!'

Silence fell. Giacomo stretched his weary little legs along the sofa, and closed his eyes. A thread of singing wavered far away.

'My wife. A very steady line . . .'

'Wonderful. What is it?'

'Something from her native village. Immeasurably old Etruscan, Tomaso, need I say?'

They both smiled.

'I have nothing to say against love-affairs, or falling in love, or what you will, Tomaso. What could I say? And I don't care who or what is the object of anyone's passing or eternal love – love as you please, a nun or a goat or a Chinaman. Fine! But only let it be love conducted normally, and kept in its right place among the realities! Oh Tomaso! These Irish crazies! You see them, how they are, how they were? Daisies, like silly daisies – like ten years old. So you begin to worry for their brains, for their work – for their natural state! I mean, such coldness, such *sisterliness*, Tomaso! With that beautiful promise of singing – these chaste icicles were a worry – a puzzle. But then at last they are disturbed – you see it happen, you hear it in their voices and in their eyes it sits. *But* – when it comes, it is all wrong! It is for the wrong person, it is at the wrong time, it is exaggerated, it is sad, it is odd and it is awkward – and it obsesses them – and it is not at all the love one wished to have them experience – as their *maestro* once wished! Oh – never mind Chiara, for the moment! Look at Rosa! Look at the fool she makes herself! Look at the fool she has taken, Tomaso! Oh, and the trouble she makes for me! And the reserve, and the silence, and the pertinacity!'

'That'll pass – Rosa's nonsense, I mean,' said Thomas impatiently. 'She's only cutting her teeth on him!'

'But at a wrong time, the little fool! She should have cut those teeth last year on Tonio. However, she too must do as I say – lover or no lover! What does she see in that pretty Frenchman?'

'His prettiness, I suppose. She doesn't argue about him with *you*, I take it?'

'Oh Heaven no! We play a complete fiction, Rosa and I! But how could she think – how either of them – that I do not know how they are living? Am I not in charge of them?'

'And, anyhow, you always know whatever you want to know—'

Giacomo smiled.

'That is so. Now, Rosa knows that I can very likely make a very good engagement for her at La Scala for November, December. *Or*, I can accept the Costanzi offer, and after it San Carlo. And she wants to take Costanzi's – and the consequences. She says to me – and she is right – that at Costanzi's she will make more money than at La Scala, because she will more often sing the leading parts – and that is true. Nevertheless, to La Scala – since the offer is serious – she will go! But she can't have her pretty Frenchman with her there. He'll be lucky if he makes a little money in and out of the Valle and the Argentina for this winter – and she knows that. And so she wants to be in Rome, to comfort and encourage him. But what he wants is to sing with her, to be seen to sing with her—'

'To be associated with her rising fortune?'

'Of course! But he has everything to learn before he'll sing in Costanzi's – so what use would it be to him then, her just being in Rome?'

'They're in love!' Thomas smiled.

'They think so, yes. And he's in love with more than Rosa – he's in love with himself as her perfectly matched tenor, and with all that can accrue from all that. But we're breaking off his youthful dream. La Scala and real work, and real tears, if necessary, are what our little Rosa needs, and what she'll get.'

'I'm glad. It's very good that Milan wants her now. But –' Thomas smiled, 'I've a rather better opinion of Chaloux's voice than you have, I think.'

'The *voice* is good; and he's been told, very often, that it is; and he's complacent. Also, they tell me that he is uneducated musically—'

'We all were when we began—'

'True. But he came to Italy when Rosa and Chiara did – where is Chiara, by the way? Is she at home?'

'Assunta said not. I believe she went to the sea-shore – to Ostia or somewhere – for the day.'

'Well, I hope she's not striding over those cold beaches at this hour!'

They both laughed.

'Forget her, Tomaso. Go on your way to Germany, and work.'

'What excuses did she give to you for the South American idea?'

'That it would be a long tour in which she would make much money; that she would like the far travelling, and the professional experience; that she would increase her repertory; and that she could continue her studies in sacred music with her *maestro*, Duarte.'

'All plausible enough.'

'Yes.' Giacomo looked weary and puzzled. 'He teaches well,' he said, 'and Chiara has a good voice for sixteenth- and seventeenth-century music. She and Luisa are studying Pergolesi's *Stabat Mater* with him – and she was working on it here the other morning. Have you heard her sing any part of it?'

'No. She has talked to me about it.'

'It is good. It suits her – and she truly likes it.'

'I know.' Thomas looked at his watch.

'Let us finish our wine before you leave,' said Giacomo. 'I commend simplicity in human loves, Tomaso. I commend flight, early flight, from any love which wears a complicated or a shadowy face. I made myself once the victim and the hero – oh, the self-appointed and delighted little hero! – of a – a human situation in which every shade and half-shade of expression or of communication grew to be far more important or oppressive or enigmatic or deplorable than any part of honest physical love need be. Well, I got lost – in an unnecessary forest that grew up and couldn't be cut down. And I played the Spenserian Knight – to no purpose whatsoever, to no one's betterment. A pompous, silly little nobleman I was!'

He lifted his glass and drank slowly.

'I don't like to see you *all* – all, mind you! – indulging yourselves in nerves and sensibility. I know the vanity of such self-wounding – I who speak. Avoid it, I tell you.'

'Thank you, sir. It's late now – are you tired?'

'I am; it's late. But I'll work awhile. The night is quiet for work.'

'Good night, sir.'

'Good night.'

The staircase of the house went steeply down past many irregular landings round a central well of darkness. Occasional gas-jets hissed, and threw greenish light here and there on shallow steps. As he rounded the first corner Thomas saw Clare's fair head and shadowy figure passing along a lower landing. The bent head expressed loneliness to him, even desolation; and looking down he felt as if he eavesdropped on the girl. He stood and waited for her, and when she came to the foot of the last flight of steps he sang softly: 'When he who adores thee . . .'

She looked up; he was shocked, not so much by her green pallor, which perhaps was caused by the bad gaslight, as by the deep accent of weariness, almost of emaciation, on her unprepared, unwary face.

'Ah! Thomas!'

'Rose told me you and Luisa went to the shore for the day.'

She nodded. She stood on the step below him now, and he saw that her eyelids were swollen and red-rimmed, and her cheeks vaguely tear-stained, blotchy. Some wisps of hair blew about her forehead and her neck. He might have said that the outing seemed to have done her little good, but he said nothing. As he looked at her he found himself invaded by distress; he was stupid and silent; also irrationally and sharply in pain. In *her* pain, whatever it is, he thought amazedly. But all he did was to put out a hand under her elbow, to support her; for she seemed as tired as if to fall.

The slight action helped her, perhaps, for at his touch she swayed forward against him and flattened her face against his shoulder. He stood rigid, apprehending with a panic and fear that startled him the suppressed, inheld trembling of her body. All he could do to help the moment and give it naturalness was to try with careful fingers to restore order among the straying wisps of her hair.

She gave a little sigh, and withdrew from him.

'I'm sorry, Thomas,' she half said, and fumbled in her pocket for a handkerchief. But she did not look up at him yet.

'What could we do, Clare? Do you want to talk about whatever it is?'

She looked up then.

'Oh, no, no, no!' she said. 'Oh Thomas, not to you!'

He did not say: yet I am the only one who knows what is the matter. Instead he gave an angry curse and took her in his arms and kissed her mouth. She stayed in the embrace a minute and even he thought that half-wearily she desired to give it back.

'Thank you,' she said then, to his surprise, and looked at him with almost normal composure.

'Would you like to drink wine, Clare? Or eat something?'

She shook her head.

'Sleep,' she said. 'If I could have a long, long sleep – I'd be all right then, I promise.'

He smiled at the childish 'I promise'.

178

'Yes, you'll sleep,' he said, and half-carried her on his arm up to the apartment.

'She's very tired, Assunta. See that she has a good sedative all the same – and make her sleep as long as possible tomorrow.'

Down in Ripetta he walked slowly past the Mausoleum of Augustus. By the bridge at Via Scrofa he leant on the parapet and stared into the river. His mind felt opaque and dead as seemed the water below him. His head ached, but stupidly, heavily; he laid it on his arms and hoped he might sleep where he stood. She'll sleep. She can't not sleep, I'd say. I'd better go and sit somewhere, I suppose – I'd better drink.

He straightened up and considered the brilliant sky. La Lanci, he thought. My God – she'll be starving.

He turned back wearily towards the Corso and Via della Croce.

The Ninth Chapter

Rose stretched herself along her rickety old sofa, across René's knees. Between lamplight and moonlight her beautiful face took variant lines and distortions, puzzling to the boy as he bent above her.

'Our last Sunday together, Rose – until when?'

'Oh dearest! Until soon! Until soon!'

Within three days Rose would be gone from this Roman lodging to Milan, to take her place in the company of La Scala for the opening season. René had secured an engagement for a month at the Valle Theatre in Rome, and afterwards must hope for circuit work in such places as Bologna, Perugia, Parma.

For Rose the honour and the ordeal of La Scala were immense, but were also deserved. That she should face La Scala now was the orthodox thing, in view of the success she had met with so far.

'La Scala *offers*,' stormed little Giacomo, stormed Ferrano. 'All right, refuse! Accept Costanzi's. And La Scala will forget you. Next year there will be others – we always have plenty of good singers. And next year's ones will be younger than you – and so every year they will be younger than you! And by next year Italy will be well used to your voice and will be hearing its faults – you will be no miracle then, if you *do* then get to Milan! Yes, we know your argument about more money at Costanzi's. What do you want? You are doing very well for an unknown Irish girl! But – have a good season at Costanzi's, San Carlo and Carlo Felice – however good, you are still not a real *prima donna*. Not for the world. Sing well, sing truly, truly well one happy night in La Scala, and you are an *assoluta* – you are in the history of opera – and the consequences are as may be! No – you do not refuse La Scala, Rosa. You go there, and you fail or you succeed. If you fail, there is still always the whole *teatro lirico* of Italy which you can serve with honour, and with profit. You are a good singer and now well-trained. You will always be able to earn your living. But this is the moment you must take with courage. You must face La Scala now. You must accept the great honour, and abide by its results.'

The argument was true; Rose had signed the contract. But she feared it. She would have feared it in any circumstances, but now she would have to undertake it in especial loneliness, deprived of the presence and habit of a love which, known only for three months, seemed now as if of always and indispensable as bread. Selfishly she loved René and selfishly would cry and hunger for him. But lovingly too, sisterly, wifely, she would fret to leave him to a vagabond life. She knew that he would fare ill without her; even in his work she feared he would lose courage, lose ground and presence without her. And she knew that for him there was in her going north to hard work and to success, to possible fame which he would not witness or share, an added poison in the knowledge that Antonio de Luca would be of the season's company at La Scala.

'They're all glad we're being parted,' said René.

'Easy for them, love. They're not the ones who're being parted!' She twisted his heavy forelock through her fingers. 'Silky head! We should talk Italian, you know.'

'I couldn't say anything that I mean to you in Italian, Rose. Let us keep French as our private language – will you?'

'Lazy. You'll *have* to work at your Italian—'

'Yes, but I don't want to work when I'm with you.'

'An old grandee in Florence told me that the way to master a language is to make love in it—'

'When I'm making love I only want to master you.'

'You've done that, René.'

'God! I wonder how? They all think I planned it – they think I'm very cunning—'

Rose laughed.

'It was I who planned it, please remember! But anyway, who *are* all these "theys-and-thoses" that you fret about?'

'Oh – everyone. Even today, in things they said, La Lanci and Silvio and Rupetti—'

With some of the now disbanded Argentina company they had spent the day on the high fringes of Lake Nemi and sharing in the traditional wine feast at Marino; and had come home at the quick fall of dark, to take supper alone together at Rose's window. The day in the hills had been exhilarating and lovely, but Rose had more than half forgotten it now in the peace and love-making of the intervening hours.

When she said, however lightly, that she had planned her present relation of love with René, she knew that somewhere in the early inclination towards him that had been true. For a long time she had sought an escape, even a positive barrier, against the strengthening passion of Antonio, but she could most certainly not seek sanctuary with any of the middle-aged or aged worldlings who offered, or would on slight encouragement offer, protection. She needed no protection; she needed love, and that she could only give and take with one of her own kind and age; some unpretentious beginner in life, like herself – someone attractive to her quickened senses. So, almost deliberately, she saw now but had earlier pretended not to see, as she sang with the young, nervous Frenchman through the summer, in *Il Barbiere*, in *La Traviata*, in *I Puritani*, she chose him, and let herself fall in love. And when on the first night of *I Puritani* she had taken René home and seduced him, she had been more in love with their tentative mood, with her own almost generalized desire for love, and with the music which they had sung felicitously together, than with the young man she took to her experimental embrace.

Often in the hardly two months since that audacious night, Rose had smiled, even if for the most part anxiously, at her own rash innocence. Where, she sometimes asked herself now, where did I think I was setting sail for on that crazy night? At any rate not for this – this puzzling, all-accepting surrender, this gratitude and pleasure, so mixed with anxiety, so irritable sometimes, so much in danger of becoming – fussy. Oh, I hadn't foreseen that I'd care in this pedestrian sort of way about an – accidental love, a wandering singer like myself. I hadn't thought that I'd be troubled with his troubles, that I'd care even more for his mistakes and humiliations than for any of my own. It seems I was a fool, she often said to herself. It seems I made a serious mistake. But whereas at first that puzzling and respon- sible-seeming idea used to sadden her, she laughed at it as it grew familiar, and took it contentedly, amusedly even, into her embrace of René. Serves me right, Clare would say, for studying everyday life in the *libretti* of Italian opera.

'What were they saying today that bothered you?'

'Oh, nothing specific, I suppose. But all that general talk about this being the last we'd see of our Rosa, that you'd be famous overnight and soar out of our reach – and all those "farewell" toasts – oh, all directed at me, I know! Just to show me!'

'Truly no, René. They go on like that when *anyone* goes for the first time to Milan. And they know that it's nonsense. It's just an empty sort of tradition – because they know perfectly well that, La Scala or not, we're all always meeting and parting and meeting again in all the opera houses of Italy. René pet, it's a chancy life – and we all just have to live it – and one season in La Scala doesn't mean that one won't be singing in La Valle for the next! Why, Silvio himself has sung in La Scala and in Covent Garden – and he'll sing there again. Meanwhile, he'll do very well in San Carlo this winter – you'll see! You mustn't mind all our wild talk, darling! If you knew Italian better you'd know when we're just putting on the flourishes—'

'Still, Silvio *did* take great trouble to tell me what it would be like singing at La Valle after singing with you. He said he supposed I imagined that other *prime donne* were as generous and co-operative as you. He thought it was amusing that I'd have to begin all over again after having been spoilt—'

'Ah, don't mind that Silvio! He's a vain, mean devil – he grudges you your good looks, my darling. He can sing superbly – but look at him!'

'Yes, indeed, look at him, my God! Still – I know what they all think. But I don't care! I hate them – blasted Italians!'

'Don't say that, René. It's silly, and no good.'

He gave her an obstinate, slow smile.

'Perhaps. But then I'm silly, and no good.'

She kissed him, because she did not like her own contempt for what he had said. She kissed him and lay still in his arms and counted ten.

'It's cold.'

She slid off the sofa, drew over the shutters and latched the big window.

'There was a man selling wood for the stove yesterday, but I didn't buy any, as it's very dear – and I won't be here to burn it.' She moved across the little room and touched the terracotta pillar in the corner. 'I'd been looking forward to lighting it.'

'They're queer things—'

'I love the look of them – yes, smoke if you want to, darling.'

She filled the glasses that stood on the top of the stove.

'Do you like this Capri wine?'

'Well – for Italian wine—'

'I adore it.' She paused before tasting it. 'I wonder if Clare is back from Naples.'

'Did she go there?'

'I told you,' said Rose. 'She went to see Luisa off to South America.'

'Ah that – of course. Does – does Clare dislike me, Rose?'

Her thought had been away from him, and this question bored her just a shade.

'Clare? Of course not, dear.'

'But – I mean, on account of you and me—'

'Oh? Oh, Clare doesn't examine other people's consciences, René. She knows I know what I'm doing – as I'd know of her, whatever she did.'

'But, you're both so – well, so serious, so Irish—'

'Oh, leave it, René, like a good boy—'

'Are you cross with me?'

Rose swept her hair from her forehead, as if to shake away some tangle there.

'Was I? Perhaps for a second. Forgive me, dearest. Look, let's eat these lovely figs . . .' She bit into one. 'I was worried for a minute about Clare. I'm too forgetful – I should have gone round to Ripetta this morning to see if she was back—'

'Why did she want so much to go on that awful South American tour?'

Rose stared at him.

'*Awful* South American tour? René darling, do you ever know what you're talking about? Do you know anything about the conductors who're going – Maioccho, Duarte, Venturi? Have you ever heard Marisi sing or Wallbach or Navaro or La Rietta, or Anna Teller, or our darling Luisa Carriaga? Truly, René – you mustn't talk spiteful nonsense! I know you don't pay enough attention to the world you're working in – but you ought to know by now that all those names *don't* set out together on an *awful* tour!'

'I didn't mean – I just thought—'

'If you don't mean how can you think?' she snapped. 'Listen, René – there's hardly a singer now in Rome who wouldn't have been glad of a place in that company. Oh, Pirazzei is a vulgar man – but he has assembled enough backing to buy all those really good names – and it means six months' secure work and good salaries in a very interesting continent, with almost no expenses – and probably a great deal of fun and fresh experience. Do you know, Pirazzei is taking all the principals for his orchestra, *and* for the chorus! He's not chancing very much about what he'll pick up in Buenos Aires! They're taking their own ballet-master and wardrobe-master – and the whole wardrobe of their repertory. I must admit that if I'd been asked I'd have been inclined to jump at it—'

'You'd never have been allowed to go.'

'I know. And neither would Clare. You see, Clare and I are still bound to little Giacomo's direction, and he'd never dream of letting Clare out of Italy yet – and he's right. It would be a mistake for Clare at present. She hasn't sung – except last year in San Carlo – in any of the great Italian opera houses yet. Any more than I have. It's different for Luisa – she has sung everywhere here, including La Scala. They know her – she's safe. Besides, she's mezzo-soprano, which makes a difference; and she's Spanish, and going to a Spanish continent, and they're going to do a very good production of *Carmen* in Spanish – for her. And she is Duarte's mistress, after all – so, it's all very suitable. But for Clare – oh no, Giacomo's right. I know he's prejudiced against foreign countries and long tours – but he's a great teacher and a great purist—'

'Some people say he's an old fogey, Rose.'

'Sillies. He's getting crotchety, I suppose. But if he likes your singing he'll kill himself for it.'

'Gioia Lanci was saying today that she didn't think he was right to thwart Clare about South America. Didn't you hear her, at lunch?'

'Indeed I did. I couldn't be bothered answering her. Giacomo is Clare's *maestro* after all – and what does Gioia know about it? Besides –' Rose smiled, 'Gioia is the best and straightest woman possible, but she *is* a great friend of Thomas, and no doubt thinks that he'd be a happier man if Clare was out of sight for a good spell—'

'Yes, of course. I think we all thought of that when Gioia was talking.'

Rose felt irritable again, unaccountably irritable and old; her fresh love of this boy was wounded often by a pathetic false worldliness in him which she knew to be of no account but which made him seem fleetingly as if he grimaced.

'I don't suppose your perspicacity bothered Gioia,' she said, and then in shame closed her eyes.

'I'm annoying you, darling,' he said very gently. 'I'd better go home and let you sleep.'

'I'm sorry, René. I don't know why I keep getting cross. Forgive me. Yes, I'd better sleep. But will you get a bus now as far as Panisperna?'

'It's not eleven yet. But anyhow I love the walk—'

Rose, in his arms to kiss him good night, started.

'What is it, love?'

'Listen!'

'I know that my Redeemer liveth . . .' they heard.

'Clare!' Rose cried, and ran to the door.

Clare stood a few steps down at the turn of the staircase, with the *portiera's* sandy cat in her arms.

'I was wondering if I could come in for a while, Rosie?'

'Oh pet – you've been on my mind! I'm delighted . . .'

They returned to the little room, cat and all.

'May he come?'

'Yes – but he won't stay—'

'I suppose I'd better be going, Rose,' said René.

'Oh, not on my account, René,' said Clare. 'I only just came round for a few minutes' company. No, do stay.'

Rose was annoyed that he took this instruction without protest. Clare's eyes were feverishly bright, and Rose was persuaded that she had come to her in a moment of exceptional need – but now, elusive as ever, was taking cover from whatever had been her impulse in this unnecessary cordiality to René. Or perhaps the politeness was forced, and only exercised lest she, Rose, should imagine any censure of her association with the boy. There was no telling with Clare – her reserves were as complicated and sometimes as silly as her affections were true.

'No, René was just going,' she said. 'We've been talking all day and I want to talk to you now, Clare. You don't mind, do you, René?'

He smiled and kissed her hand, bowed to Clare, and moved to the landing.

'Good night, dear one – safe home,' said Rose, and shut the door. Clare sat down, still holding the cat.

'There was no need to send him away, Rosie,' she said.

'Oh yes, there was! I'm going to Milan on Wednesday, and I never see you, simply never, these days, Clarabelle!'

'I know. I'm very glad about Milan, pet. You must be terrified. Are you?'

'Terrified! Ah, but you know! You can imagine! Let's forget it for a minute. Have you had supper?'

'Yes, thank you. Oh, Assunta said to tell you she's bringing some mended things of yours early tomorrow.'

'When did you get back from Naples?'

'Last night. The *Santa Catalina* sailed at about five, and there was a train to Rome at six.'

'I'm sorry I didn't know. You might have liked to come to Marino with us today, for the wine feast.'

'Thank you, pet, but I was tired.'

'You look tired now, you boldie. Drink some wine.' She handed Clare a glass. 'Did you – did you enjoy the few days in Naples?' she asked, feeling unaccountably *gauche* as she spoke.

Clare drank some wine slowly.

'I love Naples,' she said. 'You know, I was there for two weeks – Luisa and I were at the San Carlo – in April last year. It was there we first sang *Orfeo* together.'

'I remember, of course. Anyone singing there last week?'

'No, the house was dark. We were sorry.' She put the little cat down. 'Isn't he a nice fellow, Rosie? What do they call him?'

'He's Ruffo, I think. I'll hate giving up these two ducky little rooms!'

'Ah – it's going to be lonely!' Clare stood and moved about the little room.

'Will you be in Rome, then?'

'Yes. I had it all out with Giacomino this afternoon – and he's very pleased with me now, because I'm doing what he tells me. He kissed the top of my head and said I was a good girl and might yet be a good singer.'

'Dear Giaco! What's he doing with you?'

'I'm going to Costanzi's—'

'Oh good, very good!'

'For two months – until January. The usual lot of *seconda donna* work, which I like – and understudying. And some leading parts to be decided with the director next week.'

'Oh I'm glad, Clare – especially as you love being in Rome; and they pay well at Costanzi's.'

'In January I think I'm going to the Carlo Felice in Genoa; then to Nice, he said – and then to Naples for Easter.'

'Oh, all *very* good engagements, pet! I'm truly delighted.' Rose threw her arms round Clare and kissed her, hugged her; then felt her tremble and tasted sudden salty tears. She leant back from her to search her eyes, and with very gentle hand stroked and gathered up the tears as they ran down the white, embarrassed face.

'What is it, love? Please talk to me, Clarabelle? Please do! *Why* are you so unhappy?'

She pulled her down to the sofa, but Clare jumped up again and paced about.

'Where's the view? May I open the window, Rosie?'

'Of course.'

Clare turned the shutters back and leant out, taking deep breaths.

'Do you remember how we used to like to walk up there in that first summer, Rosie?'

'Often and often I remember. That's why I like this view. Oh, what lost and comic creatures we were then!'

Clare laughed shakily.

'It seems an eternity – doesn't it? – those two years and three months since we were marched into Rome by old Frau Sturz!'

'Handcuffed we were, practically!'

'How slowly time goes!'

'It seems to me to tear along!'

'Oh no! When you think of how much can happen, how positively old you can grow in a little bit of time like two years – the movement of time must really be very slow, to do so much. And it *looks* very slow. Those two years have the look of a lifetime, to me.'

'To me they only look like the beginning of a lifetime! Ah, I grant you we've both changed a lot, and pretty fast – but after all we had to do that, or else go home! We were sent here to be changed, Clare!'

Clare turned and laughed into Rose's eyes, and the latter was glad to see colour and amusement in her face.

'We were indeed! It often makes me wonder – when you think of how uniform and rule-of-thumb everyone is expected to be at home – I mean, why did they pick you and me to be sent off into the unknown and be re-made, re-fashioned altogether – and at their expense?'

Rose chuckled.

'It's very funny; makes me catch my breath sometimes—'

'But seriously – supposing we'd both been left where we were, I'd have left school in Drumcondra and gone to work, in a shop I suppose, or perhaps dressmaking with Auntie Josie – and you, what would you be doing in Lackanashee?'

'Oh, I'd have gone out earning – in Mellick, I suppose. Maybe in a shop, like you!'

'You might have got married very quickly, of course.'

'So might you.'

'Married, me? Oh no. I *might* have gone to be a nun. But anyway, whatever we did, you'd still be Rose Lennane, your exact, born self, the very girl who was sent to France – only you weren't sent. And I'd be Clare Halvey, as sure as I *am* Clare Halvey. But that Rose Lennane and Clare Halvey there at home, our identical twins, wouldn't be recognizable to us now; to us, I mean, who are trying to imagine them, here in Rome at this minute—'

'But that's true about anyone who, well, who was once definitely parted from herself, her obvious self, at any kind of crossroads. Isn't it?'

'I suppose so. Only it's queer to realize that if I'd stayed at home I'd have – well, played, if you like – one specific character called Clare Halvey all my life – and now, because I came to Italy and learnt to sing, I'll play another one – a creature known on programmes as Chiara Alve, but who simply is Clare Halvey.'

'Yes, it's queer. But it's more amusing than queer – and when you expound it like that it may surprise you to hear that I find the whole idea soothing—'

'You mean, it makes it seem easier to waive certain questions that would be immovable at home?'

'Yes, Reverend Mother, you're right. All you're saying makes me feel irresponsible, thank God!'

Clare smiled at her. That sounds happy, she thought. This Rose in love, in first love, does seem to like the new condition. And if the verb 'to like' seemed an odd one here, if one might have expected more wildness, more elation, more fever in a newly and daringly enamoured Rose, perhaps all these were indeed there, burning behind that natural screen of reserve that she accepted in her fellow countrywoman and would wish to have accepted in herself in like circumstances. At least, anyhow, the clear outward sign in Rose of whatever might be the inward mortal grace of physical love was – natural happiness, an ease that might even be called amusing in her handling of a situation which must be entirely novel to her, to put it mildly, and of a kind for which there would have been no room or thought at all in Lackanashee. However, it had long been clear to any in Italy who studied Rose affectionately that she was made for love – for love and singing. And so far, after all, thought Clare, she is only walking round the margins of her two great territories. The real conquests and discoveries are probably out of sight still. And in her choice of first love there was an interesting reflection, Clare thought, of Rose's early skill and native wit about singing. For it had been observed of Rose by many experts and from her earliest ordeals that nothing, no agitation, no underlined instruction, no first-night terror, no shouting vis-à-vis, could get her to force or fuss her singing voice. She could not be made to exaggerate whatever she had to sing. For this she was often in trouble – with bad acoustics, with imperious conductors or uncertain orchestras – and also with her fellow-singers, who knew that whatever else they did they must not drown the *prima*, but who felt, sometimes quite rightly, that they should be allowed to produce from time to time a fair round body of sound. Clare had sometimes thought that Rose a little overdid this ease, this meditative delicacy, in production of notes. But Thomas said that if it was a fault – and he would rather call it just a hall-mark, a signature – it was a fault of genius – a demonstration of musical intelligence which should take her rapidly to the skies.

So here was a parallel to all that, perhaps, in this choice and adaptation of first love.

'I'll sing *forte* when I'm ready, Tonio,' Clare had once heard her say.

'But – when *forte's marked*!' he shouted.

'I sing *my forte* – which is in proportion to my *piano*!'

'But your *piano* is *pianissimo* – it's like mice on the stage!'

'Very like mice on the stage!' said Thomas. 'And it'd be a good thing for opera if we had some more mice on the stage!'

So this *piano* first love, this tender rather than passionate-seeming choice by Rose of someone lonely and young, thin-skinned and poor and beautiful and a little silly in his beginner's vanity – to love this boy, to learn love with him, might have seemed to Rose's instincts the measure of her present power, and to give to all that in her which was tender, generous and outgoing a field of expression for what was at present the hungriest part of her heart. And perhaps she heard it all within her as a prelude, *piano* and gentle, which she could compass now.

'I'll sing *forte* when I'm ready, Tonio.'

Clare bent down to the little cat, who was chewing her shoe-lace, then dropped on her knees to pick him up. As she bent, inside her softly falling white muslin collar Rose saw a narrow, gleaming thread of gold about her neck – a gold chain. Is she wearing her Child of Mary medal in that fancy style now, she wondered idly? And then smiled. She had never seen chain or medal round Clare's neck. Where now would she have got a gold chain? And why?

Clare held the little cat against her throat, and looked about her.

'I wonder if I could afford these rooms when you leave, Rosie? It would only be until the end of December – I go to Genoa in January.'

'Surely you could. As you know – I pay fifteen lire a week. What are they giving you at Costanzi's?'

'Giaco says my fixed wage will be one hundred and thirty lire a week—'

'Very good!'

'And for every leading part I sing the terms will be from forty to sixty lire—'

'Well, you're sure to sing at the very least one lead a week – anyway, for certain you'll sing three a fortnight – so that your salary will be, say, once and a half one hundred and thirty, for sure – say two hundred and twenty lire a week—'

'Less Uncle Matt's third—'

'Yes. You'll have a safe one hundred and forty lire a week, pet! You're catching up fast on me, you boldie! Because La Scala doesn't pay awfully well – and indeed little Giaco is asking Rue des Lauriers to postpone their twenty per cent royalty on me, which falls due the first time I open my mouth on the Milan stage! He hopes they'll wait for that until my general debt is clear.'

'Heavens, yes! I hadn't thought of that! You'd be ruined if the twenty per cent was added to the thirty-three and one-third! I wish the plan was that they took fifty per cent, Rosie, off our debt. It'd be much quicker that way – and after all, we're quite used to being very poor. I don't mind being poor always – but I want to be out of debt. And it's all so slow, my God!'

'No, it isn't. And it'll be speeding up from now on! You'll see!'

'But look. When we started to earn money – I much more uncertainly than you – that's about sixteen months ago? – we owed our people at home over six hundred pounds each. Out of all the work I've done since, Uncle Matt and his friends have only had back about one hundred pounds – and I have managed to save twenty pounds, out of which I shall simply have to buy some warm clothes for this winter—'

'Indeed you must! *Nice* warm clothes, Clare – please, pet!'

Clare laughed.

'Oh, what matter? We'll fight the tramontana anyway!'

'Listen, Clare – you're worrying about money. You don't seem to understand that from now on, since you're opening at Costanzi's, you'll earn a lot of money that we can't reckon on at this moment. How many leads did you sing in an average week this summer?'

'Oh, never less than three – often four. Very welcome, at twenty lire a time. I did quite well – but that was on circuit, Rosie! You know how they work you!'

'They'll work you at Costanzi's, my girl. I'll tell you why. You'll be the youngest and cheapest of their engaged sopranos. They'll find out quickly how good you are, how seriously you work, and how much the Roman public grew to like you last season at La Valle. So – you'll be overworked. And Giaco will overwork you too – with all those sacred concerts and oratorios and Christmas holy singings, that are very well paid, and that you are mad about. No, Clarabelle, stop fussing. By the time you've finished your San Carlo season – next May? – you'll have paid back an awful lot of his money to Uncle Matt – and you'll be beginning on the twenty per cent to Rue des Lauriers.'

'Oh, I hope so. I want to be free!'

'Ah, you crazy Clare – you are free! You're the most insistently free character I've ever met. What will you be singing at Costanzi's?'

'I don't know yet. The operas scheduled, as far as Giaco knew, are *Don Giovanni, The Magic Flute, Idomeneo, L'Elisir d'Amore, Norma, The Barber, Lucia, Faust,* and *Don Carlos.* Shall I be understudying *all* the soprano parts in all of those works?'

They laughed.

'I expect you will,' said Rose. 'They'll make you earn your one hundred and thirty lire, my love!'

'As well as all the *seconde donne?* It'll exercise me, Rosie – this Roman season! Oh, I'd better take these little rooms if I can get them. I'll need peace.'

Clare paced about, looking at the room with attention.

'You'll get them. I've only to tell the *portiera.* The thing is that you have to buy lamp oil and candles, and oil for that dangerous cooking-stove on the landing – and you'll have to buy wood for the stove. But the *portiera* will see to all of that for you – she has a cousin somewhere in the Campagna who brings everything in very cheap on his cart. And he really is an honest little man. She'll get you good wine and cooking oil too, cheaper than you can get them. If you tip her well every Saturday, she'll save you bother and money. And you can get all your food in the Campo di Fiori, and it's a thousand times cheaper to eat at home—'

Clare said: 'May we have more wine? This is from Velletri? I could get rooms in Trastevere for ten lire—'

'But, Clare – how would you ever get home from Costanzi's? Have you an adorer with a carriage and pair? Mind you, from here it's far enough, but the walk wouldn't kill you if you missed the last bus—'

'I'm at the river here. Trastevere is only another five minutes' walk.'

'Too much – and not suitable. Late at night it wouldn't do, Clare.'

'Paddy's rooms are very nice – monastic. I could get rooms like them, he says—'

'Of course, he says! And would you have a minute's peace if you lived in his neighbourhood? Paddy! What are you going to do about him?'

'Why should I have to do anything about him?'

'But – he's mad about you – and that awful priest *manqué* thing is frightful. It can get unmanageable, you know. Oh, I think Paddy made a great mistake when he left the Irish College. He'll never be anything else but a priest – and he imposes his emotional madness on your sympathy – *and* engages all that's most rigid and awkward in you. You like him!'

'Yes, I do like Paddy. I thought you did.'

'Oh, he was all right, and touching – until he began to get bossy and emotional about you. But he's not good for you any more – he's bad, in fact. I didn't mind about him – I thought he was just a sort of home-figure, someone you had to be kind to because he spoke our language and was going through a hard period – and after all, there was always Thomas, Thomas the enchanter, so much more than a match for poor Paddy. But then . . .' Rose paused and reflected. She was seeking now for information, and felt mean, although her wish to know something of Clare's present state was only a need of pure love. Throughout this long and pleasant conversation she had been aware of Clare's absence – an absence not even colourless, but vividly accented while some automaton spoke for her. Playing with the cat, walking, moving, considering the room, considering the view, Clare had been excellently herself, and not present at all.

'Then what?'

'Well – then there was Duarte – and I could see Thomas getting upset about *his* influence on you. And I – oh, I don't know, Clare – but I felt somehow the same priest *manqué* thing in him that's in Paddy. And it frightened me for you. However – forgive me, pet – you were hurt about Luisa and him. God knows why, Clarabelle. Oh – I shouldn't be saying any of this—'

'No. You shouldn't—'

Clare leant out of the window and began to sing: '*E quest' asilo ameno* . . .'

But then her head went down into her hands and she began to cry and to shake all through her body. Rose ran to her and drew her into the room and to the sofa.

'What is it? What's the matter, love?'

Clare sobbed and shook, then suddenly grew still.

'No more. Forgive me, Rosie. Can I stay here tonight? I'm a bit lonely. Can I sleep on this sofa?'

'Duckie – can't you sleep in a proper bed with me? Or have you got too grand for that?'

Clare laughed.

'I haven't got grand at all, Rosie.' She got up and went again to the window. 'It seems a calm night.'

The *Santa Catalina* was abroad on quiet waters. Clare fingered the thin gold chain about her neck.

The Tenth Chapter

Clare put another log, grudgingly, into the terracotta stove.

'It's all very well, Ruffo,' she said to the little cat, 'but it burns up terribly fast. And you know what it costs!'

She returned to the letter she was writing, Ruffo in her arms.

. . . tonight I wasn't singing. It was *The Magic Flute,* and I am understudying Pamina, Papagena and the Queen of Night. Great anxiety! Next Tuesday I shall be singing the Queen of Night. It is as Rosie told me – they work us very hard. As well as singing *seconde donne* all the time, and rehearsing (as understudy) for two hours every day, I have sung the leading soprano part four times in a fortnight. Well – I've told you all about those – but it's hard work, keeping ready on all the understudy parts. And it leaves no time for dutiful expansion of the repertory. The money earned is consoling, of course – because it must please the people at home. And I told you about my extravagant purchases – my great heavy black cloak and fur-lined hood and muff and gloves – they are all one, black frieze and grey-white rabbit fur, and they protect me. So luxurious are they, they seem to protect me, not only from the Roman weather but also from the crude truth about myself. Anyway, for good or ill they cover me from top to toe on bitter nights, and I do not understand my title to such luxury. I can only pacify myself by remembering that at least I paid for it with a lot of tedious singing. You will frown on that. You think that singing must not be tedious to a singer. And I agree that singing – as an idea – is not tedious. But operatic singing – being confined to it, I mean – can be tedious. Oh, is constantly tedious! I am getting used to your not being in Italy –

that is, I don't cry any more at awkward moments. I've learnt to cry in bed. I've posted a letter every second day since the *Santa Catalina* sailed, so the Poste Restante at Buenos Aires will be getting to know you! And I, with any luck, should have a letter from you tomorrow at Ripetta. But by now of course, you must have this other address. I'm glad I took on these rooms of Rosie's. Having two rooms all to oneself is marvellous to such as me – and the beginning of adult life. Not that I count all that such a wonder – but merely it's a fact – and one has to be an adult. My grandmother wrote to me – she writes seldom, because her hands are very rheumatic – she wrote to say that she did not hope to see me again, but that she would be glad if she did, and that often when she was asleep she thought she heard me singing 'My Redeemer liveth . . .' and she told Father Ruane about that, and he said he wished he could sleep with her. Naturally no one at home even thought to smile at that unconscious, gracious joke. I don't know how it is in Spain – but in Ireland priests are good and boyish. Ah, but Grandmother is wrong! I'll see her again. Please God! If I could only get my debt much more reduced, so that I could feel it decent to ask for leave to go home for a few weeks! But both Rose and I feel prisoners to our debt, and unwilling to ask to be allowed to add to it. So, we can't go home. But I am going to slave between now and next June. I don't care what number of leads I sing, however badly; and I don't care how many oratorios and *lieder* recitals I scrape through – I'm going home to Ballykerin in June, I'm going to Grandmother. I'm going to sing whatever she wants to hear. And you'll come with me? Will you?

Your chain is round my neck. My left hand is touching it even as I write. 'I'm not giving it,' you said, when you put it round my neck. 'I'm only pledging it. It must be there when I come back.' I remember your staring, tired eyes. It'll be there. Oh, when I'm screeching away, as some mad heroine or some extremely grand, *décolletée* worldling, it can't be where you put it, darling, your lovely chain. But it's on my faithful person always somewhere concealed, be sure. And when you come to claim it, it'll be round my neck, as you placed it. I promise you.

It's very late – and a cold night. Ruffo thinks I should be more liberal with wood on the stove – but truly I have to be mean about such things. I like these rooms, as I've told you. I often have Rose's lonely René in to supper. I like him more than the Italians do, and he really does sing well. Rose is very busy and anxious in Milan – but hasn't sung anything yet – even a *seconda*. She's been taken very much in charge by the great *maestro*, Faccio – and I think they are going to make an occasion of her first appearance. In what I don't know, and her infrequent notes give me no information other than that she is overworked and very frightened.

Rome is lonely, but I love these rooms. If they weren't killing me with rehearsals at Costanzi's I'd get to know something at last about this city, since I have none of you here any more to keep me talking and arguing in cafés. Ah, how I miss you all! Rosie in Milan, you a whole ocean away, Thomas in Leipzig – and Antonio also, by the way, in Milan, to Mariana's great annoyance, she having practically signed him on with the Berlin State Opera with herself. However, he got out of that, quite dishonourably I think – and intends to establish himself at La Scala. He was in Rome on Sunday and I dined with him – and he told me that he intended to sing Don Giovanni to Rosie's Zerlina this season. Of course, he's only talking. Still, it might happen. La Scala *have* engaged him; and Don Giovanni is his mania. Also, he was full of rumours about *Otello*. He says that Rose is almost certainly going to be given Desdemona to sing this season – and he intends to sing Iago on that night. What do you think of all these hopes, you so far away? For myself – you'll hear, as you know, my doings. Nothing marvellous will happen – I can't imagine what could. I shall do my routine singing – there will be no Pergolesi, no Monteverdi, no Vittoria, no Haydn, no Glück – and no easy, blessed Tom Moore to rest me, and to please you.

Darling, good night now, I must fold up this letter, dull as it is, and say good-bye for a little time. Surely you are safe by now in Buenos Aires? When can I expect to hear from you? When do you open? What is the list? Think of me, love – pray for me. Remember my loneliness. Oh, remember, love, that I love you. Six months aren't impossible, as you said. Indeed they aren't. I can wait most happily for six months – and one is gone already!

Oh sweet, remember! Do you remember?

God bless you,

Clare

Clare picked up a large, foreign-weight envelope, and addressed it carefully and very clearly. She folded the many sheets of her letter and put them into the addressed envelope. She looked about then on her desk for sealing-wax and seal.

There was a gentle knock on the sitting-room door. It might be Assunta with some belated kindness, or it might be the *portiera* about this or that.

'Come in,' Clare said.

Thomas came in, and came and stood beside her writing-table before she had time to stand up.

She was delighted to see him.

'But – you are in Leipzig?'

'I am. Except – wait till you hear.'

Coolly he bent down and read aloud the address on the big, foreign-weight envelope. 'La Señorita Luisa Carriaga, Poste Restante, Buenos Aires.'

'Do you write to her every day, Clare?'

'As nearly as I can.'

'Is she in love with you?'

'I think so.'

'Do you love her?'

'Yes, Thomas.'

He moved about the room.

'Do you mind if I eat some of this bread?'

'I've got good cheese – wait a minute.'

She ran out to the cupboard on the landing, and came back with arms full of food. She put things down on the table, figs and cheese and butter and bread, and filled up glasses with Frascati.

They lifted their two glasses then and drank. He looked about the room eagerly, and she considered gravely his white and hungry face.

'People shouldn't be able to walk in on you as I did now. Don't you lock your door?'

'Oh yes. I forgot to. But who'd walk in?'

'Seminarists, or any other kind of lusting maniacs.'

'Poor Paddy!'

'Poor Paddy indeed! No, you should lock your door. You're very lonely up here.'

'Yes, thank God. How white, how exhausted you look, Thomas! Are you ill?'

'No. I was well, and terribly excited, until a minute ago.' He flicked a glance towards the letter on the table, and then looked hungrily at her. 'Oh, it's warm here, Clare! I'm glad I found you.'

He spread his hands out over the top of the stove.

'Were you travelling all day? When did you get to Rome?'

'Hardly an hour ago. I flung my bag into my old lodging in Via Torino – you know? – and then walked on here.'

'You haven't dined? Oh Thomas – wait a minute! Would an omelette do? And coffee? Heavens, your hands are cold! Put some wood in the stove, will you – and I'll start up the old demon cooker on the landing.'

She was glad to have something to do in a hurry. She knelt beside the cooking stove and lit it cautiously.

'Sit down, Thomas,' she called back to him, 'you must be dead tired.'

'Can't I break the eggs?'

'Ah, no! Rest. I won't be a minute.'

The omelette was good. So was the coffee.

Thomas savoured carefully the sad pleasure that invaded him within the little shabby, cut-off room. It was square and silent; soldierly clean and neat, and warmly closed against great Rome outside and the *tramontana*. The little red cat washed himself; the terracotta stove grunted; the white china globe of the lamp on the table was a private domestic moon.

Thomas ate gratefully. What am I to do about this intolerable girl? He drank a long throatful of coffee. He looked up at her then and smiled.

'You're good at life, Clare,' he said. 'It's strange – but you're good at all this –' He indicated the wine, his plate and the little cat. 'I looked for flowers when I was coming here. I even deviated as far as the Spanish Steps – but the night is too cold; there were none to be found.'

'Thank you, Thomas. Get me some tomorrow, will you? I'm always resisting them in the Campo di Fiori, where I do my shopping.'

'You're quite Roman now?'

'Well – you have to be Roman in Rome ... Why are you here, Thomas? Are you too tired to tell me? Has anything gone wrong at Leipzig?'

'No indeed. Things are going well – and I've been working like blazes. Sometimes I work so hard that for days I forget your name – let alone your face. And I like being back in Leipzig. German music people are serious and severe – they exact every ounce you have, and they will not be fooled. *Most* satisfactory.'

'I'm glad.' Clare changed his plate. 'Eat some cheese, some fruit.'

'Thank you, I will. I couldn't be bothered to eat on the train – just kept drinking wine with soldiers and their girls.'

He began to look happier as he ate.

'You had a birthday lately, Chiara?'

She smiled in surprise.

'About three weeks ago—'

'On the second of November. You were twenty.'

'Yes. All Souls' Day.'

'I was conducting Mozart's *Requiem* with a class in the Konservatorium that morning, and in the middle of it I thought of you. But it was too late to send my wishes then.'

'I wish you had sent them!'

'Do you? Well, that very afternoon by chance I saw a bauble in a dirty old shop. But it pleased me – it reminded me of you. Will you take it – with my love?' He took a little box from his pocket and held it out to her with an anxious look. 'I know that a gentleman never offers a young lady anything other than roses or bonbons – or his arm! But then I'm not a gentleman.'

Out of the cottonwool in the box Clare lifted a thin bracelet made of oval-cut aquamarines, loosely linked together in thin gold. It was simple and lovely. She let it hang across her hand; the lamplight made it seem like drops of seawater.

'When I saw it it reminded me of three things,' Thomas said. 'Of your eyes, of your maddening chastity, and of the music that you sing best.'

'Well, it's like music, anyway – oh Thomas, don't give it to me! I don't deserve it at all. I'm always hurting you, and being a bore – oh, it's exquisite!'

He laughed.

'I have given it to you. And you're not a bore.'

She came round the table to him.

'Put it on my hand then, will you?'

He took her wrist and turned the bracelet over.

'It's no great marvel,' he said, 'but it's simple – and it struck me as a thing you *might* consent to wear.'

He found the catch and clipped the bracelet on. They both looked down at it.

'Oh Thomas, why should you remember my birthday, let alone bring me this lovely present?'

He kissed her fingers and let them fall away.

'Why this? Why that? Oh God!' He stood up. 'Do you mind if I smoke?'

'Of course not.' Clare put more wood into the stove.

'It smells deliciously,' said Thomas.

'It's olive-wood from the Campagna. Imagine, there are olive trees still fruiting in the Sabines that were planted before the birth of Our Lord.'

'Have you ever been up to where Horace's farm was? I'd like to take you there, in the right weather.' He refilled his coffee-cup and looked about the room with affection. 'Crammed little place – touching – all these household goods of some unknown one! How do you fit in?'

'Happily. I'm attached to all these plaques and carvings and draperies. Although they're very Italian I find them homely, in their ugliness.'

'Yes; it's an innocent, nice room. That low-reliefed gypsy over there –' he pointed with his cigarette – 'he's vigorous! He'll convert you yet! Look out. Have you another room?'

'Through there – my bedroom. The exact same shape and kind; with a lovely picture of the infant Mozart, I thank you! Complete with his little violin, and Nannerl and the lapdog.'

'May I see it?'

'Yes, indeed!'

She took the table lamp and opened the door to the bedroom.

'No stove in here. You see, there he is!'

'And over your bedhead, no less! A most encouraging little dandy. There was a feeble little song he was supposed to have composed when he was this age—'

'I think I sang it in a play at school,' said Clare.

'You played the character of Mozart at school?'

'Yes. In an idiotic playlet by an Austrian nun in the convent.'

'How did your song go?'

'It isn't *echter* Mozart, Thomas. *Trage du,*' she sang, '*auf deinen Schwingen, O Musik, mich weit von hier! Lass' mich weinen, lass' mich* . . . Oh, I forget!'

Thomas roared with delight.

'*Da capo* . . . *Trage du, auf deinen Schwingen!* Oh, infant Mozart! How ravishing you were, with your silly song!'

'Mind the lamp,' said Clare, as he flung his arm round her.

'I'm minding it. Give it to me!'

'It's cold in here. Let's go back to the stove!'

But he examined the room.

'Orderly. I like that, though. It's like the way you sing. You're right, it's cold. Do you wash in this room?'

She laughed.

'Where else? Look at this splendid washstand! I heat water on the contraption on the landing.'

'Oo-oh! I hope you have a warm dressing-gown!' He was still marching round the little room, Clare on his right arm, the lamp held high in his left hand. 'Your too-loud clock. A clothes-brush. Your mirror. Do you ever really look in the mirror, Clare?'

'I'm not a great one for that—'

'You should be. The pastime might cheer you up. Ah, what are the *livres du chevet*?'

'They change.'

'I imagine so. Leopardi – difficult, isn't he? *L'Education Sentimentale* – I want to read that. *Fumée*. Ah, good girl! Turgenev will be very good for you. *Middlemarch – Wunderbar*.'

'I'm in the thick of that,' said Clare.

'"In the thick" is a fair description. No photographs of the family, Clare?'

'No. There aren't any. Father has a faded one of Mother that I'd like to have copied – but of course no one ever thought of reproducing Grandmother's face. I wish I knew someone who could draw her. She'll be dead soon – and then . . .'

He put down the lamp and stroked her face.

'You'll be here still. I imagine you're like her. Are you?'

'They say I am. I hope I am.'

'I'm the image of my grandmother – she's dead. She was a witty woman – what you'd call coarse—'

'Well, if *you're* the image of her! But as Rose continues to say that you and I might be twins, perhaps our grandmothers were like twins.'

He cocked his head.

'What's that noise on the stairs? The Seminarist?'

'No.' They moved into the sitting-room, Thomas bearing the lamp. 'It's my poor drunken neighbour coming home to the room at the back.'

'You have a drunkard in the back room? What sex?'

'Male. Well over sixty, a misogynist.'

'Good. Nevertheless, one more sound reason for locking your door in the evenings, Clare!' He strode across and locked it. 'Hate is love, you know, hate covers a multitude of pleasures!' He leant against the door and laughed. 'All the same, I wish the Seminarist had walked in just now – and found us waltzing round your bedroom in embrace!'

'It's not for nothing that you're attached to Italian opera, Thomas! Ah, come and sit down. Let's have some wine.'

'Nothing better. Are we safe?'

'Dead safe.' They drew up their straight-backed chairs to the stove, and Thomas leant over and filled their glasses. 'Anyway,' Clare went on, 'Paddy and I are seriously estranged at present – daggers drawn – about Parnell.'

'Parnell? Ah – there's an Irishman at the Konservatorium, and he gets excited very often about this Parnell—'

'We all get excited about him. I've been interested in him, although I don't like the kind of man he seems to be—'

'What kind?'

'Oh – dully enigmatic, silent, powerful, egotistical – and not brainy. You know, Thomas – the sort of iron man that you couldn't even talk with. A bore, I'd say, in private to you. But he has done marvellous things for Ireland in the House of Commons. Well, anyway – Paddy says that he's having a love-affair with the wife of one of his Party men – Captain O'Shea.'

'That's what Sheedy says, in Leipzig. But what has that to do with Paddy? And where does that scabrous character get his facts?'

Clare smiled.

'Paddy isn't scabrous. But he gets his facts, if you call them facts, from some angry priest in the Irish College. There's rumour of a divorce case. Thomas, I could never explain to you what that could mean in Ireland—'

'I don't care what it means in Ireland. But why has it you and Paddy daggers drawn?'

'Because I say that Parnell's private troubles are his own, and that we accepted his leadership while knowing perfectly well that he wasn't a Catholic – but Paddy blazes and screams that adultery is adultery, and that whatever trouble lies ahead is our own fault for our setting up Parnell as a false god.'

'Paddy's a self-confident fellow.'

'Why do you smile when you say that, Thomas?'

'He defines adultery as adultery. You'll admit that that's what a well-founded ass says.'

Clare laughed.

'We all plunge into fatuities when we're excited, Thomas.'

'God forbid! Oh, lovely Clare, let us cease about this dismal Paddy. I've locked him out. I've locked you in.'

Clare threw more wood into the stove.

'While you're standing up will you fill the glasses, sweet?' said Thomas. 'And then sit down.'

There was silence awhile. Clare moved about, tidying things up. Thomas watched her through half-closed eyes. If I could sleep with her tonight. If I could lie down in her bed and go sound asleep with that girl. She came and stood before him, fingering her bracelet.

'Don't say nonsense – that you're not going to take it, or that you're guilty, or any such bosh. But come here –' he took hold of her and pulled her on to his knee – 'stay there now and explain to me – explain, as you might to Paddy – why you are in love with Luisa.'

'When you drag in Paddy I resent your facetiousness,' Clare said coldly. 'Had I ever to explain my love of Luisa to Paddy, I'd do so in terms that you – an atheist flung out from Baptist chapels – wouldn't understand.'

'Don't imagine that pompous sentence worries me. My advantage with you is that I understood you before you even saw yourself. Paddy will never even see you – let alone understand you. Ah, and I love you, mad one – I love you on any terms you care to make. That's my strength . . .'

Clare kissed his forehead, and got up.

'Sitting on a knee is an absurd position, Thomas.'

'As an opera singer you are used to absurd positions. Speak about love, experienced lover. Tell me of your idea of love.'

'Don't sneer at me, Thomas. We haven't ideas, after all. We are only singers, chancers—'

'You grow up. You'd never have said that when I knew you—'

'When you knew me? What do you mean? Don't I know you now, Thomas?'

'Go on, singer, chancer—'

'My idea of love?'

'Yes.'

'Well, this morning I was working on *Otello*. You remember Gennaro? He's third conductor for this season at Costanzi's, and he's as restless and fussy as yourself. He's mad on *Otello*, which isn't in the Costanzi schedule, but which he hopes to conduct in Genoa or Trieste in the New Year. So – he ropes us all in on study of the text – *con amore*. And I'm interested –

because I think it's going to be Rosie's great part – and because I think it's a superb opera – anti-Verdi as I am.'

'You conceited girl! Continue. We asked for your idea of love.'

'I remember. You did. I think the conclusion of the first act of *Otello* is a pitifully true expression of human passion – I suppose, love?'

'You grow up, Clare.'

'But I think the voices are too much there – I think the orchestra says all that is essential – I think the singers, the two, are very nearly embarrassing – I said to Gennaro this morning – he was using the whole Constanzi orchestra, I don't know how he managed it – that the singers were too much in that expression of love.'

'Gennaro indeed! What did the ass say?'

'He's not an ass. He asked me to repeat what I'd said—'

'And then?'

'Then he laughed, and said I'd never be any good in Verdi.'

'He's not such an ass as I thought,' said Thomas. 'All the same, I'm an optimist, and I think you'll yet sing Verdi. But as to your too-clever nonsense about the voices overstating the case in the first act – that's what you mean, Clare? – you are hopelessly wrong.'

'I daresay I am. Verdi wrote it for voices—'

'Exactly. It's dramatic music – it's about two specific people – two characters. It's not about your ideas or emotions any more than it's about mine. It's strictly a presentation – that first act – of the private, personal passion of Otello and Desdemona.'

'All I meant was that the orchestra says it for me, and that the singers are – well, an interruption.'

Thomas drank a draught of wine.

'I can't understand that split in you.'

'Split? How do you mean, Thomas?'

'I mean, pet – sit down, don't look so furious – I mean, this unlucky *schwärm* you have for Luisa—'

'*Schwärm?*'

'Don't get cross. Wait. *Schwärm* is a good German word – *Schwärmerei* – for the manias girls get for each other or for their teachers – in school age. Your development has been delayed, and you are having a *schwärm* now for Luisa—'

'Oh Thomas, stop! Please stop. How dare you? Because I told you truly that I love Luisa you must not bring your clever talk against something you know nothing about.'

'No clever talk. Sit down.'

'Here I sit down. What now?'

'I know plenty about love, Clare.'

'In some ways you may, Thomas. And I have observed you, and I know your actions – but I appreciate your good manners. Still – I think you are amoral.'

'Amoral? But you, Clare? I take you to be serious and grown-up, in your own conception, when you say you are in love with Luisa?'

'Yes – Thomas.'

'Then – you are totally amoral.'

'No. I am, I suppose, a sinner – certainly I am a sinner in the argument of my Church. But so would I be if I were your lover. So is Rose a sinner – and she knows it – in reference to our education and faith. You, who come out of Baptist chapels, don't know how clear our instruction is. Rose and I know perfectly well what we're doing. We are so well instructed that we can decide for ourselves. There's no vagueness in Catholic instruction.'

'But there's a lot of disturbance.'

'That sounds witty. What disturbance have you encountered?'

'Well, love – the disturbance *you* create.'

Clare stood up. Standing she looked down on the weary, dusty young man whom she liked greatly, and to whose vivid intelligence and friendship she owed so much.

'Thomas, I've learnt fast – so has Rose – in two years of Italian life. You can argue as you like against my loving Luisa. But I can argue back all your unbridled sins. We all know the Christian rule – and every indulgence of the flesh which does not conform to it is wrong. All right. We are all sinners. You and I and Rose and Tonio and René and Mariana – and all our friends.' She ran her hand across her forehead, and the aquamarines on her wrist flashed like tears.

Thomas looked at her lovingly, and held up his glass to be filled.

'No, Clare,' he said. 'It's wrong for you to love Luisa.'

'Don't be bossy. Explain love a bit, will you, Thomas?'

He looked at her again, because her voice shook. She was crying. He put up his arms and took her down to him with the glass she offered.

'Do you really want me to explain love to you, Clare?'

She nodded.

'For me, explanation begins with my love of you. But that isn't good for argument—'

'No good.'

'Yet that is all any of us will know of it. Read the texts – Plato, Ovid, Stendhal – no good. When it's of love we think, Clare, we're alone with it.'

'That's just possibly not accurate—'

He smiled, almost as if delighted.

'"Just possibly." I suppose most human hopes have lain in that clever phrase of yours—'

Clare got up from his knees again, and walked about the little room.

'Human hopes, do you think?' She smiled at Thomas. 'I'd give ordinary human hopes more hope than that, Thomas. I was thinking of energy, imagination. The people who live on those things are only a few, after all – and they seem to know what you mean about being alone when they – when they are in love.'

He tasted the dry wine slowly.

'But what do you mean, then?'

'Oh, wait a minute! Where are we? I think I mean that that phrase – what did you call it? – that "clever" phrase of mine, that "just possibly" extends them sometimes, and makes them able to bear love, and look at it quietly even in themselves – and so it makes them write poems, I suppose, and operas—'

'Makes them sing?'

'Yes. I think so.'

'So do I.'

Clare picked up the little cat.

'All I meant was that it's silly to say romantically that when we think of love we are alone with it. Love comes from a source, and that source is its object. Ah, love is reasonable, Ruffo! If only it were a lot of operatic *cadenze*, for showing off!'

'I can hardly believe my ears!'

'Perhaps neither can I,' said Clare. 'Yet I've been listening to mine for a long time, Thomas.'

'Since you first sang in Orfeo in San Carlo, I suppose?' he said angrily.

'Since before that. Since long ago. Almost since Paris, I think.'

Thomas stood up.

'Great Christ! Oh Christ, you – you beast! You pale, self-loving ass! You – you stinking lily, you!'

Clare leant back against the wall.

'I'm anything you like,' she said, 'but I'm not a stinking lily. Take that back.'

'I don't think I'll take it back.'

'All right. But it's a disgusting idea. And it's a lie.'

He came to her and took her hands which were about the little, purring cat.

'It is disgusting. Oh Clare, can't you help me?'

'It's you who were to help *me* always, great Thomas. I often wanted you to, and not a word out of you—'

'I was afraid to speak. Come, pet – that stove needs more wood . . .'

They filled the stove.

'Proportionately, I'd say that this stove is a more serious drain on my economy than I am on Uncle Matt's.'

'Be sure it is. I'll buy you a cart of olive wood tomorrow.'

'No, dear brother. Buy me a few flowers.'

'Come and buy them with me in the morning.'

'I will. You know, Thomas, I see now some explanation of the tendency of my race – the Irish, I mean – to become nuns and priests.'

'You do? You – abandoned to sin?'

'I'm not abandoned to sin.'

'No?'

'No. But many imaginations are too extended to passion.

The Irish imagination is a bit lopsided, maybe. Anyway, it isn't at all like the Latin – we are *alarmed* by the power and stretch of feeling – oh, believe me, Thomas, we are! We don't find it at all amusing to be in love – that's why we are so awkward. We are not Mediterranean.'

'I see that. I'm not Mediterranean. But love isn't the secret of this bloody old Mediterranean, for God's sake! I don't love you just because we're knocking around in Rome – Clare, I can make love anywhere. You're right about that, darling. Still, come day, go day, I love you.'

'Thomas, you are strong. And indeed I know that you're weak too. Listen to me now. Oh no – don't kiss me.'

'I'll kiss you. I insist.'

'Ah no. I'm so lonely that nothing would be easier on this earth than to kiss you, dear Thomas. Oh, I can't bear it, I can't bear it!'

'What can't you bear?'

'Her being so far away.'

'She's probably in Duarte's arms at this minute.'

'That's what I said. She is far away. Oh! What am I to do?'

Thomas stood and stared at the bent head.

'Yes, she's far away. You ask *me* what to do?'

Clare looked up and laughed.

'Sit down. I am to be calm?'

'Yes – calm.'

'Are you calm?'

'No.'

'Could I smoke a cigar? I've got some filthy Swiss cigars that I bought off a soldier in the train.'

Clare smiled.

'He was in love, poor fellow, with the awful trollop he was travelling with. He didn't want his cigars. He only wanted her.'

'You make him sound like a happy man.'

'You think that to be in a state of lust is to be happy?'

'No. But she was with him – so he didn't want his cigars. That's to be happy.'

'Yes. You know.'

The little cat climbed up his knee.

'Oh Clare – I'm speaking out of prejudice, I know – but why this awful mistake? Why Luisa?'

'Is to love a mistake – in the end, I mean, Thomas? It can be awkward. It can be silly. But is it really a mistake – to love another person?'

'Definitely it can be. What do you want – with Luisa? What can you get? What do you want?'

'Only her. Only the one I love.'

Thomas lifted up the little cat and stared into its face.

'What is love, then? Two silly girls kissing each other? Is that love?'

'Maybe. I find it to be love.'

'Oh Clare – how all this torture heaps up love! What are we to do? Where am I to bury you, you unnatural, appalling one?'

'You can't bury me until I'm dead. But why am I unnatural or appalling? Consider your own career.'

'Darling, I'm a man.'

'I didn't think you'd be so stupid as to say that.'

'Nor did I. See how you degrade me! Stop striding!'

Clare leant against the window.

'Easily I might have loved you,' she said. 'But – *she* caught my heart before I knew what was happening, Thomas. And I think she's lovely, and I love her. I can't help it. It's true.'

'She isn't even faithful to you.'

'I know.'

'If you were a man you couldn't endure that.'

'No. Men, as you call them, don't seem to be able to endure things. I don't know what sex you suppose me to belong to, but I can endure Luisa's life. I love her, you see.'

'She's promiscuous. She's a whore.'

'Maybe. It may be for that alarming honesty that I love her.'

'Then you know more than I do about love.'

'You've never been in love, Thomas—'

'I'm in love with you—'

'Only since you discovered you can't get me—'

'I set out to get you the first day I saw you in Ripetta—'

'Did you? Still, I have this notion that you're wise and kind. Are you?'

'Wise maybe. Not kind. Love isn't kind. It's love – a firm, acquisitive excitement. Your falling in love so oddly has misled you about love, Clare. Be careful. Such a huge blunder must affect your work.'

'Oh – but love shows me how to sing the greatest imbecilities! I assure you I can sing the most lunatic ladies with understanding now!'

'Why?'

'Because I've lost my bearings, I suppose, like all those cracked sopranos! So I sing them patiently, Thomas.'

'That's amusing – but it won't make you into an *assoluta*. You must never sing any soprano *patiently*.'

'No? They can be sung that way.'

'They can't. You must either sing Verdi as he means you to, or else shut up.'

'Rose sings every part exactly as she feels her way along it – she doesn't care what the composer wanted.'

'And that is damned impertinent of her! – and she only gets it through so far because of the accidental perfection of her singing. You wouldn't do it yourself. You are too musicianly, too pure.'

'A minute ago I was a stinking lily.'

'In a different context, love.' He closed his eyes. Oh quietly, quietly, he said to his shocked and self-pitying breast. You have known this for ages. Does it matter if one obscure Irish singer is at sea and mad? 'What news out of Milan?'

'Veiled and – oh, pregnant of great things. I dined with Antonio on Sunday.'

'But . . . ?'

'Yes – he's on the Scala rota, but they're mostly lending him around at present. He was on his way to Naples to sing *Rigoletto*, and I've forgotten what else. They've already lent him to Genoa and Turin.'

'Mariana'd be obliged if they lent him to Berlin—'

'Yes, poor Mariana! He treats her badly.'

'He'll always treat women badly. He can't help it.'

'Rose, too?'

'Oh, he might murder Rose. After all, she has really made him suffer—'

'Suffer? I think that suffering is a worse thing, I mean a more positive thing, Thomas – than just not getting what you only half want.'

'That's a hard saying about Tonio. But it's true. Still, he's insane about Rose, in his way. And she's not insane about René. Really, you Irishwomen have a hideous gift for confounding simple issues. What is Rose up to?'

'Nothing. She's finding her way on queer roads. She's as good as gold.'

'She's our star, and she's going to shine! She's Giacomino's chief glory out of our year—'

'Yes – he calls us a vintage year, Thomas—'

'Ripetta 'eighty-seven – he's right. We were five good ones. And she's the best, so far. Rosa d'Irlanda! Drink to her, Clare!'

They drank and smiled.

'Poor Giaco – I must go and talk to him. Things the same there?'

'The same, in deep decline. And he hates his current year—'

'I know. How is "Casta Diva"?'

'Ah, dreadful, God help her. But forever amusing. She said to me the other day that when she listens to the practice-sounds of this year's lot she wonders why there is not an equivalent castration operation for the *vocal* organs! And then she began to cry, and she sang Schumann's *Widmung*, and told me all about Schumann—'

Thomas laughed.

'And then you wouldn't refill her glass, and Assunta came in and she threw the bottle at her.'

'More or less. Why are you in Rome, Thomas?'

'I'm not going to tell you tonight—'

'Why? Are you in trouble?'

'On the contrary. I'm being a remarkable success. There are some people we want in Leipzig and Dresden and Berlin – and I've been listened to, to my astonishment.'

She raised suspicious eyes to his.

'No more of it, Clare. You'll be hearing. Have you come across the young man Toscanini, by any chance?'

'No. I've heard Gennaro cursing and blasting about him, of course.'

'Oh, I don't want him – to blazes with the little chicken! But while I'm in Italy I'd be interested to observe his work.'

'Could you have conducted *Aída* at a second's notice, do you think?'

'I hope so. Couldn't you go on and sing *Aída* at a moment's notice?'

'I could. But that's not the same thing as to *conduct* the *opera*. And after all, I'm an experienced understudy of all those parts by now. He was only playing in the second 'cellos—'

'Oh, it was a great *tour de force*. Don't imagine I'm jealous!' They both laughed. 'Still, he's three years younger than me, the little bastard! I'd just like to see how he's shaping nowadays. Oh never mind! It's a pity the shutters are shut. I like the Roman night, don't you? I'm glad to be back in Rome.'

'I'll open the shutters, Thomas. Yes, I like the Roman night. Oh, look at the stars—'

They stood together at the window in the cold air. Brilliantly the jewelled sky smiled. The noise of human life which does not cease in Rome came up, and so did the smell of frying oil, of burning chestnuts. So came the cough and jingle of horse-cabs, and the nearby twang of an out-of-tune mandolin.

'*Gia nella notte densa . . .*' Thomas sang.

Clare smiled at him.

'What a beautiful G flat,' she said.

'From the vocal music that you think unnecessary at the end of Act I, *Otello*, Verdi.'

'I know it, *maestro*. I wonder why you're insisting on being a conductor, Thomas? Your voice is strange and pure. It's not like Italian singing at all – it's linear, geometrical somehow. If you weren't very careful you'd sing sharp.'

He laughed.

'The point is that I *am* very careful. And my voice is Welsh.'

'Why have you forsaken it?'

'Because the field of music is so wide. And I only sing well because I understand singing. The organ is unremarkable. Think of Tamagno!'

'Ah, but he's a freak! He's almost a soprano.'

'True enough. Still, I'm a musician more than I'd ever be a singer. Tonio will be a great singer, I think – but he's hardly to be called musically gifted!'

'Oh you mean, conceited fellow!'

She leant out over the cold night of Rome. She did not know the hour. Morning might not be far off. She thought of her grandmother. Grandmother would be waking now. She slept early, and woke before the last stars died. Then she always prayed for her dearest. *Before I get up in the dark mornings I always say a good long prayer for you, my darling Clare. I always ask God to mind you for me then. The early morning is a solemn time, and I worry when I think that soon I won't be there to say a prayer for you when it comes round. Well, as long as I can I'll say it, love.* That she had written in her birthday letter. Clare let the words flow through her spirit now.

'*Gia nella notte densa . . .*' Thomas sang again.

'Go on. If you get to "*Vien questo immenso amor!*" I'll try to come in—'

They sang through the great passage.

'*. . . E tu m'amavi per le mei sventure*
Ed io t'amavo per la tua pieta . . .'

Clare smiled, and waited in delight for '*Disperda il ciel . . .*' They leant together into the cold night.

'*Tarda e la notte . . .*' sang Desdemona.

'*Vien . . . Venere splende . . .*'

'*Bis, bis, bravissimo,*' yelled the gentleman on the next balcony.

'*Bravissimo!*' yelled someone from under the trees below.

The Eleventh Chapter

Thomas wandered uncertainly about the great, overlighted house. He had a roving pass, and could not yet decide where he would sit to listen. This was not an announced gala night of La Scala – but even one with less experience of Europe's opera houses than he might catch the anxiety, the curiosity which undershot the general approach to the conventionally proffered programme.

As usual in La Scala, there were too many flowers, there was too much fuss. Too many rich people, too many diamonds and loud voices. Yet why all this social brilliance tonight? He acknowledged as he moved in ill-temper through the over-perfumed and self-confident crowds that the commotion meant that lovers of opera, lovers of the human voice – dreadful though they might seem as he pressed about among them – were here with their inexplicable wits on edge tonight, to listen attentively to a new singer.

And – absurd as they might look as they swarmed in from all the world, from Berlin and New York, from London, Rome and Rio – Thomas knew that once Faccio mounted the podium they would fall still, lose their individual vulgarities a while, and simply and mercilessly listen. For that he forgave them their immediate and outward selves.

Clare was singing Lucia tonight at the Carlo Felice in Genoa. Clare could sing Lucia almost if required to sing the character backwards, by now. So it was well that she had that task tonight, when she was sick for Rose.

Thomas had seen Rose for a minute. He had brought her

Clare's white roses. *White, please, Thomas*, she had written, *and small ones. Give her my love and this note I enclose . . .*

He had brought the white roses and the note to her dressing-room – with his own tributary flowers. Rose had hugged and kissed him, but she was, as he had known she must be, unaware of all but what she was about herself. Helpless before her cold fear, he teased her gently.

'Remember – don't overdo the *pianissimo* in *Piangea cantando . . .*'

She was reading Clare's note. She looked up and tried a vague smile. There were tears in her eyes.

Pianissimo, Rosie – piangea cantando – *your celestial* pianissimo. Grandmother writes that she will be saying the Memorare for you every five minutes tonight until midnight. I'll offer up all Lucia's anguishes and madness in honour of your ordeal. *Corragio*, pet – you have it and you'll need it. We'll all be with you – so, love from Ripetta and from Genoa, and from Ballykerin and Lackanashee. Oh, love to you, Rosie – and triumph.

Clare

P.S. Paddy writes that he's praying like mad for you! So you see, you can't but triumph! – C

Thomas kissed her hands and left her. He did not visit Antonio's dressing-room. That Antonio had pulled strings and arranged to sing Iago tonight was as might have been expected. There were at least two young baritones as deserving of the occasion; but Antonio's aristocratic family, having accepted his eccentric choice of career, were not going to have him fail within it. And the de Lucas had influence and power in moderation; and a moderate expression of their power was to have Antonio sing Iago in La Scala on this especial night.

Thomas knew that Antonio would sing beautifully. He thought also that La Scala, since the intention was to present Rose to the world as the surprise of the occasion, had chosen Otello with great wisdom. Giovanni Maroni was a handsome man in his middle-thirties, who had never either failed or succeeded, but whose voice remained clear and pure, who knew his work and was a good actor, but who was now too tired and too much overridden by married life to seek climactic success. Yet he was handsome on the stage, and always sure of his music and of romantic, good Italianate style. An excellent background voice, strong and moving, for our Irish Desdemona, La Scala said.

Thomas walked against the crowds into the piazza outside the opera house. Gaslit, rain-drenched, it offered a typical January Milan night, grey and solid. We might be in Manchester, he thought. Still, this is La Scala at my back, and over there beyond those wet roofs is Il Duomo. I wonder if anyone is praying for Rose at this exact minute? Clare doesn't pray, I think. Certainly she doesn't pray for herself, but perhaps she'd pray for Rose tonight. I suppose they're praying in Lackanashee; I suppose the Committee is praying.

He smiled. He felt himself at the nadir of living, made empty and limp by anxiety. If one suffers this for Rose, he thought, what will it be when it is for Clare?

He had chosen his place in the house. In the first tier of *palcos*, near the centre, to the right of the state box. Two American gentlemen were to occupy it, and he had decided that they looked stiff and undemonstrative and would not exact anything, or seem to be there at all. He had shown them his pass, given them his card and accepted theirs, and obtained their permission to occupy a third chair in their *palco*. So now he turned back into the opera house and slowly moved upstairs. He drank a glass of brandy at the bar, and then proceeded to his seat. He hung up his overcoat, folded his opera hat, and sat down cautiously, primly. His face was white as ever Clare's could be, and his eyes burnt blackly, as hers always burnt under stress. Rose might have said that more than ever tonight he was Clare's brother and twin.

Signor Faccio came to the podium. When the prolonged applause of reception rippled down, he turned briskly to his orchestra and gathered them under his command. The lights of the auditorium went down, and the great, filled house became completely quiet.

*

Rose's life in Milan between an evening of early October in 1889 and this rainy night of late January in 1890 was a period which she would never be able to measure in terms of nights or days or weeks or hours. It was a life by itself, and unlike any life she had hitherto known, in Italy or elsewhere. This new life, with its figures, voices, scenes and sensations, was a malleable, elastic condition in which she had become as it were enclosed; and over its changes of light and pace and purpose and weather she neither had nor sought to have control. It was life within a prolonged, unmanageable and engrossing dream. It folded her in inexorably, and as a dreamer she accepted its government, no matter through what mazes and anxieties it carried her, no matter the fears, the fatigues and the recurrent astonishments she suffered. She had been, as it were, mercifully put to sleep by the enfolding power; or rather, all that rest of her slept that lay behind, beyond the new boundaries. It was not that she forgot all that other self, or any of its cares or loves or events – but simply she knew them from here, from Milan, only as if through a thin, separating veil of sleep; and she seemed content that she must know them all only thus for a while – until she woke again.

This condition accepted – and indeed it was inescapable – she was happy in Milan; and sometimes smiled absent-mindedly to think of how greatly puzzled Clare would be when someday she told her that she was happier in this grey, plain city than in Rome. But indeed she understood that *her* Milan was a small and circumscribed place, bounded by her lodgings in the Vicolo di Brera, Signor Serrano's studios in the Via Gesu and Il Teatro della Scala. A small triangle of grey stone and grey sky, which held an immense, an immortal world.

She had accepted it at once, without surprise; almost it was as if she had known that, did she ever reach this place and point, exactly as now she found it would it be.

Her lodging was in the apartment of a young musician from Leipzig who was an instructor of violin and violoncello at the Konservatorium, and whose wife gave German lessons to the students of La Scala, and so to Rose. She liked Herr Viertel and his Frau, liked her German lessons, and liked the good food and good humour in the apartment.

Work with Signor Serrano was from the first day a total exaction of all that she had of talent and of hitherto acquired knowledge – though indeed much of the latter was only extracted from her to be roared at, contemned and flung away – but much more, she had to reach springs of patience, humility, self-control and physical stamina which none of her former teachers or conductors had made necessary – and in two years of hard work in Italy she thought she had been schooled in the ordeals created by temperament, arrogance and musical fervour. However, work with Serrano was to be a battlefield, for which nothing that Luisa had said of him had prepared her; she accepted the challenge, since she had to.

And in La Scala itself she discovered that all was challenge, all was devotion, argument, ideal, pitilessness, passion, vanity and free enslavement. Here was the source; here was opera; here in this house it was born, it was fed, it was worshipped, it lived and it died and it rose again. Here she was only one, the very least and least thought of, in an uncountable throng of zealots for all of whom, from the highest and most terrifying priests and priestesses of the cult down to the most timid acolyte and donkey-boy, the tradition and purpose of this place were indeed religion; religion and love and life, and food and drink. So, once admitted at all to service, or attempted service, underneath the heavy, thick-browed roof, it would be difficult to pass even the neophyte's first day of anxious exploration, through practice-rooms, rehearsal rooms, wardrobes, corridors, wide, cold backstage staircases and terrifying giant wings and flies, without accepting the amazing principle of worship of the whole in oneself, as one apprehended it in all about.

For Rose to have hesitated would have been impossible. At the end of the first hard, extraordinary day, with her breast all full of song, she gave herself to La Scala, bent her neck delightedly to the yoke – and entered that world of dream which was to hold her prisoner until this January night – and perhaps for life.

In short, Rose was immediately at home in La Scala simply because that was the place where it was natural and best for her to be; so natural and good that, being there, she ceased to

wonder about herself. Or rather the only wonder that sometimes made her smile was that she had got there so simply –
from far-off Lackanashee. But hardly had she time to wonder.
Work engulfed and seized her predisposed ability at once and
very happily. She had to study and master, as possible understudy, one in three of the major soprano rôles to be sung in
Milan between October and April, and also one in four of
the second sopranos of the season's programme. But that was
routine; that was what she was paid for. The chief shock in
this part of her work was that in the rôles which she knew
technically – and they were many, and she had sung them
with beginner's success all over Italy – she was instructed
coldly by La Scala to begin all over again. Her singing of
them in Parma, in Bologna, in Rome, was – she said to herself
sometimes – as if she had sung them in the convent parlour in
Lackanashee. Yet, as a good novice understands the absurd-
seeming exactions of a religious rule, Rose understood La Scala.
It was the place where she must learn the meaning of her
vocation. It asked her for her very self – and that, it seemed,
was the exaction which her whole simple life had sought. But
the demand was boundless, and, like the religious claim, asked
all that could not be written down in any contract, or ever paid
for in lire or, it might well be, in later fame. It asked a total
gamble.

Rose, as she worked at her understudy rehearsals and solo
practices, was aware of this solemn, general aspect of her life
only as a kind of ambience, a condition of weather or health;
it was not a ponderable fact or set of facts. It was a state of
living which was hers. But within it she wrestled with facts,
problems and duties almost without respite, taking these as
they came, with zest or fear or exasperation or sheer pleasure,
as might be – but always with all of herself, for better or worse.

At the end of December in 1889, La Scala proposed to give
a gala performance – the first in Italy of *Die Meistersinger*.

'But why am I not to understudy Eva?' Rose asked Antonio.
   'Too much work.'
   'But they never spare us here! That can't be the reason. And

I want this understudy. Imagine the luck of coming absolutely *fresh* to *Meistersinger* under Faccio—'

'He won't direct the understudies, you silly!'

'No, but his slave-assistants will – and he'll listen to us. He's always at our final rehearsals.'

'That's true. He's listening to you a great deal. He's watching over you, Rosa.'

'Still, it's a bit annoying of them to be getting protective the very one time I don't want to be protected! It's not like them to be solicitous!'

'Oh yes, it is – for their own purposes. You wait, sweet innocent. Are you still cold?'

It was nearly midnight, and the cold rain of Milan streamed down outside the draughty little café where they sat and drank chocolate. They had been on understudy duty at the opera for Meyerbeer's *African Maid*, a long piece which wearied Rose, but in which Antonio desired to sing the very dramatic baritone part. He was satisfied that it had not been sung tonight as well as he could sing it, but the two and their colleagues had grown cold and weary as they listened to their elders and betters performing with gusto, none showing the least inclination to liven things by getting drunk, fainting, or dropping dead.

Now they had reached through bitter rain the nearest little coffee-shop, and waited on the weather. Antonio was determined that when Rose felt somewhat warmer – the stove was comforting in this little place, but the draughts were pitiless – he would go back to the piazza and find a cab to take her home. But she thought such extravagance inexcusable, as she had only to walk about three hundred yards to her lodging, and she persisted, Milan weather or not, in her Irish confidence that any downpour was only a shower and would be over in a minute.

But such optimism was in Rose, as in many of her race, strictly superficial; a part of the over-saluted and over-mocked Irish charm. In Rose, however, it might be called a positive grace. For being born most truly polite she was therefore a creature of reserve, who conceived it natural to give to passing life such gaiety and calm as she commanded; yet behind her true façade of free delightfulness, she was, indeed had been from babyhood, a realist, an anxious and a scrupulous one. And because she was good, and a good artist, she was always acutely aware of the lives and hearts of others in so far as they were associated with her. From Mamma onward and outward, as experience led her, habitual sympathy and respect worked in her for the claims and the natures of those fellow-creatures whom life drew round her. Her heart was tender, but her mind and conscience was disciplined. So, since endowed with outward graces she could not but give delight, and pain, to many; since she loved life and especially this life she had been commanded to; since she was an artist and loved love and loved to sing of love, she might be said to be in a constant dilemma. And she was, as she half-knew; and as she half-suspected she would always be.

The two drew nearer to the stove.

'Why the devil does that door not shut properly?' Antonio asked the waiter.

'I haven't a notion, sir,' said the old man sleepily.

Rose laughed in deep pleasure.

'That's like what we'd say at home. This chocolate is making me too fat, Tonio. Let's have some hot wine! I'll pay.'

'Oh, you impertinent one!'

The hot spiced wine was ordered.

'I had a letter from Clare today.'

'How is she?'

'Worked to death – and the *tramontana* is blowing like the very spirit of evil, she says.'

'Well – I'd take the *tramontana* any time rather than this Nordic slushiness—'

'And maybe you'll be enjoying it next week—'

Antonio was being let to Perugia to give two performances of *William Tell*.

'Not enjoying it, sweet! It's only where you are that a man can enjoy winter.'

'That's pretty. And you make winter better too, when you're in a good temper.'

'And since I'm a model of good temper—'

Antonio was playing his cards well during these months in Milan. He was kind and gay with Rose; he encouraged her industry, criticized her work with friendly anxiety, counselled and helped her in matters of daily life, protected and teased her, and even fussed sometimes about her health. Almost he was brotherly – save for inevitable gusts of out-of-the-blue jealousy, or waves of too sharp delight. He endeared himself, in fact, very skilfully, and from week to week gained back much ground in her heart which the angers and mistakes of the summer had lost him.

But Rose remembered René, so much less confident than this other, so vain and vulnerable, and without her now very likely again the alien waif that he had formerly been in Rome. He did not write well and – conscious of that, perhaps – he forced his style to an effusiveness that hid him from her. She wrote to him – as she wrote to anyone – exactly as she would speak to him. Even the inaccurate French she wrote was the same inaccurate, flowing French she spoke, and unmistakeably must be to him her very voice upon the page.

He could not thus send himself to her. She understood this, but it disappointed her; and sometimes it made her sharp and impatient against him as when with him she had occasionally been chilled by his unnecessary and juvenile pomposities. But she loved him tenderly; she missed him, missed the sweet habit of their physical love which had so naturally pleased her and grown upon her; and she felt responsible, and fretted about him. Writing about his work he swung from letter to letter between boasting and cursing; but Rose conceded that most people do that, in thought and even in speech, even if they do not write these fluctuant moods into such weakly florid sentences as René used. He gave her few facts about his daily life – and she needed facts always on which to build understanding and sympathy. His written effusions, pathetic or conventionally amorous, gave her nothing of the young lover she had known so well in her arms at night, or singing with her on the Argentina stage.

So she thought of him with anxiety now and, remembering Clare's good news of him, she spoke it aloud, rather foolishly.

'Clare sang at the Argentina last week.'

'Oh? Accommodating of Costanzi's!'

'Yes. They were in some fix about someone. And funnily enough she sang with René.'

'Lovely for her.'

Rose smiled.

'Clare says he was very good indeed – that he's obviously been working really hard. And if Clare says that!'

'Even Clare may nod, over a golden boy. What had she the good fortune to sing with him?'

'Believe it or not – *I Puritani*!'

'Indeed? That seems to be his lucky piece!'

'Maybe!' Rose laughed. 'But Clare would be very good for him in that – better than me by far. She can make that sort of heroine positively interesting.'

'Good. Let's hope René finds her positively interesting – far more interesting than you!'

'Oh, Tonio, don't be so silly! It's only that I'm very pleased to hear good news of his work. He's a bad letter-writer—'

'As he damn well would be, the fluting ass!'

There was a pause.

'I'm sorry,' said Rose. 'But I *was* pleased to hear that from Clare, and it seems so unnatural not to mention it.'

'I'll tell you what's unnatural, my girl . . .'

They went into a long and almost childish quarrel, under the absurdities of which, however, lay for both such confusion of passion, question and darkness that it seemed as if quiet would not return or either ever find a way back to a true and lighted reason for the strong feelings they roused in each other.

The old waiter snored; the stove cooled down. Rose's face grew white and whiter, and shadows spread along her cheekbones, but for a while she gave angry blow for blow. Then suddenly her weary eyelids closed out the whole scene, and she heard the silence of the street outside.

'The rain is over,' she said. 'I'm going home.'

'A cab?'

'There's no need.'

They walked over the bright pavements without a word to

say. Antonio had roused himself into an obstinate fury of desire of which he knew there could be no expression in this deadly, stupid moment. Rose felt only cold dislike of her own nature and of her inclination towards men and their self-centred passions. Why do I understand their manias? she wondered wearily. Shall I in fact have to understand them better? Or else go home? Oh God! Dear Mother of God!

The *portiera* opened her lodging door; Antonio kissed her hand with exaggerated, cold grace, and she went upstairs to bed.

Still they lived always in confused, exasperated attraction to each other, and in sure affection. And Rose soon understood why she had not been asked to understudy Eva – because she was to be the January Desdemona. This decision of the directors of La Scala, though often guessed at by the knowing during the summer and autumn of 1889, when at last it came to Rose in the form of a simple, routine instruction from the casting manager's office, surprised her at first, meaninglessly – as if she had never heard of the opera *Otello*. But then she stood still, alone with the plain news, and allowed herself to examine and sense its weightiness.

Giuseppe Verdi's darling, La Scala's guarded prize – this was to be entrusted to her for her beginning in La Scala itself. She stood in the side street by the stage door, stood alone in the cold December noonday, and read the clearly written command from Signor Faccio's underling. So it had come, this never quite believed-in day of climax, day of fate. She was, it seemed, to attempt to be a *prima donna*. She was to prepare herself to sing Desdemona in Milan, for the world. She had come then to this crisis, only three years away from Lackanashee and Miss French's cottage piano.

She folded the paper and put it in her purse. She crossed the piazza and walked without purpose through the Galleria and into the Piazza del Duomo. She met no one that she knew in the bitter, bright day; not Antonio, not anyone.

A pigeon lighted on her hand. She smiled into its cruel eye, and shook it off as she mounted the steps of the Duomo.

'*La tua fanciulla io sono, humile e mansueta...*' she sang uncertainly, meditatively. But she fell silent as she entered the Cathedral and made the sign of the cross.

So from day to day henceforward, every part and aspect of herself that was not of La Scala and of the opera *Otello* moved further from her centre and out to horizons of her consciousness that dimmed in fine almost to invisibility. She grew to live and work in a condition of cold joy and colder terror which seemed to allow no present life to other ways of feeling. To those working with her who did not know her well, this state of inwardness in her, of living alone with one idea, was not perhaps manifest, because as if to protect the isolation she embraced, Rose sustained all the automatic practices of good manners, good sense and self-control which always were her apparent self. But Antonio knew in those weeks of concentrated study and rehearsal where she dwelt and how sealed off and hidden; knew it sometimes angrily and jealously, but ' also, to his credit, with proud and hopeful excitement. Her *maestro* Serrano also guessed at her state, and took care to let it be, and to take her through all her hours of private work with him as if she walked in her sleep – as in a sense she did. And the great director, Signor Faccio, observed her with satisfaction.

Naturally not only Rose but the entire cast of *Otello* worked with that passion and concentration which La Scala demanded and was always given; but the principals for this production, save Antonio and Rose, had sung important parts in the great opera house before; Otello, Cassio, Roderigo and Emilia were all seasoned and celebrated singers for whom this assignment could not possibly be the enrapturing and terrible ordeal it had to be for the Irish girl.

Lisa Tevara, an accomplished and generous artist who was singing Emilia, could remember and understand such young fierce fear and delight as Rose must now undergo; but she said little of this, merely offering friendship and serenity to the newcomer. And Giovanni Maroni, her Otello, was frankly delighted with his Desdemona, and amused – though like

Emilia, with a remembering benevolence – by her abstracted passion, her air of holy dedication. Antonio also, though passionately anxious for his own success in a supremely difficult part and very naturally preoccupied, knew well what their common trial must mean for Rose, and vowed himself – 'if only for the glory of Ripetta', as he said to her – to every possible service of encouragement and brotherly love.

So the neophyte was lucky, much luckier than she might have been; and help was with her, all about her, in greater strength than she could know, and increasingly, from the first rehearsal to the last.

And at last even the last rehearsal, the *répétition générale*, from which Signor Faccio had surprisingly excluded all but those internal members of La Scala, teachers and students, who must be present – even that was over. Clouded, uncertain, unapprehended, it had passed; Rose had, she supposed, passed through it, and then she had gone home in a cab, had gone to bed in silence and obediently swallowed the sedative prescribed by the house physician of La Scala which her smiling young landlady brought to her.

'I must say my night prayers,' she whispered.

'Say them in your sleep,' said Frau Viertel.

'Oh, no. Awake I must say them, truly.'

Frau Viertel lighted a night-light and extinguished the bright lamp. She stood a moment on the threshold of the room, and heard Rose singing, *pianissimo*: '*Prega pel peccator, per l'innocente* . . .' The notes ended on a small and childish sigh. Frau Viertel smiled and closed the door.

While the applause rang through the lighted house at the end of the first act, Thomas sat as if cut in stone. He heard and knew the quality of this reception: surprise, emotion, question, curiosity – all were there; the kind of '*so far*, well done indeed' of a pleased but truly critical audience. For himself, he felt no will at all to clap his hands or shout 'Bravo'. He had listened and watched throughout the entire act with that attention which he would have had to give were he Faccio on the podium. In everything, orchestra, chorus, grouping, lighting, set, and in the individual performers, their dress and manners, their acting and their singing, he found all that La Scala could give; and it was enough. As for the love-passage on which the act concludes, believing as he did that it was the most beautiful love-music of all he knew in opera, he told himself that tonight he had heard it sung and seen it presented perhaps exactly as Giuseppe Verdi heard and saw it himself in the lonely hours of composition. Sitting motionless he listened back to the last phrases, heard them with precision, and heard nothing of the immense social din all about him.

'So far so good,' he said to himself, unaware of how his heart was pounding with relief. 'So far so good.'

At last he became conscious of the two American gentlemen on his left. The elder of them was standing up, smiling all over his face and still clapping as almost to split his fine gloves. The other, beside Thomas, sat very quietly and no longer clapped, if he had clapped at all. His long, Norman face was white, and he looked as if the effort of attentive listening had wearied him very much. Sweat shone on his forehead about the margins of his red-fair hair.

'Who is she?' he said to Thomas.

'Her name is Rose Lennane. She's very young.'

'Yes. That is clear. Rose Lennane.'

Thomas nodded, got up, and left the *palco*.

He hardly listened to the swirling comments all about him in the foyer and on the stairs; but he did hear someone say that the composer had intended to be present but was prevented by a chill from travelling to Milan, to which the reply was that it seemed now indeed as if that was a pity. As he moved back towards the auditorium he fell in line with two elderly men, one of whom he thought to be the senior music critic of *Il Corriere della Sera*. They spoke of the new Desdemona.

'Certainly the loveliest to look at that one has hoped to see.'

'Agreed. This should be an interesting night.'

'A long, dangerous night for an inexperienced soprano, my friend. How will she be when she reaches her fourth act? Has she the stamina for this tremendous opera? Has she the courage?'

'I'd swear she has the courage, anyway,' Thomas thought, as he took his seat again beside the red-haired American.

The great opera moved forward. As he listened, knowing every line, every bar, Thomas grew happy. During the second act his nerves grew so calm that he was able to appreciate Antonio's interpretation of Iago. The performance was indeed wonderful. So beautifully did he underplay the character that – his attention being released to the performance – Thomas wondered whether one-half of the audience would at all get the actor's point, or see his place in the hideous tragedy. He was indeed delighted by Antonio's subtlety. It was an amazing interpretation. Antonio seemed to fritter away the evil of his part into an easy-going charm which, blended to the accurate beauty of his singing, amounted to something like genius. Thomas was surprised by the intelligence; he had counted on the beautiful singing, but not on the interpretative brains.

But, as he grew critically engrossed with Antonio's presentation of Iago, he realized how much at ease he now was about Desdemona, who was singing and acting like an angel. In fact, after the middle of the second act, it was difficult to worry any more. Rose was in charge of her work; and every note she sang was true, charged with pure meaning.

Still remained the fourth act. And too much success, for a beginner, in the other acts, might mean disaster in that, most difficult of operatic passages.

Will she have the strength? She has the courage. But will that exquisite young voice hold for the journey? Clare, Clare, will she be able for this terrifying fourth act? Oh Clare – will Rose get through this hour?

During the fourth act, as he invoked Clare and thought of her, singing in anxiety in Genoa, he marvelled at the quite exquisite singing of Rose, before him on the Scala stage. It is alarming, he thought. This *pianissimo* is absurd. She cannot carry it through. She is too young. She will go flat. You cannot sing as she does and not go flat.

She sang through Desdemona's last hour of fear and prayer, and then of death, on that *pianissimo* which was thereafter to be famous. Quietly, quietly, she sang herself that night into fame.

Thomas listened, holding his breath like any ignorant groundling.

But when all was over he stood up and cried out with all the people. He did not shout for the emotion the story had created; he cried out to praise the singing – not Rose's alone, but Maroni's too, and Tevara's, and Antonio's. All of them had sung to his standard, and he was delighted, because it was Rose's terrifying night, and she had not only triumphed but she had been supported in triumph. It was a great Scala night – and Rose was its centre indeed – but her triumph was upheld by great general performance.

Thomas was so much delighted and moved when the last curtain fell that he wanted to kick and stamp. So he took a fierce look at his American hosts in the *palco* and then dashed away.

He walked out into the rainswept piazza; he strode up and down; he heard the comments of people who waited for their trams. All were delighted. All were ravished, it seemed, by the new young soprano. All agreed, he gathered, that it was one of their great Faccio's greatest nights, beautiful in everything.

Thomas thought that they must be right in this. He felt an intoxicated satisfaction; the more he considered the opera just witnessed, the calmer and more complete became his relief and pleasure. So, in his time, he took his way to Desdemona's dressing-room.

And there he beheld triumph. All the symbols and augurs of total success – some alarming indeed, but precise indications, as he knew – all of them were in the corridor and around the dressing-table of La Rosa d'Irlanda. The place was thronged; hot and heavy with acclamation. By the door, handsome, splendid and quiet in his everyday black suit, stood Antonio de Luca. Thomas seized his hand.

'Well, she did well, our Irish one? Didn't she, Thomas?'

'You both did inexpressibly well! Viva Ripetta! If only little Giaco had been here!'

Antonio's eyes blazed gratitude.

'Still, it was her night! Marvellous, marvellous!'

'Desdemona will never be sung like that again—'

'Except by her.'

'Can one get near her?'

'Wait awhile. She wants you and me – only us – to have supper with her at her lodgings. She has refused all the parties – and the Viertels have prepared us a feast.'

'Great idea. But I have to send telegrams to Clare and Giaco—'

'Of course. We'll compose them at supper.'

'They'll have to be full and explicit.'

'Oh, we'll send them proper telegrams, my friend! We'll leave them in no doubt!'

Thomas waited by the door and contentedly surveyed the crushed, worldly traffic in the harshly lighted room. Across it all, in the dressing-table mirror he saw Rose, wrapped in a white dressing-gown, her face, cleaned of footlight make-up, almost as white as her wrap, and her eyes shining darkly, abstractedly. She looks as if she were quite alone this minute, he thought with amusement, and as if she was enjoying her solitude with epicurean pleasure.

But she was not alone. That restless, pressing world to which tonight she had irrevocably given her voice was all about her, whether or not she saw it. And across the bobbing heads and bouquets Thomas could see Signor Faccio who stood beside her; he saw him bend down and kiss her hands. Everyone fell silent before this gesture from La Scala's greatest man; and when the master turned away, most reverently an avenue was made for him at once. As he passed through the doorway, Thomas and Antonio bowed. The old man looked for a moment at Antonio.

'Iago?' he questioned. And then he laid his hand on Antonio's sleeve. 'Intelligent,' he said. 'An intelligent performance. Good night, young man.'

Thomas stayed by the door and surveyed the throng of tribute-bearers, guessers, gamblers who pressed about the new soprano. He recognized Frühland of the Berlin State Opera, and Tring from London, and Tierhof of Vienna. He saw famous critics that he knew from Leipzig and Hamburg and Rome, and among the jewelled, clattering women two old and great *prime donne* and one notorious American duchess who, he had been told in Paris, was an infallible diagnostician of musical success, and had never been seen by the dressing-table of uncertainty or in the wings of doubt.

He smiled, and was reminded of the Americans who had allowed him to share their box. Relaxed now, he had curiosity to spare to look at their cards, which he fished from his waist-coat pocket.

Almost he whistled when he read the first card, which he remembered to have been given him by the big, silvery man who had seemed to want to split his glove at the last curtain. It bore the name of one of the most feared and renowned promoters of opera at that period in the United States.

'Ah, Rose! Von Jakob himself!'

The name on the other card meant nothing to him. Mr Silas D. Rudd, of Boston, Massachusetts. But he looked over the crowded heads in the dressing-room for the great von Jakob, and saw that he and his tall young companion had indeed made their way to where Rose sat and that the big, silvery man was bowing over her hands almost as proudly as had old Faccio. This was indeed success, and Thomas wondered idly, as he smiled in deep relief, what the gaunt and grave New Englander, Mr Silas D. Rudd, was doing on its outskirts.

The dressers began at last to clear the room, and Rose stood up, no longer absent-minded but her customary friendly self, to receive the last good night embraces of the two famous *prime donne*, and of the alarming American duchess.

After a time there was comparative quiet in the corridors of La Scala, and Thomas and Antonio moved into the night to secure a cab and to wait for Rose.

'The rain is over.'

Each was at present spent and drained of expression. That would come back, torrentially, with food and wine, and Thomas would find full and generous words to say to Antonio about his singing and acting of Iago. But for now he was content to smile silently at the radiant young man who walked at his side, his beautiful face lifted in rapture to the black sky.

'I didn't think he had the brains for what he did tonight,' Thomas thought affectionately. 'Clare will be interested in that. Right again, the maddening girl.'

Antonio, not looking where he walked, hurtled into a tall man on the corner of the piazza.

''Scusi, signor!'

The tall man smiled slightly.

'You were Iago tonight?' he said in English. He was the tall Bostonian. 'It was beautiful. The whole opera was a beautiful experience. I congratulate you, signor.' And he lifted his opera hat, and walked away after his companion.

'That's von Jakob he's with,' said Thomas.

'Von Jakob? My God!'

'Didn't you see them in the dressing-room? I shared their *palco*. That individual wouldn't strike you as interested in music, would he?'

'You never can tell, with Americans.'

'Come to that,' said Thomas, 'you never can tell anything – with anyone.'

They found a cab, and told the driver to follow them to the stage door.

At supper in the Viertels' little stuffy room Thomas sat in a state of reflection and question.

At a corner of the overladen table he sharpened his pencil and began to compose the necessary telegrams.

'Can I send them tonight?'

'No,' said Frau Viertel. 'The telegraph office won't be open until eight. It's quite near here, off Piazza Mercanti. Where do you lodge? I could send them for you.'

'Oh, thank you, no. I lodge nearby. I'll be at the office at eight.'

Rose, in a dress of grey merino, ornamented only by one of Clare's white roses which she had pulled through her collar button, in spite of the beautiful handkerchief of white silk embroidered all over with strawberries – the *fazzoletto* which had been Antonio's cleverly thought and specially woven present for her tonight and which now she held delightedly in her left hand – Rose looked exactly the child she had seemed two years ago in Via di Ripetta. She was in command of herself; she seemed even absent-minded, unaware of the storm of congratulation which it was impossible for those who cared about her to subdue tonight. The Viertels had been at La Scala, and, both good musicians, could not but exult in what they had heard.

But Rose, calm and simple, would at first have no talk at all.

'Please, please – leave it. I did my best. Oh, be quiet, please, please, my friends.'

Her friends had then been, amusedly, quiet – and addressed themselves to a very fine supper and the splendid wines that Antonio had ordered.

She sat and ate the rich food spooned to her – and stared, very calmly, into her own event. She was clearheaded, and she knew from all the side-murmurs that tonight she had succeeded in the high terms of the world.

She was not so much an artist in mood tonight as a sensible and gentle girl, who had done well in these past hours with her talent and whose great wish to justify the career into which she had been led blindfold seemed to have come true. Tonight she had answered the Committee's gamble. That much she knew. It was an immense relief.

'What are we to say in these telegrams – come on?' said Thomas.

'Oh, Thomas – as you will—'

'Do you want one sent to home, Rosa?'

'No. I think not. Mamma doesn't know what – what tonight means. And telegrams frighten us in Lackanashee. You see, they don't understand. Even Miss French didn't write to wish me good luck. So I won't upset Mamma with a wire. I'll write to her to say I'm singing here – and I'll get the criticisms translated for Miss French – and she'll show them to Mamma, if they're nice. No, I won't send any telegrams to home. After all, Mamma knew about tonight anyway – and she didn't write a line. Miss French – I don't understand – Miss French might have known

– I'll wire to René tomorrow. But I wish I'd heard from them at home.'

Rose bent down her head. Antonio strode to her and put his arms around her.

'*Rosa! Rosa di gloria!*'

'I can't bear it!'

'What can't you bear?'

'Tonight, tonight I can't bear! I've done my best! No word from Mamma, no word from Miss French!'

Antonio burst out laughing.

'You've done your best – in La Scala! – and you expect Lackanashee to hear you! Oh, my God, my God!'

The young man lifted her and carried her about the small room, as one might pace with a sick child. Thomas noticed that she sobbed as she lay against his shoulder. Antonio sang as he carried her up and down the little room – her own Willow Song. '*Piangea cantando . . .*' he sang softly, tenderly.

'My God, how clever a lover he is,' thought Thomas, going on with the telegrams.

'*O, salce, salce . . .*' came in the pure voice of Rose; they went on singing together, Iago and Desdemona, her lovely, innocent lament. She clutched her *fazzoletto* in her hand.

Thomas continued with his telegrams. He thought of Giacomo, of Mariana and of Clare. This was a night of serious triumph for Giaco and Via di Ripetta; it was a night to bring joy to Clare – and as for the Committee and Lackanashee . . .

Up and down the room, Desdemona sobbing carried in Iago's proud arms, went the pair singing as one, *piano*, *pianissimo*, the subtle, tragic *cantilena* . . . '*O, salce, salce, salce . . .*'

Thomas addressed himself to his telegrams. He would not write his telegram to Clare yet. That would be his last and happiest one, and very long; and tomorrow he would go to Genoa. If I telegraph Leipzig, he thought, I can probably stay to hear her in *Sicilian Vespers* on Friday night. He smiled. That awkward piece will surely tax her!

Rose stopped crying, and gave Antonio a grateful kiss.

'We'll drink wine now, Iago pet – and Thomas will sing Moore's melodies. Oh, Antonio, are we famous now? Isn't it awful if we turn out to be famous tomorrow? Frau Viertel – do come back and drink with us – we are celebrities! Oh, if only Clare were here – and René!'

'We can spare the latter,' said Antonio, but with good temper, and he refilled all the glasses.

Rose crossed his forehead mischievously with her 'handkerchief spotted with strawberries'.

'Which of them am I then? Cassio or Otello?'

'Cassio, most surely. Much the nicer man.'

The Twelfth Chapter

At the end of May in 1890 Clare was singing at the San Carlo Opera in Naples when the *Santa Catalina*, which had taken the Pirazzei Opera Company to South America eight months before, sailed back into the Bay with them – Luisa, Duarte, all. The tour had been on the whole a very successful one, and here they were, back on Italian earth, sunwarmed and rested from the voyage, full of strange tales and comedies, in good health and good training, and with money in their purses.

Clare was on the quay to wave them in, as she had said she would be; and in the radiant afternoon the disembarkation was a happy event. The emotion of return engendered vast and expressive delight in the whole company, some of whom besides Luisa were Roman friends and colleagues of Clare's, from the Accademia and Argentina. So they declared themselves enraptured to find her and other friends too from the San Carlo Company at the gangway, and there were some hours of truly Neapolitan boisterousness, and careless, almost impersonal, joy. In the relative coolness of the great Café Umberto in the Galleria, the crowd of re-united ones drank wine and shouted and toasted, and flung arms into the air and around each other – and cried '*Benvenuto*' and '*Viva*', and questioned and boasted and laughed; made indeed a fine, amusing scene, to the pleasure of the idling citizens about them.

Clare sat still and was well content. She had to sing *Norma* that night, and therefore must not, did she even desire to, shout or sing or drink much wine. But she welcomed the Italian, warm commotion which made adjustment to this marked day easy and gradual. She sat content, and looked at Luisa. And radiant Luisa looked at her. And Duarte stared at Clare, and spoke very little to anyone. They three, alone of the throng, were quiet, although they were, for the moment at least, happy. But none of the three was Italian.

Clare had exasperated Thomas very much, exasperated him in his professional concern for her, by her refusal to leave Italy during the winter now past, or to deviate from her set schedule. She was, in a sense, from October until the nearing end of this San Carlo season, a property of Costanzi's in Rome, through which house all her engagements for Turin, Genoa, Nice and Naples had been made. But when Thomas had come to Rome in the early winter, he came empowered to select a few voices for particular performances in Leipzig and Dresden and Vienna. And he wanted Clare for Fidelio, for Alceste and for Idomeneo. He had the authority of the opera houses of those cities to bring to them such new talent as had been reasonably tested and which he believed in. For Thomas was climbing fast in his profession, and deserved so to do, were it only because of his passionate industry.

Costanzi's had been co-operative with him about Clare. His idea was accepted, and the directors there were willing – still owning her – to lend her to Germany and Vienna, on terms, instead of to the scheduled Italian houses. Substitutes could easily be found for her already fixed engagements. And Mugnone, the chief conductor of that season at Costanzi's, had been sympathetic and appreciative, had agreed with Thomas that the operas designed for Clare in the German houses would be an excellent extension of her experience, and suitable to her voice. He thought that the adjustment of programmes should be made, for Clare's sake. Also, he said with common sense, if she sings in Germany this winter – we had not expected her to be sought by those opera houses yet – she will make more money, for us and for herself, than she will in Italy.

Thomas wooed her with the plan. But she would not have it.

'Why? You want to sing Fidelio! Already you know the score quite well. It's possible that you'll be a fine Alceste some day, so you might as well begin on her!'

'I know. I will begin on her. But not now, Thomas.'

'You'll make more money in Germany. You're always fussing about not getting out of debt fast enough!'

'Yes. But I'm doing quite well at present. They're working me very hard, and I sing the *prima* very often. No, no – leave me alone for this season, Thomas. Germany would frighten me at present. And I'd have to work very hard at German. I'm not equal to all the fuss, I tell you!'

'Oh, you're impossible! You're always mocking away at Donizetti and Bellini – and even Verdi, when you have wine taken, you lunatic—!'

'I know – I know. Give me time. I'm coming to appreciate him. Let me have this pedestrian Italian season, please!'

'Supposing I won't? Supposing I turn little Giacomino on to you? He's still your boss, you know! He could *order* you to go to Leipzig, my girl!'

'Yes. But he wouldn't. And you know why.'

Thomas knew why. He had already tried to engage the little *maestro* in this battle, but had got no alliance.

'No, Tomaso – leave her to Italy yet. She'll sing in Germany, and I believe she will sing very well there. But there is no hurry for her. She is young. And she is only a singer. You are a musician, you are four years older than her, and she wastes your valuable energies. Keep apart, you two.'

Clare saw him reflecting on Giaco's advice, which without ever having heard it delivered she could almost have repeated verbatim. She stretched a hand to him, touched by his baffled eyes.

'Thomas, let me stay quiet for these months. Forgive me, please. It isn't funk. It's that I require to stay in Italy at present. I'll study Alceste, I promise you – I'll work on it with whoever you recommend—'

'You'll study it with no one but me, you idiot!'

Tears of rage poured from his eyes, and he fell on his knees before her. With his head on her lap, her hands in his hair, he sobbed and cursed himself into a condition of border-sleep. It was warm and still in the little room. Ruffo purred, and far off a bell rang.

'I have to be in San Carlo in May,' Clare told herself super-stitiously. 'If they sent me into Germany, God knows what would happen!' She looked down at the fair head in her lap. 'I don't want this. I must be alone – I can't be stormed at. There is nothing here for him to storm.' She stroked his head and leant back in the chair, almost asleep herself in the still night.

So she had her way. And Thomas had forgiven her, stormily, but out of the exasperated love that he could not withhold from her.

The long season was indeed a time of hard and unceasing work, in which she had increased her repertory, gained the attention and good reports of some of the best critics and conductors, and had earned more money than she had counted on. So she was on her way, a true initiate now of the professional life; and she took pleasure in being much alone. But although she preferred her life in Rome to the travelling life, and had kept on Rose's two rooms on the Lunga di Sangallo so as to have always a sure base of peace, she gathered and learnt much from the periods spent in other cities. After Genoa and Turin in January she had sung in Nice during two weeks, and after-wards in Pisa, Bologna, Parma, and, to her great delight, for three weeks in the Dal Varme theatre in Milan – so that she and Rose were wonderfully and happily re-united, and she was able to see and hear the new-risen star in her first glory. After Milan she had returned to Rome and Costanzi's for April, and thence had joined the San Carlo company for the last three weeks of its season.

The months of this tour had helped her technically in her work more than had the long, hard summer of the preceding year, for the reason that, although in the natural course she made many friendly acquaintances, and even a few friends, Thomas was not there, nor could Rose or Luisa ever break in on her performances – so she had no one to whom she could jibe at the lunacies of opera, being too shy to become extravagant or mocking in speech save where she felt truly at home; and there-fore, unwatched, and none of her colleagues guessing at her questionings, she could set herself seriously to the, for her, enormously difficult business of learning to laugh like a gypsy on the stage, or flirt like a chambermaid, or hop and skip and blow kisses and peep and scream. Since no one about her knew what a fool she felt attempting lively antics, and since Thomas's amused but anxious eyes were far away, she could tackle these artificialities as it were *in camera*. And after a time she found that if she gave all, or almost all, her attention to the actual music she was singing, this vocal unity with what was going forward in the story was sufficient to cover, in some degree, her *gaucherie*, so that she even began to notice on some good nights that she was fluttering fans, throwing posies in the air and flinging her arms round soldiers with a greatly improved abandon. This amused her, but it was also a relief – since she was committed to opera life, and within it could by no means command her rôles. She knew that she would never become, in the true sense, an actress, since she did not like acting – as Rose for instance did. But she believed that she would learn to be a good actress within those parts where she was required to be consistently either grave, or mad, or tragic, or royal, or disguised as boy or man. Still, in this long season she had often to play *seconde donne* who could be very silly or embarrassing characters, and she forced herself, since no eyes she cared about were on her, to learn how to play them relaxedly, and without judging them from outside the while.

And by April she felt she had advanced in that necessary part of her work, and even looked forward with wry amusement to Thomas's seeing her play two leading rôles which she had managed successfully in Bologna and Pisa – the heroines of *Martha* and of *Don Pasquale*. He would not want to hear her in either; but if she forced him to do so some night when she was in good courage, she would hope to make him raise his eyebrows.

Now, here was Naples and the safe return of the *Santa Catalina*.

The exuberant cross-talk did not cease between all the re-united singers, friends and perhaps enemies, but friends for today. Some had got hungry now and were commanding, returned exiles, dishes they had dreamt of far away, *lasagne* and *pizze* and *salsiccia*. But Clare had lunched at her usual time, and would not eat before singing. She sipped the pale Capri wine, and answered questions of this one and that – and there were many and excited enquiries for La Rosa d'Irlanda.

It was a blessed veil, all this, that flashed between her and immediate, dangerous joy.

Had Luisa become more beautiful, or had she not remembered her exactly? She was thinner surely – and her skin had grown more gold; so had the gold-brown hair. Her eyes were the remembered green-gold, however, and shone when Clare's met them with remembered sharp sweetness. She has the sun all through her, Clare thought; she is sun-drenched, and if I touched her she would be warm like an apricot in the sun.

When the others spoke of Rose, Luisa smiled over the table to Clare.

'Not now, Clara,' she said. 'You'll tell me all of Rosa when we're alone.' And her eyes stayed on Clare's face with an expression of appraising love which seemed to exclude all about them from her wonder, her surmise. Clare smiled, to break the ring of privacy that the other had so simply curved, and she lifted her glass in salute. So did Luisa.

A little time later, having glanced at the café clock, Clare stood up and went to Luisa's side of the table.

'I have to go to the theatre now,' she said. 'The porter took your luggage to Strada Medina—'

'Yes, I know. But I won't go there until you're with me. I'm going to hear you in *Norma*.'

'Won't that tire you?'

Luisa smiled.

Duarte was standing beside them.

'I'll walk with you to the San Carlo,' he said to Clare.

'No, I will,' said Luisa.

'Neither of you, please – I'd rather – I must fly . . .'

And she sped from them. She knew that Luisa understood that even the short step from the Galleria to the theatre between the two lovers would have been a strain she could not easily have suffered on this day.

*

The opera always started late in Naples, sometimes an hour after the scheduled time. And on this night the local custom was upheld. Therefore it was after one o'clock when Norma and Pollione mounted the pyre, and the priestess was spent and very near tears by that time.

But although this was no gala night and although the tenor sang flat and roughly, Duarte, sitting still in his *palco* and listening to an opera of which only certain passages interested him, was very glad to be present.

For one thing, it always pleased him to be in this beautiful house. Whenever he either listened or conducted there he looked about it and tried to make a list of those operas which were truly worthy of so well-mannered, well-conceived an auditorium. They were few, always; and *Norma* had never been among them. Its undeniable beauties were all but neutralized for him by incongruities of almost light opera character in choral and orchestral passages; moreover he found it unattractive to the eye, and so absurd in theme as to require for its support a uniformity of greatness which its music did not possess.

Still, there were those passages of beauty, and as they were all for Clare to offer – Clare and the other soprano – he was eager to hear the opera. Moreover, opening the programme, he found that the bass who was to sing the Archdruid Oroveso was a Basque from Pamplona called Manuel Arrez who had been his friend in early days at the Paris Conservatoire and at Milan, and whom he had sought in vain in musical circles for many years. So he counted himself happy to be where he was.

Luisa loved San Carlo too.

She had sung to the noble house in the Easter season of the preceding year, and it was here in that season that she and Clare had first sung *Orfeo* together. Now as she waited for the curtain to rise on an opera she hardly knew, she looked about the gently lighted, murmurously filling auditorium with remembering pleasure.

After all the strange travels, pleasures, anxieties, mistakes and successes of eight months in a far continent, where indeed the language, with a difference, was hers, but where little else spoke of Spain to her, or at least of Castile, it surprised her that a few hours of Italy, Naples, was a home-coming.

She sighed, as if turning for sleep. The orchestra was in place at last. Soon Clare would be singing to her, to all these people. That was perhaps what she meant about home-coming – that Clare would be singing again.

'What is it like, Iago? I've only heard people rehearsing bits of it here and there. It's about druids, isn't it?'

'Yes, alas! But there are great passages of singing – mostly for the sopranos—'

'I know "Casta Diva"—'

'And in the second act listen well to the duet between Norma and Adalgisa – it's a fine arrangement for two sopranos – very difficult indeed.'

Luisa did listen. She was a good, cool listener to music, but to that duet she listened in tears.

And at last the opera was over, the ovations given and received. Duarte went to the dressing-rooms, to find Clare and Oroveso; Luisa waited at the stage door, renewing friendship with the *portiero*. Her breast and brain felt as if lighted within by the fire-clear singing she still heard. She wanted to be quiet and go on listening as Clare sang.

And when she came with Duarte and the Archdruid, Luisa took her hand and they walked into the gleaming night together, no word said. They crossed the Piazza Ferdinando and turned to the right out of Via Roma, knowing well the way to the lodging they had shared twice before in Naples. Outside the shabby door in Strada Medina while they waited for the *portiero*, they suddenly smiled at each other.

'I told Iago we were too tired for supper,' said Luisa.

'So did I,' said Clare.

The two Spaniards loitered on the wide piazza and watched the girls out of sight, Arrez amusedly.

'No good night? Did they not even need a glass of wine?'

'No. They are tired, and want to talk alone. Come, let's go

down the Partenope, Manuel. There's a good place there where you can eat sitting over the water.'

They walked by the dark palace, and descended to the seaboard.

'I'm glad to have found you again, Manuel. You were a dear friend, and I make few. You've changed little. Heavier – but that's from singing. And well indeed you sing!'

The other laughed in great pleasure.

'You were never a flatterer, Iago – so that delights me. How has life gone?'

'I've not become a renowned interpreter of sacred music – nor even the world's most famous conductor of Italian opera! Nevertheless, I work, and at Santa Cecilia I like my work, on the whole. And you?'

'*I'm* not the world's greatest operatic bass, as you know! But I've done well. I've sung all over the world in the last twenty years – since that first engagement in La Scala, you remember, which took me to Paris, and on from there – everywhere except in Italy, until this spring when I joined Costanzi's. I've made enough money – and I've enjoyed my wanderings. I'm growing tired now.'

'You didn't sound tired tonight.'

'Still – a bit of land near Pamplona! Fishing, Iago, and raising goats – and a bull-fight on Sunday . . .'

They sat down at a café table on a wooden pier. Beneath them the mildly lapping water knocked moored small boats against each other. They asked the waiter for veal and salad and a flask of Capri.

Duarte turned his dark face to the glittering bay and the night-freshened breeze.

'Naples is a flaming trollop of a town,' he said. 'But it's odd how she insists on holding a part of one's affection!'

'Trollops *can* do that, sometimes.'

The waiter brought the wine and filled their glasses.

'Idyllic, what you were saying, Manuel – about Pamplona and fishing and the bull-fight every Sunday. God, what bad exiles we are! You're married?'

'I was.'

'Ah!'

'Catalina died three years ago. We had fifteen years.'

'Catalina? Spaniard?'

'Of Santander. Manolito – our only son – is in Salamanca, with the Dominicans.'

'To be a Dominican?'

'He hopes. It is lonely – but Catalina might have been glad – proud anyway.'

'So.' Duarte smiled at the friend of early days and lifted his glass to him. 'As lives go, Manuel, yours has been good. I mean, you have been good, and have known good years and good people.'

'Yes. I have known and loved one or two good people.'

They began to eat their supper.

'You, *amigo mio*,' Manuel ventured gently. 'You *didn't* marry?'

Duarte raised his eyebrows and smiled. 'But, no! You remember my – circumstances?'

'I do indeed. But you had authoritative assurances that—'

Duarte laughed and waved his hands.

'How far away it is, that juvenile hell! Authoritative assurances against – against *her*!'

'She was very beautiful.'

'Very beautiful, and impossible. In any case, I mishandled the matter atrociously – and praise be to God!'

'No other loves, madman?'

'Oh, other loves, of course! But I'd had enough from her of seeking absolution. Never again confession, Manuel—'

'There are kind women—'

'There are, thank God. But they are kinder if you keep your secrets to yourself, and let them keep theirs. In any case, as I used to have a crazy predilection towards her kind – the beautiful, impossible, unmerciful – I've learnt to lower my sights, and frequent with friendliness. My business is my own, and buried. I cheat no one, Manuel, and I've never again reached for the absurd since that long time ago.'

'You don't go back to Spain?'

'No. Not yet. I've a house in Avila, up by San Vicente – do

you know Ávila? Two grim aunts are mouldering away in it, and they abhor me. But when they've closed their bigots' eyes, God help them – I don't know . . .'

Arrez took some cheese.

'I like Italian food,' he said contentedly.

'Singers do,' said Duarte. 'It's almost a sign of being a singer. I loathe it. This wine again,' he said to the waiter. 'Do you remember how you used to guzzle in Milan, Manuel – when we *hadn't* the price of your appetites at all! That dirty little place behind the Opera – and your mouth watering for *pizza* after *pizza*! You were a very good singer then, because you were a glutton!'

'So I suppose I'm still a good singer. At any rate, the stomach stays young, whatever about the larynx!'

When the waiter brought the new bottle of wine, Duarte asked him to bring Strega also. He swallowed a glass of it in one mouthful.

'Leave the bottle there,' he said.

Manuel looked at him out of gentle reconsideration of old knowledge, and observed that the taciturn individual he had met tonight was changing before his eyes into a fair imitation of the passionate and expressive young man of twenty years ago in Milan. The reversion pleased and touched him. He had loved young Duarte very much, and was glad to see him rise again behind the mask of middle age.

Duarte took another full swallow of Strega.

'Have you sung often in this season with this Irish girl, Manuel?'

'Let me see – when I joined Costanzi's in March she was off in Bologna and places. I think she came back in Easter week – and I believe the first time I sang with her was in *Lucia*. Yes, we were in performances together about five times then in Rome – and here I think we've sung together five or six times.'

'What besides *Lucia*?'

'Wait a minute. It's hard to remember.' Duarte smiled. 'No, you see, I'm a routine bass and I sing almost every night, because most bass parts are secondary. But she is a definite *prima*, and sings perhaps only every third night—'

Duarte laughed outright.

'Go on. Try to remember what you've heard her sing.'

'Oh, in *Faust* certainly, and *Martha*—'

'*Martha*? In *Martha* – good God!'

'*Macbeth* too. Fine in *Macbeth*, I remember. And *Norma*, of course. Tonight was our third time together in *Norma*.'

Duarte lit a cigarette slowly, lit Manuel's cigarette, filled their wine glasses, and their Strega glasses.

'You've sung all over the world? I take it in the chief opera house of the world?'

'Oh, yes. Covent Garden, the Metropolitan, all that level. I don't mean I've been the chief bass, but I *have* sung the leading bass part constantly when such people as Albani and Sembrich and d'Angieri were singing, and with de Reszke and Tamagno and Maurel. I've always worked on that level, Iago—'

'Then you have heard many remarkable voices. So have I. It is my business to hear them. Have you ever heard a soprano voice at all *like* the voice of this Irish girl? I don't mean less or more beautiful – but exactly of its kind. Have you?'

Manuel was puzzled.

'It is, come to think of it, an unusual voice – and I have heard people arguing about it in Costanzi's. It's a bit too cold, perhaps? Is that what you mean? It's perhaps like a boy's voice. Indeed, I heard a man say in Rome one day that she sang like a *castrato*.'

'Christ!' said Duarte. He flung his glass into the water below. 'Oh, Christ!'

Manuel was embarrassed.

'I'm sorry, friend. I sing with many sopranos, and I've never been much interested in the noise they make, so long as they keep in time and know their stage movements—'

'My God! And you've earned a living in opera—'

'Certainly. I sing bass correctly, and attend to my business. I was never much of a judge of voices, except to know whether or not they were in time – and I've heard too many sopranos!'

Duarte laughed.

'I can believe that. Evidently the effect is stupefying!'

'I expect it is,' said Manuel good-temperedly. He contem-

plated his friend's face, narrowed now and expressive of fierce
irritability, and he was touched. He is as vulnerable as when he
was twenty-four, he thought. But why about this young creature's voice? His opinion, I remember, was always sacred. May
one even now not see his point?

'I was never a musician, Iago,' he said. 'Explain this voice
to me.'

'Since you're not a musician, how could I? But as a journey-
man singer you must know that "Casta Diva" is an almost
impossibly difficult proposition. This is odd, coming from
Bellini and his foolish, uneven opera. An even odder thing is
that the duet for the two sopranos in the second act is a most
originally fabricated composition, very beautiful, but very
exacting indeed. In fact, Manuel, many musicians hold that
only a very intellectual musician could sing those two especial
passages in *Norma*; and since sopranos are never musicians and
certainly never intellectuals, these two parts of this unbalanced
opera are unsingable.'

'You surprise me.'

'You depress me. I had a low opinion of singers in general –
in relation to what they sing. But what I've just told you is
elementary. However, I'm going on to tell you that that girl
sang them tonight as if she were an intellectual and a musician.
And she is neither! So what do you make of that?'

'Make of it? Why – that all you windbags are wrong –
and that an ordinary soprano can sing Norma! Isn't that the
answer?'

Duarte threw his hands into the air and laughed.

'I walked into that trap! Well done, old rock of sense!'

He poured more Strega. 'I get excited seldom now, my friend.
But seeing you, and listening to your good true bass tonight
that I found I had remembered so well – that brought back
many thoughts. And then, hearing "Casta Diva" sung as it was
sung – that also – ah, forgive me. Let's not talk, Manuel.'

Manuel laid his hand on the other's.

'Tell me of yourself, amigo. Are you alone? Have you a lover?
Do you compose? Do you edit your fifteenth-century monks'
musics? Are you rich? Are you poor?'

'I am neither rich nor poor; I am a professor in Santa Cecilia, a private teacher of sacred music, and a well-enough opera and oratorio conductor. I edit my monks' musics, yes – but it's long since I composed. Still, I make notes for possible compositions. And I live alone.'

'But you skipped one question. Have you a lover?'

'Yes, and no. There is someone who is so good as to half-love me, and often to sleep with me. I admire her with affection – and I am too old for her. But she is free – she knows that – and she is lovely. That is all.'

Manuel understood that the free and lovely one was she who had gone away hand-in-hand an hour ago with Norma. He mused. The 'intellectual, musicianly' Norma, about whom his world-weary, middle-aged friend had grown so almost child-ishly partisan a moment ago.

Duarte felt sudden dislike of himself. Why all this loquacity, why this sentimental posturing? He felt the kind eyes of his friend upon his face, and he knew them to be sufficiently shrewd. But no more need be said. He could excuse this one hour of garrulousness in that he had been at once very glad and somewhat embarrassed by the unlooked-for meeting with Manuel. The latter, good and gay and modest, had too much admired Iago in the Milan days, and had been more than brother to him in the period of one great storm. So tonight though natural gladness was strong, it brought a desire to screen his present self, which had changed only to grow more what it had been twenty years ago, and he feared that this affectionate other might see his present conflicts reflected in those he had once known and witnessed.

However, enough now, a light screen was up. And hencefor-ward they could drink in peace, recount the superficial parts of their histories to each other, and talk of their professional world, and talk of Spain.

He refilled their glasses.

'Tell me about Catalina,' he said. 'Where did you meet her?'

Manuel took his cue, remembering how quick he had always had to be in taking it from Iago.

*

It was Sunday and hot noon, but Clare had not got up to go to Mass; and Luisa smiled when she reproached herself for this. The two, in their nightgowns, were loafing over coffee and fruit by an open window.

'Do you like to go?'

'I always have gone – until once or twice lately.'

'But – dearest – considering . . .' Luisa smiled teasingly.

'Considering that I'm not in the state of grace?'

'Well, yes.'

'Oh, it's a discipline. I think things over at Mass, and I read my Missal, and I wonder if Grandmother still prays for me—'

'You can be sure she does.'

'Well, anyway, at Mass I'm always sharply reminded that being happy isn't what we're here for!' She laughed and kissed Luisa's outstretched hand. 'Much good that does me!'

'Thank God!'

'More coffee? Shall I heat it up?'

This room, which they loved and had shared for their last days together before Luisa sailed away in October, was two rooms in one, with a wide, half-draped archway dividing it. Lofty, dusty and very shabby, the whole 'suite', as Mamma Lucia, the landlady, called it, was furnished in Neapolitan 1860 style. Velvet and chipped gilt, whatnots and bronze statues, and some very old and peculiar potted palms – but a few haphazard excellences too; a great, clean bed, a powder closet for the washstand, and in this outer part a cupboard with cups and plates, and a small oil-burning stove.

When Clare and Luisa had first sung together at San Carlo they had been directed to lodge with Mamma Lucia, and had occupied two small rooms on lower floors; but when they returned in October she had given them the 'suite', and Clare had made sure to have it when she came back alone to sing in Naples. She had done so because Luisa, in letters, begged her to be in the 'suite' for her return. And lived in by the two, with all their flowers and books and follies scattered, with the wine and fruit and bread they brought for supper and for breakfast, with windows open to the sky and noise of Naples in May weather, it was indeed a habitable place.

Clare re-heated the coffee.

'I'll peel us two more peaches,' said Luisa.

Clare had sung *Lucia di Lammermoor* on the night before, to Lucia's great pleasure, and the two had talked of it a long time over supper, and had gone to bed with the morning star. So now they were in no hurry at all with the climbing day.

They had been five days together. Clare had yet another week of work at San Carlo, and Luisa said she did not want to go to Rome without her.

Duarte had had to return there, or said he must, on the second day after disembarking – to Manuel's great disappointment. But the friends would meet in the capital when this season closed.

Clare poured the coffee, and came and sat on a rickety footstool by Luisa's knee.

'Have we two stopped talking at all since Tuesday night?'

'Sweet, we have. And we've slept a great deal.'

'Oh no! Not enough! Not enough sleep, Luisa. We'll have to catch up on that.'

'Ah! You look tired.'

'No, I'm not tired. Indeed it's feeling so alive that wearies me! As if burning always – as if I were some kind of flame!'

'That's what you are, I think. Iago said something like that about you once – that when you are singing very well in something that really suits your voice, you suggest a flame to him.'

'Did he?'

Both fell silent and drank coffee. If they had talked in passionate streams since their reunion – of themselves, of Rose, of Thomas, of their work, of South America, and again of themselves, they had spoken little as yet about Iago. Each had her own uneasy shyness in relation to the subject of him, and each at present felt her own kind of guilt in his regard. So now again they let his shadow pass.

Luisa fingered the gold chain on Clare's neck.

'You seem to want to wear it still?'

'I'm afraid so.'

'You wear other chains sometimes – that other for your wrist. You're well bound.'

'Thomas's chain. Yes, I love it. I often like to wear it.'

'But it's heavier than mine. And it has stones like tears in it, Clara!'

'Are you trying to be allegorical, by any chance, you silly?'

'Actually, yes – and I don't think I made a bad attempt. But then I'm still half-asleep. Sing me something.'

'A cradle song?'

'Yes.'

'At one o'clock in the day? No, sing your own cradle-song, love.' Getting up, Clare stroked the other's hair. 'You'll do it better than I, and give me pleasure while I tidy up this place.'

'What a demon you are for order!'

'I know. I can't help it. Does it irritate you?'

'A bit, I suppose. You should be more of a bohemian.'

Clare pulled on a dressing-gown and took a large enamel pan from under the stove. As she opened the door to go and fill this pan from the tap on the next landing she smiled back and said:

'If to be a bohemian is to have forsaken the moral standards of properly instructed people, then surely I am one?'

Luisa laughed and began to sing to herself.

Clare might say in those first days after Luisa's return that she was wearied by knowing herself to be too much alive, and as if she were a flame; nevertheless it was only one-half of her that lived to that degree and in relation to that image. Another Clare, the familiar one of always, was about her usual business, and was able to watch this newcomer coolly enough from the wings. And the newcomer knew this, and knew it with a sense of relief that puzzled and sometimes saddened her. One does not change, she thought, one does not escape. The heart grows and learns indeed – and gladly, gladly, Luisa. But so do other parts of soul and thought and reason – and they grow as had been expected, along the taught and fore-ordained direction; not away and outward from sequestered life, as feeling, feeling in imperious charge insisted she must travel. And travel she did – she could do no other – yet so far, it seemed, without being able to get entirely out of sight of herself.

In Naples indeed, alone with immediate delight and peace, and accepting now more strongly, more gladly that which she

had from first encounter with it always undergone in wonder –
the wild, sweet city's power over her senses – in Naples she
refused to pause more than momentarily now and then for her
familiar, watching self. And it is true that in the operas she sang
during those last eleven days at San Carlo – all routine Italian
works – *Rigoletto, Il Trovatore, Norma, Lucia di Lammermoor, La Somnambula* – she felt for the first time, she told
Luisa, free, operatic, relaxed.

'And exactly so you are singing! You are being quite superb,
my darling. Positively in command of the whole business!'

Clare laughed delightedly.

'But the absurd thing is that that is what I *don't* feel! I don't
feel in command of anything these days! I might sing flat at any
minute, for all I'd notice! Or come in on the wrong bar, or
forget to come in at all!'

'It'll be a remarkable moment when you sing flat, you
skylark.'

But Naples had to vanish at last behind a golden noonday mist,
and in hot bright afternoon Rome took charge of these two
errant, separate lives.

Clare found her rooms on the Lunga again, and entered them
in sober mood. The *portiera* welcomed her kindly, and Ruffo
skipped up the stairs ahead of her. The place was in good order,
and she looked about her with at once a desolated pain in her
heart and a creeping, treacherous sense of lonely peace.

Rose, who was back in Rome, the Scala season ended, had
flooded the little room with welcome – strawberries, roses,
wine; there were roses from Paddy too, and a letter. Two or
three other letters, one in little Giacomo's writing; one, thank
God, from Grandmother; a very thick one from Thomas, post-
marked Dresden.

Clare opened the shutters and welcomed back the western
light from the Janiculum and the small breeze from Ostia
beyond. She picked up Ruffo and while he purred against her
neck she let some sudden tears splash down on his pretty head.
Tears, for what she hardly knew, but self-indulgently she let
them fall.

Rose had found a small furnished apartment in Via dei Greci – 'on the old beat', as she said; behind the Accademia and only across the Corso from Ripetta. She was resting, but obligatorily taking refresher lessons every day, alternately with Signor Ditorre at Santa Cecilia and with little Giaco. It would indeed be a happy thing to see her again and hear all the news, and be *real*. And Clare was to go to her apartment tonight, it had been arranged, whence they would go to dine – in some grandeur, Clare smiled to note – at Ranieri's. There later Luisa would join them, coming down from the studio she had hired above the Spanish Steps, on the corner of Via Sistina.

So here were all three from Rue des Lauriers in Rome, together again, but all actually paying rent now, and, in some measure, running their own private establishments. It seemed amazing still to Rose and Clare – and also to Luisa, though she was a year ahead of them, and whereas not rich at all, had never been poor in the literally penniless sense that they two had been when they arrived in Paris from Ireland, nearly four years ago.

Clare turned from the window.

'Come on, Ruffo – there's much to be done before I go out to dine with that *assoluta* from La Scala!'

She looked at her letters. Paddy's was long, and she skimmed it. All that was necessary to read in it now was that he understood from Rose that she was engaged for dinner tonight, but that he would visit her at noon tomorrow, and hoped she might lunch with him, etc. Little Giaco's was paternal and businesslike, and desired her to call on him on the morrow, in the afternoon, as summer engagements must be discussed. Thomas's letter she fingered affectionately and put aside; it would be too interesting to hurry through, it must wait. Grandmother's – far too precious to be opened now. She would read herself to sleep on it. But there was another, in a handwriting she did not know – from Via Quattro Fontane; from Iago Duarte.

Very formal, in careful Italian. He had wished in Naples to speak to her about her singing, and had had no opportunity, but having heard her in *Norma* he desired to make a proposition to her as to her further studies, which he hoped she would agree to. When, therefore, might he see her? Would she permit him to offer her luncheon or dinner on any day within the week?

She folded the letter and put it with the others on the little desk in the corner.

Then she began to unpack.

'I must make myself look respectable, Ruffo. Signorina Rosa is a grandee now, you know.'

As she walked to Rose's lodging – past the Chiesa Nuova, through lovely Piazza Navona and by San Agostino to the Corso – she thought how little indeed of the grandee there was in Rose; and she wondered what conceivable event or set of events could ever alter that sane and simple realist.

Rose had had, since her Desdemona début, a brilliant season of success at La Scala. True, it was only a first season, and some great first seasons of the past had not been followed by sustained and mature triumph. But those well learned in opera and in the history of La Scala seemed now calm and unanimous about Rose; so her present was glittering and happy, and the future might be said to be prepared to give her all that she desired. Yet she did not change in anything, save to grow more like herself, the honest and merry and tender-hearted one, the level-headed and benevolent one, that she could have been foreseen to become in any walk of life, from Lackanashee to Milan and back again.

Rose was out of debt to the Committee now, she had announced in her last letter to Clare. *And isn't it a shame that poor Miss French will never take in the good news?* For the beloved and good Miss French had had a stroke about five days before Rose's first *Otello*, and that was why there had been no word of good wishes from her; that also was why Mamma, in the great anxiety of nursing Miss French, had forgotten the date of the month and had failed to write. So Mamma had of course long been forgiven the lapse, but meantime all these months Miss French lay in lost darkness of mind, from which she would not return. Rose often wept for her, and persisted in writing to her, although she knew that was a senseless thing to do. And it not only saddened but it exasperated her that the best and kindest one of all the Committee would not ever know that her protégée had so far done what had been expected of her.

> ... Still, I won't be able to go home yet – can you believe it? Firstly, because La Scala won't let me. I have to stay quietly studying, and getting ready for next season, they say. And secondly, I have only a little money saved, so I hope they'll let me do some short summer season, at Argentina, or somewhere – as I'll have to, really, whatever they say. Anyway, here I am in this ducky little flat which I can well afford for the present – it's cheap and shabby, thank God, as other people's grand things would worry me to death. And I'm simply dying for you to be back, Clarabelle. Rome doesn't seem natural or homely without you ...

Rome did seem natural and homely now, Clare realized, as she walked its familiar stones on her way to find Rose. She wondered how things were as to René, as to Antonio. For the two seemed still to hold their hard-fought places in the life of their beloved, despite all the now almost absurdly thronging followers. Followers great and grand, foolish and ambitious, simply amorous or simply greedy – but, as Clare could see already in March, they were persistent and very numerous; 'in all shapes and sizes', as Rose said.

Well, she would hear much of the news tonight. It would be fun.

She crossed the Corso, and walked up the stone staircase of the crumbly old house in Via Greci.

'I know that my Redeemer liveth ...' she sang, on the third landing, and out of a door on the fourth floor came Rose, who joined her singing to Clare's as she dashed down the stairs.

'... And that He shall stand on the latter day ...'

Laughing, they hugged each other.

'Come on! Come up! I thought you'd never get here! I nearly sent a cab for you!'

'Your private cab, I suppose, Adelina Patti?'

'Oh, you're looking well, Clare – too thin, though! Come, look – isn't this a lovely little place?'

It was. Its chief room, bare and simple, faced coolly north and opened to a *terrazzo* where there were basket chairs, pots of oleanders, and some sleeping cats. A wide prospect stretched beyond Via Flaminia and Monte Farnesina, to draw back into Rome the airs and moods of the Campagna; and close beside, a little above, rose the Pincio terrace and dark trees of the Borghese Gardens.

'Lovely. Are these your cats?'

'No. They're the painter's next door – but they live with me. He's a Frenchman – Dumarc – he's just finished painting me. Sit down, pet. How was San Carlo? Giaco is very, very pleased with you, he says.'

'I'm glad. I'll be seeing him tomorrow. But I want the Milan gossip, Rosie – much more exciting.'

Rose poured wine from a stone jug.

'Our own Velletri, Clare, for old times' sake.'

They drank with a smile, as they often did when alone, to July 1887, which still in its awkwardness and loneliness seemed to both of them as near to their unchanged selves as it was remote from the two accomplished young opera singers that, without conceit, they had to acknowledge themselves to have become.

'What's it like, being a *prima* in La Scala?'

'Oh – it's only my first season, and with all the established *assolute* singing to right and left and on all the important nights, you soon learn to keep your place, Clarabelle! It's lovely to be making proper money, and to be assured that one is improving and giving satisfaction. But Madame Pantaleoni wasn't after all very well pleased that they put on a new Desdemona behind her back, as it were – only three years after she had created the part for them. So they've only let me sing it twice since – that night you heard me, and one other very unimportant night. You have to learn to keep out of people's way, and not run off with ideas about yourself!'

'Yes, indeed – that would be necessary there.'

'Still, you get truly attached to the place – it's as if you'd taken vows in its service, or something! But now, of course, there's this awful shadow over everyone, about Signor Faccio—'

'Won't he get better?'

'They say he won't. Signor Boito has taken him to some new mental clinic in Switzerland – but nobody seems to have any hope. He's old, of course – but he's a god in La Scala. They say it's upset Signor Verdi very much—'

'Thomas said in some letter that they say he's working on another Shakespearean opera—'

'Yes. Isn't he an old marvel? Oh, Clarabelle, I've been looking at you very closely for these few minutes! Are you – in love at last, pet?'

Clare reached for her glass, but felt her hand shaking, so let it be.

'Whom would I have met lately to fall in love with, Rosie?'

'God knows! It's a pity Thomas is so far away. But – this is cheeky of me, Clare – you know, something has happened to you, and, well, the return of that strange Duarte—'

'Duarte? He – belongs to – to Luisa.'

'He doesn't belong to anyone. And neither does Luisa, if you ask me. Anyway, he's nearly as unsuitable for Luisa as he'd be for you. Only that doesn't bother me.'

'And truly it needn't bother you about me, pet.'

'Are you sure? Because I'm *not*, Chiara Alve.' Rose drank some wine, and smiled wisely. 'I always think that Luisa and Duarte got tangled in a love-affair simply out of friendship, and the peace of being Spanish together here. Just as you and I might have got sentimental about each other, if one of us had been a man, and we met here in Rome – the way Paddy's got so clinging and sentimental about you. You know what I mean? But I don't think those two Spaniards are in love – Luisa's too lively for him anyway – and I'm sure she doesn't even try to be faithful to him!'

Clare got up and walked over to the terrace railing.

'I don't know how you could know that, Rosie,' she said.

'Of course I don't know it. I'm only talking. But you aren't Luisa – you take things hard, darling. So I hope if you are in love, it's with someone kind and young, for Heaven's sake!'

Clare laughed, and came back to her chair.

'You sound like a sweet old aunt, my pet,' she said, but Rose

observed her brightened eyes and shaking hand, and said no
more.

'I have been intending to examine *you* about the state of
your heart, my lady,' said Clare, after a pause, 'but now all your
wisdom makes me feel disconcerted, somehow!'

'My heart? Ah!'

Rose's face and voice matched each other in sudden shadowed
gravity. Clare leant over and touched her hand.

'Rose! Shall we talk no more of love and hearts – for tonight?'

'Better not, for a while. Let's get used to being together first
– let's get like old times, a bit.'

'We find that easy enough, God knows.'

'Oh, and it's such a rest, Chiara. If it were only just talking
English—'

'I know.'

'But a funny thing – you talked French to me – did you
notice? – for the first few minutes, though I was talking English!'

'Did I? I must be going mad, Rosie.'

Clare and Luisa always spoke French together, as it was the
first language in which they had known each other.

'We're getting to be such polyglots, darling, that soon we'll
lose our identities completely,' said Rose amusedly. 'And that
reminds me – have you lost all purpose of ever going home to
Ireland again?'

'How could I have? I'm starved for Ballykerin – part of me,
that is. I wonder how I'll find it when I do get back!'

'How's Grandmother?'

'Well, I hope. There's a letter from her this evening, but I
haven't read it yet.'

Rose smiled.

'You always used to hoard her letters, I remember.'

'I'm afraid she'll be getting lonely now. Julie went off last
month to be a nun in the Presentation Convent in Tuam—'

'Surely young for that?'

'Oh no, she's eighteen, and apparently very holy. She has
brains too; she did well at school. But Grandmother will
miss her. It seems that Evie is a frivolous character, and not

simpatica, in Grandmother's opinion. She always did look a bit like Tom, whom I never could take to!'

'But he's very *holy*, isn't he?'

'Oh yes – did wonders at Maynooth. He's on the Australian Mission now.'

'Ah well, you'll have two of them to pray you in, in the heel of the hunt, Clara! Better off than me! There's no nun or priest that I ever heard of in my family!'

'Father Lucius will pray for you, pet – and Paddy, you can be sure!'

Rose stood up.

'Oh quiet,' she said. 'Clare, I want none of it. None of this praying! Please say no more!'

The simple words ended in a great cry. Yet they did not surprise Clare, who went at once and took Rose into her arms.

'Pet – I know. I know we were sent out into the dark. Be quiet, Rosie – you've taken the law into your own hands. Don't fuss. What are you fussing about?'

'How can I take the law into my own hands? What am I to do?'

'Sing away – and take the consequences.'

'That is your considered advice?'

The two laughed.

They went out to Ranieri's.

Half-way through supper they were joined by Luisa and Duarte, and later, apparently to Rose's surprise, by Antonio de Luca.

The latter, returned that evening from visiting his parents at their country estate in the Etruscan Apennines, north of Florence, had sought Rose at Via dei Greci, and had gathered, he said, from the *portiero* that one of the young ladies had pronounced the word Ranieri as they passed his lodge.

It seemed to Clare, who had been pondering in the last hour Rose's uncharacteristic brief outcry before they left her apartment – '... Quiet! None of this praying! ...' – that Antonio's unlooked-for appearance not only surprised but sharply delighted her. When he sat down beside her and took her hand in his, the two hands twisted about each other as if to express a very sure and private joy, and lay together thus enlaced a minute or more on the table.

Rose's eyes flashed happily over Antonio's gay, rejoicing face.

'Countryman!' she said. 'What a terrifying colour you've changed to!'

'Yes, indeed! You all look a pallid, footlighty lot!'

'But I haven't faced a footlight in four weeks,' said Rose.

'Nor I for longer,' said Luisa.

'In fact, I'm the only working member,' said Clare. 'And I'm out of work now!'

'Lazy creatures! Rogues and vagabonds. Ah, it's good to be back, Rosa d'Irlanda!'

'And what have you been at? Digging and delving?'

'More or less. Breaking in colts, shooting quail, and horse-whipping the peasantry!'

Antonio was no letter-writer. To Rose he was a sender of long telegrams, of frequent, gay presents picked up at random – and of peaches and asparagus and carnations from his father's gardens. But in a month of separation this gave her only his thought of her, nothing of his news.

And indeed she knew that his news from home would never be for her, that she was not to concern herself with it. She had met his parents, Count Anastasio and the Countess, when they came to Milan to hear Antonio in his and her second appearance in *Otello* in March. Clare had been in Milan then and had also met the de Lucas, as had all Antonio's chief friends at La Scala. And in both of these handsome parents, who were cousins, was manifest still much of the outgoing charm, the attack and *verve* and all-things-to-all-men quality that made Antonio at once lovable and successful. But Rose in meeting them knew that she had at last met the complete Antonio; they, without a word said, explained and expressed him to her, for as they, like him, were light-hearted, gracious, generous, pleasure-loving and of the world, so he, like them, was a member of the nobility of Tuscany; not of a very famous house, but one very old in lineage, still used to privilege and wealth and from these bastions able to look out with complete detachment, self-centredness and self-awareness upon an amusing but unimpinging world made up of several other kinds and classes of people whom it was necessary and often pleasant to meet and consider, among whom one might work and play and find friends and take lovers – but who, in the ordered nature of things, did not draw near or enter the de Luca plane of life. Rose had known this always, for indeed Antonio neither could nor ever sought to conceal his quite simple and immovable class-consciousness.

In their first year of friendship at Via di Ripetta he had sometimes puzzled with Rose over the differences he found between her and the Sicilian girl, Mariana.

'You're both peasants, serf class really – aren't you? As so many good singers have been! And that's odd too – you almost never hear of an aristocrat who's any good in any part of music or singing! But you and Mariana – Chiara, too, I suppose? – well, you're about as humbly born as possible . . .'

This reflection, which he had made more than once, always made Rose smile delightedly.

'Thomas, too, I think, Tonio! After all, a sailors' tavern in Cardiff—'

'Yes, indeed! But all I mean is that there's such an extraordinary difference between Mariana and you—'

'The difference of being Sicilian and Irish – or perhaps merely of being two different people—'

'No. Mariana is a dear girl – but she *is* out-and-out a peasant, in everything. But you—'

'Oh, so am I, Tonio. Make no mistake!'

'Are you? I can never quite remember it, Rosa. Perhaps it's only that your beauty is so exotic to me—'

'That's all, dear prince of the blood. I'm really extremely low, in all my instincts, God help me!'

But though Antonio was amused by such exchanges, Rose knew that for him a peasant was traditionally and in fact someone over whom one might, benevolently, exercise *droits de seigneur*, but whom one could not travel any distance with along the natural ways of privileged life. And having met his parents she understood better than before that this was an unalterable part of him. So, when he went home for vacation to his father's estates and to the neighbouring estates of an uncle, another de Luca, whose heir through recent family deaths he had now become, she knew that he departed into a life of which she would never be told more than its superficies, and within the frame of which her name would not be mentioned though – she could believe – she yet was not forgotten there.

But now he was back from 'horse-whipping the peasantry'. He was a singer, a trouper again, and his eyes blazed on her with the well-remembered gaiety of love – a gaiety of which at present she was much in need.

Wine flowed. Antonio ordered himself much to eat. The restaurant was quiet and cool; and the five who sat together, though each in fact – save perhaps this latest happy comer – at heart in varying measures disturbed, perplexed, desirous or sad, yet felt a passing outer mood of resignation to the lull of the hour, and also an odd, shared ambience of affection circling them.

Duarte half-closed his eyes and pondered this.

'If Thomas were here now,' said Rose, 'Thomas and Mariana – it'd be like old times—'

'And little Giaco and Casta Diva', said Clare.

'And Signor Paddy, Chiara,' teased Antonio.

'How faithful we are!' said Clare. 'After all these years, just the first few friends are all we want.'

'Four years we've known each other,' Luisa smiled to Clare.

'Not quite. It'll be four years in October—'

'And next month you and I will have been three solid years in this old Italy, Clarabelle,' said Rose. 'Oh, how old I feel!'

'Yes, Signorina Rosa,' said Duarte, smiling at her. 'You only reached La Scala in the nick of time!'

Under the gentle flow of talk, gossip of friends, professional rumours and surmises, jokes from the South American tour, from Milan, from Naples; as moths fluttered between the dreaming faces and about blown candles, as roses fell apart on the white cloth, as the street noises beyond the open door ebbed down to the singing of one child – the secret thoughts of four at least of the sippers of Frascati moved shadowily in ironic parallels.

How will it be now? I might go back to Spain at last. It's long enough. I could live, Duarte half-thought. I could have taken that Conservatoire post in Lima. Why linger about? Because I want to? Rome – Rome that I loathe? 'Strega again, please,' he said to the waiter, and smiled at Luisa. Lovely face – her beauty wears a dangerous edge sometimes – as now, when it's at its gentlest. How will it be? He narrowed his eyes, and lifted his glass appreciatively. I'm old enough to have sense, he thought. Let them be – tonight is quiet anyway. Rome seems quiet, for once.

How will it be now? Rose was asking her lifted, uneasy heart. I hope he's singing well tonight. Oh René! Two loves, no. Even I, who have become a sinner so fast – oh René, dear one – she laid her hand with involuntary hardness, as of a cry, on Antonio's beside her – and it was caught and kissed.

How will it be? How am I to live this hidden, shining life before all these pairs of eyes that know me? Oh Luisa, is it possible to go straight ahead, alone and calmly, this very day, this very night, from our golden time? Were we together when we woke this morning – were we in Mamma Lucia's those few hours ago? Ah quiet, quiet. Clare lifted her glass and drank wine with deliberation. Be sane. It wasn't life; it was a few days only, a forbidden interlude. You know you're used to being alone, it's how you are best. You must possess your soul, and learn to pray again. Be quiet. Don't look at her too much.

How will it be, here in Rome? Not this way, God, night after night – not going round in groups and trying to make her smile to me alone. Clare, you wear my chain, you said you want to wear it – you are mine. I will not be without you, love. I'll not have you withdrawing to your mountain-top. It took me long enough to sing you down to me! Luisa smiled and heard her own voice in clear memory – *Che faro* – and telepathically she found Clare's eyes and knew that Eurydice also heard her singing, far away.

Duarte too perhaps – for if he did not catch the unsung phrase he intercepted the meeting of the blue eyes and the gold.

Antonio meantime, eating strawberries, hummed his own motif of the Ripetta days: '*La ci darem* . . .' and smiled on La

Rosa d'Irlanda with the air of one who had small doubt how everything would be, and saw no cloud in the summer sky of Rome.

Rose, who sat facing the length of the restaurant, smiled suddenly with friendliness towards a distant point. Antonio, following her smile, laughed and rose to return the bow of a man who had risen to bow from a far-off table.

'Our Boston friend, Rosa! Does he never go home to his own country?' Antonio asked as he sat down.

'He went in March, I think,' said Rose. 'I didn't know he had come back. He's devoted to opera.'

Antonio smiled.

'He must be if he's crossed the ocean for our summer repertories!'

'Who are you talking about, Rosie?' asked Clare, who sat with her back to the room.

'A rich New England infatuate,' said Antonio. 'Inarticulate, but possibly dangerous!'

'Don't mind this silly fellow,' said Rose. 'Mr Rudd is a nice man, and he loves La Scala and opera in general. So he spends a lot of his time, he's told me, in Germany and Italy. He can afford to. The man he's with looks like that German baritone who was singing in Genoa last month.'

'Pity we can't look round,' said Luisa. 'Is he handsome, Rose, your New Englander?'

'I don't know. Serious, Protestant-looking.' They all laughed. 'Very tall, very thin. He was at our *Otello* first night, and afterwards he was friendly and nice to you and me, wasn't he, Tonio?'

'Perforce – to me,' said Antonio.

Duarte had looked cautiously round.

'That *is* Schelling, the baritone,' he said. 'I heard him in Berlin last year. I see what you mean, Rosa – a Protestant face, undoubtedly – sectarian.'

'What did you say this Protestant name was?' asked Luisa.

'Rudd. He's Mr Silas Rudd of Boston,' said Rose.

'And his family have always been patrons of music in North America, I was told,' said Antonio. 'Waiter, this wine again, please.'

'And bring me Strega,' said Duarte.

'Is there any news of the Argentina, Rose?' asked Luisa. 'Is there going to be a summer season?'

'Yes. A very good one they're hoping to arrange, I hear.'

'I'll get all the plans out of little Giaco tomorrow,' said Clare.

'You two will have a great summer there, almost for sure,' said Rose. 'Making money hand over fist. But I do hope they'll give me a few parts!'

'Ah, Rosie! If they do you'll put us all in the halfpenny place,' said Clare.

'Don't worry, girls,' said Antonio. 'La Scala won't let her sing in Rome this summer – for certain.'

'But what am I going to do for money?'

'You can beg, Rosa.'

'Or sell flowers on the Spanish Steps,' said Duarte.

'Ah, René!' Rose stretched her hand in welcome to the young tenor who paused behind Luisa's chair and stared in blank surprise at Antonio. 'I thought you were perhaps too tired, or had forgotten—'

'I am tired, Rose – but I had not forgotten.'

When drinking coffee with René in the Corso earlier in the day, Rose had told him that she would be with Clare and Luisa in Ranieri's for dinner, and as he expressed a wish to see Clare again she had said he might join them there after his opera at La Valle if he felt so inclined. She had not dreamt then Antonio would also be with her, and she saw now that that unforeseen presence at her side had sent René into one of those moods of his of self-pitying anger which she found hard to bear and hard to manage.

When he had greeted Clare, Luisa and Duarte, very gracefully and looking very beautiful, Clare thought, Rose made room for him at her left side on the velvet-covered bench.

'Sit here,' she took his hand and drew him down. 'You do look tired. What will you eat?'

'Oh something, anything. May I drink first?'

Rose, who knew his eyes and his mannerisms with precision, knew that he had been drinking already; feared indeed that he might have been drinking in his dressing-room throughout the course of the opera. He had not formed that bad habit; but sometimes, if he disliked his soprano or was uncertain of his relations with the conductor on any particular night, he *did* resort to brandy, not so much in order to get through a performance with credit as in defiance of the immediate irritant. He seemed too often to have to brighten and clarify his conception of himself by artificial means. Rose knew that he was a frightened young man always, and in his dressing-room an extremely frightened one. She understood this; she saw its many reasons, general, and especial to himself; and she felt very responsible towards him. Often in the year of their love she had accused herself; loving him as she did and as she continued to love him, she believed now that she had erred gravely, for him, in taking him for a lover. The decision, which had been all hers, had been for her a good one; for, whatever conscience-searching she might do, and often did, in terms of her Catholic teaching and of the catechism, she did not confuse its answers with the natural good and help and peace she had drawn, as woman and as singer, from her first experience of love. It was a sin, and she could face that; but it had also been, and still could be, a blessed and irresistible sweetness, a true explanation of life, for better or worse.

However, for René it had not been so felicitous, she feared. For him, although he loved her and because he loved her, their love had become a protracted assault upon those weaker parts of his character which it might have been supposed to help. It had by no means brought to him the rest it had brought to her. On the contrary, instead of quieting and reassuring his vanity it had inflamed it; instead of helping him to be humble about his work, it seemed to have increased his touchiness under direction and to have made him even slapdash; and as she advanced in success too far beyond him, his frightened arrogance made him parade his relationship with her so as to make his colleagues laugh, and quite stupidly despise him. Still, Rose saw that in withdrawal of her love there was no remedy now. He could not have borne either the loss or the humiliation. In loving him perhaps she had done him a wrong, but there was no help for that that she could see. He was her charge, and she must love him.

Yet often nowadays the love she gave him, although his beauty could disturb her still, was not romantic or sexual, but rather the uneasy love one has to give sometimes to a difficult and stupidly self-centred child. And one defect in him that again and again made her more impatient than she meant to be was his inability to be a good trouper. For instance, his exaggerated dressing-room terrors and stage-fright always wearied her, not because she did not know them to be authentic, but because he believed them to be an agony sent from Heaven solely for him, and not something which he shared with every other member of any opera he sang in.

'It's the same for every one of us, René, I swear to you! For every actor in the world! And will be till we take our very last curtain!'

'Oh, how can you say that! How do you know! You couldn't possibly imagine what it's like for me! And since *you* can't – what about these other cheerful sheep?'

'Be quiet, René! Don't make such a fool of yourself, for Heaven's sake!'

'Oh, you're angry! Don't be angry, Rose!'

But she could never be angry with anyone for long, and hated to be angry with this vulnerable boy. So they forgave each other again and again, and he did not grow happier. And tonight he was not happy, would not have been happy were Antonio never there.

'Drink? Yes, indeed! This lovely Soave—'

'May I have that?' He pointed to the Strega bottle.

'Of course,' said Duarte, and poured some liberally into a large glass. René took a long gulp.

'Thank you,' he said, and ordered food from the waiter, an order which Rose translated into Italian. He persistently spoke French in Rome, which was perfectly convenient, as it happened, for everyone at this table, but was bad for his work, as Rose tried vainly to make him understand. Also it made him on occasion seem more impolite than in fact he was. When he was agitated or upset, he seemed to forget that any Italian at all was required in Rome, and behaved exactly as if he were in his native Rouen. So this rapid French to the waiter was a danger signal, and Rose knew that it was one of those mistakes of René's that Antonio could not endure.

But René touched her hand gently now in apology.

'I'm sorry, Rose – I forgot. But anyhow I hate to flounder in Italian before a Tuscan aristocrat.' And he smiled with malice across her to Antonio.

'That's understandable,' said Antonio serenely.

René's supper was brought, but he seemed reluctant to eat, and drank more Strega. He smiled at Clare and at Luisa, and asked them polite questions about San Carlo, about South America.

The restaurant was very quiet now, with many tables unoccupied. Duarte's head ached, and he wished he was at home, alone at his work-table. He felt old and sceptical amid all this youth and wished he had not come here with Luisa, for he was resistant tonight to all she stood for, resistant also to Clare's unconscious exactions on his spirit, and made to feel sad and foolish by the tension which he felt between the two, and of which exasperatedly he suffered within himself the tightening pull. I wish I could get up and walk away into the night, he thought.

He poured himself more Strega. Luisa read his mood from his hand as it held the bottle, and Clare read her anxious impotence in Luisa's momentarily unguarded face.

However, the very palpable tensions at the other side of the table were of a cruder and more pathetic order.

'Do eat something, René,' said Rose. 'You really need to eat.'

'What were you singing tonight, René?' asked Clare.

'You'd never guess,' he said self-mockingly. 'An unknown piece called *Il Trovatore*.'

'Well, easy enough anyway,' said Luisa soothingly, for none of these troupers liked green beginners to sneer at Signor Verdi or at any of the hard-tried composers that they did not yet know how to sing.

'You think so, Miss Luisa? Have you ever tried getting through the piece with La Pampini on the stage?'

Elena Pampini! They all stared at him.

Rose put her hand on his sleeve.

'But she's a darling, René.'

'A fat and self-confident old darling, Rose.'

'She's a bit fat,' said Duarte, 'and she has every reason to be self-confident.'

'Indeed?' said René, afraid now that he had made a silly remark, and the more likely therefore to lose his head completely.

Antonio leant back against the velvet bench and closed his eyes as if, Luisa thought amusedly, he were asking Heaven for the grace of patience. The sooner we close this topic the better, she was thinking, for she had heard rage in Duarte's cool observation.

But Clare was too angry to hesitate.

'If you ever sing with a more helpful, a more accomplished or a more generous soprano than Elena Pampini, you'll be luckier than you deserve, René!'

Clare had sung with her in many opera houses in her two years of travelling round, she sometimes *seconda donna* to Pampini, Pampini sometimes supporting her. And it was always a blessed thing, as every singer knew, to have her in the cast. She was a soprano now in her middle thirties who had missed full success only because of an unfortunate marriage which had made it necessary for her to support her children by singing here, there and everywhere in any kind of engagement during the years when, by her merits, she should have been choosing her work with reserve and caution. Nevertheless, despite the enforced rough-and-tumble of her professional life she was still held, by judges such as Duarte who had directed and conducted her, to be one of the most musicianly and reliable of living Italian singers, and among singers themselves there was hardly one in Italy who did not hold her in love and gratitude. She was always especially good to young singers, and could correct and guide them, out of her wide knowledge, with benevolent good sense. Rose saw now that it must have been by some kind direction on to René of this good sense that La Pampini had offended him — that he had failed to understand her benevolence, and being no judge of musicianship of any kind, did not appreciate her artistry. It was merely another instance to her of the lonely, nervous habit of his days, the vague detachment which he wrapped around himself at the centre of his professional life. Oh, the more fool he, she thought now in an access of impatience. But even as she did, she still saw his peculiar difficulty of nature, and blamed herself for its increase in him; blamed herself too for Antonio's happy and unlooked-for presence here tonight.

That Clare, who always befriended him, should attack him so contemptuously made René furious.

'I don't see how you can possibly know that, Miss Clare. After all, you're not a tenor!'

'But we all know,' said Luisa. 'We've all sung with her!'

'And yet you won't agree that on the stage she's the most self-confident and domineering of old women?'

Duarte uttered under his breath a Spanish imprecation which made Luisa laugh out loud and clutch his hand in warning.

'But dear, dear René,' said Rose, 'what has Pampini done to you that you should so totally misunderstand her?'

'I do *not* misunderstand her, I tell you!'

Antonio sat up and turned squarely towards the Frenchman.

'Chaloux,' he said, 'this is Italy. You go home, and try to get a job at the Paris Opéra.'

'I'll do that when I'm ready, de Luca.'

'Oh, you'll never be ready, even for that. But go, I *beg* you. You're not wanted here.'

'Antonio, please—' Rose stretched a hand to him imploringly, and he took it in both of his.

'I'm sorry, sweetest Rose, but we have borne enough—'

'You call her "sweetest Rose", and to my very face—'

'We all do that,' said Clare.

'Let go of her hand, you profligate! Let it go, I say!'

Antonio laughed cruelly, kissed Rose's hand and let it go.

René was shaking now; he took another mouthful of Strega, and then tried to speak calmly.

'Come, Rose. I'm sorry about this disturbance. Come, I'll take you home.'

Rose thought that perhaps she owed it to the others to go with him now, since he and she between them had spoilt the happy evening, Clare's and Luisa's first evening with her after so long. So she moved as if to find her gloves and purse.

But Antonio laid a detaining hand on her, and spoke to René.

'Rose is my guest this evening, Chaloux, and I shall take her home. In any case, I allow no drunken man to take a lady home.'

René stood up.

'You call me a drunken man?'

'Yes,' said Antonio, rising also.

'I don't permit you to, de Luca.'

'That alters nothing.'

'You'll take it back.'

'Never. It's true.'

'Sit down, you two,' said Duarte. 'Or better, you come out for a breath of air with me, Chaloux. We could walk home in peace together – I am also a little drunk,' he ended tactlessly, with a brotherly smile. But he was not heeded.

'We'll settle this outside,' said René.

'The work of a moment,' said Antonio, who was now as foolishly angry as René – and as they spoke the two had swept from the table and were striding to the door. Duarte could only laugh. Rose was exasperated and felt very tired. Nobody moved or spoke.

A shadow fell across the table.

'Miss Lennane . . .'

Rose looked up.

'Ah, Mr Rudd . . . ?'

'You will forgive my intrusion, I hope – but it just occurred to me, as there seems to be some, some slight disturbance – I mean, if a carriage is what you require, Miss Lennane, I have one waiting nearby, and I should be delighted—'

But Antonio came striding back, wearing a radiant smile.

'Mr Rudd?'

'Mr Rudd has very kindly offered me his carriage, Antonio—'

'That is indeed kind, but fortunately it is not necessary to trouble you, sir. I have a carriage waiting, Rose, and as I'm sure you're tired—'

Rose knew he had no carriage waiting, but the farce was getting out of hand and she could no longer resist the delighted mischief in Antonio's eyes.

'Yes, I'm tired, Antonio.' She laughed in rueful apology to Clare and Luisa. Antonio thrust money into the waiter's hand, took Rose on his arm and swept her from the restaurant.

Silas Rudd stood and watched them depart.

'The other young man, the Frenchman – he has a delightful tenor voice – ah, here he is!'

They all saw René come in, tousled and dusty as if he had taken a fall, looking beautiful and angry.

Mr Rudd went towards him.

'Monsieur Chaloux, I heard you sing in *L'Elisir d'Amore* the other night – I was enchanted. Will you do me the honour of drinking a glass of wine with me and with Herr Schelling?'

René blushed and smiled, and went with the kind American to his table.

The forsaken three, all their own stresses and desires forgotten in this comic moment, broke into enchanted laughter and surmise, and poured more wine.

The Thirteenth Chapter

'Is he going to die, Thomas?'

'I'd say not. Pneumonia is a devilish thing, of course. Still, I'd say he'll overcome it.'

Clare and Thomas were standing at a window of Signor Giacomo's dusty studio in Via di Ripetta. They had been allowed to look at the grey face of their *maestro*, who was fighting for every breath at the other end of the corridor, in the bed which had been Clare's and Rose's during their first months in Rome. Oxygen containers were stacked in the corridor; heavy druggets were spread everywhere, and Assunta and Signorina Caterina tiptoed about on the various uncertain errands that the menace of death suggests. But a Blue Nun sat in calm at the foot of Giacomo's bed; she was Sister Baptist, she was Irish and from Limerick, and irrationally Clare was comforted by these irrelevant facts. But even more was she comforted, irrationally, by Signora Vittoria. Casta Diva marched over all the druggets, clad in a lacy, tattered peignoir, and singing her Etruscan village songs.

'That's the one she called "Her Music on His Tomb" – do you remember, Thomas?'

Every few minutes the tall singer strode to where her husband lay, and bent and kissed his forehead, and said: '*Corragio, amore mio!*' and then swept away, singing again, in a young voice.

'I have tried to prevent her, Signorina Chiara! But you know how she can be! And Sor Battista – amazing, Signorina! – she says to let her be! She says that the Signora is *good* for Signor Giacomo! She says that he listens for her, and that when he doesn't listen any more we must then get anxious. But I – I think it too much, Signorina – and I cannot control the Signora!'

So said Assunta. La Signora could be heard singing now, far off along the corridor.

'What is their story, Thomas?'

'A love-story. Almost a good one. Anyway, it's true. Little Giaco always warned me against love. But damme, it must be something to have the woman you were once insane about simply singing you back out of the valley of death.'

'I don't think she loved him at the right time – do you?'

'No. But he got her, and he endured her and he understood her – and she loves him now—'

'She wasted him.'

'Ah, who's to say?'

It was October. Thomas was in Italy examining talent for Germany, having spent August at home in Cardiff, assisting at his father's deathbed and assisting his mother and sisters to wind up his father's affairs.

'I'm well left, Clare. My father was a man of great sense, for all his outbursts. I had a few clear talks with him before he died, and he made me read him his will in the hearing of my mother and sisters, so that we'd all agree, before he died, that we were satisfied. We protested, but he said: "Hell to that! Agree now, in my presence, that I've done justly." And he had. He left his public house to my eldest sister, quite rightly – and of course to her husband, who had worked his place in the business and is a very good fellow. He also made generous provision for my mother, and for her life-time rights in the place. But it's amazing the money that quite wild little man made in investments and property-buying. I had always thought that in his generosity to me about Leipzig and Rome I'd had all that was due to me, and my sister Maddie, who has her fine little confectionery business in Cardiff, thought she'd had her share too – but not at all! We were both left a fine lump of stock and house property and gilt-edged. Amazing. I protested to him in astonishment when I read the will – because he was always a disorderly and wilful kind of man, and his generosity made you feel that he'd leave little behind him. He laughed at me. "You're disappointed that I turn out to be a good business man," he said. "Well, I'm disappointed that you're too superior a musician to be the great tenor I was looking forward to!" You know, Clare, in Wales music is the human voice; and my father was a fair tenor himself, and at one time his heart was set on my being the great tenor of my time. But, he let me have my way in everything. And now he's left me quite liberally well-off. I don't know exactly yet what I'm worth – but it means that I can proceed as I like, and with all the people at home off my mind. It's amazing, isn't it? Out of a very low-class public house on the Cardiff waterfront?'

'Did your father have a happy life?'

'Yes and no. I don't think Mother was any use to him – and I think he found that out early. But he was lively himself – a bad, wild man, many people said. But I thought him grand and good. All the same, his consideration of us all in his will and on his deathbed amazed me. In those last days he used to say to me: "Sing, you traitor, sing – if you can keep in tune." And, of course, he only wanted simple Welsh songs, and, to my surprise, Moore's Melodies. Do you know what he liked best, Clare – what I sang every day to him, and last song of all before he died? "When he who adores thee . . ." Wasn't that odd?'

All this had been part of a long conversation of two nights before, when, heralded by a telegram from Genoa, Thomas had presented himself at Clare's rooms on the Lunga. She was very happy to see him again, and in the two intervening days, of which he spent as much time as was possible with her, she noted how sustained and vivid was her pleasure in his company and how truly he stimulated her, as always he had done. On that first night of reunion they had walked over to Trastevere for supper, which they ate in the garden of a house said to be the dwelling of Raphael's bakeress, his Fornarina.

'I expect they made love under this very same fig tree,' said Thomas.

'Rather an exposed place?'

'Not in the deep night. Look how heavy and huge these fig leaves are! Clare, have you ever come across the Trastevere poet?'

'Belli? I was just going to ask you if you knew him. I bought a volume of him lately. I like his work. Don't you?'

'Not exactly verses for young ladies.'

'No. But I wasn't born a young lady. I gave a copy to Luisa, too – she's delighted with him. I knew she would be.'

Thomas lighted a cigarette with slow care.

'You and Luisa are consistent rule-breakers, aren't you? Yet two more sharply contrasted people one couldn't observe.'

'That is true, I suppose.'

If there was a very slight inflection here of – hardly sadness, hardly even anxiety, but of repressed question, Thomas gave no sign that he heard it.

They strolled back to Clare's rooms, and as they crossed Via dei Fratti Thomas was reminded of the 'lusting seminarist'.

'Oh yes, Paddy's still there in the old rooms. But they're crowded with books now, and he's made them comfortable, in a suitably seminarist style. He's doing well. He teaches history in the Collegio Romano, and lectures to all kinds of learned bodies, and he takes a tutorial class in English at the University. Rome is really getting a bit small for him, I think. I mean, he'd never get a chair among so many ecclesiastics – so he's sounding American universities. But sometimes I think he may go back and get ordained in the end.'

'He might as well,' said Thomas. 'Still got his inflamed eye on you?'

'Well, if you call a watch-dog's eye inflamed? He dislikes me by now, you know, Thomas. But he's certainly an awful busybody.'

'Don't fool yourself, Chiara mia. Your parish-pump Savonarola doesn't what-I'd-call dislike you.'

They sat at her window and talked almost until dawn. Clare should not have done this; she had at five o'clock the following evening to take a rehearsal with Luisa, in Duarte's studio, of the Pergolesi *Stabat Mater*, which the two were to sing in their master's sacred music concert at Santa Cecilia on the following Sunday. The occasion would be a critical one for the two singers; always Duarte set a very high standard for his academic concerts, which were renowned in Rome; to be allowed to be a soloist in any programme of his was at once a test and an honour. And this *Stabat Mater*, difficult, lovely and rarely performed, was alertly anticipated by the *cognoscenti*.

So Clare felt guilty about the next evening's rehearsal; but she had been a long time deprived of Thomas; she was in more need than she admitted to herself of his sheer brotherliness – though indeed, she often thought, his was a kind of brotherliness not in the common competence of brothers. And she would sleep and be silent all through the morning and the early afternoon.

She told Thomas of this anxiety.

'I should think you hardly need tomorrow's rehearsal,' he said. 'You knew the Pergolesi *Stabat* very well a year ago – and Sunday is four days away. All you need is a run-through on Saturday.'

Clare smiled.

'If *you* were conducting it you wouldn't say that. Besides, it's one thing to know the music; it's another to give a performance that will satisfy Iago.'

In June Iago Duarte had persuaded Clare to take private tuition from him in church music. She resisted and argued awhile because she could not afford his customary fees, which were high. He desired to give her lessons without fee, insisting that her voice was particularly suited to the music of his especial field, and, if developed as he intended to develop it, would be a rich investment for him. So at last, tempted by what he had to offer, and incessantly argued thereto by him and by Luisa, she had agreed to study with him, paying what she knew was only a token fee.

All through the burning summer, therefore, although she was singing an average of three *prime* a week in the Argentina season, as well as occasional *seconde donne* – the Spaniard made her work harder and with more humility than she had yet been asked to give; but with rich gain, as after three months she could acknowledge, indeed with immeasurable gain to her in knowledge and judgment. Technically, theoretically and in the history and examination of European religious music, Duarte taught her with speed, impatience and merciless accuracy; indeed with a compressed passion in every instruction that compelled her wits to race with him, and that brought – she could hear and feel herself – great elasticity and extension to her voice.

She was grateful to him, for he was opening horizons to her talent, horizons she had always known were discoverable but which, in her dutiful resignation to nineteenth-century Italian opera, she had not expected to explore. Moreover, from Duarte she was learning something that could engage her for her life-time, and which she could study, teach and happily pass on to others, if she ever did decide, as she knew she would always be tempted to, against the life of a *prima donna*. She was at last in this hard work justifying herself to herself, she thought; whereas hitherto, in spite of some occasions of delight or of amuse-ment in her strange career, she had most generally felt that her voice justified her only to her sponsors at home, Uncle Matt and the rest.

Nevertheless when in September the Argentina had lent her to the Goldoni Theatre in Venice for three weeks, her relief and pleasure had been boundless. It was not only that she was seeing Venice for the first time; it was not only escape from the long-drawn, savage Roman summer, or respite from excess of concentrated work; nor was it altogether – though it was this in greater degree than Clare would measure – absence, brief absence, from Duarte and from Luisa. The joy and rest she took in speeding off to those three weeks came in great part, as for every comer it must, from Venice itself. Also there was the sweet, accidental luck that La Scala had so far yielded to Rose's clamours as to allow her to sing in the short Goldoni season – it was hailed by the two from Ireland as miraculous fortune to be singing together at last, and in Venice. But, for her amuse-ment, Clare knew that her real delight during the three Goldoni weeks was in being an ordinary opera-trouper again, in lodgings and free, with only easy work to sing; escaped awhile from having to take one's talent at the highest level of seriousness; escaped from the presence of love.

Venice had indeed been a holiday. For Rose too, Clare felt it was a happy, necessary respite. She also, explicit as Clare was not, was glad to be away from love, from the angers and the presumptions of lovers. Not that Rose could ever any more be free of love, or lovers. And in Venice, too, admirers crowded round. But not – for the interlude – the only two who troubled her, who now were troubling her deeply. Free of them, she did indeed once or twice in moods of great anxiety talk to Clare of her bewildered and bewildering heart, its contradictory passions and her confusing weaknesses of desire and pity and self-pity. But, for the most part she gave herself, as Clare did, to the brief escape. And they sang in *Figaro* and *The Barber* together with a quite reckless sense of fun; and on Rose's nights Clare sat in a stall and applauded *La Traviata* with all the strength of her hands; and on Clare's nights Rose did as much for *Lucia*.

For the rest, they fooled about the lovely town, with their fellow-singers or with stray admirers; in gondolas, in steamboats or on foot, they travelled over Venice and the lagoon and the islands; and they were enchanted to be quite simply together in this magic interlude, and free, both, for a brief time, of all the precious and troublesome associations that Rome had brought about them.

Among Rose's 'followers' in Venice there appeared, to Clare's amusement, the American gentleman, Mr Rudd of Boston, who had intervened with kind intention on that June night when Antonio knocked René down in the street outside Ranieri's. He was very kind to the two Irish girls; he arranged pleasant, small supper parties for them in Florian's and Danieli's, and took them on expeditions to Murano and Torcello. Clare, who read a great deal more than Rose did, recognized him, out of her light acquaintance with Hawthorne, Emerson and young Mr Henry James, as a typical New Englander. He was a Harvard man, and a citizen of Boston. He told them, in his dry and reluctant way, a great deal that was interesting about Boston and Harvard. It was evident to Clare, for all his modesty of speech, that he was an important man at home, and probably very wealthy. More remarkable she found was his real and informed interest in music. Music in all its large expressions, orchestral, choral and operatic, not merely attracted him but took his critical and knowledgeable attention. She gathered that he had grown up in appreciation of music; she did not understand why, and could not ask leading questions of a man so reserved and monosyllabic. But she did discover, and hardly with surprise, that he loved the music of Johann Sebastian Bach; when they fell on the subject of Bach together it seemed to Clare that his narrow, masked face was lighted up from within, and certainly his eyes flashed into pleasure. But when Rose laughed at Bach he took her mockery quite gaily.

'You are entitled to your folly, Signorina Rosa,' he said. 'You are music itself – so how can you judge music?'

Clare puzzled over that abandoned jest – which came oddly from Mr Rudd. But it was clear that he admired Rose's singing without reservation. And one night he told Clare that, reared though he was in admiration of oratorio, choral and symphonic music, that which moved him above all else was the human voice, the tenor or soprano, in solo performance, dramatic or lyric. Therefore, he said, he was an addict of opera, and had developed a passion for Italian opera. He added that in years which were now nearly ten of listening to the best opera in Europe, wherever he could find it, he had never heard soprano singing to match that of La Rosa d'Irlanda, in *Otello* at his first hearing of her – or in anything he had heard her sing since then.

Clare pondered him compassionately. Compassionately, because after some surprised observation she believed him to be most gravely in love with Rose.

In this judgment, dissociating from it her naïve compassion, Clare was right.

Silas Rudd had arrived, at this time in Venice when he talked with Clare, to fatal certainty about Rose. His condition of infatuation made him indeed unsure during those weeks in Venice whether he lived or dreamed.

He was a grave and good man; he was one who moved through the fortunate circumstances of his own life with measured gratitude, and who considered and adapted himself to those of others with an acceptance which was unflurried and sane. Life had been well ordered for him, and he never had to question his happy duty in giving back to it a reciprocal order, of good will and good manners. That was his tradition, and his nature embraced it, since in truth he was to its manner born.

There had been one vivid thread through the respectable good warp and woof of his days. But he had recognized that from earliest childhood, had allowed it to be a part of all he was, and had made it one with the rest of his excellent Boston life. A permissible decoration; a flower renewed each morning on his dark lapel.

Silas D. Rudd was a wealthy Bostonian, owning the banking house founded by his grandfather in 1836. He was an only son, and his father had died at the age of fifty-three, leaving the family affairs in perfect order, with Silas, aged twenty-seven then, firmly in the saddle and already perhaps a shade over-scrupulous and responsible in habit of mind. He was a distinguished-looking man, in the New England tradition, with narrow eyes, fair hair inclined to red; a long, Norman face. He had worked well at Harvard, reading constitutional history in general, and American history in particular. Also he rowed and swam for the university, and he liked to race small yachts and to ride a good horse. But he sowed very few wild oats, to his mother's vast relief. She, a Boston Wainwright, was everything that the wife of a Boston Rudd should be – correct, Episcopalian, every inch a lady; but well-educated for her time and place – and very handsome.

When Silas found himself master of his father's house, with his mother and his unmarried young sister Agatha under his protection, he was well content to be a good son and brother, and to proceed correctly with the Rudd way of life.

This, besides its private and business duties, embraced civic responsibilities and charitable interests; and to the latter, the last especially, the family brought traditionally a liberality, a progressiveness and generosity which was not entirely approved by other Bostonians. The Wainwrights indeed, who had no other fault to find with the Rudd connection, did sometimes shake their heads (behind Madeleine's back, because they saw no need to hurt her) over the Rudd method in directing the various foundations and trusts to which they put their name. But about the Rudd hobby in benefaction they were indulgent

– because, oddly enough, Wainwrights were also traditionally inclined to it. Grandfather Silas – Silas the First, as they
called him – had loved music, and had been generous to the
limits of his power in promoting music for Boston. Sacred
music, orchestral, chamber, operatic – to all of it he gave his
warmest zest, and his name stood high in all subscription lists
and on all committees which concerned it in his city, or anywhere in Massachusetts. So, the mantle which he had flung
about so widely and freely in the eighteen-forties, -fifties,
-sixties, his sons continued to unfurl. And his eldest grandson,
his direct heir, Silas the Third, was glad to continue in the
obligation.

He never spoke of the joy he took in his inherited patronage
of music, because he was a shy, laconic man. But he did not
have to discuss it with his mother, whose Wainwright tradition,
as has been said, was with the Rudds in this especial civic
interest. Yet in manhood he sometimes considered – desolately
– that he had been slow-witted, and even loutish, in that he did
not decide in time to go to Europe and *study* music. Not to
become an executant of any kind; he knew that he could never
have interpreted music himself, let alone have composed it. But
he should have learnt to know it. He saw that was so, when it
was too late. The New Englander, the Episcopalian in him had
shrunk in fear – as he came to understand – before European
expressiveness, European ease and genius. So he had pursued
his obvious tradition, and became its excellent exponent.

Yet always, from earliest childhood, there had been the one
golden thread. He had been taken, early and constantly, to the
concerts and operas of Boston. He had met musicians and
singers in his grandfather's house, and afterwards in his father's,
in the library of which he was to assemble in his own time a
collection of musical scores and of works on music which was
at once his consolation and his grief, and which he would leave
at his death to the citizens of Boston.

Always then there had been this rose for every morning.
Music. Above all, the music of the human singing voice. Early
in his life, song had become his cult; it was his private, guarded
window to the upper skies.

Clare, simply pitying him, knew nothing of the closed-up man she compassionated. But one night, tired and half-asleep, for she had sung Queen of Night in *The Magic Flute*, she awoke in a *trattoria* near the Goldoni statue to hear Silas Rudd speaking to Rose.

'You sing the Italians exquisitely,' he was saying. 'Perhaps too exquisitely for Italian taste. But, when I think of you – forgive me – I always hear Bach – happy, pure music, Miss Rose – I know Bach annoys you—'

'No,' said Rose. 'Bach only means someone I haven't had time to grapple with – goodness, can't you understand? Now, Clare – wake up! Has there been time for us to deal with Bach? I ask you – has there?'

'No, no,' said Clare. 'There's been no time at all.'

'You don't have to "deal with" Bach, Miss Rose. I only mean that his music reminds me of you – it expresses, well, it expresses – goodness.'

'Goodness,' said Rose, and then she laughed and threw the word up again in gay astonishment: 'Goodness!'

'Still, I mean it,' said Silas Rudd, smiling at her joke.

'I know you do,' said Rose, and with gravity added: 'Once I was good.'

Clare got up and strolled away in silence, towards her lodgings. Something of suppressed piteousness, or fear, in Rose's face made her anxious, as also did the devotion in the New England face.

But that had been Venice and September, when moments of doubt or cloud had been wisps in a gold sky. Now it was late October, and the days for Clare were Roman, hard worked, realistic; pressed upon close by the exactions of others, troubled and made shadowy by her own. And Rose had long been gathered back from sped Goldoni brightness into the fogged and faraway disciplines of La Scala.

Ripetta was sad in this cold dusk; the druggets spread, the pianos closed, the autumn pupils scattered to the care of other *maestri*. The trees beyond the Belle Arte roofs shuddered in the wind, and as Assunta came into the studio with a pot of chocolate, Signora Vittoria's folk song floated after her, from the *salottino*.

'It doesn't seem right,' said Assunta.

'It's probably good for him,' said Thomas. 'The Blue Nun says it is.'

'Oh, thank you for this, dear Assunta.'

'I've written to tell Signorina Rosa about the *maestro*, Signorina Chiara. I didn't want to trouble her, but I know she'd wish to pray for him. How is our Signorina?'

'I hope she's well, Assunta. I must write to her tonight.'

'Ah, give her my love. I miss her – so much, Signorina! Coming, coming!' she answered to a shout from the *salottino*.

Thomas was late for an appointment at the Accademia. So, having scalded his mouth with a gulp of chocolate he leapt to his feet and cursed, then laughed.

'Sorry, dear one. Ah, I must fly. You're not singing tonight?'

'No. Not even understudying – which is lucky, as tomorrow's the *Stabat Mater*, you know.'

'Indeed I do. So – you'll go to bed early?'

'I hope so.'

'Do, Clare. And – don't be too sad for Giaco. He'll get through. For awhile anyway.'

He hesitated at her side, reluctant to leave her as she was reluctant to have him go. Each sensed melancholy in the other, a melancholy not altogether arising from the gravity of little Giaco's illness, but seeming to be inescapably inhaled from the cold, darkened air, and to chill breasts that were uneasy and felt empty.

'The *Stabat* will be beautiful, Clare. Don't be anxious at all.'

'Ah! But I am anxious.'

'Of course. I wish I were conducting. However, Duarte will be in his element – and you'll sing divinely – both of you.' He smiled at her. 'Be sure you do, young lady.' Then he stroked her head lightly, and was gone.

Clare sat a while in the familiar, dusty workroom, taking physical comfort from the hot chocolate, and listening until the Etruscan singing in the *salottino* dropped into silence. The signora's eyelids were down now, as she lay on the rickety *chaise longue*. Assunta would be relieved, but possibly little Giaco's half-delirium was saddened by the silence, Clare thought, as she took her way across the corridor and down the dim, cold staircase.

By the bridge at Via Scrofa she passed Paddy near enough to touch him. He was striding towards Via Ripetta, and she marvelled in relief that, absentminded and myopic, he had not seen her, although her uncovered fair head was always, so Luisa said, like a trumpeted announcement of her in a Roman street, even in October twilight.

She smiled after him as he vanished northward. What with the miserable characters of Parnell, Duarte and herself, to say nothing of his sad suspicions of Rose and his uncanny loathing of Luisa, Paddy was at present a difficult and tiring companion, unhappy in himself and a creator of anger and exasperation in Clare. And tonight assuredly she could bear none of him. Let him go and sit with the Signora awhile, in expression of his love for little Giaco.

She drew her cloak about her against the chilling night. She felt cold enough within its shelter, cold and sad, from sad Ripetta. I wish I had told Luisa to come to supper, she thought. She needn't have stayed late, and it would have been a comfort. And she smiled at herself – because the one who was always now a trouble, a perplexity to her, remained also, paradoxically, her dear consolation against that trouble, a sweet light that could scatter the darkness she created. Clare laughed. It's because she understands about it, I suppose, she thought. After all, I can talk to no one else of her and me.

As she turned into the porch of her house she found Iago Duarte, who was leaving a message for her with the *portiera*. In the dim light she thought he looked ill and weary; she was glad to see him.

'I shouldn't have called, Clara. But I was passing near here – and I wondered if perhaps you'd dine with me tonight – early, so that you can get a good night's rest?'

'No, thank you – I won't go out to dine, Iago. But come upstairs awhile. I hope the stove is warm. It's a horribly cold evening.'

'Yes, indeed. It would be good to sit by your stove.'

Clare lighted the lamp on her table. The stove was burning well, and the small room glowed comfortingly. Ruffo stretched himself and purred.

'I'll put some more wood in.'

'I'll do it,' said Iago.

Clare flung her cloak into her bedroom.

'Shall I heat some wine? I'm afraid I have none of the strong things you like!'

'A glass of wine, thank you. But there's no need to heat it, is there?'

She poured two glasses of red wine, and brought him one.

'Sit, won't you, Iago?'

They both sat down, and Ruffo jumped on to Clare's knees.

Iago had been visiting Manuel Arrez nearby in the Via Giulia; their talk had not gone happily, and they had drunk much brandy. Leaving his friend and feeling dejected, Iago had uncharacteristically followed an impulse to call on Clare – and now was wishing he had not been such a fool. She, for her part, observed that he was not only tired but somewhat out of control of himself, and she was surprised at his coming to visit her alone and uninvited, something he never did. She wondered what they would talk about; she was never alone with him save at her lessons, when their interchange was severely professional. But she was glad to see him sitting there; glad to be in out of the cold and to have his sympathetic company, if she could not have Luisa's.

'You didn't go to Julie's concert?'

'No. Luisa went. There are too many Chopin programmes – even in Rome.'

Julie Constant, friend from the days of Rue des Lauriers, had recently arrived in Rome as pianist of a small French chamber music orchestra which had won some success in northern Europe and now was touring Italy. Julie herself as a soloist had some minor fame already, and had been this afternoon playing Chopin and Scarlatti for eclectics in the palazzo of the Principe dei Fortibelli. Clare had been sent a card, but had felt sad, and uninclined for Julie's brilliant playing, of which she had heard enough in the preceding week.

It had been amusing to meet Julie again, to recall her kindness in that awful week before she and Rose had been swept away into Italy, and also to note how the French girl's natural sophistication, combined with her pianistic gift, had carried her into a worldly brilliance which was measurable and attractive – which might have been foreseeable, and was indeed a gay encouragement; until Clare heard her play alone, apart from her quintet.

After Julie's first solo concert – she had been engaged for a few by *cognoscenti* of the piano – Clare had felt unhappy. She was no judge at all of pianoforte performance, and had gone to hear Julie's Beethoven and Chopin programme in innocent goodwill, and secure in her inability to criticize. Iago Duarte had refused to attend that first solo concert. 'I am indifferent to the piano,' he said to Clare. 'And in any case, I assure you, Clara – don't be feministically offended! – I assure you that whereas no woman can play Beethoven, what is worse is that there is a general understanding that they *can* play Chopin.'

Clare *had* been 'feministically' offended by this Castilian nonsense.

Nevertheless, whereas she thought that Duarte's male generalizations were defeated by Julie's brilliance in performance, she did not like her playing, which surprised her by its arrogance – its leaning towards what she feared was vulgarity. She was sorry to feel this doubt, because she wished to counter Duarte's impertinent assertions about women in relation to music. But she dreaded too much his musicianship to venture on a feminist lie. So, when he had asked her, during a lesson, what she thought of the concert of Mademoiselle Constant, she had hesitated.

'Go on,' he had said. 'It's almost that you're a musician. Your hesitation differs from the salutes of the critics.'

'I haven't read them. What did they say?'

'They were definite. What do you say?'

'Oh – don't glare at me. I didn't like her playing as much as I thought I would.'

'Wait a minute. Did you know the music she was playing?'

'Well, yes. It wasn't unusual. I'd heard the two Beethoven

sonatas often, in Paris, and in Milan and here. And most of her Chopin was everyday stuff, in the Accademia and everywhere, all these years. Now, had it been Scarlatti – whom I hear she plays very well – the younger Scarlatti—'

'You're interested in the Scarlattis?'

'Yes. Why?'

'No why. Except that there's no reason why you should be interested – or differentiate between them.'

Clare smiled.

'You forget how hard and fast you teach, Iago. You fling out information – and I try to follow up. I read a great deal now, from your suggestions.'

'Where do you get the books?'

'Well, Paddy gets many of them for me—'

He laughed.

'Your crazy Paddy!'

'Paddy isn't crazy. He's fanatical – a different thing. Anyway, he gets me books.'

'All my books are there, Clara.'

'I see them. But I haven't dared to ask.'

Now this evening he pressed her again about Julie's playing.

'Oh – I'm no critic.'

'Still – what did you think, Clara?'

Clare got up, lifting Ruffo to her shoulder. She brought the wine-bottle across the room and filled Iago's glass.

'Don't pester,' she said.

'Pester?'

'As to Julie – Oh!'

Iago sprang to his feet.

'As to Julie, as to Luisa – Clara, what lunacy brought me here tonight?'

'Tell me.'

'The mistake I repeat.'

'I don't know about your mistakes,' Clare said. 'But I know you know where my love is. Luisa has told me that she told you.'

'Luisa told me. Long ago in Buenos Aires she had to tell me, poor child. She was so lonely. She thought it was news then. Clara, how obtuse we are in love!'

Clare was delighted by what he said.

She opened the stove and flung more wood into it.

'What a pet she is! The innocent!'

'And you are innocent,' said Duarte angrily. 'Or else a sinner.'

Clare turned a grave face on him.

'Innocent? No, Iago. I only used that word in fun, in affection. If you are moralizing – none of us is innocent.'

'And suppose I am moralizing?'

Clare looked at him coldly.

'Moralize then. Sit down. I shall listen.'

He sat down, and looked about the room, embarrassed, perplexed.

'Would it be very rude of me to ask your permission to smoke?'

'Not at all. People sometimes do smoke here – even Paddy!'

'Thank you,' said Iago, and he lit a Turkish cigarette.

'I've less right than anyone I know to moralize, Clara, if by that you mean to take up a preaching or even a questioning attitude about – anyone's private affairs. And God knows I've less intention. It was wrong and ill-mannered of me to trip you up over your use of the word "innocent". But perhaps you've noticed that I'm sometimes irritable – and impertinent?'

'Irritable, yes. As my teacher, you could hardly strike me as impertinent, I suppose?'

He smiled.

'You remember Manuel Arrez? That ageing bass who was with you at the San Carlo last May? He's a Basque, and a good character. We were friends when we were young men at the Milan Conservatoire – ah, nearly twenty years ago. Well, he's thinking of going home for good now. He's lonely for Spain and he has saved money, he says. Anyway, he's going on a search-trip to his native Navarre, to look for a small farm or *quinta* – and I lunched with him today, to wish him well.'

'Is he happy?'

'Very happy, I think. You see he's a widower and his only child is training to be – a Dominican priest. Manuel's homesick and he's done enough singing.'

'His going saddens you? Do you envy him?'

'I do.'

'So should I, I think, if I were you. But only with half of myself, of course. This – this life we're trained to – in my part of the profession anyhow, Iago – is still most truly exotic to me, when I think it over in cold blood. And yet it masters one; it imposes its idiom and habit on the old native, gawky self! So – there seems to be no escape!'

'For you there *is* no escape. Your voice has been put in command of your life. You have to stay in the places where opera is sung, and keep on singing it.'

'It sounds depressing.'

He laughed.

'You know it isn't, Clara! Why – if you went back to live where you grew up – where was it?'

'Ballykerin.'

Iago picked the word up as he might a curious shell or pebble at his feet.

'Bally-kerin? So. What would you do there?'

'Not earn a living as a singer, anyway!'

'You might marry the love of your childhood, of course.'

'Had he ever existed!'

'Such people don't exist – I agree.' Silence fell. It was as if under effort that Iago spoke again. 'You've heard of this young Spanish musician, Albeniz? You've heard me talk of him?'

'Yes – Luisa too.'

'She is very admiring of his work – and indeed it's brilliant. *Muy español*. He's much my junior – I don't think he's thirty yet – but we've met and corresponded. He's teaching at the Madrid Conservatoire now. Well, he and some of the younger people there are anxious that I should apply for a post that is vacant now, in sacred music. He wrote to me again today about it – I don't know if I'd get it – some of the Madrid people seem sure that I would—'

'Do you want it?'

'It's my work, the same as here, save that I'd be in Spain. But, I think that I want nothing any more, Clara. Nothing that I've any right to, that is.'

'You said just now that you envy Manuel Arrez?'

'Yes – I envy him for being himself, for knowing his own wishes and being free to pursue them. I envy him the goodness and the quiet temperament that have created this peaceful prospect for his middle age.'

Clare laughed.

'Forgive me – but for you to covet Arrez's temperament – what a lost cause, Iago!'

He did not laugh with her.

'He gave me a piece of his mind just now. Oh, nothing that I don't know of myself far better than he does! Good Manuel! He's angry with me – but what does that change?' He stood up. 'Why do I bore you? May I pour more wine?'

'Of course.'

'Thank you. I'm sorry to have to ask you and Luisa for this run-through concert in the morning – but the strings are young, and my scoring for them isn't easy, so I think it wise to keep the music to the forefront of all our minds all day tomorrow, even at the risk of tiring you.'

'Oh, I welcome it.'

'I wish now it were something of Morales I had chosen. But Italians like their own people – and I hope Pergolesi has been educative? Have you ever studied *La Serva Padrona*?'

'Thomas and I have skimmed through it. He finds it amusing music; it's not the kind of thing I care for at all. But Thomas is an educator, like you!'

'He seems ambitious, certainly,' said Iago in a cold voice. 'I've not been ambitious. In any case, I am not gregarious enough to make the usual assaults on success. However, I am industrious, and that suffices for me. Manuel thinks that I should offer myself for the Madrid post. He knows I have never liked Italy – and he's good enough to say that so far as he can observe I'm no better than an ageing mischief around here now – and that it would be better for everyone if I went back to Madrid where I'd have to behave myself, he thinks.'

Clare could find no answer for that speech, so she made none. Iago paced about.

'There are some reasons – and Manuel knows them – why a decision for Madrid cannot be easy.'

Clearly the man wanted her to comment on his private business. Uneasily therefore she spoke.

'Luisa is, one supposes, a chief reason?'

'Luisa is, naturally, the first and chief person I've discussed the question with; but she isn't a reason against it – or hardly at all.'

Clare looked at Iago through a veil of careful wonder.

'Luisa has never been in love with me – as you know, Clara. And indeed it would have been wrong and grotesque had she been. But from her arrival in Rome I was rashly and selfishly attracted by her – well, she's lovely, and my own Castilian kind. So, I put myself more or less in charge of her work in her first year, and we became greatly attached to each other. And there came a time – during the summer of last year – when we became lovers. I think we both thought then, or I did for a while, that we were indeed what is meant by in love. I had no right at all to take advantage of a mood in her that I thought I understood at the time. But I see now –' he smiled – 'I've said this to her and she agrees with me – that she it was who was taking advantage of me! I wasn't to understand that until much later, and long after our "being in love", let's call it, had changed to what it has been since, an affectionate but rather untidy attachment. What Luisa thought she was doing when she made me her lover was to set up guards for herself against a kind of love she knew about already and which frightened her – for herself and another. But the trouble was, of course – she couldn't know this – that she was already *in* that love before she took me.'

Clare answered slowly.

'She told me that always she has been attracted to women – and afraid of the attraction.'

'I believe that is so. Still, in the spring and early summer of last year she must have known that she was – in love, and that she had travelled beyond such artificial barriers as, say, a love affair with me was to erect. Dear Orfeo!'

Clare said nothing. She felt now almost intolerably embarrassed and at bay, and feared to move or speak lest a shaking of hand or voice betray her disturbance. She fingered the gold chain round her neck; silently she implored her heart to keep still.

'So you see,' Iago went on, 'my going to Madrid would not affect Luisa seriously, since I hope our affection can survive distance and time. But indeed, had we been in love, there could of course never be any question of Luisa's life being attached to any one place, or group. As your life is, so is hers commanded by her singing voice, and she will have to go and come around the world as it takes her. And to love, say, her or you, or any of your kind, is to have to share your imposed wanderings and restlessness.'

He looked down at Clare fixedly; the hard-drawn mouth seemed to say that he grudged her whatever he might see ahead of her 'imposed wanderings and restlessness'.

'Do have some wine, won't you?' she said, for want of anything else that was easy to say.

'My – exile in Italy has long been imposed on me – by my private judgment. But I have of course become very much interested in Luisa's voice, and in yours; and both are excellent instruments for the work I give my life to. Instruments after my heart indeed – they could become.'

Clare was touched by a sudden change to uncertainty of tone, dreaminess, in the last sentence.

'We both owe you immeasurable gratitude,' she said.

'Nonsense, Clara. To hear those polyphonic works with one's ears of flesh is a rest sometimes from having to listen to them so much with the ears of the brain. And you and Luisa and my small group of zealots here are my – my restitution, dare I say? – to – life.'

He laughed.

'I'm sounding pompous. May I smoke again?'

'Of course. The smell is delicious. Would you put more wood in the stove? I hate to disturb Ruffo.'

He attended to the stove.

'Luisa is, as you know, a wonderful and quick learner. She has of course an advantage in regard to such composers as Victoria and Soler and Ortello in that she was hearing them from her birth almost, in Segovia and Leon and Valencia cathedrals – and long before she heard a bar of Italian opera. Her father is, as you may know, a church organist and a music master—'

'Yes, she's told me about him.'

'He's a good man – a humble musician, but very sound. I met him many years ago, as it happens. But Luisa of course will sing anything that she's properly taught and that she's not allowed to get bored with – simply for singing's sake, and because singing is what she does well—'

'Yes. It's delicious. Rose is like that too—'

'True. But she is *purely* operatic, and I say *purely* with admiration. Luisa is endowed to sing everything – lieder, oratorio, liturgical music, opera, gypsy songs. Everything, I believe, except Wagner. And for my part, I offer her no condolences on that exception.'

'She's lucky in being such an adaptable singer,' said Clare.

'I have thought so,' Iago answered. 'But I am not sure that I do now. Your case is very different from hers – and I begin to think that in full maturity you will be the better singer—'

'Oh, no – that never—'

'The more serious, I think—'

Clare laughed.

'I am always that—'

'You are,' he said gravely. 'It makes one anxious. Luisa's temperament is very like her talent, Clara – indeed it is a part of it – very adaptable, very exploratory and non-analytical – very unwilling to pause over things, to be bored, to be restrained—'

Clare looked up; her hands moved over Ruffo's little body on her lap.

'– It is difficult to look forward for her without some uneasiness,' Iago went on. 'She'll travel, of course; she'll have adventures; she'll hurt people—'

'And we must suppose that she'll be hurt,' Clare said softly.

'Not very much, I think. Not as she will hurt – more serious natures.'

'How do we know? There are chances that have to be taken, Iago.'

'There are some that should not be taken. There are errors against which people must discipline themselves.'

'There are indeed.'

'Luisa is hurting you already, Clara – as she would have had to. You will suffer and be injured; she will not.'

Clare stood up, desiring only to ask this man to leave her.

'Julie Constant, for instance—' he said.

Clare laid Ruffo on the table. She shook all over as she tried to speak.

'I beg you—' she began.

'I speak as I do because I must – Julie Constant isn't the first—'

In blazing anger Clare spoke at last.

'I'll learn from Luisa herself whatever she tells me of what's in her heart, or gone from it!'

'She is incapable of fidelity!'

'And are we in charge of her, Iago?'

'I used to think I was. I am sorry to distress you!'

'Distress me?' Tears poured down Clare's ash-white face. 'Oh, go away!'

'Yes, Iago – go away.'

Luisa, who came and went in Clare's rooms as she pleased, was on the threshold now. Clare turned to her in joy.

'Yes, I will go,' said Iago. He moved to the door and bowed, looking old and almost sheepish. 'I have spoken stupidly, perhaps, but you know why, Luisa.'

'Yes, poor Iago. I know you're hopelessly in love with her. Go please.'

He left the two.

Luisa kissed Clare's eyelids and ran her hand over the white wet cheeks.

'I'm frozen, love. Give me some wine.'

They turned together to pour it out.

'Lucky I came up, my darling one. I felt I had to see you for a little time tonight – as I'm so nervous about tomorrow. But now I feel –' she laughed – 'that we should both refuse to sing in his old concert!'

Clare watched Luisa drink.

'He was trying to tell me things about you that I know,' she said gently.

'A rash, misguided man,' said Luisa. 'But I think he has always been that.' She held out her glass and Clare drank from it.

The lengthy student concert came to an end none too quickly the following afternoon. It was a full programme, much of its earlier part made up of early Spanish and Flemish music, which exacted perhaps more care and experience than it was just to ask of first- and second-year Accademia pupils. Thirteenth-century *Cantigas* of great and difficult beauty; new scoring of old quartets and quintets for oboe, flute and strings; some agreeable but tricky singing of *seguidillas* from early Catalan *zarzuelas*. Clare, listening, felt tired, unhappy, and hardly even frightened, but far-away rather, and desiring to be far away from all these carefully produced and attentively heard noises. She had taken part in several concerts such as this during her own two student years, knew what work, anxiety and hope went into their preparation and execution, how jealousies and partisan strifes flared all about them, in suppression. Also she knew how dreamy and tremulous was the awestruck envy of the student-participants for the successful, or said-to-be-successful professionals – on this afternoon Luisa and herself – who were usually invited to perform, as encouraging examples – in the chief large piece of the day. Vaguely, wearily, almost as if she dreamt what was going forward, she could only hope that she and Luisa would not dishonour their year, or cause juvenile brows to lift in question.

As she watched Duarte on the podium, where he was always a reassuring model of calm and serenity, she could see no sign in him that he remembered that twenty-four hours ago he had made a fool of himself – even to the point of endangering the performances, yet to be faced, of his two carefully selected soloists.

Naturally, personal life and its mistakes were flung out of reach, as they must be, when he took up the baton. Yet this cool, bitter-faced musician had done an unprecedented, a stupid, perhaps almost an unforgiveable thing to two whose master he was, and who now, with this confusion of his making in their breasts, would have to stand up before all of musical Rome, and under his direction sing – for his glorification – the most difficult composition either had yet had to take part in in public. Though he gave no sign whatever as he stood erect in his place of being aware of anything on earth but the piece of music it was his business to produce from the persons and the instruments in front of him, Clare could not but smile inwardly, in weary suspicion of some exasperated shame making uncomfortable this 'rash, misguided man', making him dread now their inescapable *Stabat Mater*. For herself, however – she knew that she loathed the occasion, its absurd juxtaposition of three of them – three of us, she thought sickly, who have cared so much about each other – in a public ordeal immediately after such a foolish private shame. She wished she was miles away, and indeed only trouper-discipline kept her waiting for her turn. And she was unable as she sat to recall a bar of what she was about to have to sing. However, she thought, Luisa will be marvellous – sound and ready and exact as she always is. She'll give me back my wits, please God. So she closed her eyes and listened, half-listened to the lovely Tirana *seguidilla*, which seemed to be refreshing the tired Sunday afternoon audience, of which she supposed Thomas was a part. She hoped, vainly, that he would not listen to the *Stabat Mater* with his customary attention.

'There's little time left now,' Sister Baptist said.

Thomas had been wrong; pneumonia was taking Giaco quickly, quickly out of life on that cold Sunday night of October.

At the conclusion of the concert in the Accademia, Clare and Luisa stood demurely, one on each side of their *maestro*, and surrounded by participants, orchestral and choral, of the programme. All had had to bow, curtsey, bow, kiss the hands of great ladies and the rings of cardinals; they had also to take accolades from the director, from their professors, from critics and colleagues and friends and foes. It was the usual amiable conclusion to such occasions. Clare took it this time with more relief and grace than she had expected to find in herself – for it seemed that, against the odds, they had done well, well enough at least, in their *Stabat Mater*. As she stood and bowed and kissed hands and murmured polite nonsense – watching Luisa the while getting over similar antics with so much more brilliance; watching Duarte, Castilian and cold, but pleased, it was clear, by a few of the compliments which were being mouthed – she marvelled that they had come through safely; and she was momentarily unable to recall any part of the just ended music. But she amused herself – in relief and for peace sake, as before on occasions of worldly-seeming success she had done – by thinking of how she would describe this kind of plauditory hour to Grandmother. Dukes, you know, Grandmother – and princes. I don't have them kiss my hand a quarter as often as Rosie, of course – because they swarm in from all over Europe to La Scala. Did you ever hear of a thing called the Almanach de Gotha? Grandmother would tell her that almanacks were calendars, she thought – ah, and so on. They would have fun over all these bishops and princes. Your uncouth, neglected grandchild, Grandmother. And who neglected you, child of grace? And where did you learn to be uncouth, behind my back?

A wizened old gentleman squeezing her hand reminded her with monkey-smile that he had heard her sing in Rue des Lauriers. The Pope's cousin in person once again! Ah, Rosie would laugh.

'You sang Handel, Signorina. "My Redeemer Liveth." I shall not forget it. It was the same voice greatly enriched that we heard just now. It was a dramatic occasion when we heard those two very young Irish voices in Paris. La Rosa d'Irlanda – she travels fast. I heard her last season at La Scala! But you – you sing differently! When you sing you make a saint of a man,' said the little old monkey.

Clare laughed.

'If I believe your great compliment, Signor, I fear I'd grow depressed for my future.'

I must remember all this for Rosie and for Grandmother, she thought. But where is that wandering Thomas? Was I then so bad that he won't face me?

Julie Constant came and pressed her hand.

'Oh, Clare! You really do sing like a seraph now! That was what you always threatened us with!'

'But when have you heard the seraphs, Julie?'

'*Touché*. I'll never hear them. But I can hear you! Forgive me, but were you talking just now to a simian admirer from that terrible day in Rue des Lauriers?'

'What a memory you have! The Pope's cousin, someone said—'

'Yes. And Rose saw him crying when you were singing "My Redeemer Liveth".'

'He has sore eyes, the poor little man.'

'You could cure them, Clare—'

Go away, Clare was thinking. I don't want your easy manners mazing round me. And then she saw Thomas's face far off, and his hand raised, beckoning her. Even across the room his eyes burnt with unusual urgency. She signalled back to him.

'Forgive me, Julie . . .' and she left Duarte's side.

Thomas snatched her hand when she reached him.

'Why do you look like that? Was I so bad?'

He stared at her.

'No! You were great. There was something unusual – wrong, maybe? – but not musically. Musically the whole pack of you were great. But of that another time.' He kissed her hand. 'Clare, little Giaco is dying. Will you come quickly?'

The two ran, hands joined, over the familiar distance. From the back door of the Accademia, across the Corso, down Canova, and home, as Clare always called Ripetta – home, and like hares up the long, ill-lighted staircase. In the routine to-and-fro of the student time they had never hurried as now. Still, as they sprang along the crooked, wide stone flights, Thomas laughed and said:

'You never did do it on C in alt.'

'You forbade me to.'

'And you are so obedient! However, while the little tyrant breathes, don't try the mortal sin, Clare!'

Assunta let them in.

Over the druggets they tiptoed to look into the *maestro*'s

little withered and surrendered face. He was not gone yet; he battled darkly for those last few breaths that Sister Baptist and her colleague would conscientiously find for him, out of the oxygen tubes.

He looked unhappy, but not agonized, Clare thought.

Thomas looked down at him.

'I suppose he's not hearing any more, in our sense of hearing? Yet he had the most agonized fine ear in the Italian schools, I'd say. That mightn't be much. Still – he could listen to music.'

Sister Baptist did not want a crowd of breathing mourners round her fighting charge. Clare and Thomas moved away along the sad corridor to the studio of the two pianos. On the bench before one of these were seated La Signora Vittoria and Paddy.

'I try to help Signor Paddy,' said La Vittoria.

'But Paddy, you don't want to sing?' said Clare.

Paddy laughed as it were behind La Vittoria's back.

'No, Clare,' he said softly in English. 'Signor Giacomo's so upset about her – about leaving her – I promised I'd do what I could . . .'

Thomas was talking meantime to La Vittoria.

'He'll be gone soon, Signora. I think he still hears us, perhaps – do you?'

'I am certain he hears when I sing to him, Tomaso.'

The *maestaro*'s sister, Signorina Caterina, came into the studio with a tray of coffee-pot and cups. She had always been old and angry in the days when she taught Italian to Clare and Rose.

'I shall continue to sing to him – oh, Signor Paddy, thank you!' Paddy had, with a deftness that surprised Clare, brought a glass of spirits to La Vittoria's waiting hand.

'She will not continue to sing to me,' said Signorina Caterina.

Assunta came into the studio. She took Signora Vittoria's arm; she spoke directly to Signorina Caterina.

'Sister Baptist says to come at once, Signorina,' she said.

Paddy went quickly to Signora Vittoria's other side, and escorted the three, wife, sister and domestic servant, to the deathbed. Thomas opened the studio door.

Paddy turned back on its threshold, towards Clare. He looked almost tragic in his ascetic youthfulness as the intoxicated, peignoired *diva* leant against his shoulder.

'He has had the Last Sacraments, Clare,' he said. 'Everything has been done, I promise you.'

Clare smiled at Paddy; following Assunta, the procession left the studio.

Thomas poured out coffee. Clare opened a shutter. The cold, familiar, Roman night lay there, beyond this room whose occupant was about to leave earthly life and habit.

The trees shuddered over the roofs of Belle Arte. Lights stirred on the cold slopes north-west. The sky was jewelled. Clare turned from all the too-familiar and almost ran to Thomas for the coffee he held out.

'It's over now. Ripetta's over, Thomas.'

'Yes. When he dies you and I aren't students any more.'

'What will happen here? What of Assunta?'

'Sh!'

A solitary, soprano cry rang through the house – a long C in alt, which broke into a rakish, trailing sob, then rose again to singing, and then ceased.

Assunta came into the studio.

'He's gone. The little signor.'

Thomas closed the two pianofortes very gently.

On Paddy's arm La Vittoria came down the corridor.

'*Dite alla giovine . . .*' she was singing softly, drunkenly.

It's a pity he can't hear that for the last and lucky time, Thomas thought.

The Fourteenth Chapter

It was an evening of early May, in Milan, in 1891.

Rose stood at the window of her apartment in Piazza San Stefano and looked down gratefully at the old fountain and the plane trees of the courtyard. Sunlight fell coolly about stones and doorways; afternoon blue was paling from the clear sky; a dove cooed somewhere near. That is a tedious noise for a bird to make, the *prima donna* thought.

She had returned from walking in the public gardens, where it was her habit to take the morning or the afternoon air each day – preferably alone – for health's sake and pleasure's sake. She had grown attached to those gardens; even in Milan's worst weather she liked them and was grateful for assaults of wind and rain there. But this afternoon they had been laughing and lovely in first leaf, and crowded by children, lovers and dogs; and she had thought that Clare, who save for La Scala found Milan uninteresting, might today have had a kind look to cast on the Lombard town. She'd like this courtyard anyhow, Rose thought, as she turned back to the *salotto*, and pulled off her pretty hat.

'Ah, Assunta, please! *Not* any more!'

Assunta laughed.

'I'm sorry, Signorina – but these are so very beautiful.'

With care the girl placed an urn of golden roses on a *guéridon* by the window, where the sunlight fell about them.

'They have only just arrived, Signorina. There is a letter with them.'

Rose had sung *La Sonnambula* the night before, and the assault of flowers which the kind and flower-loving Italians

made on this as on other favourite singers on a night of performance and on the day that followed it had during this season
become a problem and a joke between Rose and Assunta.

Rose did not like at all to be crowded and thronged, either
by people or by their gracious flowers. But neither did she think
that it would be suitable or mannerly of her to send her overflow
of tributes to hospitals or churches. 'Time enough for that sort
of showing off when I'm Grisi or Albani,' she would say to
Assunta. 'Why can't we start a little corner stall somewhere?
Quite anonymous, you know. We could send the weekly profits
to Nettuno, to your mother! They'd come in handy.'

But Assunta could only laugh, and continue to arrange roses,
lilies, violets, carnations, discreetly about the theatre dressing-
room and the quiet apartment.

'All right then,' Rose would say. 'If the plot is to destroy my
breathing – go on! All I have to live by is this mysterious set of
works in my throat, Assunta – *and* my nerves! And this excess
of foliage is bad for both! Come on, let's go out and look at a
few flowers in the public gardens!'

Rose's second season at La Scala, which had run through the
winter and spring of 1890–91, was now in its last weeks. It
had been a period of the hard and unrelenting work which she
understood and embraced, and had contained its fair share of
days of discouragement, anger, despair and all the rest. But she
had sung and sung and sung on the great stage, to the great
house. She had got to know its pitch and mood and to understand her own varying reactions to these. She had quickly
become a favourite with La Scala's routine audience, and as she
was a scrupulous zealot at her work and never, even on bad or
dull nights, sang technically below La Scala's standard, she was
allowed her turn, as the season rose to flood, at every one of
the *assoluta* parts in the year's repertory.

It was a great, sustained opportunity. Health, courage, self-
control, co-operativeness were all repetitively tested week after
week through the hard winter, and against the foreseeable
annoyance of the established *assolute*, and the impatience of
contemporary rivals.

But more, and more important, Rose's musical educability and her range within all the arts arising from musical execution, from operatic expression of music – all of this was tested and retested, and over and over again.

She had known what it was all about. She had known by the end of her first season in La Scala that were she recalled for a second that would be the severest test which the world could impose upon an intending grand opera soprano.

She had come through. Even *she* admitted that to herself, in amazement, as the months of music swept her along. I've done what they got into their heads in Lackanashee! Whatever possessed them to think of such a thing? Ah, I suppose they hadn't a notion really of what they were talking about! Still, here I am! It just shows you! Oh dear Miss French! Oh dear, oh dear! Oh my dear Miss French, how are you now, I wonder?

Before the close of 1890 Rose had been out of debt to her Committee, and thereafter the sole extraneous claim on her earnings was the twenty per cent due to Rue des Lauriers. The business management of La Scala had taken charge of this deduction and payment for her since Signor Giacomo's death. So she felt, and was, solvent and although in her own view quite amazingly rich, she was sane and even what she self-mockingly called 'careful' about money, so that she was able to send now a quite substantial monthly allowance to her mother, and also had a savings bank account – mainly to make further provision for Mamma and Aggie. This savings account and its pleasant increase from month to month gave her comfort, and helped her to feel in touch still in her troubled heart with far-away Lackanashee. Shall I ever go home, I wonder? she sometimes asked herself. Do I want to go home now – or ever?

She had become twenty-one on the fifth of April of this year, and on that day Signor Giuseppe Sandroni, a Milanese merchant prince who, in the tradition of his family, was a generous patron of La Scala, had held a luncheon party in her honour.

Gracefully her host had given to this party a formal air, a character of quite grave occasion, as if as much to salute her high place in La Scala as her having attained womanhood. So his guests were carefully picked for their importance in Rose's newly conquered world, and they ranged from the Scala director himself and Signor Arrigo Boito through some foreign impresarios then in Milan on the business of their state opera houses, to an unknown young composer from the Conservatorio, a protégé of Signor Boito, called Puccini. Among the impresarios was Mr Karl von Jakob of New York, who had been present with Silas Rudd at Rose's first appearance in *Otello*, and of whom Mr Rudd had written to her from Boston that he would be in Milan in April and looked forward very much to hearing her sing again.

During this luncheon party he was very kind indeed, and he and each of the other important gentlemen made small and almost solemn speeches to her, praising her and wishing her fame and happiness, before they lifted their glasses to the birthday toast of 'La Rosa d'Irlanda'. 'La bellissima Rosa', her host beside her said under his breath. Rose was touched and exhilarated, and hoped that the tears she felt in her eyes would not brim over untidily.

Young Signor Puccini made no formal speech; but he leant towards her after the toasting, and said: 'What a solemn occasion! And you're only twenty-one!'

Rose smiled at him.

'How old are you, Signor?'

'Thirty-three, Signorina! And I haven't got started yet – with life half over!'

'You don't look as if life is half over, somehow,' said Rose.

As Signor Sandroni escorted her home from the party in his beautiful open carriage behind a pair of silky greys, Rose thought ungratefully, while she smiled and thanked him, how much more happily she would sit in such an equipage with Antonio. Where is he? she wondered. Will he remember the date?

At the door of her apartment, as Assunta held it open, Signor Sandroni bowed and kissed Rose's hand. If he was hoping to be asked to sit awhile in the *salotto* and talk the party over, he gave no ungentlemanly sign, and Rose merely thanked him again with a radiant smile, and sped indoors alone, in deep relief.

Her host descended the shabby staircase, smiling also – and

perhaps also in some relief. He was by now wilfully and, to his surprise, persistently impassioned of Rose. But although young and handsome of aspect, he had long been soundly married, had many children, and was an exemplary part of Milan's respectability. This meant for him that he might, could he not help himself, indulge illicit sexual pleasures with discretion – but that he would have to be a madman, which he was not, to seek to be the lover of a very beautiful and universally observed young *diva* – an Irishwoman, at that! Poor Giuseppe Sandroni! He knew always, in business and in the secret business of his own feelings, what were the risks he was prepared for, and which the mistakes he would not make. Moreover, for all his self-confident and handsome eye, he did acknowledge that some of life's best things might be beyond his reach. Still, he could love a singing voice, without danger? And generously indeed he devoted himself to promoting the cause of this new voice out of Ireland. So the luncheon party had been well planned, and might be said to augur happiness, happy returns. Yet the fifth of April 1891 had not been a happy day.

Rose had indeed of late gone astray, and often into panic, about happiness. Not that she had ever been obsessed with possession for herself of what she understood it to be; but that, without reflection, she had always tended in her own nature towards zones of clarity, goodwill and good temper which contain happiness. Feelings, which naturally governed her, had never been confused; and even when she first invoked and accepted adult love, passion had been somewhat unusually at the disposition of tenderness and wonder. But perhaps that very fact which had made first love seem an easy thing had been no good omen, but rather a cloud the size of a man's hand. Assuredly she knew now, had known before long, another passion; and its truth had made it compulsory in her to wound and if possible to kill that first, which she had shamelessly evoked and fanned and cherished.

Truly in this dark confusion, of her own making, between two clamant loves, she had lost sight of serenity, and so of what she had always meant by happiness. And much of her loss was because she knew she did not want back the lost immediate past, which she had invented, almost, for her own pleasure, and which René would not, or said he could not, forgo.

But that was only a part of what she was having to learn of the blindness and intractability of adult feeling, or rather of how bafflingly the needs of the heart are at the mercy of conventions, fixed ideas, self-protection, wilfulness, fear, and the thousand hard, insistent claims and irrelevancies of general life – all unacquainted with the immediate, puzzling life of the inner breast. She had been learning lately how self-confident an innocent she was, and how sentimental; and she saw that innocents like herself make their share of trouble for some of their fellows while seeming too often to be the aggrieved ones.

'Would you have ever taken me for fatuous, Assunta?'

'I don't exactly get your meaning, Signorina.' Assunta smiled. 'In Rome I always thought you singularly young in spirit.'

It is probable that only Assunta of all her world knew at this time that Rose was unhappy. That self-control which she was rigorously trained to in her work, and which could reach a condition of smooth and even radiant self-disguise, was already native in Rose, as it is in many Irishwomen. She never felt inclined to talk of herself to others; the hard concentration her work exacted kept her alert and unselfconscious, and youth and health shone undefeated still from her clear eyes. So the confusion of heart she carried about and was trying to learn to live with was indeed most deeply private and concealed.

But Assunta knew of it. Without a word said, Assunta knew, because she loved her, and had known her since she was an innocent.

Rose was fortunate to have Assunta with her now; and to be Rose's personal servant and housekeeper made Assunta happy as she had not expected to be again.

After the death of Signor Giacomo there had been a period of grotesque and terrible confusion in the apartment in Via di Ripetta.

The little *maestro*, characteristically scrupulous, had left his modest affairs in excellent order; his will, his life insurance and savings, instructions as to his pension – everything, including his accounts for Clare and Rose. His sister and his lawyer were left in charge of the simple and honourable estate, and of his beloved wife, Vittoria, whom, her health being uncertain, he entrusted to the faithful care of Signorina Caterina Buonatoli.

Clare's debt to Uncle Matt and his friends being still unresolved, Signor Dirotte of the Accademia – little Giaco's great friend – took over management of it from Signorina Caterina, and Rose's remaining obligation was henceforward, as has been said, discharged direct from her earnings at La Scala. So their two Irish names passed out of the dusty story of Ripetta.

But what of Casta Diva?

Her immense grief, Clare wrote to Rose, filled the now far too vast apartment as it had never been filled. She drank and sang, and marched and pitched about the place, and told her love – which had not been love of Giaco – in every doorway and to every corner. Assunta, Clare said, had found in herself the strength of her people, physical and moral; but Signorina Caterina, dutiful in all the legal part of her new responsibility, refused, and for ever, to leave her quiet small apartment on the floor below, where she had lived thirty years in peace with her cats, her visiting pupils and her religious practices. So, what to do with the poor Signora in the large, and now purposeless, apartment? There had been a moment of tragi-comedy, Clare wrote, when Paddy – truly in great grief at the loss of the little *maestro* – when Paddy, martyr-like, had asked to be allowed to take rooms in it – 'if he could be of any help to the dear Signora?'

Both Clare and Assunta had refused to listen to that quixotry, and indeed when it was suggested to Signorina Caterina, she made clear that she was shocked. But Signorina Caterina, after years of mousey independence, was not going to lose its quiet now. She held control of the money that her brother had bequeathed for his wife's support. So, she saw to that support. She commanded the transfer of her sister-in-law into the care of a community of nursing nuns. She had the grace, perhaps the ironic whim, to choose a quiet retreat high up near Volterra, in Etruria. So home she went, whether she willed or no, the Etruscan, singing and drunk.

And on the day of that departure Signorina Caterina gave Assunta a month's wages and a railway ticket to Nettuno, where her mother lived.

After a little time, Assunta came to Milan to look after Rose. And for the present they talked seldom, and then only briefly, of Ripetta, because both grieved very much for it, and Rose knew that Assunta's mind and heart were sore with puzzled memory.

For herself, she thought with woe of Casta Diva, bewildered in a strange, high place, amid a great flock of nuns, and seeking darkly, always more darkly, that once so vivid noonday.

'*Dite alla giovine* . . . When did I first? Was it in 'sixty-nine, dear husband? . . .' Ah, why could she not have died before him?

'Assunta,' Rose ventured once, 'do you think those nuns – do you think they'll give her enough – enough wine?'

Assunta seemed to wince.

'I don't know, Signorina.'

If to have taken Assunta into employment was a daring gesture and sometimes struck the thrifty Rose as self-indulgent, it was at least an indulgence based on gratitude and pity, and sure knowledge of what would make the other happy at this time. And it was indeed a modest expression of a *prima donna* way of life; for the good Assunta proved to be not merely a comfort that Rose could afford, but a surprising economy. For she was not only the shrewd and excellent housekeeper that she had had to be in Ripetta, but in all the crafts and skills of lady's maid she showed herself as clever and economical as she was devoted.

An immediate proof of this latter talent was that almost from the day of Assunta's coming to her Rose began, to her own half-embarrassed amusement, to present in her dress and grooming a quite marked and simple *chic*, an orderly rightness which would henceforward, according to Assunta, be expected of her, but which in the stress of her working days – and indeed in the unself-consciousness of her nature – the young singer could never have attempted by herself. So that now she was not only beautiful, but under her maid's unrelenting care, quite truly elegant. Rose herself hardly knew what all the dressing-table fuss was about – but she bore it gaily, and even gratefully, and enjoyed the comments and compliments aroused by her coiffed and manicured perfection, her always immaculate gloves and laces.

... *You'd demur at my show-off grandeur, as well I know, my lady* ... she wrote to Clare; and Clare, smiling, knew that very likely she would. Yet she was glad of the gay ring of that sentence; for often lately she read an unwritten sadness – more than sadness, something like frightened sorrow – in Rose's letters, which covered the pages as eagerly and confidingly, it might seem, as ever, and which yet confided nothing.

Clare had not seen Rose since their happy weeks in Venice in the past September; nor nowadays did she see either Antonio or René, although the two names, especially Tonio's, flew in and out of Rose's news, as they had always done. But since October, after little Giaco's death, with the ending of Ripetta and Thomas's return to Germany, her own life in wintry Rome had taken an uncertain tone of wintriness. On *her* twenty-first birthday, the second of November, All Souls' Day, she and Luisa had sung in Verdi's *Requiem* in the Augustea, under Duarte's baton. And for all that great honour, she had not counted it a happy birthday. She was working very hard, however, throughout the whole season – at Costanzi's, and in concerts, and oratorio productions. She was working hard, and making more money than in the preceding year; and all this pleased her and was useful to her troubled spirit. But she knew that she was much troubled in herself, and that made her fearful of peering out towards forebodings of the griefs or mistakes of another – of dear Rosie – whom she could not reach, and upon whom perhaps she was casting unnecessarily a shadow from her own morbidity?

But now it was May and in Lombardy, for this hour at least, there was no winter. Rose did not have to sing tonight, and Antonio, who had been absent from Milan for fourteen days, was returning and would be with her in a little time. That was sure and true, and on this sunny evening and after a separation which with anxiety she had known to have seemed to her too long, it was above all else what she desired.

She must go to her room, and make ready for him.

'Supper will be perfect, won't it, Assunta?' she called towards the little kitchen.

'Never doubt it, Signorina.'

Still lingering at the window, Rose admired the sunlit yellow roses on the *guéridon*, and her eyes fell to the envelope beside them. With a small gasp she picked it up and opened it.

It was from Silas Rudd, announcing that he had arrived in Milan at noon, that he saw with regret she was not to sing tonight; but that that gave him a little hope that she might be free to allow him the honour of taking her to dine – and in such anticipation might he call at her apartment at eight o'clock? There followed a few expressions of pleasure at having regained Italy before the close of the season, wishes for her health, and he was, as always, her devoted and happy admirer.

Rose smiled, looked again at the roses, and even laughed very gently. Then she went to the writing table.

She scribbled rapidly there for a minute, and crossing to the kitchen while she licked an envelope flap, said:

'Assunta, whatever about your sauces and things, I'm afraid I must ask you to take this letter at once to the Grand Hotel! Can you?'

'Of course, Signorina.'

'You'd better take a cab! It's urgent. And besides, we don't want supper spoilt!'

'That won't be spoilt, I promise. No need for a cab, Signorina. I'll get a tram on the corner. Just as quick.'

'Thank you. You're an angel.'

Assunta was gone.

Rose smiled still as she went towards her bedroom.

That would have been a *contretemps*, she thought.

Supper, eaten by the open window of the *salotto*, was all that Assunta had promised, and the wines and fruits which had been sent by Antonio's command made heightened festival.

The cover removed then, and the window shuttered against the cooling night, coffee was brought.

'Good night, signor. Good night, Signorina.'

'Good night, Assunta. Thank you.'

'So, shall I put a teaspoon of brandy in your coffee, Rosa?'

'Please. I haven't thanked you for all the extravagant, lovely things – but then, your generosity is – well, like your fingernails, Antonio.' Rose smiled at these, the strong, immaculate ovals, as she took her cup from his hand. 'One forgets to go on thanking for a natural attribute.'

'Silly Rose!' He drank some coffee slowly, and looked at her the while. 'No matter how I try,' he said after a moment, 'no matter how I try, Rosa, I forget your lovely face when I'm away from it.'

'That's a pity, if you think it lovely, love.'

'Yes, it is a pity. It's very hard on me. I suppose I lack imagination, or something?'

They both laughed, and he came to her and lifted her up into his arms.

'It's been longer than ever this time. It's always too long!'

'Yes, I think so too,' said Rose.

During ten months now, since the last sped Roman summer, these two had been lovers. Lovers infatuated, against – for Rose – all scruples, qualms and difficulties. For Antonio there were none of those. He was simply and triumphantly in love, as by unassailable right; and with every day of it his certainty, his command, his gratitude and delight expanded. Although he was arrogant, perhaps, still he was young and had good manners in feeling; and he knew with all that was true in him that he worshipped Rose. More now than he might have hoped for, more now that he, as he would calmly say, owned her, did he appreciate and enjoy his total devotion to her – and hers, it went without saying, to him.

For Rose, love of Antonio, which when at last guiltily admitted and expressed, had overborne her senses and then, in quiet, her heart – for Rose this passion was as far from simple as for Antonio it was noonday clear. But she understood this difference between them, which he did not allow. So she never explored with him – since he would only have laughed and embraced her into silence – all the grouped shadows and questions in her mind that accented, perhaps too dramatically, her bright, clear passion for him.

With her plain Catholic scruples she would trouble no one. She had not troubled René with them, nor would she begin now with this other much more dangerous Catholic pagan. Her mortal sins were her own, and nothing to pester others with. But her true sin, her dark mistake and cruelty, she knew, was her offence against René.

To speak of René to Antonio was to invoke absurd and boyish outbursts which she could forgive, but which bore nowhere on her guilt, her anxiety. So, she lived alone with her great offence; and in Antonio's arms resolutely and gladly she chose to live with him.

Rose was more honourable than men incline to be, in that she took her guilt by herself, her several kinds of guilt; and if she sometimes ventured on an alleviation of self-pity, that also she tasted alone. But, like every well-taught Irish child, she knew her catechism; so she knew where she stood, she knew that she alone was responsible for her sins, and that she had no legitimate consultant outside the confessional box. Certainly she had no consultant in Antonio, whose indifference to her conscience delighted her.

Their first greeting of each other tonight had been rapturous and gay, but perforce almost conventional, since neither could at once quite focus the sweet truth of the other – too blind and silly was the gladness. Also, Assunta would be in and out, with aperitifs, with canapés, and in arrangement of the supper-table. So, for all their delight, Rose felt as if they were playing their reunion in opera, before the Scala audience. And so it had been through supper, as Assunta hovered with her crayfish and her ducklings.

However, Antonio had talked as he ate, of the activities of the long fortnight. For the first week he had been singing at Bologna; *William Tell* and *Don Giovanni*.

'*Don Giovanni* is a lost cause in Italy, Rosa. Oh, I wasn't bad. At least I adore the music; what's more, I know it. You can't imagine how unknown it was to the conductor and orchestra in Bologna! Mariana Fogli and I were the only two, I think, in the whole organization who knew the opera—'

'But what did Mariana sing in *Don Giovanni*?'

'My dear, don't faint – but she sang Zerlina. They're frightfully short of sopranos in that extraordinary company, and poor old Abrigi – afraid of nothing! – actually shifted Zerlina to mezzo! Lovely for me, wasn't it, arriving just in time for two rehearsals? However – Bologna didn't seem to notice – and Mariana is as clever as paint.'

'She must have enjoyed herself,' said Rose, with a glint of irony. This was not lost on Antonio.

'She did, of course. So did I. But she's a respecter of Mozart – and she saw the joke.'

She is much too sensible not to see that happy joke, thought Rose.

In the second week Antonio had devoted himself to his newly bequeathed estates in northern Tuscany. His aged and wealthy uncle was now senile, and more and more his wide and well-husbanded properties required Antonio's direction, which he gave to them with enthusiasm and intelligence. Since his accidental inheritance of these estates of his father's eldest brother – an inheritance which carried with it eventually the chief title of the de Lucas of Tuscany – Antonio had become more interested in his landlord duties and privileges than in operatic work. He still took singing engagements, still worked with his Milan *maestro*, and sought for any opportunity to sing with Rose. But the governors of La Scala perceived that he was losing professional passion, and although they held his voice and his natural musical taste in watchfulness, it was unlikely that they would promote him now against serious and totally committed singers. Antonio understood this, saw its justice, and was content. He was free and rich, and so long as he could come and go about La Scala while Rose was one of its glories, that was enough. He would take proffered engagements still, because he knew he sang well, he loved to work at opera, and he loved the life of a singer. Also, still to be a singer kept him closer to Rose in sympathy than he could be were he to become merely the amateur patron, the connoisseur-visitor to La Scala. He would like to sing Iago once again to her Desdemona; very much he would like to sing his beloved Don Giovanni to her Zerlina. But he guessed that neither of these two delights could ever now be his. La Scala rightly accepted no half-measures; but he could neither help being a landed aristocrat nor his natural and growing interest in the life arising to him from that social state. So if in recent months he looked in half-farewell upon his opera-singing, in exchange he welcomingly embraced his obligations to the orchards, vineyards and husbandmen of his Tuscan lands.

Now in the quiet room he moved about his love in peace. He lowered the flame of the lamp.

'This isn't a good wick. You need a better lamp, Rose. I'll look for one tomorrow.'

He paused by the piano.

Rose was gathering up the coffee-cups to take to the kitchen.

'Play for me, love,' she said.

'Not unless you sing. Ah!' he studied the open music sheets on the stand. ' "Nuits d'Eté"! You are studying these?'

Rose came back from the kitchen and came to him singing Berlioz's first phrase. He sat and began the music, but when she laid her hands on his head he leapt to his feet and put his fingers across her mouth.

'Love, love! No singing now!'

They kissed as if for the last time on earth – and then they laughed together.

'Your singing is the last straw sometimes,' Antonio said. 'You are yourself too much. Don't sing tonight, my darling.'

'I don't want to. I hardly ever want to.'

'Oh you liar! That rose – do you see those yellow roses?'

'Yes.'

'They're not hardy – look at them. We have that identical rose at home – I'd have brought you some, but they don't travel—'

'Their smell is glorious,' said Rose, bending over them.

'Yes. That's what is good about them – but you know our

flower-gardener and my mother between them can't trace that rose's catalogue name. Where did you get these, darling?'

'Mr Rudd sent them to me.'

'Mr Rudd? Oh, the American? He has returned?'

'Yes. He seems to have arrived in Milan today—'

'And you not singing! Poor Mr Rudd!'

'La Chiarini is – exquisitely – in *Cenerentola*.'

'Happy man! Still, I wish I knew the name of this flower! Not that it's a bit like you – except for the exquisite perfume.'

Throughout the night Rose, used now to love-making, indeed accomplished in it, yet marvelled almost amusedly at herself, as always in this predicament she did. No delight that her senses could bring her would ever, she was now persuaded, overcome her certainty of wrong-doing when she made love; but neither would that certainty dissuade her from a necessity she found so sweet, in herself and in her lover. Were it not for René, she thought with grief now and then as she moved in shameless peace in Antonio's arms – oh, René, what I do myself is nothing, but what have I done to you?

'What is it, love? Why did you sigh?'

'The candles are dying, Antonio.'

'I'll fetch some from the *salotto*.'

The new candles seemed too bright for the languid hour.

'Do you hear the birds? It must be daylight.'

'It's daylight, love. Lie still awhile. I'll soon be gone.'

'I don't want you gone.'

'But then you'll sleep.'

'Yes. I'll sleep indeed. And you, my pet, will you?'

'Like death, Rose. Forgetting all about you.'

'Yes. That's what saves one's reason, I suppose.'

Antonio laughed.

'When do you sing again? You told me – I've forgotten.'

'On Tuesday night – *Don Carlos*.'

'Ah! I wish I were singing Posa.'

'I wish you were. And I wish Luisa were singing Eboli. They say Luisa is a wonderful Eboli. La Matucci sings finely, but she's an awkward sort of actress.'

'Mariana would be good—'

'But she's not mezzo! Is she developing a freak voice?'

'Well, she sang Zerlina!'

'Outrageous. Oh, I'm sleepy. Love, you must go.'

'I know. I'm glad I'll be here for Tuesday, anyway.'

'Why? Are you having to go away again soon?'

'Yes. I'll have to be at San Damiano with Uncle Riccardo and all his lawyers – before Saturday.'

'More lawyers? What are they arranging now? Don't you yet own San Damiano?'

'Well, conditionally, as you know. Conditionally to my making the marriage Uncle Riccardo desires.'

'Yes, I know. And is his old heart still set on that poor little girl who's at school in Switzerland?'

'It is indeed. But Giuseppina's home now – she's eighteen and she left school at Easter. And Uncle Riccardo feels death approaching – as well he might! And he and the Barriacas are anxious to have the enormous business of our alliance fixed and done with. Hence a huge gathering of the families at San Damiano next week! I am to become betrothed, my Rose!'

Rose sat upright in the bed, and pulled a silk robe over her naked shoulders. She looked in wonder for a minute about the disordered, happy, candle-lit room.

'Will you open the shutters, Antonio? Blow out the candles, please. They're hot.'

Morning was still silver and uncertain in the courtyard; there seemed no sound from other windows, but the birds in the plane trees announced the day, and Rose heard the monotonous dove already at her exercises.

'Betrothed? Do you mean, Tonio, that you're going to become engaged to be married next week – to that little girl?'

'Yes – that's it. But in families like ours and the Barriacas getting engaged, as you call it, isn't an ordinary *bourgeois* matter. It has nothing to do with falling in love and going courting – as say a young clerk might go after Assunta and take her to the nearest padre—'

'I know. Go on.'

'When one of us is directed into betrothal – especially if he is Uncle Riccardo's heir! – an enormous mass of machinery creaks into motion! Because although the two families may know all that there has been to be known of each other since the thirteenth century, and although they may have decided on a certain union even before the parties to that union were born – nevertheless, when the moment seems to ripen – oh, Rose, the affair it is! I've seen it through with my brothers, my sisters, my cousins, my friends! Now it's my turn. The examinations of estates and title-deeds, the searching of muniments, the discussion of jointures and trusts, the matter of quarterings and family jewels and dower houses; the progeniture arguments, the plottings as to issue, male and female; the heavy consultations with archbishops and with senile great aunts; the acrimonies about titles, baptismal names, and beds and wine-cellars and family portraits and family tombs . . .'

Rose sat still. As she had not slept in the night and it was morning now, sometimes her eyes closed and she lost a word or two of Antonio's humorous grandiloquence. Momentarily now – as sometimes in the lonely Paris days when falling asleep – she thought she heard water lapping under the bridge at Lackanashee, and she thought she heard the whirr of her mother's sewing machine.

'Go on, Tonio. It's interesting.'

'Oh, when you're at the centre of it it's hardly interesting, Rose! It's a heavy, conventional fuss – but it's just got to be got over. It's our traditional way. It can't be altered, and it can't be helped.'

'But – about this little girl—'

'Giuseppina?'

'Yes. You are going to engage yourself to her next week, to be her husband for ever, and the father of her children—'

'Exactly. That's what all the fuss will be about.'

'Then – you must love her?'

Antonio turned on his elbow and looked up at Rose. His face, she noticed, was grave and beautiful in the rising light of day.

'No,' he said. 'It would be silly to say I love Giuseppina, now.

I've known her since she was born, and I know she's as good as gold. Very certainly I shall love her later on, within the requirements of my bond—'

'But the bond of marriage takes in everything, Tonio – there's no "within" about its requirements, is there?'

'Marriage is marriage. It's not everything. It's very important indeed. But that granted, it's not everything. It's solemn and irrevocable, and its solemnity will be sweetened by the love that one will share with one's wife for one's children.'

Rose shivered. Antonio drew closer and put an arm about her.

'Are you cold, darling? We must mind your throat. Shall I shut the window?'

'No, no. It's going to be a lovely morning.' She paused. 'You have often talked of this future betrothal, pet, and of little Giuseppina in her school in Switzerland. But why is everything now happening next week?'

'For the usual good traditional reasons. Uncle Riccardo is aware that he is very near death. He has no intention of leaving his beloved San Damiano to an unmarried man – and he'd like – if possible, but it won't be – to see a great-nephew born to the inheritance before he departs this life. Anyway, he has long set his heart, his cupidity, on our marriage into the Barriaca estates. And the point now for him is this: Giuseppina will be entering society in the autumn. She is not beautiful and she is indeed excessively naïve. But taken in hand by some high-born Roman aunts that she has she will be made very presentable in a couple of months, and on the Roman marriage market she is well known to be a good match. She would be snatched up quickly by any worn-out Calabrian prince, or more likely by a parvum industrial prince from the north. The Barriacas would have no objection. Their line, though old, is not as old as ours – and they are wealthier than us. They have properties about Turin and Genoa that are very valuable. But they like the old neighbourly alliance, and they know that we are still rich people, and that our name is older than theirs.'

'My goodness! What a lot of words about your just marrying a nice little girl!'

'Ah, Rose!' he laughed. 'It's only that Uncle Riccardo doesn't want to let the age-old plan slip. And I see his point. The formalities are being rushed – I was certainly surprised to find that they were hatching the betrothal ceremonies for so soon—'

'For when are they hatching the wedding?'

'I suppose, since they're all being so cunning, I suppose before Christmas.'

'Have you been asked about this?'

'I? No. Uncle Riccardo knew that I've taken his plan for granted. It's obvious and right.'

'What does Giuseppina say?'

'Giuseppina? Why, nothing. What would she say, pet?'

Rose's eyelids fell in heavy weariness.

'But look, Tonio – she must have something to say!'

Antonio pulled Rose down into his arms.

'I think you're talking in your sleep,' he said. He kissed her immoving eyelids.

'Go, darling,' she said. 'Go, Tonio.'

He rose, covered her over, dressed, and stole away.

Rose lay a long time without moving; light and noise crept up beyond the window; shutters rattled open and the smell of coffee rose. There was a shout or two, a jingle of harness somewhere; church bells began to ring for Mass.

Shall I get up and go to Mass, Rose asked herself, but was ashamed of the theatrical idea even as it crossed her.

No. She must stay still and be quiet. In any case, she had no easy claim on Mass or prayers.

She had had her love tonight – without guessing at all what sword hung over her – she had had her love, her true, sweet love and all its sweet expression, for the last time. For the last and lucky time, as Mr Chris used to say at home. Lucky. Lucky time. Lucky in that neither of them had known that it was to be their last embrace. Tonio did not know that yet. Poor boy, he would learn. She could not cloud his innocent ease tonight, or seek to explain to him plain facts of the heart that he would never accept. Let him be, let him rest – and for the past happy and translucent night of joy let her not diminish gratitude. But

– she would never be so revisited. Antonio was gone; and all his reasonings and all his guile would never bring him back into her arms.

Marriage is marriage. The little girl commits herself to you. I have no aristocratic training and no dower houses to be arguing about – I only know I'll never have you again. I love you, I love you, I am dying now, Antonio.

She turned face down on the pillow, and crying took her crazily. Over, over, over, she sobbed – all I do is wrong and over. I broke you in pieces, René; I'm breaking myself in pieces now. I am made of sins. I do nothing else but commit mortal sins – for sentimental reasons.

She began to laugh hysterically at her 'sentimental reasons'.

'Oh Tonio, darling, darling – wait till you know! Sleep, sleep – let us sleep. Let us sleep . . .'

The Fifteenth Chapter

Since I am to be an opera soprano, of no great brilliance, Clare reflected, shall I always be so fortunate as to sing in Naples in May? Fortunate, she asked herself with memories twisting, and conscience always questioning? Yes, fortunate, for I am faithful. I welcome memories. And life turns out to be an unceasing argument with conscience everywhere. So also here.

She lived now in Naples in a respectable hotel overlooking the bay. Never again, without Luisa, would she occupy 'the suite' at Mamma Lucia's. But Luisa was gone. Gone in April on a worldwide tour. The north-European capitals first: Berlin and St Petersburg, then Hamburg and Stockholm and Christiania; afterwards London and Dublin and Lisbon and Madrid. Then, for the winter, the whole of South America once more, and when spring came, probably New York and Boston and Montreal.

One half of the world would hear her sing, and pay well for the pleasure – for Luisa was going on this round in excellent company, and as a rising star. She had to go; she had to be, like everyone else, about her business.

'For every reason, love, I must be gone. I've always fled from guardian angels—'

'And am I one, Luisa?'

'No, no! A thousand times no! But he is – Iago! And all the more because of you, poor man!'

'There's nothing of "poor man" about him, is there? He's very much his own master, I'd have said.'

Luisa seemed to hesitate, to choose between possible replies.

'Has he ever talked to you about himself, Clare? About his youth?'

'No. He has sometimes seemed a bit pompous, I suppose – and I've gathered that there was a tragedy somewhere.'

'That is true. There was. But he has turned his personality into too much of a re-enactment of it. He symbolizes overmuch his unimportant past. I've told him this – so it's no disloyalty now!'

Clare laughed.

'All the same, love, it's an unkind thing to say.'

'I give him only kindness; I owe him nothing less. But as I love you both – and I do! – I warn you against him, Clare! Have mercy on the man, and keep him at bay!'

'But he's not asking for mercy! And as for keeping him at bay – Luisa darling! You talk as if we were all tigers!'

Luisa kissed Clare's mouth.

'I wish we were,' she said. 'Then we could get into a nice warm cage together, and I needn't have to go and roar my throat out in Berlin!'

Yet to Berlin she had had to go, and now she was in Russia.

'Here is your chain, love,' Clare had said in their night of farewell. 'No, no solemnity or harshness meant – only, I couldn't wear it now. Would you want me to, you free, cool customer you – in common honesty?'

Luisa took the chain, but she did not laugh. Clare was touched to distress by her stricken eyes as she weighed the little knot of gold in her unwilling hand.

'Don't hand it out too often, or too carelessly, will you, love?' she said, 'After all, I've worn it with devotion for a year and a half.'

Luisa began to cry. Clare took her into her arms, gold chain and all.

'I'll be back with it. You'll see, Eurydice – I'll force it round your neck again.'

'*Che faro* . . .' Clare began softly. 'Sing, Orfeo – please . . .'

So Luisa was gone in April, and here was the end of May, and here was Naples, empty of her.

Not Naples only seemed empty. Clare thought sometimes of late, in heavy-heartedness, that now in the fifth year of their singing life, years wherein they had been, after all, only students, beginners, and enclosed within a little narrow circle which had sufficed to them and sometimes seemed, indeed, too full and crowded an arena – she thought sometimes in this lovely May that not only was her world emptying suddenly, almost emptied – but that Rose's too, so much more brilliant, so shining and full, seemed to have grown bleak, to have been by some elusive treachery denuded of its now long customary graces and gaieties. In a few weeks of spring.

During twenty-one days Rose had not written to Clare at all. That in itself was not unusual; but it was not like Rose to have ignored Luisa's departure from Italy which she knew was grief for Clare; nor was it like her to forget to salute Clare's lonely and anxious opening night in San Carlo.

Then Iago Duarte said one day as they walked by the shore at Bagnoli:

'If Antonio de Luca *is* intending to marry the baby daughter of his Barriaca neighbours – and they say he is – that will certainly put an end to his singing life. The Barriacas will not be as indulgent of his bohemian whims as his parents have been.'

Clare guessed that this was said of kind intent, to warn her for Rose's sake. But the suggestion surprised and frightened her, so that she could answer only perfunctorily.

'It was always clear that he'd have to do his duty by his family quarterings! Poor Tonio! And he sings so well!'

'Indeed he does.'

One night not long after this she had to sing the foolish opera, *Martha*, with René Chaloux, who had been sent in haste from Rome to substitute for a sick tenor.

René liked Clare, who was kind to his vanity, and sorry for him about Rose's infidelity. And she allowed him to speak French to her. And feeling that they had sung well together, and in a French opera, which he liked and in which he was always well received, the young man had asked the *prima* to have supper with him. So, her thoughts very much with Rose, she went to supper with Rose's first love. He took her by chance to a restaurant in the Galleria where night after night in the May of another year she and Luisa had loved to eat and talk.

René seemed surprised by the welcome Clare received from the waiter.

'Oh, we're loyal in Naples, René. And I'm one of the old hacks at San Carlo now.'

The beautiful young man laughed delightedly. He was conscious that his beautiful guest was a distinguishing foil for him, and no old hack. He ordered supper with his customary French fussiness, and when the waiter was gone he said disarmingly to Clare:

'It's not for nothing that I am the son of the best *charcutier* in Rouen.'

Clare liked that observation.

'And looking like Tristan,' she said. 'But why not?'

They ate well, and while they did so Clare observed the boy carefully, and made him talk about himself. Indeed this, as she knew of old, was easy, as René had little idea that there was anything else to talk about. It appeared to her, who had not seen him for some months, that he had rallied well from what she could only call his 'jilt' of ten months ago. In the early autumn of 1890 when Rose, after a summer sojourn nobody knew where, had reappeared in Venice and afterwards in Milan as Antonio's declared and open lover, many of René's colleagues who had far less patience with him than had Clare, feared for him in this insulting grief; for they knew, as Clare did, that he was not a man to take such punishment, such public punishment and loss, as Rose's change of heart had flung upon him. And indeed throughout the winter, wherever she sang, in La Valle or on tour, he had made scenes and theatre. He had been troublesome and absurd.

Clare believed, as many, La Lanci and others, did not, that Rose had truly wounded his heart, that her sudden leaving of him had lacerated his natural affections. But she did agree with the less patient that the blow to vanity and ambition seemed all but lethal for a time.

Rose had made him her lover; together on the Roman stages they were the very expression of human beauty and romance; she could already sing and act more exquisitely, more movingly, more powerfully than any soprano of her generation then to be heard in Italy. As her proclaimed lover and her heaven-ordained physical match, he should have been swept with her to where, in the days of her love, she had dreamt to take him. Had she been true, he thought – sometimes in the winter he had shouted this, in his distress, in his drunken wretchedness – had she been true he would have been at La Scala with her in this, her great *assoluta* season.

His informed listeners winced when he went so far. To say such a silly thing was simply to proclaim oneself an ignorant Frenchman who knew nothing of La Scala.

'My God, René!' La Lanci had burst out shouting one night in a café on the Corso, 'if Tamagno himself, or young de Reszke, were Rose's lover, they'd have to *sing* themselves into La Scala! Oh, do be quiet! How *could* she go on loving you, you fool?'

The foolish days were past, Clare thought. René was hard and calm, and she learnt, from measured questioning, that he was working more seriously than he had been wont to, was making sufficient money, and had reasonable hopes for the immediate future.

He had recovered. He was his own man now, and becoming easy at last, Clare thought, in management of his vanity – even in enjoyment of it.

She smiled to herself as she considered that.

How vain am I? she wondered. How much is it a concealable defect? What pleasure do we take from dreaming of ourselves?

'You're smiling. What are you smiling at?' René asked. Clare thought that there was a hint, barely a hint, of peppery suspicion in his voice.

'I was thinking about vanity,' she said. 'My own vanity.'

'Are you *vain*, Clare?'

The intonation was amazing and amusing, but Clare let the obvious protest float away.

'I don't know,' she said peaceably. She was sorry he had caught her smile. 'I don't think I am. Why should I be?'

This idle query seemed good sense to René. He poured more of the beautiful Capri wine into the tall glasses.

'It's madness to order a French wine in Italy,' he said.

'But this is lovely, René.'

'Ah – Italian!'

'I love the Italian wines. But then –' she smiled at him – 'I'm not a daughter of the best *charcutier* in Rouen.'

'No,' he said nervously. 'You – you are some kind of aristocrat, I imagine.'

'My grandmother is *my* kind of aristocrat. But my father is a lazy clerk in the Customs and Excise. I don't remember my mother – but Grandmother smokes a clay pipe, and is bi-lingual.'

René raised his eyebrows.

'In Irish and English.'

'Then you're a peasant?'

'Yes, indeed.' Clare looked in amazement at his puzzling face. 'Is that a shock to the son of the Rouen *charcutier*?'

He laughed with grace.

'It could be. We're snobbish in Rouen.'

He asked the waiter for coffee.

'What are you doing when the Roman season ends, René?'

'I've got a good touring engagement – you know – Bologna, Parma, Genoa, Torino – and in the autumn I believe that I may sing in France, in Paris.'

'Oh, good!'

'It will please my mother,' he said.

Silence fell while the waiter poured coffee. 'Brandy, Clare?'

'No, thank you.'

René indicated brandy for himself.

'Rose,' he said suddenly, seeming to underline the name – 'Rose will still be hanging round La Scala?'

Clare was taken by surprise. How little we know of sickness or cure, she thought confusedly. This that René had just said sounded, from his beautiful red mouth and gleaming teeth, the remark of a stupidly sick man. So she took her time and looked at him before she framed an answer.

'People don't hang round La Scala, René. They wouldn't be allowed to. Everyone is there to work. It's the Mecca of all of us, as you know. There's no hanging round. If you're admitted there and allowed to sing, you have begun to be a *given* singer.

Rose is there – and assuredly she's never had to hang around, as you call it, in any opera house. Rose is an *assoluta*, after this brilliant season.'

René, mutely seeking Clare's permission, lit a cigarette.

'You're loyal,' he said. 'I suppose that is because you are both Irish.'

'Loyal? To what? To success? To brilliant success? What occasion is there for loyalty, René? Wait until Rose is in trouble before we talk of loyalty.'

He smiled.

'Don't you think she is in trouble, Clare?'

'In what trouble?'

'She lost her throw with Antonio de Luca. He's marrying into his own class, in October.'

Clare, among a thousand startled and angry answers to this smirking, vengeful statement, could not find a best, a neat one. Almost, in despair, she decided to strike the face across the table. But instead, guardian-angel guided, she flung the vulgar gloating from her, and remembered that if what this fool said was true, then Rose, seeking no marriage, no coronets or rings or honours, was indeed in trouble. Because Rose loved Antonio; and it would go hard indeed with her before she would take again a lover who had pledged himself in marriage to a girl who was to be the mother of his children.

In a second Clare saw and felt Rose's silence. Looking into René's stupid, beautiful face she understood that the blue-eyed fool had spoken truly. Rose has lost her throw. She is in trouble. Antonio has wounded her too soon.

Clare could find no answer to the triumphant, vulgar boy.

She stood up. He rose with her.

'No, sit down, René. Finish your coffee. I require to walk home alone.'

'I – have said something wrong?'

'I hardly remember. But you seem to have said one right thing – that Rose is in trouble. Remember that, René – if you have loved her.'

Clare departed from the Galleria, and walked home.

*

Iago Duarte was the chief conductor of the San Carlo season in that sad spring. He chose Clare's work with great care, but the last week of May, which concluded the season, he had arrogantly and arbitrarily devoted to Glück. The management of the great opera house was not enthusiastic about this idea, as they feared that Naples would not welcome in one week the two *Iphigenias*, two performances of *Orfeo* and two of *Alceste*. But it seemed that this concluding programme had been Duarte's pound of flesh. It was to be his reward to himself for giving Naples for many weeks his brilliant and exact directions of their darling Bellinis, Donizettis and Verdis. And it was possible that as his hard-drilled and clean-sung season had pleased the Neapolitans, they would support his eccentric concluding week.

Clare was grateful to him, however, that he had not cast her to sing Eurydice, even if she suspected that his restraint was as much in concern for his own nerves as for hers. She did not attend his rehearsals of *Orfeo*, let alone the public performances – and although she understood that the latter were beautiful and successful, she and Duarte did not speak of them to each other.

Alceste she had to sing, on the two last nights of the San Carlo season. She had long studied the score, the story and the character of Alceste, and early in the spring Duarte had worked with her rigorously on the music. Sometimes she had thought, as she learnt the opera, of Thomas, whose great favourite it was, and who had used to swear that she would sing it first under his direction, or he would require to know the reason why.

However, Thomas now seemed to have decided on farewell. Since his return into Germany after little Giaco's death he had become only perfunctory in his salutes. A birthday telegram, a Christmas card, a rare, flying note or postcard. All the old brotherliness was vanished, and he seemed anxious, Clare thought, to make its ending understood.

So, she was hurt and at a loss; and if she was to sing Alceste for her Spanish director, so be it. She would learn and sing.

Alceste suited her voice and temperament. At present in

rehearsal she felt as if it suited and fitted her whole state and nature. It was to her mood of loss and loneliness consolatory music; and if only Naples was to hear her sing it – Naples was, after all, very nearly as old as the story her voice would tell, old as Euripides – and she hardly cared just now if Naples listened. She would sing the high, cold story for herself – and for one who could not hear.

At the end of the second performance of *Alceste*, which concluded the San Carlo season of 1891, the applause of Naples had indeed justified Duarte's obstinacy; and even he, taking call after call at the end of the opera, had looked pleased in a boyish, surprised way – as Clare, standing by, thought she had never seen him look. As again and again, in answer to the shouting, he took her hand and the hand of Admetus and presented them both to the dark and storming auditorium, Clare thought with amazement, out of the depths of her reactionary fatigue: 'How amazing he is! What a boy this ageing man – and here am I, an old woman by the end of the night, in his service!'

The boy, the ageing man, had engaged her to sup with him, when all the noise was done. And as they drove along the Partenope in an open carriage, and viewing the starry night, they carried in their breasts the peace, the momentary peace, of being satisfied with what had just been done. Both were tired, yet each exulted. Both knew, apprehended, the weariness and questions of tomorrow. Still – for tonight, they had done their best, and it had seemed good.

'Partenope? She was a siren, wasn't she?'

'Yes,' said Duarte. 'The sirens sang around here.'

'Just as well we don't think too much about that in San Carlo! Where are we going, Iago? I'm hungry.'

He laughed.

'You've earned a classic supper, so we're going to a place not far from where Lucullus had some banquet. He would have liked the situation. But the cooking – well, I hope you'll find it good enough, Alceste?'

'I'd like a chop and some floury potatoes!'

'Sounds more Irish than Lucullan. I'm afraid we didn't think of a chop and potatoes, Clare. But there's one thing that may please you in this garden over the sea – the rose-trees are real trees, trees that you can sit under, bigger than olive trees – and the roses hang down and drip on you, and on a summer night the perfume almost makes you think you're drowning.'

'I've never seen rose-trees like that.'

'I wondered if Luisa and you had ever come here – La Torre Fiorita it's called.'

'We didn't travel so far at night. We couldn't afford these carriages. Was she here with you, Iago?'

'No. I found it when I was alone. I was walking back from Pozzuoli.'

The garden above the sea was set indeed as Lucullus might have desired it. The hour was late now, even for Neapolitans – rather it was early, not far from three o'clock. But the two were expected, and the head waiter led them to a flowered and ready table, under just such a rose-tree as Iago had promised, and flung out high above the sleeping Mediterranean.

There were some groups at supper still among the roses; of these many were in evening dress, which meant that they had been at San Carlo; so as Clare and Iago crossed the garden they could not but feel the sense of pleased recognition of them that moved through the scattered tables; and indeed as they sat down they heard some gentle '*bravos*' and '*vivas*', towards which the *prima* and her conductor had to smile and half-bow. The head waiter was delighted with this grace and pleasure among his clients, but he knew better than to stress or more than lightly to acknowledge it.

The two sat down and subsided into granted privacy under their own tree of drenching-heavy roses. Clare felt young and embarrassed.

'I've seen Rose sometimes have this sort of – well, reception – in public places in Milan and Rome. But it's never happened to me. It must be that I'm with you.'

Duarte smiled.

'You've been singing all of Naples' favourite heroines on the immense stage of San Carlo for the last three weeks. Last night and tonight you have absolutely distinguished yourself, once and for all, in Alceste. You've been performing before the whole of Italy last night and tonight, in clear, harsh lighting. As Alceste, if I may say so, you have looked glorious, accented and exotic; and you have sung like a god – as I taught you to.' He laughed affectionately. 'Yet, you think that these sophisticated opera-goers recognize you and applaud you because you walk in here with me! Oh Clare!' He laid his hand lightly, briefly on hers, 'Clare, you are mad. You became famous last night. You sealed your fame tonight. You are a *prima*. Let La Scala say what it likes, after tonight you are an *assoluta* – even if you're never going to be the perfect Verdi unfortunate!'

Clare smiled resignedly.

'If you say so, then I suppose you're entitled to your opinion.'

'Entitled to my *opinion*?'

'Anyway, if you're right, Iago, it's the least that might happen, I suppose – after all the fuss and bother.'

Duarte laughed almost in an ecstasy of surprise.

'The *least* that might happen, did you say? The *least*? To become a great operatic singer, to be the living instrument through which difficult music comes, to be able to produce through your small, vulnerable but perfectly constructed vocal organs the tenuous work of immortal men – to be able to make that incredibly delicate and complicated work sound almost simple, even to the dullest ears in dullest, dustiest opera-houses!' The Spaniard whirled into laughter again. 'So you think that that perilous destiny is merely the *least* that might happen to you, after what you call the fuss and bother? Oh, Clare! Oh you Irishwomen! What are you made of? Along what systems do you try to think?'

A young waiter had filled their glasses with green-gold Capri. Another boy was serving Clare's plate from a smoking dish of aubergines and shrimps. Duarte sipped Strega.

'Crude of me,' he said. 'But I must. Tonight was a strain. Tonight, after last night's *réclame*, every important judge of opera in Europe either was in San Carlo or had his appointed spy there. We made your fame tonight, Clare, after all the "fuss and bother"! It was, as you say, "the least that might happen".'

He lifted his glass of Strega. His eyes glittered; he was laughing still.

Clare understood that her foolish phrases had hurt him.

She lifted her glass of Capri in response to him.

'Don't mock me,' she said. 'And don't ask by what systems I try to think! That's unfair. I'm not a fool, but I certainly don't seek to think. If I did, the only system that's ever been explained to me is the Catechism – and even I know, Iago, that that isn't a philosophy!'

They both laughed.

'I wasn't mocking, Clare. I'm forever puzzled by the split in you.'

'Split?'

'Leave it. Drink, Alceste – drink and eat.'

They did so. Small red mullet – 'the little *salmonetes* of Spain,' said Iago, 'and never perfect unless caught and cooked at once off the Viscayan coast. The *salmonete* is not a Mediterranean fish. Very few good fish are, you know—'

'This Mediterranean fish is good enough for me,' said Clare. 'I didn't know you were a gourmet, Iago?'

'My God, I'm not!'

'I find them bores – the few I've met.'

'I also. But we grew up on the Catechism, and in poor countries, Clare.'

'Italy is very poor.'

'Is she? She teems with everything – including children. Italy's not naturally poor. Spain is.'

'So is Ireland.'

They were silent, and ate.

Eastward the sky paled, and below them the water lay without a breath. There was as nearly silence as can be in Italy; only the far cry of an uneasy bird, and, nearer, the clink of glasses being washed.

'I wonder what you'll do next,' Iago said.

'Whatever Mugnone tells me, I suppose.'

'Do you return to Rome tomorrow?'

'Yes. On the evening train.' Clare looked back over the bay and the scattered, thinning lights. 'I love Naples.'

'Without Luisa?'

Clare turned eyes on her questioner that fixed him by their expression of honesty and loneliness.

'Because of Luisa.'

'She will not come back to you.'

'She and I are not sure of that,' Clare said, with a turn of insolence.

The plates were changed.

'We seem to be eating excessively,' said Clare.

Iago paid no attention to her attempt to restore lightness and to shut out from him her awareness of an absent one.

'When you spoke coldly now – when you were seeking to dismiss me from your – association with Luisa – I got the shock that you've given me before. Usually you've given it to me when you've been singing. I remember my amazement when I heard you sing "Casta Diva" exactly a year ago, here in San Carlo—'

'I remember.'

'Your tempo then – one would have said almost your eccentric speed, were it not that you were precisely with your conductor – that very individual timing, and the quite rare character of your voice – not sexless at all, but geometrically clean and very nearly impersonal, very nearly violin singing – which the human voice shouldn't be; they are instruments both, and should not be confusable, as you know – well, in "Casta Diva" that night, and often since, in the *Requiem*, in *Stabat Mater*, in *The Magic Flute* at Costanzi's at Easter – I have been invaded, you have invaded me, Clare, with pain that had been a long time dead. And in Alceste, though I believe she never sang it – you sang for her. I heard her. *O femesta Dea . . .*'

'*Nume fatal*,' Clare sang very softly; '*non io placar . . .* Who was this singer, Iago? Where is she now? Is she famous?'

'She isn't anywhere. She isn't even dead.'

'But she's some time ago, isn't she? Was she your only love – or why are you always hinting about her?'

Duarte shook a branch of the rose-tree, and petals fell about. He pulled a great open rose from over Clare's head and laid it in her hands.

'I never hinted about her until you brought her back – you

couldn't help that. I had forgotten her, almost forgotten the *ennuis* of that faraway time – until I heard you sing.'

Clare stood up.

'Let us walk.'

They walked over the harsh grass to a parapet on the edge of the cliff.

Clare pondered with distaste and anxiety the latter passages of this conversation. We are being theatrical, she thought uncomfortably. But then he, by his refusal of theatre, has perhaps made himself into an attitude. And after all, what am I but some kind of actress? And these two fevered nights of *Alceste* have been much; and we are tired.

She turned compunctiously to look at Iago, but found that he was looking at her with what in plain daylight she would have called excess of expression. Now the dark lines of the man's face and the narrowed shining of his eyes embarrassed her, and whatever kind platitude she had had in mind stayed unsaid on her mouth.

'I have been in love with you since last year, since here in San Carlo,' Iago said. 'I think I was in love with you before then. But since then – beyond doubt. You have known that?'

'I have sometimes thought it might be so.'

'No man of my age – and circumstances – should allow himself to be devoured by passion for a girl, a good girl, who could almost be his daughter.'

He said this as if there was no more to say. Awkward silence fell again between them. Clare looked diffidently towards Iago's face, and thought how perverse and strange it would be to kiss a mouth that Luisa had known and kissed – had kissed by habit and goodwill even when she was Clare's sworn lover. Would I find her there, the villain? Would I find any trace of you, Luisa, in so wrong a place?

'I am not what is called a good girl, Iago.'

'I find you good.'

'Neither I nor the Church agrees with you. But since none of us is good—'

'Indeed! Indeed! Come back to the table – I need coffee.' They moved over the grass. 'Had we stayed there, you looking in your white dress so mercilessly *Alceste*, I'd have become an angry old fool and tried to kiss you.'

'Angry old fool,' said Clare in soft amusement.

They sat and watched the boy pour coffee. Clare took some strawberries in her hand and ate them. Iago poured Strega.

'Will you have *fine*, Clare?'

'Thank you – I'd love it. I feel anxious – irrationally anxious. Oh no, I'm not a prophetess or witch, Iago – indeed I hate witches and their antics. But, just this moment I feel afraid. Do you think – everyone's all right?'

'I don't for a moment think that everyone's all right! How could such a tidy thing be?'

Clare laughed and tasted some brandy.

'God give me courage,' said Iago, slowly and with, to Clare's ears, an almost suspect gravity.

'For what?'

'Luisa has *never* spoken to you of me? To tell you of my history, I mean?'

'But, Iago, why should she? What do you take us for, Luisa and me? As I know that she has never talked of me to you – beyond admitting that she has loved me – so, as we are civilized, please—'

'I beg your pardon, and Luisa's. Listen then. I am what is called an unfrocked priest.'

'You said?'

'I was a priest. I was unfrocked.'

Clare listened after the words were gone. She picked up the dying rose on the table and looked into its centre wonderingly.

'You are a priest for ever,' she said carefully.

'Yes. But, rightly, you surrender on oath, when you are unfrocked, priestly powers and duties.'

Clare stared into the rose.

'You have said a terrifying thing. I'm afraid you must say more now. When did you tell Luisa that you – that you are – a priest?'

'I didn't have to tell Luisa. When I was young, when I was a novice, I was sent to the house of our Order in Segovia—'

'What Order?'

'Augustinian. The oldest of the Orders. I was sent to Segovia to study some fourteenth-century unedited liturgical music in the Cathedral library. Luisa's father was the organist there, and he was very kind to me. He wrote to me about music often over the years – he's dead now. But, naturally, his household knew my story. Luisa knew it when we met in Rome. She made that clear quickly, kindly – at the beginning of our acquaintance. But everyone in Castile church and church-musical circles knows about me.'

'I see. What happened? Why was it?'

'I was born in Avila. I was the only child of my kind and elderly parents, who were very pious and spared nothing on my education. I was sent to a very great Augustinian school. There was a gifted choirmaster there – a celestially pure musician. Before I was ten he had turned me into a near-fanatic about liturgical, mediaeval music, and the whole polyphonic science. I lived for it – to my mother's delight. And when I entered the Order, at sixteen, my superiors spared no pains or expense over my training in music. I was moved from house to house of the Order, wherever the instruction best suited to my talent was to be found. After periods of early study in Segovia and El Escorial and Toledo, I was entered at the Conservatorio in Madrid. But there they had little to give me, so I was sent, when I was twenty-two, to our house in Paris, and to study with a very great scholar of Flemish Church music in the Conservatoire.'

'Yes?' Claire said. 'You were happy in Paris?'

'I was zealous, and happy. After a year there – I was ordained. After ordination they sent me to Rome – to our famous old convent in the Piazza del Popolo—'

'Ah, in the corner there! Luther's convent!'

'Yes, poor Luther. It was in that house that I gave up, and asked to be unfrocked.'

'I've passed it so often; I've even prayed there, and thought of Luther. I like the Sansovino tombs. Some Popes' tombs . . .'

She knew she was talking nonsense, out of the terror of her embarrassment. She was ashamed of the unreasonable shock she was undergoing; she desired to listen to this story as a detached and intelligent person should.

342

'Ah, go on!' she said wearily.

'There's little more. I went to Milan. My action certainly hurried my mother's death. Yet she forgave me. They both forgave me – though I never saw them again. My father had some modest means and house-property in Avila – so I was able to continue my studies. My Order forgave me too – to the generous extent of using, and publishing, certain of my arrangements of twelfth-century Augustinian Masses.'

He paused. Clare felt his question – but she did not look at him. She kept her eyes on the delicate western sky, whence stars were vanishing as the east brightened.

'In Milan I met a girl who was studying both at La Scala and at the Conservatorio. I think it is just to say that our falling in love was simultaneous. Truly for me it was a total passion, my first, and such as I was not to know again, until I was too old to bear or face it. This girl sang like the morning star, or a skylark, or as perhaps we imagine the seraphim sing. Her voice was pure as ice – and she was a natural scholar of vocal music. Almost at first meeting we were sure – and in a disgracefully short time we were living together. She had some means, I rather less – but, as students reckon these things, we were not poor. We had all we wanted.'

Silence again. Clare did not move. She heard the noise of pouring into a glass.

'This girl was, like me, an hereditary Catholic, though, like me, not keeping to the rules. But, as our love grew and was impregnable, she began to desire a child. So she thought we should marry. She would not have an illegitimate child, she said. I had to tell her then—'

'You hadn't told her? Loving her as you did?'

'No. I hadn't told her. I was afraid.'

'Afraid?'

'I was right to be afraid. I told her my story, after a long time. Ah! I was right to be afraid! The distortion, the grotesque, the inferno! The change of beauty and love into some kind of mediaeval, witch-driven fury. After all these years – don't let me remember what became of that most lovely woman.'

'But what did become of her?'

'She vanished. One day I came home and she wasn't there. I never saw her again. It took me a long time to forgive that cold cruelty. And the death of love was slow – and made me dull, and I became a dull old man. But then Luisa shot across the monotonous Roman life. And she was the voice of home and Spain – and she was Luisa. And then you came – and your singing carried back that other voice – the only voices of their kind I've heard. My idea of true singing.'

He filled his glass again. Clare shivered.

'Ah, it's cold, it's morning! Where is your wrap?' He lifted the old black cloak and put it round her. 'Forgive me. I love you. Come, I'll take you home.'

They drove the long road through the cold rising of day in a silence that Clare could not break – for fear in her great fatigue that she might cry.

Iago made no effort either. Kindly and politely he took her to the door of her room, and bowed over her hand.

'Thank you, Alceste,' he said.

Clare took the noonday, not the evening, train to Rome.

In her rooms she found letters that troubled her; and while she was reading them, with Ruffo on her shoulder, Paddy came to visit her.

Almost she cursed at the sight of him. But he told her that he had gone on the previous Saturday to Volterra, to visit Signora Buonatoli. This kindness, which he repeated from month to month as he could afford it, always touched Clare while it puzzled her. She took it to be an act of devotion to the little *maestro*, to whom Paddy had taken a real attachment on that drunken morning when he had had his first singing lesson. Also, she thought it might be a sentimental tribute to the Ripetta days, and vaguely thus to her. But why or why not, the faithfulness was good in Paddy.

'How is she?'

'You wouldn't know her. She seems to get smaller. She's not herself at all.'

'Are they kind to her?'

'Oh, yes. Signorina Caterina pays the nuns well, you know –

and they take great care of the Signora. She has a very fine room.'

'Does she – do they give her wine – and so on? Enough, I mean? Rose often worries about that. She says that Assunta says they'll kill her if they don't give her what she's used to.'

'I don't think they give her enough, really. But she's not what she was anyway. She won't be long now, Clare. It's just as well.'

'Ah, Casta Diva!'

Paddy was desirous of a very long evening of confabulation. He was anxious about many things – about Rose and Antonio; about gossip arising from Clare's *Alceste* triumph in Naples and her suspect friendship with the sinister Duarte; about Parnell and his absurd, wrongheaded attempt to fight his bad cause; the madman, in Holy Ireland. And about himself: should he shake Europe off his nerves and see what to do as a teacher in Australia or in America? Or would he dare attempt the religious vocation again, and seek admittance to Maynooth or Salamanca?

'Salamanca,' said Clare – who had had her recent surfeit of priests and half-priests.

Paddy stood up.

'I can see you're not in patience with me,' he said.

'No, I'm not. Forgive me, Paddy. But do write your news of Casta Diva to Rose and Assunta – won't you?'

'I've never been on writing terms with Rose, as you know – and really, in view of the way she lives—'

Clare stared at him.

'Oh, Paddy! Please go away!'

When he was gone she re-read her letters. One small letter, from her grandmother in Ballykerin, she read three or four times. Then, with Ruffo for sole company, she stayed up nearly all the night, with her window open to the noises of Rome and the bright stroke of morning across the green Janiculum. She wrote a number of letters during the night, the only long ones being to Rose and to Luisa.

In the morning she made all the orderly arrangements that were necessary, with the *portiera* and with her bank. She stamped her many letters, and at three o'clock, while Rome still drowsed in siesta, she found a cab and placed her luggage in it.

'Goodbye, Ruffo. Be a good boy. Perhaps we'll meet again.'

The drowsy *portiera* brought her a flat, well-packed registered parcel, for which she had to sign and give a tip. She took it, gave her last tips to the *portiera*, her last kiss to Ruffo, and got into the cab.

She would post all her letters at the station. What was this package? It was wonderfully and efficiently bound up, and it came, according to its label, from a publishing house in Vienna. It must be a present from Thomas – some score that he thought she should study.

The Sixteenth Chapter

After Rose left her, Clare sat a long time on the *terrasse* of the chocolate shop. It was the same one where they had feasted with Julie Constant in the July of four years ago. It was September now, and not so warm as Clare remembered that other anxious, childish day. Rose and she, sitting here, had recalled it all – the collars and cuffs, the shiny belts, the francs left over for chocolate eclairs in a 'fashionable' place.

In the cool light of the September afternoon she watched Rose until she vanished along the Boulevard de la Madeleine.

'I have to do this, Clare,' she had said. 'It may be a mistake, and La Scala are angry with me. But – before he marries I must be oceans away. This huge American offer is perhaps – don't laugh, Clare! – perhaps God's way of showing mercy to my sins. I mean, it's removing me from – from an occasion of sin in the only way I can manage to be removed!'

Rose was as beautiful as ever – more beautiful than a year ago, maybe, because a truly searching argument had engaged her senses. She had suffered guilt and pity in her juvenile sentimentality and resultant cruelty to René, but gladly had learnt how the wound she gave had festered outwardly and cleaned itself, becoming hatred, which cauterizes love. She suspected that all the more did this vulgarly expressed hatred mean that she had injured René – but, in her own deeper trouble, she could not have much patience with that early mistake, however heavily it was hers. René's heart was closed and hard against her now, quite rightly; and he had taken an older, wiser mistress, and no doubt could laugh in her arms over his mistake with the Irish soprano. To be able to laugh over a love that has failed is not, Rose guessed, a fortunate ability. But if she had created such a hardness in René, against her intent, then she was to blame for what he was and might become.

So she thought; so she worried foolishly. René would have been the first to laugh at an anxiety which he would have dismissed as silly conceit. Clare, however, understood scruple. And Clare thought she saw how that scruple, even more than her true woe for loss of Antonio, was working on the very structure of Rose's face. Not by any means that years or disappointments had carved furrows there – time enough for those still remote insignia. But the bones of Rose's face had in this winter and spring come to command and almost to dismiss the flowering, summer fairness of one summer ago.

This might be sad. But Clare welcomed the accent and control it brought into a face which soon might have to bear the worship of a wide swathe of the world.

Rose had said lightly, sadly: 'I've played enough *Traviata*, pet. Except that Uncle Riccardo hasn't come to Milan to sing Germont père in my *salotto*, and also excepting the hacking cough – I play Violetta too much these days!'

She was going now. At some risk to her future with La Scala she was crossing the Atlantic before Antonio took his marriage vows in the parish church of San Damiano. Mr von Jakob had made an offer of a long and splendidly paid tour of the chief cities of America and South America. And with Assunta, and escorted by Mr Rudd, she would sail from Le Havre the next morning.

Mr Rudd. Clare pondered him and reached no conclusion. He was rich, young, well-mannered, and learned in music. He seemed to be frequently where Rose was, and at her side, and she seemed relieved that he – by coincidence – would be aboard her liner on the morrow. For all his excellencies, Clare hoped that Rose would go on grieving for Antonio at a safe distance – and then she could only smile, half sorrowly, half in pleasure.

She opened the heavy volume of songs which lay on her lap. She had brought the book to show to Rose, and perhaps to Mère Marie Brunel.

It was Thomas's first publication of a work of his own composition; it was the packet which had reached her from Dresden on the day of June when she was leaving Rome for Ballykerin. It was entitled 'Songs for Clare', and it was dedicated thus:

'On the fifteenth day of May 1888 we sat on the Pincio terrace, dear Clare Halvey, and admired the little acacia trees, and heard the bells of Trinita dei Monte. I boasted then that I would write a song for you about those white acacias. Here are twelve that have arisen from a musical theme that I wrote down even while we talked. The acacias are not literally represented, but they control this sequence. And since songs require words, I have taken words that I found singable – that I thought you would possibly like to sing.

'Learn these songs. They are not worthy of the voice that you will one day let us hear. But as they are my first published work and as you inspired them I offer them to you with devotion.

Thomas Evans'

At home in Ballykerin she had studied the twelve songs. She had a tuner out from Galway to put Father Ryan's piano into order, and there in his parlour she had worked at the 'Songs for Clare'.

They were beautiful. They were difficult to get into outline at first; their design seemed arbitrary, and too firm and eccentric for the basic inspiration suggested in the dedication. Where on earth are those poor little acacias? Clare asked as she took her first surprised surveys of the twelve randomly worded songs.

She could find no reasons in the music, or between each other, for the poems Thomas had made into songs for her. A verse from here – rarely the first or last verse of anything; half a verse from there; two songs set to Welsh, without translation; one prose passage about a swan that seemed like a translation from the German; one verse from Goethe. Lines from John Clare, from Shelley, from Poe, from Tennyson, from Landor.

'A shadow flits before me . . .' one song began; 'Stand close around, ye Stygian set . . .' another. The arbitrariness of arrangement annoyed Clare at first. This is arrogance being silly, she thought. But as she learnt the songs and learnt, stumblingly, to find her way in their firm, clean structure, she heard by degrees what Thomas had heard and remade through his erratic pattern – Rome on that especial day, Rome quite hardly and cleanly cut into the music which supported the voice – the voice, supposedly hers – she smiled – expressing the contradictory and random-true emotions of an individual, to which Rome does not listen.

Clare knew that these songs required a musician to expose them to her, at Father Ryan's piano. But there was no musician in Ballykerin. So alone and slowly she taught herself the songs – laughing to think of Thomas's rage when, if, she ever sang one of them to him. The one she liked best, or found easiest to learn unaided, was made on two verses of Shelley: 'As music and splendour . . .' it began – and the song disturbed her very deeply. So did another; lines from John Clare which ended '. . . The grass below; above, the vaulted sky'.

Grandmother had liked that one. She used to practise these songs by Grandmother's bed at night. But over and over again she would have her sing: 'As music and splendour survive not the lamp and the lute . . .' right through the two verses of which Thomas had made his song Grandmother would have her go. She had to learn the words, apart from the music, and would repeat them wonderingly.

'Shelley! I never knew of him, child. It's a queer name, isn't it – Shelley?'

Clare spent a lonely summer, cold and lonely, in Ballykerin. She was shocked at how difficult she found the primitive life of her own people, and it saddened her to realize that, *prima donna* or not, she could not ever live now the simple, clean, courageous and uncomforted life from which her grandmother was departing in holy and collected peace.

'Thank God you came, love. Ah, you're my pet, God bless you. And when I open my eyes I'm surprised and delighted to see you sitting there. Ah, thank God. You'll tell me more about Rome and all – won't you?'

'Yes, Grandmother. But you must try to sleep now, pet.'

'I'll sleep enough when the time comes. You're a good child, aren't you? You look good anyway. May God keep you so! But soon I won't be there to pray for you, love.'

'Won't you pray in Heaven?'

'Faith and I will! But I don't know – I won't know the ropes so well there.'

The old eyes closed.

'I know that my Redeemer liveth . . .' Clare began softly. Grandmother's hand groped out and Clare took it and sang as softly as she could.

And one night at the end of August Grandmother opened her eyes as Clare sang, and said 'Jesus, mercy'. A minute later she was gone. And with her going Ballykerin ended, and Clare had no choice but to return to the world.

And here indeed she was going back.

Tonight Rose would fetch her at her *pension*, and see her off at Gare de l'Est, for she was on her way to Dresden. For the autumn and winter seasons she was engaged to Dresden and Vienna. Thomas had had his way; her contracts were good, and he would choose her operas and in the main conduct when she sang. Tomorrow, after almost a year of half-silence and separation, he would meet her on the station platform in Dresden. Professionally, for a time at least, he would be her master.

She closed her eyes against the pleasant afternoon. An experience of an hour ago was still making her feel faint and sick, and had made her vague, she knew, with Rosie, to whom she desired to be at present all that was possible of help and love.

Reluctantly, but disciplined by Rose who was inclined to be 'correct' in such matters, she had agreed to go with her after lunch to call on Mère Marie at Rue des Lauriers.

They had been most cordially received at the dreary old house – 'As well we might be,' said Rose, 'with all those twenty per cents still to collect!' – and old, lazy Mère Superieure had kissed them ripely and given them each a miraculous medal. Mother Bursar was almost affectionate, and Frau Sturz, who chanced to be in conference with Mère Marie, insisted that they go to the music room and, to her accompaniment, sing for the gratification of their first directress.

Mère Marie, very gracious, had smilingly asked that each

sing the piece she had chosen to sing on that July day of '87 which had fixed their fates.

So they had done – Rose's 'Last Rose of Summer', sung, as Mère Marie observed, with exactly the same fresh delicacy which had made it lovely on that other day. And Clare's 'My Redeemer Liveth'.

'You have learnt a great deal, Clare. This is no longer what you need most in sacred music, is it?'

'No, Mère Marie. I've been studying with Señor Duarte—'

'I know. I can hear that in your singing now.'

As Clare looked in some surprise at the beautiful, cold nun whom she had never liked, she heard Iago's voice in the garden of the Torre Fiorita.

'She isn't anywhere,' he was saying. 'She isn't even dead.'

So she was here, in Rue des Lauriers.

Clare groped through thoughts, through parallels and confusions. She was amazed at her own *naïveté* and slowness. The disturbance in her breast she had to take for granted. But the social occasion, the gracious reunion which Rose had insisted upon came to a graceful conclusion – and in the hall, as long ago when they two were being forced away in tears to Italy, they said goodbye to Mère Marie.

She kissed them both, more affectionately than had been her wont. She patted Clare's shoulder.

'*Vaya con dios*,' she said. But Clare knew now, as she had not known four years ago, that that is what the Spaniards say.

She sat and pondered. She felt too sad, too almost elegiacally sad, about the sadness of this year of success, to be over-bothered with her own surprise about Mère Marie. After all, why should it not have happened thus?

Ah Luisa – where are you now? Were you here would I tell you this strange story? I believe not. You protected Iago's, even from me. I must protect hers, even from you. Yet, how you'd laugh! If you were here, how we'd both laugh!

But today was not a day for laughing. Today Rose and she, after five hard years of friendship, were having to say a real goodbye. Today, this summer, all of it, was a scattering – no matter how the heart protested.

And did the heart protest? Was it not good to sit *alone* under city trees, and know that love, plaguy love, was far away, and could not touch you? Rose, with her sick heart, would not agree. She was fleeing a temptation to which she would not yield, but she was running from its precious brilliance into a kind of polite twilight that could be at least as dangerous a source of sin.

Sin. The word came now from far enough away. Yet it was the word of all. What would Thomas say to that?

> '. . . As music and splendour
> Survive not the lamp and the lute . . .'

Clare sang the first two lines without satisfaction to herself. Still, I have studied them. I'll sing it as he hears it in his own head.

'*Vaya con dios*.' Mère Marie Brunel. 'She isn't anywhere. She isn't even dead.'

She gathered up her heavy book of songs and went her way down the Rue Royale. The Place de la Concorde struck exaggeratedly against the sad quiet of her heart.

Roundstone – London.

1957